From the Golden Era of Paperbacks,
three novels originally published
by Gold Medal Books:

THE VENGEANCE MAN

Jim Wilson has a problem. His rich wife takes a fiendish pleasure in banging every guy in town. But Jim has a plan. He hires a detective to follow her. And the next time Mona steps out on him, he's ready. Because Jim is a man with a bigger plan than dealing with an unfaithful wife. Jim is thinking big—he wants power, he wants respect, and if he can pull this one off, he just might be able to get it. Trouble is, the plan has to start with murder.

PARK AVENUE TRAMP

During one of her blackouts, Charity McAdams Farnese walks into a downtown bar named Duo's and into the life of Joe Doyle, second-rate piano player and a man with a bum heart. Yancy the bartender knows that she's trouble, a rich girl with an itch, but Joe won't listen. All he knows is that Charity wants to love him. But Charity has a husband— Oliver Alton Farnese. Oliver is a creature of habit and allows Charity her flings. But when this fling turns serious, Oliver has his own way of dealing with the situation.

THE PRETTIEST GIRL I EVER KILLED

Accidents happen, but the town of Sherman seems to have more than its fair share of the fatal kind. Someone falls into a well, another drowns, another is killed by an exploding stove. Curt Friedland comes back to town to clear his brother of murder, convinced there is more to all these deaths than mere coincidence. Enlisting the aid of Velda, whose sister was supposedly murdered by Curt's brother, the two of them gradually begin to attract the attention of a very ingenious killer, a man well versed in the game of Death.

The Vengeance Man
BY DAN J. MARLOWE

Park Avenue Tramp
BY FLETCHER FLORA

The Prettiest Girl
I Ever Killed
BY CHARLES RUNYON

A TRIO OF GOLD MEDALS

STARK HOUSE

Stark House Press • Eureka California
www.StarkHousePress.com

A TRIO OF GOLD MEDALS: THE VENGEANCE MAN /
PARK AVENUE TRAMP / THE PRETTIEST GIRL I EVER KILLED

Published by Stark House Press
2200 O Street
Eureka, CA 95501, USA
www.starkhousepress.com

THE VENGEANCE MAN
Originally published and copyright © 1966 by Dan J. Marlowe
Copyright © renewed 1994 by Dan J. Marlowe

PARK AVENUE TRAMP
Originally published and copyright © 1958 by Fletcher Flora
Copyright © renewed 1986 by the Estate

THE PRETTIEST GIRL I EVER KILLED
Originally published and copyright © 1965 by Charles Runyon
Copyright © renewed 1993 by Charles Runyon

Dan J. Marlowe by Charles Kelly copyright © 2007
Fletcher Flora by Charles Kelly copyright © 2007
Interview with Charles Runyon by Ed Gorman copyright © 2007

ISBN: 1-933586-14-1

Text set in Figural and Dogma. Heads set in Bodega Sans.
Cover design and book layout by Mark Shepard, shepdesign.home.comcast.net
Proofreading by Joanne Applen

The publisher would like to thank Charles Runyon, Ed Gorman, Charles Kelly, Barry Malzberg and Catt LeBaigue for all their help in making this book come together.

First Stark House Press Edition: September 2007

0 9 8 7 6 5 4 3 2 1

Dan J. Marlowe
BY CHARLES KELLY

Dan J. Marlowe (1914-1986), an almost-forgotten master of the gun-and-fist suspense novel, is again taking a turn in the spotlight. He's been called "hardest of the hard-boiled" by horror writer Stephen King, who dedicated his 2005 novel, *The Colorado Kid*, to Marlowe. Los Angeles novelist Hugh Gross, who owns the rights to Earl Drake, the writer's strongest character, is working to get two of Marlowe's novels made into movies. Readers are increasingly seeking out details about Marlowe: not surprising, since he led a fascinating life—writing some of the toughest Fawcett Gold Medal paperbacks, befriending bank robber Al Nussbaum, falling victim to amnesia, then fighting his way back to complete one more novel before he died.

Marlowe was a complex mix. An unathletic sports fan, he created he-man characters who could dive, shoot, and copulate with the best of them. Though chubby and unattractive, he himself was hell with the women. He studied to be an accountant and was proud of his business skills, but also spent years as a professional gambler. Though a conservative who served as a city official, he loved booze and a good time. He castigated one popular novel as "filth," but praised the book's literary qualities, spoke out against censorship, and quietly wrote pornography himself. And—at least professionally—he was quite interested in the spanking fetish.

Marlowe was born in Lowell, Mass., in 1914, the son of a printing-press mechanic. His mother died after falling ill in the flu epidemic of 1918. Afterwards, Dan and his brother Don (who went on to become a celebrated scientist), were raised by their grandmother and two aunts. Dan Marlowe attended parochial school in Woburn, Mass., and high school in New London, Conn., then received an accounting certificate from Bentley School of Accounting and Finance in Boston in 1934. For the next seven years, he lived mostly as a professional gambler—playing poker and betting on horses—though he also found time to work as assistant manager of two Connecticut country clubs. Marlowe later worked at an aircraft company and in 1945 took a job as an office manager and credit manager for Washington Tobacco Co., in Washington, D.C. He married during this period, but after 11 years his wife died suddenly of acute hemorrhagic pancreatitis.

It was 1956, and Marlowe was 43 years old. He had considered the idea of being a writer up to this point, but had been too busy. Now he had no constraints. The following year, he moved to New York, rented a hotel room, started working on a book-length story and took an evening novel-writing class at New York University. Near the end of 1958, he sold his first two books, *Doorway to Death* and *Killer with a Key*. They and the three Marlowe novels that followed featured Johnny Killain, a tough military veteran who works as a bellhop in a New York hotel and solves mysteries.

Marlowe wrote one non-Killain novel, *Backfire*, before producing his masterpiece, *The Name of the Game is Death*, which was published in 1962. The novel tells the story of a callous bank robber, embittered by social injustice, who finds and kills the people who tortured and murdered his partner while trying to get the partner to reveal the hiding place of stolen money. *The New York Times* called the book "tensely plotted, forcefully written, and extraordinarily effective in its presentation of a viewpoint quite outside humanity's expected patterns." The protagonist, known by the false names Roy Martin and Chet Arnold, takes the name Earl Drake in a subsequent novel and uses it consistently in the rest of the Marlowe novels about him.

The Name of the Game is Death was so realistic that it impressed a real bank robber, Al Nussbaum, who read it while he was on the run from a bank job in Brooklyn, N.Y., in which Nussbaum's chief partner, Bobby "One-Eye" Wilcoxson, had machine-gunned a guard to death. Using an assumed name, Nussbaum telephoned Marlowe, who by now had moved to Harbor Beach, Michigan, and asked for tips on writing fiction. Later, Nussbaum followed up with a letter. When the FBI caught up with Nussbaum, they visited Marlowe, suspecting he was an associate of the robber. Marlowe laid their suspicions to rest, but was intrigued by Nussbaum's cleverness and genuine desire to become a writer. While the robber was serving a long stretch for multiple crimes, Marlowe helped him by critiquing his work, offering writing advice, and helping him sell his stories. Nussbaum, in turn, helped Marlowe by advising him on the technical aspects of firearms, burglar alarms, and explosives.

As his relationship with Nussbaum developed, Marlowe was also forging more conventional social ties. Already a member of the local Rotary club in Harbor Beach, from 1967 to 1970, he served on the City Council. Meanwhile he continued to churn out paperbacks and garner acclaim. In 1967, *The New York Times'* Anthony Boucher called him one of the country's top writers of original softcover suspense, numbering him with such authors as John D. MacDonald, Brett Halliday, Donald Hamilton, Richard Stark (a pseudonym for Donald Westlake), and Edward Aarons. Though he was a master of craft, Marlowe always said his primary motive was making a living. "I'm a creature of the marketplace," he told the *Harbor*

Beach Times in an interview following publication of the Boucher article. "I'm a businessman in the business of delivering salable words to editors. When I know what an editor wants, that's what an editor gets from me."

It was no doubt this practical turn of mind that made it easy for Marlowe to collaborate with others, as he did occasionally with Nussbaum and extensively with retired Air Force Col. William C. Odell, a highly decorated World War II veteran considered an expert on night aerial combat. In 1964, Odell was running an advertising agency in Mansfield, Ohio, and trying his hand at fiction when a literary agent he was dealing with, who also represented Marlowe, suggested Marlowe might be brought in to help rewrite an Odell manuscript. That book apparently never was published, but Marlowe and Odell began a relationship that continued for years, working together on about a dozen books. Despite the collaboration, Odell got co-credit with Marlowe on only one of those novels, *The Raven is a Blood-Red Bird*, published in 1967. James Batson, a mutual friend of Marlowe and Odell, said the two writers decided it was better to give sole credit on the other books to the far-more-marketable Marlowe.

Odell, with his extensive knowledge of military tactics and equipment and foreign settings, was particularly helpful in the production of the "Operation" books (*Operation Fireball, Operation Breakthrough*, etc.) in which the bank robber Earl Drake is recruited by a government agent and becomes an operative himself—a change-in-direction of the character requested by Marlowe's editors to cater to the reading market.

For one of those books, *Flashpoint* (later issued as *Operation Flashpoint*) Marlowe won the 1971 Edgar Allan Poe Award for Best Paperback Original from the Mystery Writers of America. In 1977, Marlowe was still hard at work, with 25 novels under his belt. But that year he fell victim to terrible headaches while doing research in Florida for what he hoped would be a "breakout" novel to be published by Bernard Geis, maverick publisher of *The Valley of the Dolls*. Marlowe managed to drive back to Harbor Beach, but three days later suffered an attack of amnesia that caused him to forget all the people he had known and everything he had written. The amnesia probably was induced by a stroke, though physicians at the time believed the cause was psychological.

At 62, Marlowe's writing life appeared to be over. But Nussbaum, who by now had been released from prison and was working as a writer in Los Angeles—turning out short stories, stories for TV, and educational books—convinced Marlowe to move to LA and live with him while trying to regain his writing skills. Marlowe did so, and managed to produce a few new stories, a number of easy-reading books for the educational market, and one full-length novel—a generic adventure yarn called *Guerilla Games*, written as "Gar Wilson" for the Phoenix Force series published by Gold Eagle—before he died of heart failure in August 1986.

Marlowe's work falls roughly into three categories—the Johnny Killain novels, stand-alones (in which I include the bank robber novels before the robber—as Earl Drake—becomes a quasi-government agent), and the "Operation" books. Despite getting the Edgar for an "Operation" book, *Flashpoint*, Marlowe did his best work in several of the stand-alones, particularly *The Name of the Game is Death*, *One Endless Hour*, *The Vengeance Man*, *Strongarm*, *Never Live Twice*, and *Four for the Money*.

In my opinion, *The Vengeance Man* is his second-best book, behind only *The Name of the Game is Death*. The protagonist, construction company owner Jim Wilson, demonstrates a ferocity matched only by Earl Drake. The kinky overtones of the sex-and-power relationship Wilson has with Ludmilla Pierson, his murdered wife's friend, provide the most offbeat example of Marlowe's heavy-breathing eroticism. The corruption of virtually every important character in the book is thorough. The theme of betrayal is relentless. *The Vengeance Man* starts with a bang, ends with a bang, and gallops like a desperate racehorse in between. Hold on tight. You're in for a hell of a ride.

—Scottsdale, AZ
October 2006

Charles Kelly, a veteran reporter for The Arizona Republic, *is researching a biography of Dan. J. Marlowe and has written about him for novelist Allan Guthrie's website* Noir Originals. *Kelly's first novel,* Pay Here, *is being published by Point Blank Press.*

The Vengeance Man

BY DAN J. MARLOWE

CHAPTER 1

The low-lying, late afternoon, Moline, South Carolina, sun streaming through the windshield nearly blinded me as Wing Darlington swung his fender-dented Galaxie into Shadylawn Terrace. His bronzed, corded forearms cradled the steering wheel. He was talking about our chances of being low bidder on the Edmonds Road job. When I saw that my mud-spattered station wagon was the only car at the curb in front of my house, and that my wife Mona's Pontiac wasn't in the garage, either, I felt a tingle. Maybe today was the day. "Carry me on over to Perry's, Wing," I said, interrupting his disparaging remarks. "I'll walk back."

He jammed his foot down on the accelerator again and the Galaxie leaped ahead past the big house I couldn't afford. Wing drives like he does everything else, fast, hard, and often, because Winfield Adair Darlington is a hard-charging country boy who also manages to look like a movie idol. He's a lean sixfooter with perfect features, perfect teeth, and crisp blond hair that curls even when he's in the water. When he smiles his go-to-hell smile with the white teeth splitting the Spanish-leather hue of his suntan, the women fall down in rows. Although I'm the same mahogany color as Wing, I have more trouble with my women. It might be because my hair is black and I wear it in a flattop. Or because, while I'm just as lean as Wing, I'm two inches taller and twice as wide. Or because I've never been asked to enter a Mr. Apollo contest.

He was still needling me as he pulled up in front of Perry's Liquor Store, a quarter mile from the house. " 'Pears like with your father-in-law's political connections, we should be gettin' a better smell on these county bids, ol' salty dog," he said.

" 'Pears like with your ex-girl friend ownin' a bank an' your ex-best friend a vice-president in it, we shouldn't be so stretched out for financin' "—I gave it back to him pork gravy style. He grinned at me. Wing and I have been partners for four years in the Darlington-Wilson Construction Company. I'm the engineer and he's the superintendent. We're a maverick outfit, specializing in road paving when we can get it, but willing to sink a tooth into anything we get turned loose on. I don't know any two men in the state who work harder, but that isn't what cuts the mustard around Moline, South Carolina. If a man who knew his business were asked to rank the contracting firms in and around the city, the DarlingtonWilson Construction Company wouldn't even make his list. I'd made up my mind a long time ago that I wasn't going to let it stay that way.

"See you in the mornin', hoss," Wing called back cheerfully as he drove off.

I went into the liquor shop. Doug Perry had seen me coming and had a fifth of Jack Daniels sacked up beside the cash register. "Hot one this evenin', Jim," he said as I paid him. He was a round man, with a shiny, sweating, bald head. "Must be rough on a big man like you."

"Not for us local boys," I said, deadpan. "It's only you carpetbaggers from Richmond who mind the heat."

"I've lived in this town twenty years!" Doug began indignantly. Then he laughed as I walked out to the street. "Always kiddin'," he called after me.

I took my time going back to the house. Not a breath of the August air was stirring the drooping leaves of the magnolia tree in the front yard. There was a note from Mona on the kitchen table: "Shopping with Lud. Back by eight." I read it twice. She *could* be shopping with Ludmilla Pierson, her best friend, although on the last two Wednesday afternoons, she hadn't been. I glanced at the kitchen clock. Ten after five. If it was going to happen, this was the time for it to happen. Mona's father, Judge Tom Harrington, the political bête noire of the Darlington-Wilson Construction Company, had gone over to Charleston on Monday for a prostate operation. With the old wolf out of the way, I just might have a chance. If Andy called... I crumpled Mona's note and threw it into the garbage bag under the sink.

I ignored the sacked-up Jack Daniels and had a bottle of gin down from a shelf and a tray of ice cubes out of the refrigerator when the telephone rang. I could feel my stomach muscles tightening as I went into the front hall to answer it. "Jim?" It was Andy Martin's slow drawl. "'They're in room twenty-four at the Stardust. I'm leavin' this instant to pick up my witnesses an' come by an' get you. You be ready, y'hear?"

"I'll be ready," I said. Then I hung up. Andy Martin was as much as Moline afforded in the way of a private detective, but it seemed that he was enough. It would take him at least fifteen minutes to drive from the Stardust Motel to my place, plus however long it took him to round up his witnesses. I had plenty of time.

I went to the sink and retrieved Mona's crumpled note from the garbage bag and placed it on the table. I removed the Jack Daniels from the sack, split the plastic seal around the cap with a thumbnail, removed the cap, and took a long double swallow. Then I poured half of the fifth down the sink drain, being careful not to splash it, and rinsed the sink out. I left the still-open fifth and the melting ice cubes on the counter. The gin, I returned to the shelf.

I went back to the telephone and dialed the Pierson number. "Jim, Lud," I said when she answered. "Is Mona there?"

"She left just a few minutes ago," my wife's best woman friend answered promptly. As always, when she spoke to me, Ludmilla Pierson's voice took on the bright, hard tinkle of crystal. Lud and Mona had been roommates

in college. Ludmilla was the only daughter of the deceased town banker;
Mona was the only daughter of Judge Tom Harrington, the wheeler-deal-
er politico who ran things in the county. Wing, Ludmilla, Mona, and I had
been in high school together; we were all within a year either way of thirty. We'd knocked around as a group with some crossover dating. Wing
hadn't finished high school, let alone gone to college, but even so, Lud had
waited a long time for him to propose to her. When he didn't, she married
George Pierson, whom she was now pulling by the ears tip through the
bank hierarchy. George and Wing had been best friends in school, but
Ludmilla skillfully split them up. I'd seen her still looking at Wing occasionally when she thought no one was watching. I didn't think she was in
love with him; he was just something she'd wanted and hadn't got yet. I'd
never asked Wing how he felt about her.

Mona and I had kicked a few gongs during those years, but eventually
we drifted apart. Five years ago it had flared up again unexpectedly, and
one weekend, we'd driven down to Georgia and got married. Ludmilla
hadn't approved. Judge Tom Harrington—the "Judge" was a courtesy title
from a tour on the circuit court years ago—hadn't approved, either. He had
bigger game in mind for his only daughter. From bankers and politicians
in Moline, I'd had nothing but a hard way to go ever since.

"I believe Mona had another stop or two to make on her way home," Lud
was saying.

I'd known she'd lie about it unhesitatingly. I just wanted her to remember my call afterward, "She should be along soon, then," I said before I
replaced the receiver.

I went into the living room and opened the safe behind the picture of
the four-masted schooner on the north wall. I scooped up an elastic-band-
ed roll of money and closed and locked the steel door again. I replaced the
picture and carried the money to the Queen Anne desk that Mona had
inherited from her grandmother. I sat down gingerly in the matching chair
that had never been constructed to hold my weight, and rapidly made out,
in duplicate, a deposit slip for the total of the amounts shown in a rent collection ledger I took from a drawer. Collecting rents was one of my keep-
ing-the-cookies-on-the-table sidelines. I counted out enough bills to make
up the required amount, folded and elasticked them into the original
deposit slip, and shoved the bundle into my hip pocket. I stuffed the rest
of the money into a side pocket.

From another desk drawer, I removed a Smith & Wesson .38 police special,
clicked off the safety, thumbed a cartridge up into the empty chamber, slipped
the safety back on, and dropped the heavy weapon in my jacket pocket. I left
the living room, leaving the rent collection ledger and the duplicate deposit
slip on the desk top. Ten minutes after receiving Andy Martin's phone call, I
was out in front of the house again, getting into the station wagon.

I drove directly to the Stardust. Mona's Pontiac wasn't there, but Bailey's car was. I parked beside it, got out, and approached the door of number twenty-four. The sun was almost down, but it was still light. The shades were tightly drawn, and I could hear the rasp of the air-conditioning. I bent down to get my left shoulder on a level with the door's lock, and then I rammed against it solidly. A panel of wood splintered noisily, but the lock held. I backed off and hit it again. The lock burst with a whining screech of metal and the door flew inward to hang, sagging, on a broken hinge. I drew the .38 from my jacket pocket, flicked off the safety, and stepped inside.

Every light in the room was on. Whit Bailey, the mayor's son, was on his feet beside the bed, his pretty-boy face blank with shock as he stared incredulously at the .38. With a position disadvantage to overcome, Mona was still rising. Both were needle-naked. Mona came toward me, squarely into the teeth of the Smith & Wesson. That was part of her trouble; she was convinced that all ordinary laws were suspended for Mona Harrington Wilson. I pulled the trigger twice, just as she started to say something. I'll never know what it was. For a fraction of a second I could see the double dimple in her sweaty flesh just below her left breast where the slug caught her; then the dimples exploded outward in a froth of blood. She staggered sideways and slid to the floor in a long diagonal. The only sound she made was a kind of questioning mew. I knew what she meant. This couldn't *possibly* be happening to *her.*

I walked over and looked down at her. Even if I hadn't seen where the bullets stitched her, I'd have known from her eyes that she was gone. I turned and looked for Bailey. He was standing petrified, goggling in horror at Mona's body. He felt rather than saw me turn toward him. Screaming hoarsely, he jumped back onto the bed, face down, his head wrapped in his arms. I stepped up to the side of the bed and put single bullets through both his buttocks, deep. His screaming soared, and he flopped onto his back like a grassed fish. The scream choked off in a gasp as his new position put pressure on his wound; he rolled onto his side. I leaned down over him, reversing the .38 in my hand. I turned him onto his back again, unpeeled his arms from his head, and went to work on his face with the butt of the Smith & Wesson.

I was still busy when the first wave of gabbling fools rushed through the shattered door and grabbed me by the arms. I shook them off, tossed the .38 onto the bed beside the unconscious Bailey, and sat down in the room's only chair.

"Call the police! Call the police!" someone was yelling hysterically.

Eventually someone called the police.

I sat in the chair looking at Mona while I waited for them to get there.

It was just as sticky as I'd known it was going to be.

"Don't turn a wheel 'til Chet gets here," was the first thing I heard from the uniformed police, who were the first to arrive. This was when they found out who was involved. Chet Dorsey was Chief of Detectives and one of Tom Harrington's boys.

When he got there, Dorsey supervised Bailey's removal in an ambulance before turning his attention to me. "Smells like a distillery," he snapped after shoving his red-veined nose into my face. "Take him downtown."

Five plainclothesmen made the trip with me. They were handicapped by the fact that quite a few onlookers had seen me leave the motel intact, and also that with so many of them in the cruiser, they got in each others' way. I knew three of them personally, too, which made them a bit conservative, but I was lucky that it was a short ride. Sometime during the trip, my jacket split right down the back. When we reached the station house, they rushed me into a small room that was bare except for a single chair. And the questioning began.

"How did you find them, Wilson?"

"You planned it all, didn't you?"

"You waited for this chance, didn't you, Wilson?"

"Admit that you planned it. Admit it."

"Will you talk, damn you?"

"You're going to make a statement, Wilson. Make up your mind to it."

I told them nothing. Dorsey was nowhere in evidence. The personnel asking the questions kept changing. They'd cleaned out my pockets at the admitting desk but hadn't booked me. For some reason they'd left me my watch. After four hours of hacking around with nothing out of me, a new team of three men came in. I knew two of them: Zeke Williams from the west side of town, and one of the younger Moody boys. There were five or six boys in the Moody family, look-alikes, all with the same wide-spaced eyes and lantern jaws.

I'd seen the third man around, although he wasn't a local. He was a lean-faced character with a five o'clock shadow. He stood in front of me, smiling, pulling golf gloves on slowly over his hands. Williams looked uncomfortable, and young Moody looked like a man trying to look like a man doing his job. They took hold of my arms and pulled me back in the chair I was sitting in. "You don't need to make a statement, Wilson," the third man said. "All you got to do is sign the one they're puttin' together for you now. Let me know when you're ready."

He had fast, hard hands, and in slow time, he hooked and jabbed me, giving each time to take effect. He worked the belly, the chest, the arms, and occasionally the face. He wasn't punching solidly, but he knew how to snap them off. He took his time, and he kept it up. All my life I'd never doubted my ability to stay the course over any racetrack I was dropped down on, but this boy had me wondering. Although my plan didn't call for it, I was just about to rare back and slam both heels through to his back-bone when he stopped and went out, pulling off his gloves.

I spoke for the first time since he'd entered the interrogation room. "I'll talk to Dorsey," I said. "Alone."

They couldn't get him in there fast enough. They took just time enough to clean me up first. I waited 'til the Detective Chief's bulky body was planted right in front of my chair. He was carefully avoiding looking at me. "You know me, Dorsey," I began. He started to pout; it wasn't what he wanted to hear. I continued before he could speak. "Better make the 'accident' fatal because if I make it to the street, I'm holding you responsible. You, personally. Understand? You can't hide from me, Dorsey. Not in this county."

He turned on his heel and walked out; his beefy face was brick-red.

The questioning was renewed, but without the calisthenics. Chet Dorsey knew me all right. Seven-eighths of Albermarle County knew me.

Around three in the morning, they tired of it and slung me into one of Fat Jack Grissom's detention cells. Grissom is the city jailer. The cell furni-ture consisted of a steel cot without even a blanket on it; but compared to where I'd been, it looked almost attractive. I was soaked with perspiration and would have relished a shower and a change of clothes. Since it wasn't to be, I sat down on the cot, took off my shoes, probed at my ribs ginger-ly, and tried to organize my thinking.

First, there was the cell.

Ten years ago, in my ridge-running days, I'd huddled around with a boy named Tony Lawton, who surprised me by turning square and joining the police in the next county. For a while he kept coming around on his days off, in uniform, until he realized I didn't feel comfortable around a cop, friend or no friend. He stopped coming finally, but not before he told me stories about police routine and procedure that I've never forgotten.

The only light in the entire cell block was from a head-high, green-shad-ed light bulb in my cell. No matter where I stood in the cell, its light was in my eyes all the time, while the ceiling was in comparative darkness. I stood up in my socks on the steel cot, put my head above the rim of light, and waited 'til my eyes adjusted to the absence of glare. When they did, I saw it right away. Not the bug itself because I couldn't get high enough, even on the cot, but I could see plainly two thin wires bradded into a sup-porting joist. They trailed oil into the next cell before disappearing into the ceiling.

I climbed down from the cot and stretched out on my back on the cement floor. I chose the corner of the cell that promised the most protec-tion if someone opened the outer door and sprayed a magazine into the steel cot. It wasn't too likely, with Harrington in the hospital and unavailable for decision-making, but it wasn't impossible. Tom Harrington drew a lot of water in Moline, South Carolina, and someone might take a notion to show Tom he was on the team. I'd figured originally that if I stayed alive for eighteen hours after being taken into custody, I had it made, but I still had half of that to go.

The cell was cooler than the night air outside, but the humidity was high. I shifted position from time to time on the damp cement and listened to the jail sounds. Gradually my inner turmoil subsided. I became more conscious of aches and pains, but I surprised myself by dozing off a few times. When I saw daylight at last through the barred window, I had it all figured out: I was in roughly the fourteenth hour of the problem, and I had to think I was on the downhill side of the action.

Nobody came near me 'til Wing showed up at nine o'clock. "Goddam, I jus' now heard it, almos' by accident"—I could hear his furious voice outside the cell block. "Don't you bastards ever *notify* nobody, Grissom?"

"Next of kin," Grissom answered. He sounded nervous. There was a clank of keys, and Wing walked into the cell block. He was looking back over his shoulder at Grissom following him.

"Next of kin!" Wing snorted. He turned his head and saw the locked door of my cell. "Open this heah door, you fatass slug!" be demanded.

"I cain't do it," Grissom whined.

Wing's right hand drew back swifter than a striking water moccasin. "Hold it!" I shouted. "One of us in here is enough. At a time, anyway."

The hand dropped reluctantly. "I ought to bust you right down the middle anyway, Grissom, jus' for luck," Wing said softly to the white-faced jailer. "Now haul yourself the hellan'gone out of here."

Grissom needed no second invitation.

I was sure that the only reason Wing had been let inside was so that they could hear what we had to say to each other. He had moved closer and was staring at me through the bars. Before he could say anything, I put my hands to my ears and wiggled my fingers, then pointed to the ceiling. Wing's mouth tightened, and he nodded. There was never anything slow on the uptake about Wing Darlington. His mother had raised no foolish children.

"God almighty dog, Jim, boy," he burst out, his eyes on my face. "You must've—they must've—" He choked it off, swallowed, and started again. "Great smokin' blue hemlock, it scares me to think how close I come to wildassin' it out to the Sunset Lane job 'thout knowin' a thing about this. If"—his glance flicked ceilingward—"if a friend hadn't called—" his voice died out. "They let you call a lawyer?" he resumed abruptly.

"First time I've heard the word."

"I thought so, after the runaround I got on the phone this mornin'," he said. "So I brought you one. If you can call him a lawyer—he's on'y a kid.

Soon's I got the message, I called Vic Cartwright, an' you know what he did? Hung up on me. Our own lawyer, scared green. So were the next two I called. Goddam lawyers in this town don't pull down their pants to crap 'til Tom Harrington"—he paused and spat toward the ceiling—"tells 'em it's time to unbuckle their belts. So I got this boy, if you'll have him. He prob'ly ain't tried but a half dozen cases, an' all of 'em in civil court. He's got it here, though. Wing patted his slim stomach. "That I'll guarantee."

Even a kid lawyer was more lawyer than I'd thought I'd have available. If he wasn't a plant. They could hardly have planted him on Wing, though. "Get him in here and let me talk to him, will you, Wing? Another thing— there'll be some kind of arraignment this morning. Make sure someone from the *Clarion* is there. It might help later on if the public knew I was comparatively healthy to that point. Something else you can do for me. There's a hatchet-faced type on the detective squad, mean-looking but a smiler, a twenty-minute egg. I've seen him around, but I never did know his name. I'd like to."

Wing nodded. "Got you." His grin was wolfish. "An' I'll go get my boy. He's only 'bout yea big, understand, so don't be expectin' Dan'l Webster."

"If he's got his ticket and his nerve, he's good enough for me."

"He's got both," Wing said. "I'll be right back."

It wasn't that easy.

For thirty minutes I could hear scattered phrases of frantic telephoning on the part of Jailer Grissom, interspersed with Wing's hard-voiced sarcastic comments and an occasional softer voice asking Wing to please let him handle it. Finally I heard the clank of the keys again.

"—want you to know I'm only doin' my duty!" Grissom was declaiming passionately as he opened the outside door.

"*Aaahh*, shut your fat, lyin' mouth," Wing said disgustedly.

"Only the lawyer goes into the cell," Grissom said defiantly. "That's orders."

"Orders?" Wing flared, whirling on the balls of his feet. "Whose goddam orders? Grissom, I'll crawl your blubbery—"

"It's okay, Wing," I said. "Keep things afloat, will you?"

"Well—" he said uncertainly. "If you say so." He glared at Grissom, then raised his hand to me in a half-salute and went out.

The lawyer came in and shook hands when Grissom unlocked the cell door. I was probably only five or six years older than he was, but God, he looked young! He was slight in build, but with a good chin on him, and he had sharp blue eyes behind heavy horn-rimmed glasses. "I'm Manley Sloane, Mr. Wilson," he said. "Sorry to make your acquaintance in such circumstances." His handshake was firm.

I had no time to waste. "Who are your folks, Manley?" I asked him.

He was expecting the question. In Albermarle County, where two-thirds of the populace are cousins to each other, it's one of the first asked. "My daddy, Richard Sloane, farms in South Hollow, the other side of Edgemere," he said. "And my uncle, Peter Sloane, sells real estate and is first selectman over in Wiggins."

As I knew just about everyone else in Albermarle County, I knew Dick Sloane and his wife, June, too. Good, solid, reliable country folk. I'd never heard they'd bred any culls. Plus Wing had vouched for the boy. And what choice did I have? "You're my lawyer, Manley."

"Fine," he said briskly. "Let's find out where we stand."

While he was speaking I took him by the arm and led him to the center of the cell. He looked puzzled, but without saying anything, I stooped and took hold of him by the thighs and lifted him straight up in the air—he didn't weigh much more than an average-sized woman—until he was looking right at the bug. He grunted in understanding, his body stiffening in my arms. His voice rose like a bugle. "Jailer! Grissom! Damn your fat soul, I'll have you up on charges for this! You know the lawyer-client relationship is a privileged one! GRISSOM! I'll have your—"

He was bellowing right into the bug, guaranteeing a listener a tin ear. I let him down, and he rattled the cell bars, still hollering. He had a lot of noise in him for a little one. Grissom came trotting in, shaking. He'd had a hard morning. "What's—what is it now?" he pleaded. "What's the trouble?"

"Trouble!" Sloane roared. "Any time you plant a listening device in the cell of one of *my* clients—!"

"Oh, that ol' thing." Grissom didn't even look aloft. "That's just in case a drunk tries to hang hisself. It's—it's not even connected up now, I'm sure. Almost sure."

"Get us out of here," Manley Sloane said grimly.

Grissom hurriedly moved us to another cell, but even after he'd left us again and Sloane and I had carefully inspected the new location without finding anything, we stood in its center and talked in undertones.

"Have you made a statement?" Sloane asked me first.

"No."

He raised an eyebrow. "No? Nothing at all?"

"Nothing."

He shook his head slowly. Like Wing, he'd been looking at my face. "I must be fated for a short life, Mr. Wilson. Our instructor in criminal law was always telling us that some day we'd have a client who hadn't already made a complete confession before we talked to him for the first time, and the day we did, the end of the world was at hand."

"Let me tell you how it happened," I suggested.

I told him, properly expurgated.

He listened until I finished without interrupting. "I don't believe the coroner's jury will even recommend passing it on up to the grand jury," he said then. "Unless"—he frowned. "There's the personalities involved, of course. There'll be pressure." He was silent a moment. "But even if they bind you over, a trial jury will never convict. Not in this county. Not after what you've told me. But I'm positive it will never come to a trial."

That had been my thinking, too, but it was encouraging to hear it from the little man.

We talked a while longer, and then Sloane left. Before he did, he made so much racket about the bugged cell that Grissom didn't put me back into it. When Sloane finally departed after a superfluous admonition to talk to no one but him, I drew a long, long breath. So far, it had gone almost exactly the way I'd hoped. There were still a lot of things that could go wrong, and not much chance to become overconfident, but as I paced the cell and thought it all through again for the hundredth time, I really began to feel that I might beat Tom Harrington's odds board.

For some reason I've never understood, coroner's juries in Moline, South Carolina, meet at night; and five days after the fact, I appeared before one. The puffiness had left my face, and my skin is so dark anyway that the remaining marks could hardly be seen. The atmosphere in the small, side courtroom was informal, Sig Jacobus, the coroner, was in his shirt sleeves with a big black cigar in his face, and Manley Sloane was the only man in the room—including the spectators in the back of it—who wore a jacket. I knew every man on the six-man jury—in South Carolina, women aren't allowed on juries—and they all knew me. In Albermarle County, it couldn't have been any different.

Our jurors are supposed to be selected from a full panel, but actually, all Sig does is go out on the sidewalk and tap the first six property owners he finds. If he happens to have told six men to be walking in the square that time of evening, old Sig is going to get the verdict he wants. Two years ago, a friend of Tom Harrington's had been involved in a nasty hit-and-run manslaughter case. Harrington's lawyer, taking over for the friend, and wary of Sig's jurors, had demanded that Sig call a new one from the full panel. He'd made it stick, too, although Sig protested that it was just an additional expense to the county. Everyone knew Sig was afraid of the precedent that might loosen his grip. There'd been a distinct coolness between Sig and Tom Harrington ever since. I was counting on it. Sig didn't have to be for me; I just didn't want him to be against me.

Old Bart Simmons, the straw boss at Crater's Sawmill, was appointed jury foreman. The procedure was just as informal as the atmosphere, and the whole thing went along rattle-de-bang. Bill Craddock, the prosecutor, and Sloane continually interrupted each other via verbal harpoons while Sig Jacobus smoked his cigar, asked an occasional question, and took an occasional note. Craddock did a lot of talking to the jury, a wide smile plastered on his face, but Sloane leaned toward me. "He doesn't like it," he whispered. "He wouldn't be pushing it if someone weren't twisting his arm."

Before I could reply, Craddock stopped talking and looked in our direction. Sloane got to his feet and strolled toward the half dozen loosely grouped chairs that held the jury. "Gentlemen," he began easily—the little man's dignity was impressive—"I believe you're aware that most of these hearings are almost a foregone conclusion In their result, with the prosecution presenting just enough evidence to persuade you to hold the defendant for the grand jury, without disclosing in full the evidence it has, and with the defense correspondingly sitting on its hands to avoid tipping off its particular line of defense. Contrary to custom, however, you've just heard the prosecution present a great deal of evidence, adding up to not much of anything, in my opinion, but proof in itself of the prosecution's knowledge of the inherent weakness of its case. In turn, gentlemen, I'm going to make an exception of the defense's standard gambit of silence.

"You're all busy men, and I'm not going to waste your time. I'm not going to parade my client before you for you to see the marks on his face. I'm not even—"

"Exception!" Craddock roared, bouncing to his feet.

"Sit down, Bill," Sig Jacobus said in a bored tone.

Craddock sat, fuming.

"I'm not even going to refer to the listening device placed in his cell so that his conversations, even with his lawyer, could be overheard," Sloane resumed. "I'm just going to stick to the facts. In my summation, I must necessarily touch upon matters distasteful both to the defendant and to myself, matters that the prosecution's mistaken zeal to indict forces us to take up. You have heard the case described as one of deliberate, premeditated murder, gentlemen, but I submit to you that Mr. Craddock's own witnesses have proved it was nothing of the kind.

"Consider: the defendant's business partner has testified that on the evening in question, less than an hour before the tragic event, the defendant was in excellent spirits. You have heard Douglas Perry, proprietor of Perry's Liquor Store, testify to the same effect. Douglas Perry testified also to the defendant's purchase at that time of twenty-five point six ounces of a ninety-proof alcoholic beverage. In testifying to the condition of the Wilson kitchen immediately after the tragic event, the prosecution's own witnesses inescapably support the conclusion that the defendant drank some twelve point eight ounces—half the total content—of that same beverage within moments of receiving Andrew Martin's telephone call."

Snow them with figures they know to be right early in the proceedings, the enthusiastic Sloane had confided to me while Grissom was bringing us across the street to the courthouse, and they'll begin to believe everything you tell them. The little man made his figures sound impressive. I must have drunk a thousand fifths in my lifetime without knowing that one contained 25.6 ounces.

Sloane's voice deepened as his glance roved the chairs. "I have listened along with you, gentlemen, to the prosecution's remarks—surely no more dignified a term can be applied to them—to the effect that in the city of Moline in the county of Albermarle in the sovereign state of South Carolina we no longer operate under what was somewhat grandiloquently referred to as 'the barbaric inheritance of the doctrine of the unwritten law.' You heard me object to the remarks as irrelevant, since they bore on no evidence as introduced. Nevertheless you heard them, and you will weigh them as they deserve to be weighed.

"Mr. Jacobus has informed you that your duty consists in binding the defendant over to the grand jury, or releasing him, as you see fit. I will say in passing that, although to this moment you have heard the prosecution speak solely in terms of an eventual indictment for first-degree murder, if you so desire, Mr. Jacobus will inform you that alternative choices exist in profusion, including second-degree homicide, manslaughter, and aggravated assault."

Sig nodded to the jurors. Sloane sauntered up and down before the chairs, his arms clasped behind his back. "Most important of all, gentlemen, you have heard the action branded as premeditated, the most easily refuted point in the prosecution's entire rambling presentation. Consider again: the defendant returns home and finds a note indicating that his wife has gone shopping with a woman friend. I won't bore you with the details of the difficulty I had in tracing the note to have it introduced in evidence. It had been—ah—mislaid. At almost the same moment that the defendant reads the note, he receives a phone call from a private detective pinpointing the wife's actual location as a motel room liaison with another man, the final deterioration of a domestic situation that had led the defendant to employ the private detective in the first place. And bear in mind, gentlemen, that it was not the first such phone call.

"Unquestionably affected by the rapid assimilation of twelve ounces of the ninety-proof alcoholic beverage readily to hand, the defendant loses his head. Instead of waiting for the private detective and the witnesses as directed, and as planned, he drives himself directly to the specified location. Unfortunately, he has on his person a gun. You have heard the prosecution try to make much of the presence of that gun, and you have heard the simple explanation. The defendant collected rents for a number of landlords, and because it was general knowledge that on certain days he carried large sums of money on his person, on those days he carried a gun. He had a permit for the gun. I repeat: HE HAD A PERMIT FOR IT. And you have heard the prosecution somewhat unwillingly concede that, when apprehended, the defendant had upon his person some three thousand dollars wrapped in a deposit slip of current date, prima facie evidence that the defendant was on his way to the night depository of one of the local banks as usual; and as usual the gun accompanied him."

Sloane lowered his voice, and I could see two of the jurors lean forward to hear better. "As a result of the telephone call, the defendant's mind and emotions became inflamed. He burst in upon the woman who was his wife and the man who was with her. You have heard the ugly details. Surely none of us can presume to know what was in his mind at that moment. Premeditation? Say, rather, the simple explosion of a primitive reaction sparked by a sight never intended for husbandly eyes. It was unfortunate that he had access to a gun at that particular instant, BUT HE WAS ENTITLED TO HAVE IT. There was no premeditation involved. You have, in fact, heard a prosecution witness admit that if premeditation had been involved, both parties could have as easily been killed, instead of the defendant's, in the case of his wife's bed partner, resorting to an outburst of impassioned violence highly indicative of his disturbed mental condition. Premeditation? For the prosecution in such circumstances to even raise the question seems to me a joke, and one in extremely poor taste."

His voice rose again. "In conclusion, gentlemen, I will say to you only that in the light of all the evidence presented here this evening, you cannot in good conscience recommend that this man be held for the grand jury."

He bowed, smiled confidently at the jury, and walked back and sat down beside me.

There was a stir in the back of the room, a rustle and buzz amid the scattered knots of listening people.

The jury retired, and we settled down to wait.

They were back in eighteen minutes. "No finding," Bart Simmons said in his harsh voice when Sig put the question to him. "Unan—unan—" He took a breath and started over again. "All of the same mind."

Bill Craddock glared at Sig Jacobus, who smiled winterly. Manley Sloane and I shook hands. Wing rushed up to me with a jubilant congratulatory handshake, but there weren't too many of them; the long arm of Tom Harrington reached into this room, too, although not as deeply as he might have thought five minutes before. "Taylor," Wing said to me, still pumping my arm.

"Taylor? Taylor what?"

"The name of your hatchet-faced detective. The one you asked me to find out for you. Hawk Taylor."

"Oh. Yes. Fine. Hawk Taylor. Thanks, Wing."

"Nice goin', boy," Wing said to a beaming Manley Sloane.

"I got in a few licks never would have been permitted at a trial," the little man confided. "Sometimes strict legal procedure gets bent all out of shape at these preliminary hearings."

"A beautiful job," Wing said emphatically. "An' he's not goin' to be sorry, is he, Jim?"

"That he's not. In fact—"

"You just clear out a corner of your office for a few filin' cases," Wing continued to Sloane, anticipating me. "You're our lawyer, boy. The files'll be over soon's I catch up with Vic Cartwright an' cut the ground out from under him."

I was looking around for Grissom. I saw him finally, standing off to one side. "Am I supposed to go back with you?" I called out to him.

"Don't see why 't should be necessary," he replied. with an attempt at a jovial smile. "You can pick up your belongin's at the station house when you're ready. No hard feelin's, Jim?"

I looked right through him. "Good night, Manley," I said. "Good night, Wing. I'm going to walk. I feel like stretching my legs again." Wing grinned sympathetically. "See you tomorrow." I left the hearing room, turned left on the oil-darkened wooden floor of the long corridor, and descended the outside marble stairs to the street.

On the sidewalk, I drew a deep, relishing breath of the night air. I looked up at the stars overhead. For an outdoor man, there are not many places worse than where I'd been the past few days. If necessary, I'd been prepared to sweat it out all the way to the trial, but I'd be lying if I said I enjoyed the prospect. This had been the consideration that had held me back the longest.

My thoughts turned to the house on Shadylawn Terrace, the empty house to which I'd be returning now. Naturally, Mona's image came into focus. What did I feel about her now? That was easy. I felt nothing, one way or the other. I'd been feeling nothing for a long time about Mona. For six months after we were married, she'd stood me off about having children. Then she stopped standing me off, but we didn't have any children. It was three years later before I found out by accident that the "minor" female operation she'd had just after the six-month mark in the marriage had been to make sure she'd have no children. I almost divorced her then, but I was already looking ahead. And in the long run, it turned out to have been only Strike One on the marriage.

Mona? No. Mona had already been gone for a long time.

I set off up the street at a fast walk.

CHAPTER 2

I intended to go directly to the station house, pick up my wallet and car keys, and get myself home. Tom Harrington might have lost a battle, but he hadn't lost the war, and if one of his boys could line me up properly in a gunsight, he didn't have to lose it. Until I had an umbrella in place, the area around Moline, South Carolina, was no place for me to be exposing myself.

I changed my mind when I saw a light in the second-floor corner office of the three-story building alongside the jail. I detoured to the building's doorway and climbed worn stair treads to the second floor. I opened a door lettered CARTWRIGHT & MILLER, ATTORNEYS. I hadn't made any noise. "Working late, Veronica?" I asked as I entered.

Veronica Peters, Vic Cartwright's redheaded secretary, looked up from her desk, startled. "Oh!" she exclaimed, half-rising. She glanced quickly at the closed door of the inner office. "He's—Mr. Cartwright isn't in right now!"

I started around her desk. She ran out from behind it and stood between me and the door; her violet-colored eyes were wide. "Don't, Jim!" she pleaded. She was breathing heavily, agitating a considerable bosom. I was familiar with the bosom; I'd been getting to it and adjacent precincts for the past eighteen months.

I placed my nose inches from hers. "Get back behind your desk, Veronica," I suggested, "before I feed you your gluteus maximus in one-inch strips."

She tried to stare me down. Failing, her eyes dropped, and she stepped to one side. Her full lower lip was trembling. I advanced to the closed door, opened it, went inside, and closed it again. Vic Cartwright was bent forward over his desk, studying a sheaf of papers. Above his thin, pinched features, his gray hair was straggly. "Yes, Veronica?" he inquired absently. "What—" He turned his head and his eyes came into focus on me. He paled as he stumbled to his feet. "Jim! I'm delighted—that is, I just learned—it's good to know—" His voice ran down.

"Send our files around to Manley Sloane's office the first thing in the morning, Vic," I said. "No excuses or delays. If I should get the notion you were stalling to photostat a few items, you wouldn't enjoy it."

His lean throat worked convulsively. "I know you're upset, Jim, and I don't blame you, but circumstances—isn't there some way—"

"There isn't. When I know who my friends are, Vic, I act accordingly. You get the files over to Sloane."

"Wait, Jim," he called as I started for the outer office. I turned and looked at him. "All right, you're entitled to feel the way you do. I let you down." He passed a shaky hand along his jawline. "I want you to know there was nothing—nothing personal in my refusal to act for you when—when Wing called me." His Adam's apple bobbed again. "There was—there had been a prior call." He cleared his throat heavily. "I imagine I'm not giving you any news when I tell you that Tom Harrington has my balls in his nutcracker, to use the vulgate. And I thought—we all thought—well—" He shrugged. "We were wrong. Although—"

"Although you think all the votes might not be in yet?" I asked when he hesitated. "You still think you might have signed up with the winning team?"

He flushed. "I'm raising a family, Jim. I have—well, problems."

"Let me tell you something, Vic. If you were twenty years younger, your family would have the problems because I'd hospitalize you."

"You—you don't mean that—"

"No?" I stared right at him, and he couldn't meet my eyes. "You get those files over to Sloane's."

Veronica was hovering just outside the outer door when I opened it. She circled me quickly and looked in Vic's door, gave an audible sigh of relief, and closed the door. Finding herself standing right beside me, she retreated to her desk, one hand unconsciously smoothing out her skirt. Veronica is more than a little blocky in the butt, but I happen to like them that way. "I'd never have forgiven you if you'd—if you'd—"

I moved toward her, and she put the desk between us. "If I'd what, Veronica?"

"You know. Attacked him."

I advanced around the desk, and she plunged into her swivel chair like a rabbit into its hole. I put a hand under her chin and tilted her face up. "I'd rather attack you, Veronica. Since I figure this office owes me something. Let's have dinner tomorrow night."

Her strange-colored eyes widened again. "You—how could I—you don't mean—"

"Maybe I don't mean dinner," I agreed. "You're wondering how a girl can afford to be seen with such a notorious specimen of wife-killer?" She blinked. "We can fix that," I continued. "I'll meet you at six-thirty tomorrow evening in the parking lot behind Rowley's. We'll go on from there in my car." Rowley's was a roadhouse two towns away.

She was staring up into my face. "I couldn't, Jim. Just because we've—can't you see that things are different now? That you—that you're different? I can't do it. I'm—"

"Rowley's at six-thirty," I said, and I walked out of the office.

I was positive she'd be there.

I picked up my things at the police station after signing a release—someone had light-fingered forty dollars off my roll, but there's a time and a place to make a stink about that sort of thing, and this wasn't it—found my station wagon on the police lot, where it had been towed down from the Stardust, and drove home. The light was on over the portico, and Frank Garvey, one of Chet Dorsey's men, met me on the front steps and handed me the house keys. He had a two-inch cigar stub in one corner of his mouth and a well-chewed toothpick in the other. "Y'hear tell 'bout the burglary?" he asked me.

"What burglary?"

"Yore burglary. Seems as how someone busted into yore livin' room safe the other night an' like to cleaned it out."

"With the police watching the house?"

He shrugged. "Embarrassin', ain't it?"

He followed me inside. I looked at the battered safe without saying anything. Tom Harrington had been too little and too late with that move. Mona's will and a few other important papers hadn't been in the safe since I'd made up my mind three months ago what I was going to do about her and Whit Bailey. I'd driven over to Palmetto and rented a safe deposit box in the local bank under the name of Joseph Winters. Judge Tom Harrington might have the reputation locally of not having made a mistake since 1908, but he'd made one with me. Still, the attempt on the safe was a good weather prognosticator. Harrington was conceding nothing.

When I turned away from my inspection of the damage, Frank Garvey was eyeing me speculatively. It must have been a surprise to a lot of people that I was still walking around Moline, South Carolina, five days after killing Judge Tom Harrington's only daughter. People are always watching to see if the old lion is losing his teeth. Probably no one in Albermarle County thought seriously at the moment that Harrington was losing his, but—there I was, walking around.

He hadn't had a real chance at me yet, of course, except for the first few hours in custody, and he hadn't been around himself to give a direct order that would have let him capitalize on it, something he was entirely capable of doing, judging from past performances. And underlings don't accept that kind of responsibility. It was what I'd been counting on. Afterward, it was natural for Harrington to let the law do his work for him if it would. Since it hadn't, it was into the trenches in earnest.

I hadn't planned to leave the house again until daylight, but the look of the safe changed my mind. What I needed first and foremost was a life insurance policy. I knew where to get it, and sooner, rather than later, seemed to be the sensible order of the evening. Paying no attention to the sleepy-eyed but observant Garvey, I went back outside to the station wagon and drove to Ludmilla Pierson's house. Garvey's car noodled along half a block behind mine. There was a three-quarter moon in the north-east quadrant of the sky, and I hummed to myself as I drove. With a break here and there, the good citizens of Moline, South Carolina, were due for further surprises, starting with Frank Garvey when he saw into whose driveway I'd pulled the station wagon.

The Pierson housekeeper's face expressed shock when she recognized who was ringing the bell. She left me standing on the outside steps while she went to tell Lud who her caller was. I knew Lud would see me, if only to spit in my face. She swept out to the front door in the dramatic manner she'd had even in high school. She's a tall, cool-looking blonde, and while not quite as regal in appearance as she imagines, she makes an impressive entrance. As usual, she was looking down her patrician nose at me. "You've got a nerve, coming here," she started in on me. "You're not going to get away with what you did, you know." Her voice was calm. "You may have bulled that red-neck jury with your tough-guy image and your unwritten law, but there's an older law: an eye for an eye. You're a dead man, Jim Wilson."

"I came over here to tell you why I'm not, Lud. Can we talk? Privately?"

She hesitated before leading the way inside and turning into a small, poorly lighted sitting room crowded with heavy, old-fashioned furniture. "Be quick about it," she said, facing me again. "I despise the sight of you."

"I'll be quick," I said. Looking at her—she was smooth as cake frosting—I found it hard to believe that since her daddy died Ludmilla had been the brains behind the bank, although she never set foot in it. Her classification of southern lady wasn't supposed to know the meaning of work or the odor of perspiration. "You know I'm Mona's heir?" I went on.

"I know." Her lip curled. "An unfortunate residue of the early days of the marriage. You won't live to enjoy her money."

"You talk a hell of a game, Lud, but your needle's stuck. I'll tell you what I'll do: I'll debate it with you tomorrow morning in the high school audi-torium." She sniffed. "No? Then listen for a change, instead of talking. You might learn something. You remember eighteen months ago when it looked as if Tom Harrington might finally have put a foot down wrong before the chief witness in the Crescio case disappeared?"

"I remember," she said, her gray eyes narrowing.

"Twenty-five years ago, he'd have lighted up a fresh cigar and forgotten it, but this time he must have decided he'd come too close to a financial feather-clipping party. He has too much to lose these days, so he began transferring quite a few of his assets to Mona."

"Oh, good God!" Lud exclaimed. She was way ahead of me. "Then you're—"

"When we get out of probate, Lud, I'll be worth more than Tom Harrington."

"Now I *know* you're a dead man," she said flatly.

"Wing Darlington's my heir, Lud. You think Harrington's going to feel any better with Wing on his back? Besides, it's not quite the way you see it. When I'm ready, and that will be damn soon, I'm taking over from Harrington, with a little help you're going to give me."

She was staring at me. "Taking—you're insane!"

"So I'm insane. To change the subject just slightly, Lud, didn't it surprise you when the blackmailer stopped coming around for his money a few months back?"

Her lips thinned. "I don't know what you're talking about."

"Have it your way. I just want you to know you've got a built-in interest in keeping me alive now, Lud, because if anything happens to me I've made arrangements to have the film delivered to someone who doesn't like you. For the sake of your own dear, velvety skin, you'd better get the word to Harrington that, dead, I'm going to smell up a few peoples' front porches."

A slim, white band was at her throat. "Film?"

"Film. Spelled M-O-V-I-E. The movie in which you and Mona share equal billing as a pair of accomplished perverts."

Her face was gray marble. "I'll—" She had to stop and begin again. "I'll buy it from you."

"It's not for sale. Just convince Harrington it's better all around to keep me alive, though, and you're in good shape."

"And how do you think I'm going to convince a vendetta-minded man like Tom Harrington of that?" she cried out passionately.

"Explain to him you've just learned of this movie that would be so damaging to Mona's memory."

"After his forcing you to blacken her name at the hearing, why do you think the idea of the movie would affect him?" she snapped. "I was dead against pushing the hearing, and not only for that reason. I *told* them they couldn't make it stick in this county."

"You preferred to have Harrington hire himself a rifle shot aimed at me from the brush on a side road?"

"Exactly," she said coolly.

"You're lucky you didn't win the argument"—I smiled at her—"because perversion is regarded differently in these parts than good, clean old cuckolding. Harrington's own reputation could be involved, and when he simmers down, he'll realize it. You don't need to say anything to him about your own role in the film, of course. Just tell him I came to you about it because you were Mona's best friend. After the old goat has chewed on it a day or two, you and I will go down to his office and smoke a peace pipe."

"I won't do it!" she blazed. "You're not making *me* a pawn in your harebrained schemes! I refuse absolutely to be seen in public with you, in effect, sponsoring you!"

"Smarten up, Lud. You'll do it or I'll ruin you." I paused for a count of five. "And enjoy myself. You're supposed to have brains. Get it into your head that whenever I say so from now on you'll be seen in public with me, or under me if I take the notion. I'm not playing tiddledywinks with you goddam people. You get on the phone to Harrington and get him straightened out." My voice had started to heat up. I started for the door.

"Wait," she said. I halted. "How did you get—you killed that awful man, didn't you?"

"Killed?" I said. "I just bought the film from him when he came around to blackmail Mona."

She was rallying from the shock I'd given her. "If I couldn't buy it, how do you think you could?" She shook her head decisively. "No. You killed him." She was nibbling at her lower lip. "I want that film."

The imperious note in her voice got to me—Lady Bountiful among the poor. "I wouldn't give it to you even if I didn't need it, Lud. You're the one who took Mona away from me, you and all the rest of the laughing people, laughing at poor ol' stupid Jim Wilson. Snickering up your sleeves for years. You remember the sequence in the movie with you and Mona performing squarely in front of a picture of me, both of you laughing fit to kill? I must have watched it fifty times. Nobody laughs at me, Lud. Nobody." I tried to pull up on the reins as anger surged over me.

"I suppose I'm next on your list, then," she said defiantly.

"I've already told you that I have a better use for you. You're my lily-assed lightning rod."

There was a fifteen second silence. Lud's bands were knitted together in front of her, the knuckles showing white. "You're still angry at Mona, Jim," she said swiftly. It was the first time in ten years she'd used my Christian name without my surname. "The film can't do her any harm now, but think what it could do to me."

It was so exactly the sort of self-centered approach I should have expected from her that I boiled over. "Just what the hell do you think I owe you, Lud? I blame you for the whole rotten mess. You're an out-and-out lesbian, or so close it makes no difference. Was that why, when I had your pants down back in high school, I could never get it in you? I used to think then that you were just a natural-born teaser. How do you keep George in line? D'you make a big sacrifice and lay for him once in a while? Or d'you take care of him some other way? You're no good, Lud, not one damn bit of good. I blame you for what happened to Mona."

"I'll kill you myself," she said between her teeth.

"It'll be the most expensive luxury you've permitted yourself in some time if you expect to look the people of this county in the eye again."

Her voice was shaking. "I want that film! That damn man—I was drunk, the only time in my life I was *ever* drunk! I've *got* to have it! I want—"

"You just keep on wanting. And turn Harrington's juice off until I'm ready to take care of him myself."

She was staring at me again, as she had previously. "You planned it all deliberately, didn't you?" Unexpectedly, she burst into a flood of tears. "I don't c-care," she sobbed. "You didn't n-need to *k-kill* her. D'you realize sh-she's *dead*, you big b-beast?"

I couldn't have been more surprised if a fountain had erupted through the cement of the front walk outside. Crocodile tears? Or the real thing? Who the hell ever knew with a woman? I turned to the door again. "Keep it clean in the clinches, Lud, because I'll be watching you."

She was still sniffling as I went out into the front hall. Whatever else I had expected from the interview, the sight of Ludmilla Pierson in tears hadn't been one of them. I was still trying to figure it out on the drive home.

There was a car parked in my driveway. I pulled in behind it and sat looking at it for a minute before I recognized Wing's Galaxie. It made me realize I had to keep the screw down tight on my nerves. Wing climbed out of the car, carrying a bag. "Thought you'd be along soon," he said cheerfully, following me up the front steps. He slid the bag into a corner of the front hall as we entered it. "Reckon I'll bunk down in your guest room for a few days," he said casually, leading the way into the living room and appropriating my armchair.

"I don't need a bodyguard, Wing."

"The hell you don't, partner."

"I don't want the wrong people thinking I feel I need a bodyguard," I continued patiently. I went over to the liquor cabinet and fixed Wing a drink. As an afterthought I made one for myself.

Wing spoke to my back. "In case you ever get to feelin' you did the wrong thing—"

I didn't turn around. I looked down at the bottles I was returning to the cabinet.

"She made a play for me last year. She didn't want me, but she made the play."

I closed the cabinet door.

"I almost told you because I wasn't the only one. Reckon I was afraid you wouldn't believe me."

I carried him his drink. "I still don't need a bodyguard."

He cocked an eye up at me over his first swallow. "Listen, ol' salty dog, all the goddam heroes—"

"I know where the heroes are."

"You tellin' me you don't want me around, Jim?"

I could hear the hurt in his voice. In the past four years there wasn't much that Wing and I hadn't done together. "You know better than that,

Wing. There's nobody I'd rather have around, but not right now. Not until a few things get settled."

"You're makin' it sound like a blood feud," he grumbled, tossing off half his drink. "All the more damn reason I should be here."

"Thanks, but no." I changed the subject. "How are we doing out on Sunset Lane?"

"No worse'n usual. Only a dozer an' a back hoe broke down today. An' I caught ol' Willie totin' water from a salty spring, spite of all I've warned him. Ruined the mornin' batch of ce-ment Jus' lucky I caught it before we had it down on the road." He briefed me in detail, but his heart obviously wasn't in it. When he finished, the silence stretched out between as.

"I won't be out on the job for a day or two," I said at last.

"Good idea." he said, looking relieved. "Goddam brush grows right down to the roadside all along there. But what difference is a couple days goin' to make?"

"A big difference. I'll have an umbrella up."

He waited, but I didn't elaborate. He finished his drink, changed position uneasily in his chair, and rose restlessly to his feet. "Well, if you're sure—"

"I'm sure. Thanks for the offer, partner."

He shook his head dubiously. On his way to the door he retrieved his bag from the hallway. "Seems like you're playin' a lone hand on this all the way," he said on the steps. His tone was aggrieved.

"It only looks that way right now, Wing," I said, trying to soothe him. "You know I can't give the appearance of hiding from Tom Harrington."

"You're s'posed to sit up for him like a gopher at its hole?"

"I have reason to think there won't be any of that."

"You ain't thinkin' or reasonin', boy," he snorted. "With a polecat like Harrington? I know a man's got to play his cards the way they're dealt, but—well, you change your mind, you call me, y'hear? Anytime. Any damn time at all." He went down the walk, grumbling to himself.

I'd intended to go to bed, but I didn't feel sleepy. Might as well sit up a while longer, I decided. I went over to the liquor cabinet and picked up my neglected drink. Through the window, I could see the moon outside. I sat down, drink in hand, and began to think.

Whatever he'd heard about me, he wouldn't be expecting me this soon.

When I made up my mind, I nursed the drink for better than an hour.

It was after midnight when I left the house again.

The station wagon bumped down the rutted road that was no more than two wheel tracks, its headlight bouncing wildly from mucky marshland and swamp greenery. I kept watching for the lightning-blasted pine, and when I saw it, I stopped the car. I got out and went around to the rear of the wagon, lowered the back gate, and slid Hawk Taylor, tightly trussed, out to the end of it. I put a shoulder under him, carried him around to the front, and dropped him in the track in the glare of the headlights. His eyes stared up at me. They didn't look the same as they had the night at the station house.

I went to the back of the wagon again and lifted out a crowbar. Then I walked back to Taylor and broke his shinbones with two swings of the bar, first the right and then the left. To give the devil his due, he didn't make much noise. I cut him out of the rope, and he sprawled there, sweating. His eyes were closed, and his chest was heaving as if he'd run a mile.

I hunkered down in the track beside him and waited until his eyes opened so I would be sure he'd hear me. "You're two miles from the highway," I told him. "If you've got any guts, you'll make it. But take a piece of advice: when you can walk, leave town. If I see you around, the next time I pack you out into the swamp you'll be bait for the land crabs."

I walked away from him. By the time I had the wagon turned around and headed back the way I'd come, Taylor was already over on his belly and crawling toward the highway.

I drove home and went to bed.

The buzzer wakened me.

My first glance was at the alarm clock: three thirty-five. My second was at the indicator on the chair beside my bed. A red "x" glowed silently in the square, showing that someone had just stepped on the metal plate inside the back door. I'd had a problem after the blackmailer had showed up looking for Mona; since I'd built it, the doors of my house had never been locked, and I couldn't start then without having her ask questions I didn't want to answer The solution had been to get her out of town for a weekend and install the alarm system with its warning box in my first floor bedroom. Mona's bedroom was on the floor above.

I found an electrician in Greensboro, North Carolina, to do the job, and I'd driven him both ways myself to make sure he didn't do any talking about it. He slid a thin metal plate under the linoleum at the kitchen door in the back hallway, a plate under the rug at the front door, and a strip under the rug in front of each of the downstairs windows. The only problem was in the back hall where we had to take up the old linoleum and replace it with new, but it wasn't too much of a job. Mona was surprised to find new linoleum there upon her return, but it wasn't enough of a deal to cause her to comment much. The electrician also put floodlights in the dining room after I convinced him I was serious about it. From then on, the last thing I did each night was to go into the dining room and remove the heavy folds of Mona's draperies that I kept over the lights in the daytime, then set up the indicator box beside my bed. I kept it in a locked closet, and nothing was activated before I set it up and turned it on. If Mona had been any kind of housekeeper at all, she'd have been almost sure to notice the new arrangement of her draperies; but she never did.

I groped for the .38 under my pillow and eased myself out of bed. To reach the bedroom, the intruder had to come through the dining room, and in doing so, he was making a surprising amount of noise. I waited just outside the dining room door, with my finger on a special switch. When I heard a stumbling step well into the room, I touched the switch. A bank of floodlights turned the room into a goldfish howl. The slight figure in the room's center yipped aloud and pivoted in surprise. I just did stay off the trigger. The man was Albert Brown, a not-too-bright-in-the-head colored boy who did odd jobs around town. He had a gray blanket on his arm, and his color nearly matched it as he stared at me. "I sure didn' know you was home, Mist' Wilson!" he blurted out at last. His bulging eyes were on the .38.

"What're you doing here this time of night, Albert?" I asked sternly.

He held out the blanket. "Mist' Wheeler done stopped me on Pearl Street jus' now an' took this outn' his car an' ast me to fetch it here an' leave it. Seem like they borreyed it when they was watchin' the house while— while you was away. They want it put back, he say."

It was my blanket, all right. Billy Wheeler was another of Chet Dorsey's men. If I hadn't had the floodlights rigged, or if I'd fired without getting a good look at Albert, another coroner's jury getting a look at me in quick succession might have had an entirely different recommendation to make concerning the killing of a harmless, simple-minded, local colored man. "All right, Albert," I said gruffly, shaken by the close call. "You run along."

I followed him out into the kitchen to the back door and watched him go down the path.

Then I went back to bed, but not to sleep. It hadn't been a bad move on Harrington's part, I thought. Not a bad move at all. Evidently a slug from the brush wasn't the only thing I had to fear from the old wolf.

I'd have to check with Lud and see if she'd given him the word. The smart thing to do might be to go and see him right away, although it was earlier in the game than I'd intended. Waiting on a battle-scarred old coyote like Harrington, though, could turn out to be not quite bright.

I'd see him soon. See him, and begin the tooth-pulling process.

The decision made, I fell asleep again.

CHAPTER 3

The next evening, I pulled onto Rowley's semi-deserted parking lot at six twenty-five. At midnight the lot would be jammed. I almost hadn't come. What had seemed like a fine idea the night before, when in juxtaposition to Veronica Peters' lush amplitude, had in bright daylight seemed a much less pressing matter.

A bare arm waved to me from Veronica's blue Dodge, and I walked over to it. The redhead sat in silence as I approached her and opened the door of her car. "We'll come back for your car," I told her.

"Where are we going?" she asked, sliding out from under the wheel and pulling down her rucked-up skirt as she straightened up. I didn't answer her. She led the way over to the station wagon. She was wearing a sleeveless pink dress. Redheads aren't supposed to be able to wear pink, but I couldn't see anything wrong with the color scheme parading across the parking lot in front of me. There was a lot less strain on my eyes than on the back seams of her skirt. I was beginning to look with favor upon the program again.

"I really don't know why I came," she said as I handed her into the wagon. "I couldn't explain it to—to anyone. But here I am." She turned her head to study me, as if expecting to find the answer printed on my forehead.

I didn't say anything. Women are always trying to justify themselves to men. And to themselves. A waste of time and breath. A lot of foofaraw for nothing.

"You—scared me last night," she went on. "And after—after what happened—well, I shouldn't have come. I don't know why I came."

"You came because you like getting shafted, puss."

"What a thing to say!" she said indignantly.

"Well?" I challenged her. "What's wrong with a roll in the hay?"

She pursed her full lips. "With a man who so recently—so recently—" She didn't try to finish it. "Sitting in the car waiting, I couldn't find an excuse for myself, let alone expect anyone else to. But here I am. I'm—"

I tuned her out. Conversation wasn't what I wanted from this one. I boomed the wagon down the road. Three miles from Rowley's, a smart farmer had thrown up half a dozen well-separated three-room cabins in a grove of jackpines. No highway signs advertised the place, but there were never any vacancies anyway. Wing and I split the rent on a cabin, year-round, and the others were similarly spoken for. I'd never brought Veronica out here before. Once in a while I used to come out alone for a weekend's quiet drinking, but usually the atmosphere was communal and hectic. I turned into the unmarked driveway and continued along it to the last cabin. If Wing's Galaxie had been parked in the slot, I'd have swung right around onto the highway again and gone to a motel, since in my present state of ripe odor in the town I could hardly expect Veronica to try to smuggle me into her apartment as before. The stall was empty, though. I parked the wagon, got out and fished for my key.

"My, it's quiet here," Veronica commented. She teetered on her high heels in the pine-needled soft turf, and I took her arm. When I had unlocked the cabin door, I ushered her inside. "Isn't it nice," she exclaimed.

Wing and I had spent a few dollars outfitting the interior. We'd hauled a couple of loads of furniture out from town, including a ton-and-a-half air-conditioner. "You like it cool, honey?" Wing used to say to his little pullets. "You jus' let the ol' Wingman push this heah button down an' in fifteen minutes your maidenhair'll be frosted, sugar. You won't have no complaints about the de-froster, neither."

The place had two bedrooms, a john with a fully tiled shower, and a completely equipped kitchen. Veronica tap-tapped from room to room in her high heels, inspecting everything. I had turned on the air-conditioner and had my shirt off already when she came back into the first bedroom. I took hold of her and turned her around and unbuttoned the three little buttons on the neck of her dress at the back. I looked at my watch, stooped, and took hold of the hem of her skirt; and in fifty seconds I had her shucked out of dress, slip, girdle, and bra without tearing a thing. Wing and I used to have contests for cases of beer.

Out of her clothes, there was a hell of a lot of Veronica. "My God!" she said, kicking off her shoes and sitting down on the edge of the bed in her stockings. "I couldn't have undressed that fast myself."

I stripped and joined her. I tipped her onto her back and filled my hands. Then I flipped her onto her belly and filled them again. My response was automatic. "You really do have a big ass, girl," I told her. "Let's put it to work."

One reason I kept coming back to her when I kept telling myself I really didn't have the time to fool around was that she was good in bed. She enjoyed it, and she worked at it. "Not so—fast!" she protested breathlessly, but she popped her weasel before I did.

"Like to shower?" I asked her after we played the last half of the first inning without changing sides.

"Together?" she said archly.

"Sure."

"Don't get my hair wet," she cautioned as she bent over to remove her stockings. She yelped and bounded eighteen inches into the air when I whacked her.

We didn't get her hair wet.

Any that showed in public, that is.

Back in the bedroom, I looked at my watch. I had a nine o'clock appointment with George Pierson. Veronica came up behind me, put her arms around me, and massaged my stomach with her palms. We gravitated back to the bed. Veronica certainly discarded her inhibitions with her clothes. She instituted a couple of new variations on the theme. I responded in counterpoint. *"Owwww!"* she squealed shrilly, bucking wildly and trying to roll onto her back.

"Hold still and I'll match it for you," I told her, turning her onto her stomach again.

"Ooooooh!" she squalled. *"Jim!"*

"Show those to your girl friends," I suggested, letting her scramble free.

For the next few moments the action was voiceless but not soundless. Where the script called for a grunt, Veronica grunted. She was an earnest laborer in the vineyard. Out of the shower again—singly this time—I took another look at my watch. "Sorry to break up the party," I said. Obediently she reached for her clothes. I sat on the edge of the bed and watched my teeth marks disappearing into her girdle. "What's new at the office these days?" I asked.

She shrugged into her slip. "Not much, unless you count Mr. Harrington sending Mr. Cartwright over to Spartanburg for a couple of days," she replied muffledly.

It was a good thing she was enveloped in the slip and couldn't see me; I had half-risen from the bed before I thought. The blackmailer had been from Spartanburg. Had Lud known it? It hardly seemed possible. Cartwright wasn't Harrington's lawyer, though. Sounded as if the old buzzard wasn't letting his right hand know what his left was doing.

Her slip in place, Veronica had turned around and was looking at me. "Which will give me some extra time off," she said.

"We'll have to take advantage of it," I said, and I thought even better of it as I heard the sound of my own words. A foot in the enemy camp wasn't a bad idea at all, even if the foot had never worn a shoe. Perhaps especially if it hadn't.

From Veronica's seat in the grandstand—hell, from any woman's—I was now an eligible target, of course, once a few niceties had been complied with. And she had to figure she had the inside track. I wondered how long it would be before she took to hinting about marriage. It would be the end of a beautiful friendship. I wasn't about to marry Veronica—or any other woman, for that matter. I'd been that route and learned the hard way that in the Dollar Sweepstakes single-saddle carried the least weight.

I had Veronica back at the blue Dodge in a hundred and twenty minutes, portal-to-portal time. "It's been great," I said, and I was surprised to find myself speaking the truth. I'd unloaded a whale of a lot of tension on that plump white body, tension that had been building up for some time. Why on earth couldn't it have been like that with Mona? I backed away from the thought. It never had been, even at the beginning. "I'll call you, Veronica." She gave me a big smile, and I watched her drive out of the parking lot.

Since Cartwright was in Harrington's pocket, there was always the chance that she'd been planted on me.

I didn't think so, though. Even at her apartment, we'd always been discreet. Although you never can be sure about a thing like that, I didn't think anyone knew about us. But the idea of her having been planted was something to keep in mind; there was no point in becoming careless now.

I made my nine o'clock appointment with five minutes to spare, but George Pierson didn't. I waited thirty-five minutes before giving it up as a bad job and heading on home.

I began telephoning Ludmilla Pierson the middle of the following afternoon when I hadn't heard from her. The fifth time that the housekeeper told me Mrs. Pierson wasn't in and it wasn't known when she was expected, I piled into the station wagon and drove over there. I could see Lud's car in the garage, which was all I needed to know.

The housekeeper opened the front door and stepped into the entrance, blocking it, when she saw who it was. "Mrs. Pierson is—" she began.

"In," I said, cutting her off. I shouldered her aside, and an indignant gasp pursued me down the hall. I toured the ground floor rooms rapidly, but there was no sign of Lud. With the hard-breathing, matronly housekeeper on my heels, I turned to the ornate stairway leading to the second floor.

"You can't go up there!" the woman exclaimed behind me on the stairs. "I'll call the—you have no business in this house!"

I didn't answer her. I went down the second-floor hallway, opening doors. I found Lud in a bedroom at the end of the hall. She was half-reclining in a lounger with a sheaf of papers on her lap and spectacles perched on the end of her nose. A bulging briefcase was beside her chair.

"I couldn't stop him, Miss Ludmilla!"—the housekeeper's shaken voice came over my shoulder. "He's like a—like a steamroller!"

"It's all right, Margaret," Lud said quietly. She removed the spectacles, folded them, and slipped them into a glasses case. "I'll take care of it."

The housekeeper looked doubtful, but accepted the implied dismissal. "What's with the business-tycoon act?" I asked Lud when the door had closed behind the housekeeper.

"Doing George's homework for him," she said. She methodically stuffed papers into the briefcase. Finished, she leaned back and looked at me. "Don't you think you'd better leave?"

The mention of George had sidetracked me for an instant; I wondered if Lud had had anything to do with George's breaking the appointment last night. I shunted myself back onto the main course. "Did you call Harrington?"

"Yes." She wasn't as much at ease with me as she was trying to pretend; the tip of her tongue emerged and flicked lightly over her lips. She had on no lipstick that I could see.

"Did you tell him I wanted to meet with him?"

"No," she said defiantly.

"Then get on the phone to him, damn it. We'll go clown to his office right now."

She flushed and started to say something, then changed her mind. "He's not at his office," she said finally. "He's still at home, recuperating."

"It won't kill him to go down to his office for thirty minutes. Call him and tell him we're on our way down there."

She swung her feet to the floor and sat up straight on the side of the reclining chair. "Jim, why don't we—"

"Call him, Lud."

She flared up like a roman candle. "If you think you can—"

"I *am* pushing you around." I made my voice override hers. "Call him. I haven't got all day."

The telephone was on a marble-topped table beside the bed. She got up slowly and went over to it. I was just a step behind her. She had on a bright print dress, and I could see a faint sheen on her bare shoulders and beads of perspiration on her upper lip. It wasn't that hot. I knew it was grinding her down that she couldn't think her way out of the cat's cradle I'd landed her in. She was so used to being in control of a situation that with someone else's foot on the horsepower she didn't know up from sideways. "Hold the phone so I can hear him, too," I told her as she dialed.

She didn't look at me. "This is Lud, Tom," she said swiftly into the phone. She sounded anxious to get it over with. "Jim Wilson's here and he wants to meet you down at your office right away."

She held the phone away from her ear, and I could hear Harrington's cracked voice plainly. "Pushy bastard, isn't he?" he said drily.

"I really think perhaps you ought to do it," Lud said. "We could come right down."

"*We* could come right down?" Harrington repeated, emphasizing the pronoun. "For the record, Ludmilla, whose side are you on?"

"You know whose side I'm on!" she retorted angrily.

"Do I?" There was an audible grant. "I wonder. You're pushin' me hard on this, seems as though."

"You know how I feel—felt about Mona! I'm just trying to do what's—
"

"No sense in our fussin' at each other," he interrupted. "Could be just what Wilson wants. I wasn't goin' down to the office today, but I reckon I can manage it. These damn doctors an' their carvin' on a man—" He stopped. "Half an hour all right?"

"Fine. We'll be there." She replaced the receiver, stood with her back to me for an instant, and stared across the room at the far wall. Then she walked to the door, still without looking at me.

I followed her, feeling the same familiar upsurge of adrenalin I experienced when the bouncing dice rolled down the table top.

Soon I'd know whether I actually had Judge Tom Harrington where I wanted him. I was almost sure that I did, but with an old gray wolf like Harrington, how could I be positive?

Out on the front walk, Lud headed for my station wagon, which was parked in the driveway. "We'll take your car," I said.

She was already stooping to slide into the passenger's side of the station wagon's front seat. Her dress and slip were so thin I could see plainly the outline of her pants on the round bulge of her fanny. She straightened up slowly. "You and your goddammed pound of flesh," she said bitterly when my meaning became clear to her. In my car, there just possibly might be an acceptable explanation for her being with me. In hers, there was no question that she was with me all the way.

We walked to the garage and her car, and she started to head for the driver's side. "I'll drive," I told her. She started to protest, but thought better of it. I backed her car down the driveway, around my station wagon, and out onto the street. I was still thinking about Lud's underwear. It was hard to believe that years ago I'd sweet-talked her out of it, even though nothing had come of it. What had it been like? I couldn't remember. Whatever the sensation had been, it had long since blended with a thousand others.

We headed downtown. She sat erectly beside me, her hands tightly folded over the handbag in her lap. In the square, I parked across the street from the bank. Harrington had his suite of offices above it. "On a day as hot as this, you can certainly park closer," Lud said irritably. She turned suddenly to glare at me. "If you think you're going to parade me around the square like a—like a Roman triumph—!"

"Glad to see you're up on your history, Mrs. Pierson. Prepare to parade."

"I won't do it!" she stormed. Her gray eyes were blazing. "I won't go with you!"

"You're not calling this square dance, Lud. If I have to, I'll carry you. Or if you think your hole card's better than mine, call my hand." There was an electric silence. "Now get the hell out of the car."

She did so, and she was an actress. Before she hit the sidewalk, her thin-lipped mask of anger had changed to her usual smooth-faced, patrician hauteur. Side by side, we marched around two sides of the square to

Harrington's office, and to look at her you'd think she'd been doing it every day of her life.

I could picture the rush to the front windows of the shops we passed.

"Isn't that—?"

"What in the world?"

"Why, I thought—"

"Ludmilla Pierson and Jim Wilson, of all people! What do you suppose—"

In Moline, South Carolina, it counts more than in most places whom you walk out in public with.

I knew that Lud could see the picture, too, but her veneer never cracked. We entered the door to the right of the bank entrance and climbed narrow stairs to the second floor. She was two steps ahead of me, and I was again able to observe at close range the play of sleek hips and long legs beneath her skirt. She didn't appear to have gained an ounce since high school. She led the way down the second floor corridor and opened a door with Harrington's name lettered on it.

There were three desks in the first office, two of them empty. Judge Tom Harrington sat at the third. He was a big-framed man, but he looked shrunken, somehow. His hair had been white ever since I could remember, but it had been cut recently by an inexpert barber, probably while he was in the hospital, and the flowing mane that had usually lent him dignity looked like chopped cotton. His face was deeply lined, more so than I remembered it, and his prow of a nose subordinated the rest of his seemingly diminished features. His eyes had a yellowish tinge. I realized that Lud was staring at him, too. Tom Harrington looked old.

"Pardon my not risin', Ludmilla," he said. "These damn doctors an' their whittlin'—" he didn't finish it, and he didn't look in my direction. Even his voice was different. The familiar resonance was missing.

"You'd like to get this over quickly," Lud said. It was a statement, rather than a question. She remained standing.

"Reckon I would," Harrington agreed. One hand rubbed the back of his neck slowly. The yellow-tinged eyes still hadn't come to rest on my face. "No doubt about this heah movie, Ludmilla?"

"None, Tom."

"An' he can do what he threatens?"

"I've seen the—the evidence. He can do it. Dead or alive."

Harrington's expression didn't change. "What's his proposition?"

I opened my mouth for the first time since leaving the sidewalk below. "I'll make my own proposition, Harrington."

The yellow-flecked eyes hit me a glancing blow before returning to Lud. "Reckon you'd best step into the other office for a minute," he said to her, and he waited for the door to close behind her. "Well, Wilson?"

"I want the Edmonds Road job. For a starter."

"You've got it."

It took me by surprise. "I'm talking about the whole contract: grading, drainage, culverts, bituminous paving—"

"I said you've got it."

"Well—" I said uncertainly. The old goat had certainly taken the wind out of my sails. "Then I guess I'll just walk across the street to the *Clarion* office and give them the item." I couldn't resist trying to harpoon him. "Should I tell them we weren't the low bidder?"

For an instant, the glare was back in the tawny eyes. "They know it!" he snapped. The glare subsided. "Tell them anything you damn please, except about one thing," he continued wearily. He appeared to be turning something over in his mind. "I could be a loser all the way around in this jackpot, Wilson. Suppose Whit Bailey's friends get to you?"

"I don't happen to think Bailey's got that kind of friends. If he should, though, don't you think you ought to convince them you have priority?"

He growled something deep in his throat. "If I was—"

"Yes, I know. If you were twenty years younger, you'd exercise the priority."

"If I was a year younger, damn you!" He subsided again, staring down at his desk top.

"We'll have more to talk about later," I said. He didn't answer me. I went over and knocked on the door of the inner office. "We're leaving now," I said to Lud when she came in.

She looked at Harrington for confirmation. "Pardon my not risin', Ludmilla," he said.

At this left-handed corroboration, she preceded me through the outer door. She couldn't wait to get downstairs to the street to find out what happened; she stopped in the middle of the stairs. "Well?" she demanded.

"Wing and I get the Edmonds Road job."

She cocked an eyebrow. "Just like that?"

"Just like that. For openers."

She didn't appear to hear the needle I intended her to get. "He's an old man," she said. There was a wondering note in her voice. "An *old* man." Her eyes focused on me again. "What's the rest of your bargain? Me staked out naked over an anthill?"

"Too good for you, Lud."

She smiled. "Do I have to drive you back to the house?"

"You run along," I decided. "I've got a little business downtown. I'll catch a ride out later and pick up the wagon."

We descended the rest of the stairs, and out on the sidewalk she walked away from me without a backward glance. I watched her go, then glanced around the square. Nothing was moving; people were standing. Standing and watching. I headed diagonally across the street to the *Clarion* office.

They wouldn't be surprised at my news item. Tom Harrington had been top dog in the county for a long time, and he worked hand-in-glove with the city's politicians, the people who mattered. And he had pipelines into the important state offices. The *Clarion* people might be puzzled over the reason for Harrington's giving me the job, but not at his ability to do so.

Reb Dunleavy, who had some kind of job in the mayor's office, came hustling out of Abbott's Drug Store and angled to meet me. His jackal face was alive with curiosity. "You walkin', Jim?" he asked eagerly. "Give you a lift somewheres?"

I started to refuse, then changed my mind. Let the word get back where it would do the most good. "Give me five minutes with Roy in the *Clarion* office and you can run me a couple miles out to my car, Reb."

"Sure, Jim. Sure. I'm parked in front of the bank."

Twenty minutes later I was climbing into the station wagon again, after watching Dunleavy's beady little eyes widen when he recognized where it was parked. When Reb rushed back to town and checked on the item in the *Clarion,* and with his other news, he was going to make the *Clarion's* next edition superfluous by the time he finished broadcasting.

I started back to my house to get my boots before driving out to Sunset Lane to tell Wing about the Edmonds Road job. On the way, I thought about Tom Harrington. The whole affair had gone so easily that there hadn't been nearly the pleasure in it that I'd anticipated. Was there a warning in that? Had Harrington given in too easily? A factor I hadn't considered previously was slowly coming to the surface as one of prime importance: it would be twelve to fifteen months before Mona's estate was settled, twelve to fifteen months before I swung any kind of financial leverage against Tom Harrington. Could he be thinking in terms of sabotage on current jobs that could break me before I got my hands on Mona's—and his—money?

I was going to have to tell Wing to be careful.

There was a black sedan parked in front of my house, and a man got out of it as I drove up. He was tall, rawboned, and young-looking. He had large ears and a high-cheekboned face whose expression was solemn. For an instant I couldn't place him, and then I did. He was the Moody boy—I couldn't call his first name—who'd held my arms the night Hawk Taylor worked me over at the station house.

He shambled over to the station wagon and leaned in the front window. "Reckoned you'd be lookin' for me," he said stiffly. "Thought I'd save you the trouble."

He'd heard what had happened to Taylor. This was a country boy, right out of the clay hill canebrakes, and the worst thing I could do would be to ha-ha him that he'd just been doing his job and Taylor was the only one I was interested in—which was true. If this type got to brooding afterward and decided I was soft-soaping him against the day I toted him out into the swamp, too, he'd be likely to mount a scope on his deer rifle and do a little stalking of his own.

"Let's go around to the side yard," I suggested.

"Fine," he said. He looked relieved.

We walked around the house to the twenty-by-thirty Anchor-fenced enclosure, unbuttoning as we went. Mona used to keep her dog in the side yard before she got rid of it because the dog paid more attention to me. Moody and I stripped to the waist. On the street he'd looked skinny, but squaring off, I noticed he had long arms and a slab-sided pair of shoulders. In the first thirty seconds, he rattled my teeth three times with punches that seemed to come out of nowhere. It dawned on me then that he was a southpaw and I was circling right into him. I reversed and went the other way, then found I still couldn't get past his right jab. He ticked me off with it steadily until I bulled inside and whaled him with both hands to the belly. It dropped his guard, and I decked him with a chopping right.

He bounced right up again and charged me. We ricocheted off the fence a couple of times, and I could feel skin staying with the fence. After his quick round trip to the turf, Moody wouldn't back up and he wouldn't cover up. He just planted himself, leaned in, and traded punches. He had knotty, plowboy knuckles that cut when they landed. Once I had his style figured, he landed only one to my three, but he threw them steadily from out in left field. He was a willing workman.

It took me another three or four minutes to time his left hand and drop my right over it consistently. Each time I landed after that he went down, and he kept getting up more slowly, but he kept getting up. He was leaking blood from half a dozen gashes, but he kept trying doggedly to land that left hand again in a meaningful way. I feinted him once, then twice. When he reacted, off-balance, I nailed him a lick that sent him staggering backward into the fence. As he reeled foreward again, I caught him with a right that picked him up and turned him around. He landed flat on his belly.

I thought that was it, but his knees scrabbled busily, as he tried to get himself started upright again. This kid was really something. I knelt down beside him, then sat on his head. He kicked steadily for a minute, trying to dislodge me, and then ran out of steam. I waited another minute to be sure he'd petered out before I got up. It took Moody a while to stumble to his feet. His arms dangled straight down at his sides, and his tongue licked at a trickle of blood at a corner of his mouth. He kept shaking his head. " 'Fore—God, Wilson, you hit—a mean lick," he panted. He was looking over my shoulder. When I turned to see why, people were lined up two deep against the side fence. No one said anything, and no one had come into the yard to break it up. In Albermarle County it isn't done.

I turned back to Moody. "Let's go inside and clean up."

He nodded, and we picked up our clothes and walked to the gate. My legs felt like lead. The side yard turf was badly torn up. It looked as if a drunken elephant had been taking dancing lessons. Inside, I showed Moody the downstairs bathroom. "Take your time," I told him. He nodded again. I didn't feel up to any five-minute speeches myself.

I went upstairs to the big bathroom and took inventory. I had a cut over my left brow, a swollen nose, a puffed lip, and purpling bruises on the ribs on my right side. Plus I'd scraped a yard of skin from my back onto the fence. I washed up and took care of the oozes with a styptic pencil. Downstairs again, I went to the liquor cabinet, and when Moody came out of the bathroom dabbing at his face with a wet towel, I handed him the styptic pencil and a three-ounce jigger of bourbon. He tossed the jigger's contents back in a swallow, then stood as if he was listening to something. In forty-five seconds he was green. He dashed back into the bathroom, and he was really racked. He didn't know it, but the bourbon-induced nausea was a part of his licking.

I sipped my own drink slowly, letting it trickle down to my still-churn-ing stomach. It was another five minutes before Moody emerged again, very pale. He'd made good use of the styptic pencil. He had only one slash—high on a prominent cheekbone—that was still bleeding. He also had some lumps that would get lumpier.

"I reckon that was a real kid trick, tossin' that bourbon down," he said, getting into his shirt. If his arms felt like mine, I could sympathize with his grimaces. Our breathing was almost back to normal, though. When he had his jacket on, I put on my shirt and walked out front with him to his car. He looked almost cheerful as he got behind the wheel. He squinted up at me from one half-closed eye. "Good day to you, Wilson," he said. Then he drove off.

It made me wonder what it felt like to be that young again and without a worry in the world. Moody had taken his licking and had lost no face. Around Albermarle County there's nothing more important. Tonight he could walk down Beauregard Street and, in response to joshing queries about his appearance, say easily: "Oh, I drove over to see Jim Wilson this afternoon." Nobody would ask any foolish questions. And if his friends expressed the hope that he had done all right, he could say just as casual-ly: "I reckon he messed up a time or two."

It seemed a long time back to the days when I'd been like that.

With no further need to act like an iron man, I went back upstairs and stripped. I stood under the shower's hot water for twenty minutes, soak-ing out the major aches. Dressed again except for shoes, I went down to the back hall and routed out my cement-encrusted snake boots. After I had pulled them on, I set out for Sunset Lane and Wing Darlington.

CHAPTER 4

At my uncle's place on the edge of town, the barn stood four times as high as the house that had been home to me from the time I was five until I was thirteen. The front parlor had a fireplace twelve feet wide; there were fourteen-foot ceilings in all the rooms, and sixteen-inch oak planks for flooring. People restoring houses would pay upward of ten dollars a board for that flooring today. From the weathercock on its roof to the washtubs out in front, the barn, which was the largest in the neighborhood, received a fresh coat of paint every third year. The house, a shabby, peeling gray-white, was never painted in my time there.

My father died when I was four, and my mother ran off with a traveling man. Or so my uncle told me; I was twenty before I learned she'd married a farm machinery salesman and they'd been killed on their honeymoon when he drove his car into the side of a freight train during a heavy fog. The same party who told me that also mentioned that my uncle had courted my mother for six months before she married the salesman. After the things he'd had me thinking about her, it was a good thing for him he wasn't available to me the day I found it out.

He was my father's half-brother, actually, and a slob. He had to depend on good hired help to keep the farm going. He and my father had never got along, although I didn't find that out until years later, either. My uncle was a God-fearing man; I heard him say so often enough. He had other favorite sayings. "Preventative medicine," he used to say, snapping his galluses over his pot belly—I've never liked fat men since—and rolling his eyes toward the dog whip on its handy nail in the kitchen. "Preventative medicine. Catch 'em young an' train 'em right That's the ticket, ain't that kee-rect, Lucy? Ho-ho-ho."

Lucy, his wife, was a wraith of a woman. When two minutes away from her, I couldn't remember her features. She would smile timidly at each such sally of her husband and say nothing. At thirteen, I was six feet tall, but I weighed only a hundred and fifteen pounds, and in any losing jousts with my uncle's authority, I learned that he could take off a right smart bit of skin with his damned dog whip. Since even then I had what could be called an independent nature, the dog whip and I were no strangers to each other.

Not that I felt particularly abused. I knew plenty of kids who had it tougher than I did, and from their own folks. My trouble was that I never learned to keep my mouth shut. Measured against the output of the hired hands on the place, my work was a man's work, even though I was only thirteen. I knew better, since my uncle was tighter than a tractor tire to the rim of its wheel, but out in the barn one day, I told him I'd appreciate a few coins to jingle together in my pocket at the four-corner store come Saturday evening. He turned scarlet. "Just like your Jezebel mother!" he trumpeted, grabbing me and snaking from his pants the belt that always reinforced his galluses. "I'll teach you to want to hang around with other no-goods like yourself, sniggering over Satan only knows what!"

I was afraid of him, but that time I fought him. I think it surprised him that he had so much trouble. When it was over, he stood there panting, glaring down at me on the rough barn flooring between his feet, "Reckon——you need—t' be shown—a little oftener—who's boss—around here!" he said, wheezing. "Now go tend t' the cows like y' should've been doin'—in the first place!"

I tended to the cows, and sometime during the process, I decided I wasn't having any more of that. For a week I thought of elaborate schemes, then on impulse acted upon a simple one. I came in from the barn one night with a half a dozen two-foot lengths of baling wire under my shirt. I carried them up to my attic room. My uncle's house was an early-to-bed house, and by ten o'clock it was silent. I made a bundle of my things, then sat by the window so I wouldn't fall asleep. When the grandfather clock in the front parlor chimed midnight, I tiptoed downstairs to the kitchen and acquired the dog whip and a chunk of cordwood from the woodbox. With the baling wire in my hip pocket, I walked boldly into the bedroom of my uncle and aunt.

I'd counted on the fact that he was a heavy sleeper, and he never moved; but my aunt raised her head. "Get out of bed," I whispered to her between his heavy snores. I thought she might scream, but I didn't care. That's why I had the cordwood chunk—for him, not for her. She slipped quietly from the bed, though. I placed my chunk nearby, in case I needed it, then reached for my baling wire. I had my uncle tangled up in the sheet and his forearms wire-wrapped together before he began to come to at all. It took me longer to wire his kicking feet.

I'd been watching my aunt from the corner of my eye, but she had seated herself in the room's only chair. I picked up the dog whip and worked the sheet over from end to end. The sounds that came from beneath it only stimulated me to greater effort. During the whole performance, my aunt never said a word or made a move. I dropped the whip finally, went back to my room to pick up my bundle, and left the house.

I didn't stop walking until I reached the county line; and I slept the next day in a ditch under a cottonwood tree. The second night, I walked across another county and slept out in a cornfield. The third morning, I hired out to a farmer. I told him I was sixteen. I wasn't too much concerned that anybody would come after me and try to bring me back. Anybody official, that is. In Albermarle County, no one was going to interfere with my uncle's dog whip, but no one was going to interfere with my getting out from under it, either.

The second week I was with the farmer, I was bulling a gang plow behind a span of three horses in a field at the edge of the county road. An Albermarle County cruiser drifted by and Deputy Jed Matthews looked me squarely in the eye and then kept on going down the road without a sign of recognition. Years later he told me that after I'd disappeared and they'd seen the shape I'd left my uncle in, there'd been some concern that he might have buried me out on the back forty. When they found out he hadn't, official interest lapsed. No one ever told my uncle where to find me.

I stayed with the farmer for two years before moving back to Albermarle County. I got a room in Moline and a job in the jute mill unloading hundred-pound sacks from freight cars. I'd grown another two inches and put on fifty hard pounds. After a couple of months at the mill, Jed Matthews came wandering into my freight car one day, mumbling that I had to go back to school. I wouldn't have paid any attention to him, but he went to my boss, Rafe Larkin, too. Fortunately, Rafe liked my work well enough by that time to work out a deal. I worked two shifts at the mill, from four to seven in the morning and from four to nine in the evening and in between I went to high school. At first I had trouble picking up in school after a two-year lapse, but I finally caught on to it again.

My algebra teacher was Miss Eleanor Townsend, a middle-aged old maid with a spirit to match her pepper-and-salt hair. She kept telling me I should go on to college, and I kept saying 'Yes,' but I paid no attention. Then I heard she'd tackled my uncle about it on the street one day—he and I didn't speak the few times we met—and he'd said for the world to hear that I didn't have brains enough to pound sand in a hole properly, and he wasn't about to waste money sending me to college, even if part of the farm *was* to be my inheritance at twenty-one. That was the first I'd heard of it.

So naturally I went to college to spite him. Rafe Larkin got me a job in a cotton mill in Charleston, and that carried the load. I'd always liked figures, so I went the engineering route. Summer jobs were easier to get with that background, too, when the mill slacked in hot weather. I was no ball of fire in the classroom, but I burned enough midnight oil to finish in the top third of the class.

Even with my job at the mill, I didn't have money for weekends at home, and not much to go home to, anyway, but my third year at school, I met a good-looking girl who didn't run from me. We had a few dates, and kid-like, I had to show her off. I borrowed a car and drove her to Moline and paraded her around town. The Larkins put her up.

That should have been all there was to it, except that I was me. In one of our walking tours of the town, the girl and I passed the Salisbury Tavern with its usual quota of loungers out front. There was a chorus of whistles, and a heavy voice said distinctly: "Lookit the ass on *that!*" I turned to see who'd said it. That was Mistake Number One—and the only one I really needed to make because the speaker was Luke Johnson, the bully boy of the county. If I ignored the remark after identifying the source, I was branded, and if I didn't, I was guaranteed a great deal more than I could handle.

The girl's hand had tightened on my arm as she tried to walk me past the Salisbury. I shook her hand off and walked over to Johnson, a hulking, black-browed giant with shoulders like a mule's hindquarters. "Maybe you'd like to apologize for what you just said?" I asked him. I was so mad—and so scared—my voice cracked in a falsetto. Johnson laughed, then slapped my face with a contemptuous backhander I didn't even see coming. Furious at myself, I nailed him solidly with my best shot. It moved his head back maybe six inches. He grunted and went to work on me in earnest.

For years afterward, people told me solemnly how they'd kept count of the number of times I got up from the ground. Depending on the teller, it varied from thirteen to twenty-one. Toward the end, Johnson's voice changed from a snarl to a plea. "Stay down, you sonofabitch! Stay down!" he kept saying. He was still almost unmarked when he turned abruptly and walked up the street.

I rocked back and forth on my heels, sick and dizzy, trying to remain upright. The girl had disappeared, as any sensible girl would have done. I took an uncertain step, and then another, found I could walk, and wobbled through the Salisbury's swinging doors. The crowd followed me inside, no one saying anything. I hooked my elbows over the top of the bar, trying to look casual and not as though the bar was holding me up. "Whiskey," I said to Al Gershon, the bartender. I'd never had more than a beer in my life, but I tossed the shot of bourbon down the way I'd seen others do. I barely made it into the men's room before spraying it off two walls. When I could breathe again, I mopped the blood off my face with my handkerchief, left the Salisbury without speaking to anyone, and took the back streets to the Larkin house.

The girl had returned almost in hysterics, and Rafe, that patient man, had dispatched his wife to drive her back to school. Rafe patched me up himself, and after a night's sleep, I felt almost human again. Before Rafe would let me drive myself back to school, though, I was two days overdue.

I never saw the girl again, but I never again had trouble in Moline like the Johnson trouble, either.

Out on Sunset Lane, the scattered backhoes, graders, and bulldozers were sputtering, fuming, and smoking. I found Wing holding up a line of cement trucks, their huge drums revolving, while he tested a sample of the cement poured from a drum. He used a hollow steel cone, twelve inches high, eight inches in diameter at the base and four at the top. He poured cement into it, tamped it down vigorously, and repeated the process several times. When the cone was packed solid, he lifted it up by projections on its base and watched the wet cement settle. A two-inch slump was permissible; anything more meant an inferior mix. The county inspector performed the same test at our batching plant before sending the trucks out, but we usually checked it again on the job site, too.

Wing waved the line of trucks ahead to the paver with its maw waiting to receive the trucks' cement, tossed the cone aside, then turned and saw me. His eyebrows lifted comically. "What'n'ell happened to your face?" he wanted to know.

"Young Moody came by to see me," I explained. "He was one of the ones at the station house that night."

"Aaahh," Wing said softly. He had never asked me about Taylor. He was wearing nothing but boots and cement-stiff work pants, and he hadn't shaved that moaning. One side of his beard stubble was crusted with dried concrete. "Thought you were stayin' the hell away from the job," he added as an afterthought.

"My umbrella's up."

"You hope." His glance went up and down the raw gash of the gouged-out road. Thick brush grew down close to its edges on both sides. "Makes no sense, your comin' out here, Jim."

"I tell you the umbrella's up, Wing. But let me tell you something really important: we've got the Edmonds Road job."

"Who says?" he asked instantly.

"Tom Harrington."

"That's—great," he said slowly. Then he was silent.

I couldn't understand it. "That's all you've got to say? I thought you'd be turning handsprings in the newest-laid concrete segment. You know what it means to us."

"Sure, I know." White teeth gleamed in his beard-stubbled face, but his usual cheerful grin was rueful. "I just wish I felt I'd a little somethin' to do with our gettin' the job."

It was the last reaction in the world that I'd expected. "Don't be a jackass, Wing. What difference does it make who got it? Who landed the Pulsifer job? I didn't. I didn't have a single—"

"The Pulsifer job was mighty small potatoes an' not very many to the hill, compared to this'n."

"What difference does it make?" I repeated. "For once we're standing out in a rain of soup with a spoon instead of a fork."

Wing was looking thoughtful. "How'd you squeeze the old bastard, Jim?"

I'd already decided how to answer this question I had known it was bound to come up. "I'm Mona's heir, you know."

"So? Mona didn't have—" He stopped. "You tellin' me she left you some real money?"

"Harrington had put a lot of his own money into her name recently. Ironic, isn't it? He's got to be nice to me now."

Wing stood with his head to one side as if testing the sound of my words. "It don't sound like him," he said. "He should be fixin' to slab you up in one of these segments an' leave you as a permanent part of this heah Sunset Lane Extension."

"I told him that you're my heir, Wing," I said patiently. "That's the umbrella. Should he feel any better dealing with you than with me?"

"Reckon not." He considered it for a moment before grinning faintly. "I reckon not. How's it feel to be worth more dead than alive?"

"I'm not used to the idea yet. And it won't be true until a year from now, when the probate court makes the transfer final. In the meantime, if you're right about Harrington, don't you think we should be keeping an eye out for some kind of reaction aimed at crippling the outfit financially before I get that far?"

"I see what you mean." Wing's hazel eyes had narrowed. "We got to hold the lid on, right? Watch ourselves?"

"Watch the jobs," I emphasized. "That's where we can be hurt. How do you feel about your crew?"

"The old timers I'll guarantee," he said immediately. "Shorty, Jerry, Bill Edwards, Willie—hell, they been with us since I used to borrow from one to pay another. No problem there. The newer ones—well, how can you be sure?"

"And we'll be hiring more for the Edmonds Road job," I pointed out. "Plenty of chances for Harrington to slip in a weasel or two on us."

"Yeah." Wing shook his head, then grinned suddenly. "Why'd you have to go an' load us up all of a sudden with these problems of wealth, pardner? When I been so used to cuttin' it as a poor man?" He had built himself up from the flatness of his mood when I'd given him the news. Wing always responded well to a challenge.

"Since the Edmonds Road job is bituminous instead of concrete," I continued, "and neither of us has given it a serious thought up to now, I'd better get back to the house and the drawing board and work out all the figures we'll need for the changeover. Drop by the house this evening and we'll kick the details around."

"Sure will." Wing sounded animated again. His glance had moved up the road where a T-shirted workman was balanced precariously over the big sluice gate of the paver, probing at a congestion in its mouth with a rake while a cement truck dumped its load into the capacious maw. "Lookit that idiot, will you?" He raised his voice. "Hey, you-all on the sluice! Git yore ass down from there less'n you want yore family to be tippin' their hats every time they drive down this stretch of road!"

A rumble of laughter swept through the crew, and the workman sheepishly backed away and stepped down to the ground. "Another thing, Wing," I said. He turned and looked at me. "How do you feel about Steve Curtin?"

"The county inspector? No ball of fire, but he's honest enough." Wing paused. "Or has been up to now. You think he could be bought?" I didn't answer. "Most can if the price is right," Wing answered himself. "Man, he could really put our tails in the gate if he started okayin' bad mix comin' out've the plant. 'Course, we usually run a doublecheck out here anyway—"

"From now on let's make it routine. And have the scales at the plant checked each night to make sure the interlocking device is working properly. A few pounds too much or too little of this or that could cost us some real money. And I mean check the scales when Curtin isn't around."

"You're really expectin' trouble, huh?" Wing sounded almost eager.

"I think Curtin might find temptation placed in his way. When has Tom Harrington ever taken a situation not to his liking lying down?" I didn't wait for Wing's answer. "Come on over to the house around eight."

"You bet, boss."

I walked back to the station wagon over the cushion of sand and three-eighths inch stone awaiting its overcoat of concrete. Properly wary, Wing wasn't going to let anyone put anything over on us out on the job sites. It was up to me to see that no one put anything over on us off them.

When I got back to the house, I found one letter in the mailbox. It was in an official-looking envelope. I opened it and took out a bill from the city's police department for towing my car from the Stardust Motel to the police lot. I readdressed the envelope to Chet Dorsey, care of City Hall, and put it back in the box for the mailman to pick up on his next round.

The telephone was ringing when I went inside. "Yes?" I said when I picked it up.

"I've been trying to reach you for an hour, Jim," Ludmilla Pierson said. "Drive over and have dinner with us."

Not 'will you or won't you' or 'can you or can't you', I thought. Just come. It was one of the things about Lud Pierson that had twisted my cork for years.

"George wants to talk to you," she added, as if reading my mind.

If George really wanted to talk to me, he'd have asked me to stop in at the bank. "Hold it a second, Lud," I said. "I just walked in and I'm running through the mail." I cupped a palm over the mouth of the receiver while I thought. There had been nothing special in her voice to indicate what she wanted; it could have been a social invitation except that from Ludmilla Pierson I didn't get them. There was nothing I could win talking to her. I uncovered the receiver. "There's a couple of letters I really should answer tonight, Lud—"

"Do you consider your financing on the upcoming Edmonds Road job important?" she interrupted.

"I guess I don't have to answer that one." What was the woman getting at? "Are you—"

"Come over and have dinner with us. You might learn something."

She hung up without waiting for a reply. Typical of her. I tested my beard growth with a knuckle while hanging up the phone. I decided to go, the clinching factor being that George would be present. I had plans for George. I'd watched Tom Harrington's operation carefully for two years now, and observed that he funneled his financing through a single banker most of the time, in his case, Bob Carmody of the Second National. I was aware that a contractor was a lot better off tying in with one bank and one banker than spreading all over the landscape; but operating on a shoe-string the way we'd been, it just wasn't possible. If any one banker knew the shenanigans I'd gone through in the past four years to keep us afloat, I'd have been the poorest credit risk in Albermarle County.

I shed my clothes on the way upstairs, then showered and shaved. I rarely wear a tie, even on so-called dress sessions, and I didn't put one on this time. In our latitude, open-throated sportswear is at least semiformal attire, anyhow. I drove over and parked in the Pierson driveway, and George met me at the front door. Like Wing, his eyes lingered on my face. "Ran into a boom out on the job"—I forestalled the obvious question.

He nodded. "Sorry I had to disappoint you the other day, Jim," he said as we engaged in the perfunctory bankers' handshake. George is a stocky, round-faced man with steel-rimmed glasses shielding owlish eyes. I wondered if Lud had had anything to do with his disappointing me, and whether the dinner invitation represented a change of heart on her part after she'd seen how I'd handled Harrington. George led the way into the living room, where Ludmilla reclined on a chaise longue in four ounces of green chiffon, looking every inch the Lady of the Manor. "Cocktail?" George asked me. "Martini? Manhattan?"

"Martini," I said.

"Dear?"

"Martini," Lud said. She was inspecting my face. "The most *interesting* things seem to be happening to you all the time, Jim."

"Now, dear," George said. He was already on his way over to a portable bar in a corner of the room. The ensuing silence was broken only by the clinking of bottles. Lud seemed to have nothing more to say, and I was saving my own *bons mots*. George advanced toward us, carrying the drinks carefully. In school I'd always thought him a lightweight, but rather a pleasant one. Seen up close, he seemed pompous. His sandy hair was already graying. Nothing like working in a bank to make a man look like a banker, I thought.

We had two drinks apiece before the housekeeper announced dinner. I tried steadily to get through to George conversationally, only to have Lud monopolize the small talk. One reason I'd asked for the appointment with George that he hadn't kept was the hope of sizing him up. If I was going to use him for the purpose I had in mind, I needed to know something more about him than the color of his socks. Whether Lud guessed my intention or not, she did a good job of stifling the leading questions I aimed across the table. Midway through dinner, George announced that he hated to be a member of the Eat-and-Run Club, but he had a previous engagement. That smacked of Lud's doing, too, and whatever was on her mind, I could do without. I decided to leave with George.

The dinner conversation convinced me of one thing; I was going to have to change my mind about using him. He'd always been around, but I'd never paid much attention to him. Watching him in action at his own table, it was obvious that there was nothing much to pay attention to. All through dinner, he never said "fire" 'til Lud said "hell." I've known men who could stand up to everyone in the world except their wives, but I couldn't give George the benefit of the doubt, even in that respect. He looked and sounded like an amiable jerk. He didn't even appear bright. For the life of me, I couldn't see how he could be expected to stand up to anyone in a tight business situation. I remembered Lud upstairs, with a briefcase full of papers, "doing George's homework for him." I didn't doubt it. What a hard-nosed type like her had ever seen in him to make her want to marry him in the first place was beyond me.

We adjourned to the library, and as I might have expected, Lud outmaneuvered me. I was just stretching my legs out comfortably with a pony of brandy in my fist when George spoke up. "I shouldn't be more than an hour, dear. Sorry to run out on you this way, Jim."

I gulped my brandy and started to rise from my chair, only to find Lud beside me refilling my glass. "Jim and I have a few items to discuss, anyway," she said.

"Another time," I said. and then I thought: What the hell? Why postpone it? I settled back into the chair. "I can spare you a few minutes."

"Thanks," she said drily. George had left the room without our being aware of it. Lud sat down in the high-backed chair opposite mine. Somehow it didn't dwarf her as it would have most women. She crossed her legs and went to work on her own brandy. With her skirt length what it was, it guaranteed me a flash of tanned thigh.

We sat and drank brandy silently for a time. Lud got up continually to keep our glasses filled. When conversation did ensue, it was elliptical, glancing off subjects without coming to grips with any of them. We had four brandies apiece before I tired of it. If she wanted to demonstrate she had a hollow leg, she could hire a hall. Despite the steel under her eggshell facade, she could hardly expect to drink me under the table head-to-head. I wondered if she was trying to loosen up my inhibitions. I wondered what made her think I had any. "Buttons off, Lud," I said. "What's on your mind?"

She smiled. She could have been drinking tea to that point except that I'd been watching it come from the same decanter. "What did you think of George?" she asked. "I saw you inspecting him during dinner."

"He's a nice fellow."

"Isn't he, though." There was no particular inflection in her voice, and she continued in the same tone. "I'm sure you know better than to come to dinner without a tie, Jim, so I can only consider the lack of one to be a deliberate affront to your hostess."

It raised my hackles. "For that particular hostess, I'm loaded with deliberate affronts."

She smiled again. "With the Edmonds Road job and the others you seem to think you'll be getting, you'll be moving in circles where a tie is *de rigueur.*"

"Sorry I never studied Russian. Speaking of the Edmonds Road job—"

"I don't wish to speak of it."

"No? On the phone you said—"

"I don't care what I said on the phone." She was still smiling. She uncrossed her legs in a manner guaranteeing me a flash of untanned thigh, got up to refill our glasses again, and retreated to her chair.

"So?" I said impatiently. "What *do* you want to talk about, Lud?"

"George," she said. Her voice had turned husky, the only indication the brandy was having any effect on her. "But first, let's go upstairs and tie into each other. Just for fun."

"I'm not wearing a tie, remember? You like them couth, Lud." It made me curious, though. "Have you ever in your life had a real honest-to-John shagging? From a man who could make you say 'ouch'?"

Her smile was poised above the rim of her brandy pony. "You're applying for the position?"

"God forbid."

"I'm so disappointed." She took a slow swallow of brandy. "Or should I feel relieved? At not having to confront your ravening masculinity?"

"Stop kittening it around, Lud," I said impatiently. "What's on your mind?"

"George," she said again. Her voice had turned lazy. "I want you to kill him for me."

"That's all?"

"No, that's not all. Then I want you to marry me."

The goddam woman means it, I thought. It's not the brandy talking. "Sorry," I said. "Both of those engagement books are filled right now."

She set down her glass carefully. "I want to run things in this county, Jim, but I need a man to do it. You saw for yourself that I'm not going to be able to reach the goal with George. If you take over from Harrington, and I'm surprised to find that I believe you will, you and I could make a winning team together. I'd bring you social and financial contacts you could never hope for otherwise."

"And a handy knife under the pillow."

Her smile was lopsided, but recognizable as such. "Wouldn't that merely add spice for a big he-man like you?" Her expression changed. "Wouldn't you like to get me on a bed, absolutely at your mercy?"

"I don't happen to think you've got the talent for the job."

Just for a second her claws showed. "*Damn you! I'm better—*" She chopped it off and immediately slipped back into her hostess veneer. "More brandy?"

I held out my glass, mainly to see if she could get up and walk. She could. "You don't seem to smarten up very fast about blackmailers," I went on. "How are you going to explain this interesting conversation to George when I play him the tape from the miniature recorder in my shirt pocket?'

That reached her, but the girl had a concrete gut; not a crack showed in the varnish of her composure. "*If* you had a recorder, which you haven't, I'd simply say I was plumbing the foulest depths of your foul nature." She grinned at me, pleased with herself.

"Okay, I haven't got a recorder," I agreed. "But I'm not taking on your propositions, either." I tried to move away from the subject. "I've got problems enough. Wing is mad at me, for one thing."

She was interested. "He is? Why?"

"He feels he's not carrying his share of the load, which is foolish."

"You men," she commented. But then she was right back at the other thing. "What I've said makes sense, Jim. For both of us."

"Thanks, but no."

"Are you afraid I might have a recorder in the room?"

"The thought did cross my mind."

"All right. Just keep on saying 'no.' " She rose to refill my glass again; I put my palm over the top of it. "But arrange an accident for him."

"Speaking of Wing, I asked him to be at my place at eight," I said. I looked at my watch, and it surprised me. "And it's now ten-fifteen. I'm leaving." I rose from my chair, and she followed me out to the front door. She was glassy-eyed, but she had yet to slur a syllable.

She put a hand on my arm as I opened the door. "An accident," she said urgently.

"You're out of the foulest depths of your foul mind, Lud," I said as I started down the walk to the station wagon.

As I was pulling out of the driveway, George Pierson pulled in, in an incongruous white T-bird. I glanced back at the house, but Lud had disappeared from the doorway. If they slept in the same bedroom, I wondered how she'd explain her brandy-laden aura. Although she wasn't the type to do much explaining.

I didn't lack for subjects to think about during the drive home.

When I pulled up in front of my house, Wing was sitting there in his car. He remained in it while I walked over to him; then be started in on me angrily. "The next time you tell me to come by your damn house at eight o'clock—"

"I had an unexpected dinner invitation, Wing."

"You couldn't have left a note? I wasted the whole damn evenin' waitin' on you."

From the sound of him I guessed that he'd had a whiskey bottle for company. "I forgot, that's all. I'm sorry." It sounded lame, even to me, but I couldn't understand his anger until his next words.

"I don't like the way you're actin', pardner. When you didn't show, I took a turn around town lookin' for the station wagon. An' guess where I found it parked? Your old friends ain't good enough for you, man?"

"It's business, Wing. We—"

"Don't you 'we' me, Jim." He turned on his ignition. "I haven't felt like a 'we' in our setup for longer'n I like to think about." He gunned the motor viciously. "An' from the looks of things, it don't feel to me like I'm goin' to." He slammed into the accelerator and roared away in a squeal of tires.

The measure of his anger was the measure of the loss of camaraderie in our personal relationship. Four months ago he'd have cheerfully waited out a weekend. All too well I knew the hurt pride of a man like Wing. But what could I do?

I locked up the station wagon and went into the house.

CHAPTER 5

I stepped into the drugstore pay phone and reached for my change. For no good reason at all I felt fine; I felt loose as ashes. I dialed the seven-digit number and listened to the ring at the other end of the line. "Victor Cartwright's office," Veronica Peters said.

"How'd you like to have your pants taken down tonight, Veronica?" I asked her. "Not for the same reason your old man used to take them down?"

"Approval of the matter in which you're interested appears to be merely a question of time, Mr. Jackson," she replied.

"Mr. Jackson" was the signal that someone was sitting in the anteroom, within hearing distance, waiting for Vic, and that she couldn't speak freely. "And have your belly rubbed?" I continued.

"Nothing out of the ordinary has been noted in your proposal, sir."

"And your butt rousted all over a king-sized bed?"

"I believe I'm quite safe in saying that your proposition meets with general approval, Mr. Jackson."

"And your curls braided?"

"The—ah—details of the indicated course of action promise to be quite satisfactory."

"Rowley's at six-thirty?"

"That will be fine, sir."

"Bring flesh, Veronica. Heated."

"Oh, that's easily managed, sir. You have no idea of the present status in that regard."

"Six-thirty."

"I've made a note of it. And thank you for calling, sit."

I hung up the phone.

I was ten minutes early reaching Rowley's back parking lot, but Veronica was there before me. "I'm going to have an accident someday when you talk to me like that on the phone," she greeted me.

"You like to hear about it, puss?"

"Well—part of me does and part of me doesn't. Does that make sense?"

"Perfectly. Let's go."

She transferred to the station wagon, and we drove to the cabin. Veronica took several deep inhalations of the soft air under the pine trees. "It's so nice out here, Jim," she said when I unlocked the door and we went inside. "I know we've had some good times at my place, but I was never able to fully relax there. I was always waiting for the phone to ring, or someone to knock on the door, or—well, there was always a knot in my stomach that never seemed to dissolve completely."

"Never?"

She laughed. "Only when the noncerebral part of me took over. And never for very long, unfortunately. Here, I feel"—she flung out an arm—"well, *relaxed.*"

"Yon have me curious to see what form this new-found feeling of relaxation is going to take."

We were in the larger bedroom, facing each other. She put her arms around my neck and drew my face down to hers. When she removed her lips from mine, and unbuttoned my shirt and pulled its tails from my belt. Her expression was sweetly serious as she unbuckled and unzipped my trousers. She guided them downward, and I stepped out of them. She slipped down my shorts and placed my apparatus on her warm palm. "Stretch out on the bed," she whispered. "I'll be right with you. She hesitated. "Can I be the engineer?"

"Be my guest."

Her hands went to the tiny loops at the back of the neck of her dress, then paused. It seemed she had other preparations to make first. I sat on the bed and removed shoes, socks, and undershirt while she went to the bureau, dragged it alongside the bed, then angled its minor downward so I could see myself in it. She undressed quickly. Crease marks from her underwear were faintly visible on the undersides of her big, firm breasts, around her waist, and across her upper thighs.

"Let me do it all," she breathed, joining me on the bed.

I found it no hardship to let her do it all.

Her preliminary arrangements made to her satisfaction, she turned her head to consider the slow undulation of her own milky flesh in the mirror. She went from a languorous glide to a plunging attack to a slow-motion diminuendo before subsiding altogether. For a few seconds our rapid breathing intermingled; then I reached around and slapped a sleek haunch. Obediently she slipped down beside me. *"Aaaahhh, that was good,"* she said quietly. Her eyes were closed.

Granted that this girl had a lively curiosity and a healthy aptitude for bedroom acrobatics, why should a session with her be so incomparably better than it had ever been with Mona? I had no real feeling for Veronica; she was a nice kid, and a superlatively good lay, but there it was. There'd been at least one time in my life when I was in love with Mona, if I knew the meaning of the word. I'd broken my neck with her to achieve and give just a part of the satisfaction attained so effortlessly with this plump red-haired girl, and I had been met by total indifference. Indifference at first, followed by increasingly irritating slurs.

It didn't make sense.

Still on my back, with Veronica's even breathing warming my shoulder, I stared up at the ceiling...

We'd been married about a year when Mona and I went to one of the Saturday night dances at the country club. It was the usual sort of thing: a lot of drinking, strolls in the garden by mismatched husbands and wives, and occasional disappearances by same. There was damned little dancing. Mona sat at our table for hours with the same warm beer in front of her and the same cool smile on her face, so fixed that it must have hurt her ears. She didn't want to dance. She didn't want to drink. She wanted to sit there feeling sorry for herself. Why? I was never able to extract a reason. I sat there drinking for us both.

The Moline Country Club incorporates several social strata in its membership. People rub elbows there who never meet anywhere else in town. Mona's gaze lingered longest on the Pierson table, where Ludmilla, resplendent in a floor-length gown, presided over a changing coterie of admiring males while George beamed fatuously and smoked a cigar. Ludmilla had shed her usual chilly demeanor to become the belle of the ball. Wing Darlington danced with her twice, his mahogany-tinted blondness complementing her silvery sheen.

Mona, resplendent also in a floor-length gown whose cost I'd spent a third of the evening estimating, rose abruptly to her feet. "I want to go home," she announced. It was a familiar gambit. I started to argue, then changed my mind. In a year, I'd learned I couldn't win any arguments. If I came out ahead on points on a technicality, I was saddled with a silent martyr around the house for a week. I hadn't the temperament that could afford such victories.

On the ride home, her mood could fairly be described as sulky. "What was the matter tonight?" I opened with the Ruy Lopez. "You wanted to go."

"I have a headache."

"I don't mind your not dancing with me, but when you refuse fellows like George Pierson and Charlie—"

"I said I have a headache!"

There were no surprises in the dialogue. It was like a high school play in which everyone knew everyone else's lines. At home, Mona shed her clothes just inside the front door and began to prowl restlessly through the house. She had this thing about stalking pantherishly through all the rooms, upstairs and down, naked. She had on earrings with dangling pendants, a double strand of pearls, and blood-red, high-heeled dancing pumps.

I was at the liquor cabinet when she passed me on one of her circuits, the dimpled, high-pointed cheeks of her behind twinkling. I reached out and took her by the arm. She stopped and went into her act; without quite collapsing, she became as limp as it's possible for a person to be and still remain upright. She had a trick of booming as boneless as an eel. Opposition I like; cooperation I love; compliance I detest. Mona fed me compliance in a steady dose. The first time, she rose from our bed with the single comment "Messy!" I almost hit her. It might have been better if I had.

I let go her arm, and she went upstairs. I had two fast drinks that demolished the bottle's contents and went to bed in the downstairs bedroom. It was the first time, but not the last.

Two years of it drove me to a psychiatrist in Wilmington. He hadn't wanted to see me, but a friend wangled it. The psychiatrist was a lean man with watery-looking eyes behind heavy glasses. "I have your check, but I haven't cashed it," he began when I sat down across from him at his desk. "This can't do any good. Nothing constructive can emerge from a generalized twenty-minute interview."

"You said all that on the phone, Doc," I said. "I'm trying to get a picture. I'm not making it with my wife, and I'd like to know why."

He sighed, then leaned back in his chair, fixing his eyes on a point somewhere above my left shoulder. "I'm not even the best psychiatrist you can find," he went on. "Merely the best you can afford. And catch-as-catch-can opinions are notoriously dangerous. If I saw you for a year, and your wife for the same length of time, I might possibly be able to tell you something that would help you with your problem." He cleared his throat. "An opinion ventured on insufficient data might be the worst thing I could do for you."

"Let me worry about that, Doc."

He placed his hands on the desk top, palms down. I was surprised to see that he bit his fingernails. "Are you potent?"

"Yes."

"With your wife?"

"So far."

"Are you oversexed?"

"I don't think so."

"From what do you derive your greatest sexual pleasure?"

"Ramming it home."

"You're a big man. Your hands are calloused. You admit to an impatient attitude. Do you consider yourself sadistic in your lovemaking?"

"I've had women tell me I was rough. I never had one refuse to try it again."

"What is a typical behavior pattern in a sex situation with your wife?"

"Me charging and her like a rag doll."

"Always?"

"Since about a month after we were married."

"Did you engage in premarital intercourse?"

"Twice."

"Satisfactorily?"

"No, but I thought it was because of inexperience. She was a virgin."

His eyes came down from their point-in-space vacant stare over my shoulder and settled on my face. "Scarcely the commonest commodity these days."

"She was a virgin."

"She has men friends?"

I'd been watching his hands drumming on the desk top. I looked at him. "Not really, if you mean does she run around. My friends come to the house—"

"Women friends?"

"A few. Two or three."

"Hen parties?"

I started to say "Yes" automatically, then stopped and thought. "Well, no, I guess not. She doesn't play bridge—"

"Does she ever fight you off in the sex act?"

"No."

"But she derives no gratification from it?"

"If she does, she's an actress at hiding it."

"What gives her pleasure?"

"Sexual pleasure? Nothing. With me, anyway. Unless you'd say she gets pleasure from parading through the house in her skin, waving it at me, then turning as dead as Kelsey's nuts when I go after it."

"You've stopped going after it?"

"Almost."

The incisive questions continued for a solid thirty-five minutes. I told that man things I'd never fully admitted to myself. The sweat poured off me. And finally he sat back in his chair, shaking his head. He opened a drawer, took out my check, and pushed it across the desk to me. "I can't do you any good," he said. "I'm not an M.D. who can say 'Take a yellow pill.'
"

The check remained in the center of the desk between us. "Is it me, Doc?"

"I haven't seen your wife," he pointed out. "I believe you tried to be honest in your responses, but in that on area people rarely are, at least not completely. That's why repeated sessions are recommended."

"Is it me?"

"There is a pattern," he began; then he stopped. "Basically you seem an uncomplicated individual," he resumed. "With perhaps an overcompensatory drive a certain type of woman might find repugnant."

"A certain type of woman?"

He hesitated again. "Snap judgment, and not valid. But a woman with a bit less than average interest in men."

"It doesn't sound fatal, Doc."

"It needn't be. I'd recommend counseling for you both, however." He slapped his hands down on the desk top, "That's it, Mr. Wilson. I've probably done you no favor with an off-the-cuff interpretation of what in the ultimate case could be a deep-seated traumatic condition or a comparatively simple case of maladjustment. If you'd come to me from anyone other than whom you did, I'd not have gone this far. And I'd suggest a decent measure of restraint in any course of action you contemplate taking."

I left his office still not sure.

It was another year before I was sure.

Veronica rolled over against me and blew gently on my neck. "I have to get dressed," she said.

"Let's stay here tonight," I suggested. I placed a palm in the center of the inverted bowl of her substantial belly and rotated the palm briskly. White flesh danced in rippling waves. "I'll run up the road and pick up a couple of fried chickens and a case of beer. We'll have an orgy. I'll swipe some grapevine leaves for garlands."

She was watching her own gelatinous vibrations in the bureau mirror. "I'd love to, Jim, but I told—ooooh, stop it!—I told Mr. Cartwright I'd come back to the office tonight for some special dictation."

"You're the stinky type who puts business before pleasure?"

She laughed. "I'm a working gal."

"Hardworking," I agreed. I leaned up over her. "Care to give another demonstration?"

"Love to."

"Which charm school taught you not to press a gentleman for a reengagement?"

"The school of soft thumps," she said demurely.

We went to work, and in each ensuing movement of the waltz, Veronica met me just a little better than half-way. She was a *prèmiere danseuse*. "I'll turn on the shower for you," I said a few minutes later, and I left the bedroom to do so. When I returned, she was still on the bed, stretched luxuriantly. "What's so important about the dictation tonight?" I asked, dropping down on the bed beside her.

"Nothing, really, except that with Mr. Cartwright out of the office two days a week, we're falling behind with the routine work." She sat up reluctantly, swung her legs over the edge of the bed, and stood up.

I wrenched my attention from the sight of my fingerprints in her tail to a fuller appreciation of her words. "Why should Vic be out of the office a couple of days each week!"

"I thought I'd told you. Mr. Harrington is using him in Spartanburg on some kind of job." She stooped quickly, kissed me, then trotted to the bathroom, jiggling pleasantly.

I stared after her for a moment before dropping back on the pillow with my hands behind my head. This business about Cartwright's spending so much time in Spartanburg—not for the first time did I wonder if Ludmilla Pierson could have known that the blackmailer came from Spartanburg. If she did, and had told Harrington—although how could she without revealing the source of her information, namely herself? It didn't seem likely, but it wouldn't hurt to get a line on Harrington's interest.

"Is Harrington interested in the Blackwood subdivision over in Spartanburg?" I asked casually when Veronica came back into the bedroom.

"I don't know," she replied as her hips disappeared into her panties. "Mr. Cartwright never mentions what he's doing there."

"No dictation on Spartanburg?"

"None. So far, anyway."

It was hardly the type of answer to leave me feeling overconfident.

I dashed in and out of the shower, dressed, and drove Veronica back to her car.

The next three weeks were as busy as any I'd ever put in. Except for one date with Veronica, I stuck to cost-sheet estimates and material-quantity breakdowns. I spent a lot of time also with suppliers and subcontractors. Wing and I had handicapped ourselves by getting off on the wrong foot on the Edmonds Road job. Not only was it five or six times more extensive than any we'd taken on before, but our original bid, made at a time when we hadn't a prayer of getting the job, had been made on a superficial analysis of the problems. Since we hadn't been the low bidder, I wasn't afraid of losing money; as far as economy went, I was sure we could match performance with anyone. But since this was our first big slice of pie, I wanted to wring all the water out of the job costs to make sure some of the money stuck to us.

Wing's attitude remained surly during my trips out to Sunset Lane to confer with him. I ignored it because I was sure he'd come around. Although I felt that most of his feeling of dissatisfaction was based on my recent outmaneuvering of Tom Harrington without awarding Wing what he considered an appropriate role to play, part of our trouble went back considerably beyond that. Wing couldn't accept his own limitations. He was a hell of a good construction superintendent, but be started and stopped right there. He had a much better relationship with our work crews than I ever did; he could jolly them along. I'm no jollier. A road does-n't get paved only at the job site, though, and almost from the beginning of the partnership, I'd carried more than my share of the preparatory load. Originally, the division of labor between us called for Wing to be our liai-son with suppliers who, being human, had a way of trying to take advan-tage of a small operator. After Wing blew his stack and tipped their desks over on a couple of these people, it was agreed that I'd take over that aspect of the work, too. Not that my temper was any better than Wings's; it was just that I'd learned to smile—and wait.

When we were only ten days away from the completion of the Sunset Lane job and the changeover from concrete to bituminous, I took my job breakdown across the state to a man whose judgment I trusted. On a big paving job, a firm doesn't get any second guesses, none they can afford to live with, anyway. Bill Moore was a retired contractor who'd given me my first job out college. He was a self-made, man, tough and shrewd. He went over my figures carefully, and finally tossed his pencil aside. "It looks all right," he said. "If you're sure you're not running into anything more than a heavy clay base."

"I'm sure. I drilled the test holes myself."

He nodded, studying the specifications sheet. "Ten-inch sand cushion, six-inch gravel coating, two-and-a-half inch stone topped by three-eighths-inch stone, two inches of asphalt—" His voice died away as he leaned back in his chair. "Who's doing your financing?"

"Are you volunteering, Bill?"

He smiled and shook his head. "If I wanted to risk my money, I'd still be in the game myself."

"Fair enough. I've got six or eight people I've been using right along that I can go to. I'll hit them harder this time, and more of them. I don't antic-ipate—" I stopped. Moore was shaking his head. "What's the matter?"

"This is a big job, Jim. You can't afford to nickel and dime it like that. It hurts your image. One of the hardest things to learn in this business is to start thinking big enough to avoid being a little man all your life. You've got to promote yourself a real line of credit. It shouldn't be a problem, since it's a county job and everyone knows the money is good."

"But the county takes its own sweet time about paying, Bill. If I sign a paper with a bank, they want their money at 3:00 P.M. of the designated day. I'd rather do business with people I can go to and say 'Jack, I'm going to stand you off another ninety days on that loan.' "

"I appreciate your thinking because I started out that way myself, Jim, but from where you stand now it's all wrong. You're going to be bidding on work in the future where the first thing the prime party will want to know is your bank reference. What are you going to tell them? Sand Hill Bank on Shadyside Lane? What you need is a friendly banker, one who knows the problems of the business and is prepared to go along with you."

"I don't know any friendly bankers."

"Naturally. You never had anything to offer them before. Go talk to a couple now. You might be surprised."

So after the drive back home, I dropped in to see George Pierson. He was cordial and heard me out, then removed his glasses and polished them carefully. "Ludmilla thought you'd be in about this, Jim," he said. "Why don't you run out to the house and talk to her about it?"

It took me a minute to get it. "You mean you, personally, can't make the decision?"

It didn't faze him a bit. "Different areas of a bank's operation require different viewpoints, Jim."

I wondered if his area consisted of counting the postage stamps. This was the banker I'd considered using when I took over from Harrington? I must need bifocals. I got to my feet. "Thanks for listening, George."

He walked with me to the door of his office. "Talk to Lud, Jim. She has a good head on her shoulders for that sort of thing." He was totally unembarrassed at the admission of his own incapacity. It takes all kinds to make a world.

I took a couple of days to think it over. I wasn't anxious to put my head in that particular lioness' month. Still, everything Bill Moore had said made sense. We couldn't penny-ante along forever. And if I went to an out-of-town bank, the first thing they'd want to know was why the local bank wasn't accommodating me. I called Lud, finally, and arranged to see her. I'd had so much on my mind recently that it wasn't until I pulled into the Pierson driveway that I recalled the details of my last visit. After the load of brandy she'd taken on, I wondered how many of the details Lud recalled.

She received me in her upstairs sitting room; she was surrounded by little stacks of paper on the floor around her chair. Her peach-colored dress was cut low under the arms, and she was wearing her glasses, which oddly made her look younger. If I hadn't known her, she'd have looked good to me.

"George said you'd been in to see him." She started the ball rolling. "What's the total figure you'll need to swing the job without wondering where your next payroll is coming from?"

"Three hundred seventy-five thousand."

She reached down to pick up one of the piles of paper, and I could see a very pretty bulge of breast. "I have a figure here forty-five thousand higher than that," she said.

"We cut corners, Lud. We try harder."

She didn't smile. "The credit could be arranged."

"It could? What would it cost us?"

She waved a hand. "Standard charges. You couldn't do any better. This method of financing, though, is not the way I'd prefer to see you get the money."

"No?"

"No. What have you done about the proposition we discussed the other night?"

"Which proposition was that?"

"You know which proposition. If you were married to me, Jim, financing could hardly be a problem."

"You forget that I saw George in action at the bank. I don't care for the jobs you get your husbands."

"You're not George, for God's sake." She rose from her chair and paced the room impatiently. "Can't you understand, Jim? It could be a big thing for us. Ever since I was a little girl, I've wanted to be a part of the power elite in the state. I had a good start with the family money, but I needed a man. I thought I could make George into the man, but you saw what happened to that idea. You have more rough edges than a shagbark hickory tree, and they'd have to be planed down before you could pass in the type of society we'd be entertaining, but it could be managed." I opened my mouth to tell her I didn't care for her managing, but she continued right on. "We could be married three months after George has his accident. We could even—"

"Three months!"

"Well, four or five. What's the difference? People are going to talk, anyway. Then someone runs off with someone else's wife and we'd be out of the public eye again. And we'd have what we wanted."

"You'd have what you wanted."

"All right, let's get down to cases. What would *you* want?"

"From you, nothing. If George is bugging you so badly, Lud, why don't you divorce him?"

"There'd be too many loose ends if he were still around."

"You mean it might cost you a few dollars?"

"There'd be too many loose ends," she repeated.

"About the loan, Lud—"

She shook her blonde head. "You're talking business, and I'm talking success—power. Can't you see it, Jim? You're going to take Harrington—he's ripe to be taken. I can see it now that you've pointed it out. Together we could run the state, Jim."

"I'll admit it, Lud: you're too fast for me. I can't keep up with your thinking. Just tell me 'Yes' or 'No' on the loan."

"Oh, you can have it."

"Okay, then. I'll be leaving now."

She offered no objection but walked downstairs with me. "I thought you showed me something a while back. but I guess it was just a flash in the pan," she said as I went out the front door.

"I save my energy for pulling my own chestnuts out of the fire," I told her as I went down the walk.

I thought it was a silly conversation. The only good thing I'd heard in it was that she thought I was going to take Harrington. As long as she kept on thinking it, it should make her less interested in Spartanburg, assuming Spartanburg had been her idea originally. I must remember to get Veronica to root around in Vic Cartwright's private files and see what the hell was going on in Spartanburg. I didn't like loose ends any better than Lud did.

The next day, I saw George at the bank and filled in and signed about twenty-two forms giving my pedigree, financial and otherwise. I stuffed a batch of them into a folder to take to Wing to sign, too. There is no shortage of paper work in banks. "I'd say two weeks," George replied when I asked how long clearance would take.

A week later, I was driving home at night with the car radio on. I was thinking about Wing. He'd signed the papers all right, but morosely. I was going to have to do something to get him back to the good-natured, roughhouse, kidding attitude that was an integral part of him usually and had been so noticeably missing recently. The news announcer's half-heard words jolted me into a state of awareness. "—high rate of speed. The car was totally demolished. Mr. Pierson was thirty-two years old and vice president of the Commonwealth Bank. Funeral arrangements have not yet been completed."

I pulled the car over to the side of the road and stopped. After a minute, I turned off the radio.

It was quite a while before I restarted the engine and continued the drive home.

CHAPTER 6

George Pierson's death left me in a position with Lud where I didn't know whether to back up or go ahead. Instinct told me to grab the cow by the udders; caution argued that my stance was poor. In the end, I did nothing but go to the funeral, as half the town did. If I was right in my estimate of the situation, I'd be hearing from Lud without any necessity on my part for pushing the issue.

I heard in a week. She called the house one afternoon when I was enmeshed in a maze of figures. I didn't even recognize her voice. "Oh," I said finally. "Lud. Yes. What d'you want?" The second it was out I realized that the tone of complete unawareness could only be considered lese majesty.

As it was. "I want you to come out to the house," Lud said, slivers of ice crackling in every syllable.

All the former imperiousness was back in her voice. I was tempted to give her an argument—it had been that kind of day—but there didn't seem to be any point in it. "I'll be over," I said. I hung up my T-square and went out front to the station wagon.

As I drove over to the Pierson house my thoughts weren't pleasant. Until he was gone, I hadn't realized what a buffer George Pierson had been between me and Lud. Despite her high-and-mighty indifference to public opinion, there were things even she couldn't do. The number of these had been sharply diminished, and I didn't care for the prospect of the consequences.

She received me in a black dress, whose color was its only concession to mourning. I could have spit through the fabric, which clung to her like wax to linoleum. "I've had a discreet investigation made," she began without preliminary when we were installed in her upstairs sitting room. "There's no question about it. Someone tampered with the steering knuckle on George's Thunderbird."

"We both know you didn't need an investigation to find that out, Lud."

She ignored it. "Facts have emerged that could lead the authorities to want to ask you some questions. If the facts were called to their attention."

"Oh, I see. *I* killed George, is that it? Do you mind telling me my motive?"

"Revenge because he had turned down your application for a line of credit."

That reached me. "Turned down—? What the hell are you talking about? George *okayed* my application."

"You have it in writing, of course?"

"Of course." I bluffed.

She smiled. "You must be a formidable poker player. George never signed anything before I looked over the details."

The woman had had her husband killed. It would have made a lot of sense to her to arrange the facts so the evidence pointed toward me. "So?"

"So unless you marry me, I'm prepared to turn over the results of my investigation to the authorities."

It probably should have had a greater impact on me than it did. I couldn't stand a noise like this; my current odor in the community was bad enough. All I felt was irritation, though. "Why don't you get off that button, Lud? If it's a good jabbing you want, I'll line up a half dozen young bucks for you, one for every night in the week."

She refused to take the needle. "Much as I detest you personally, it's you I want to marry. I need your ruthlessness to move ahead with plans I've had for years."

My ruthlessness? That was a good one. I made another try; if I could get her mad enough, I might yet see daylight on this. "Why bother me with trivialities now? All I'm interested in is the line of credit. Everything is ready to go—"

"*If* you marry me, there'll be no difficulty about the credit," she interrupted. "If you don't, there'll be nothing but. You can't obtain it from us now, anyway." She smiled again. "Since that would permit you to name me as an accessory after the fact if I later had to use the revenge motif as substantiation for your killing him. The people who count know, you see, that if George refused you, it was with my knowledge. So I could hardly grant you the credit later, could I? Without being vulnerable?" She leaned back in her chair and considered me. "But assuming you agree to cooperate, I've already made other arrangements—quiet arrangements—for you to get the money."

The damn woman thought of everything. "Do you think this town is going to hold still for the kind of three ring circus you're suggesting, Lud? You're underestimating—"

"A nine days' wonder," she said briskly. "Who's to question it? Seriously? And what do we care what the public thinks or says? No, there's no problem."

"But why get married, for God's sake? I can bulldoze just as many people for you without living under the same roof."

"There are several reasons. In the area we're both interested in, a woman without a husband can't reach the type of men I want to listen to me. A woman with a rough, tough, nasty husband gets an excellent hearing, especially if he has financial and political weight to add to his avoirdupois. With the muscle we'll have to go with your nerve"—she paused to regard me over the tops of her glasses—"if you haven't lost it, we're going to own this end of the state." She said it with complete confidence.

I had no great respect for public opinion myself. In different circumstances, and if Lud had been anyone but who she was, I might have jumped at the chance. She had looks and brains. She represented money and power. But—she was Ludmilla Pierson, and I'd known her for years.

As usual, she was thinking right along with me. "When you think it over, Jim, you'll have more reasons for wanting to than I do. We can be married in four months. Say the end of December." Another quick smile. "Mustn't forget the tax advantages. And meanwhile, a truce to all the sniping. You've got the credit, and you can go ahead with the job."

I was groping for something to slow her down with. "What do you think Tom Harrington would have to say about your marrying me?"

"I stopped worrying about what Tom Harrington had to say the day I was in his office with you," she said crisply.

If it was a fight, I'd lost every round of it. I decided to get out while I was still alive. "I'll be running along, Lud."

"Start dropping by the house evenings," she said, swinging herself up from her reclining chair in a swirl of diaphanous skirt that revealed sleek legs. "We should have a proper courtship, you know. I'll let you know which evenings."

I choked down a reply. She was too confident, and I had to find out why before I tackled her head on. At best, she should have figured our situation as a stalemate; we each had something on the other. She was acting, though, as if she were completely in the driver's seat, and it might not be just her natural cussedness.

She didn't follow me downstairs; and getting into the station wagon, I looked back at the house.

When I was in the upstairs sitting room, it appeared that Lud had thought of everything. Sitting in the car, I wondered if that were true. If I couldn't think of an angle, and if she pushed me hard enough—

One thing was clear: if Ludmilla Pierson had a fatal accident, the last stone was off my back and I was home free.

I called Vic Cartwright's office from my house later that afternoon. "Veronica?"

"Yes, Mr. Jackson?"

"What's the chance of your getting into Vic's file and finding out for me what he's up to in Spartanburg?"

"That's the most difficult request you've ever made of this office, sir."

"He keeps it locked all the time?"

"That's right. It is."

"But you must need to get into it occasionally?"

"Rarely. And usually with supervision."

"One time is all I need, baby. It could be worth a couple of dollars to me to know."

She hesitated. "It will be difficult, sir. I don't see how—"

"For the home team, Veronica."

"Well—I'll put it at the top of the list." She still sounded doubtful. "Don't expect too much."

"You'll find a way."

"I honestly don't see how. Without—without—you know I'm not retiring soon, sir."

"Don't worry about Vic firing you. I'd like an excuse to line him up in front of the firing squad, anyway."

"You couldn't get along without it?"

"It would mean a great deal to me if you found out."

"Well—"

"You'll find a way," I repeated.

She didn't reply, and I hung up. Veronica promised to be no exception that people were wonderful until asked for something, but I had a feeling she'd come through. Even though she hadn't thanked me for calling this time.

I stood there in the front hall, conscious suddenly of the sticky, late afternoon heat. I went upstairs and took a shower, then came back down in slippers, slacks and T-shirt. I went into the kitchen and built myself a collins in the tallest glass I could find, then carried it outside to the patio, which was shaded at that hour by a butternut tree.

The kitchen's sterile, unused appearance reminded me of the womanless state of the house. I ought to get someone in to clean on a regular basis. I'm neat enough—Mona used to be amused at my obsession about a place for everything and everything in its place; she lived in a discarded-clothing-on-the-floor atmosphere—and I'd made several tours of the house with vacuum and dust mop, but a home gets a frowsy look without some serious housekeeping to keep it licked into shape. Not that Mona was ever a serious housekeeper, but she had kept a sharp eye on the various maids she'd brought in to do the work. None of them had ever lasted long on the job. I was continually coming home and running into a new one.

I sat down on a flimsy wickerwork chair on the patio, put my feet up on another, dipped my bill into the collins, and settled down to some serious thinking. The afternoon's conversation with Lud had been disturbing because it had crystallized a few half-formed notions that had been floating about in the back of my skull. It wasn't her monomania about marriage that bothered me; I'd deal with that situation in its own good time. No; the item that had been looming larger and larger ever since I'd heard the radio report of George Pierson's "accident" was the identity of the man she'd conned into tampering with the steering mechanism of George's car.

Granted she'd planned it, but she hadn't crawled under the car and done it herself. Someone had done it for her, and I very much needed to know the name of the gentleman. An unknown, sharp-edged cutting tool like that was a dangerous commodity in the neighborhood, especially if she took a notion to turn it loose against me at some time in the future. I had to find out who had done it for her, and the sooner the better.

She wouldn't have tried to hire a professional; that would have opened her again to the same sort of blackmail deal that had already scorched her patrician butt. It almost had to be somebody local, on whom she had a hold of some kind. With the bank behind her, a lot of people were obligated to her in one way or another, but how many would have the nerve and skill to bring off such a coup? It took a certain amount of mustard, even grant-ed the attractiveness with which she could festoon the deal. I wondered if her fair white body had been a part of the contract. If it had, the guy had been a big loser on that end of the proposition, at least.

I thought myself around in circles right down to the bottom of the collins glass, and got exactly nowhere. I couldn't think of anyone's being obligated to Lud and having the chilled-steel nerve requisite for loosening the steering knuckle of a man's car, leaving it operating by a thread. I gave up the problem in disgust, finally. When I glanced around the yard, I was surprised to find that dusk had enveloped the patio. I realized suddenly that I was hungry.

I went to the garage to get out the portable charcoal grill. As I rolled up the door, I was brought up short by the sight of Mona's Pontiac. I'd had it driven in from where she'd left it the afternoon she'd met Whit Bailey. I wasn't supposed to dispose of any of her property until the probate court made the settlement final, but in a year, the car would depreciate more than its book value by standing idle. I'd have to find out from whom I needed permission to sell it.

Looking at the Pontiac reminded me that I'd never checked it out for her personal belongings. I opened the door and took the keys out of the igni-tion, then went around to the rear and opened the trunk. It was empty except for the spare tire. Next I tried the locked glove compartment. There was nothing in it but a shriveled-up candy bar and the automobile insur-ance policy that went with the car. One reason I'd been able to proceed against her with confidence was that we'd had only one small policy on her life and I'd quietly let that lapse eighteen months ago. I locked up the Pontiac and put the keys in my pocket.

I rolled the grill out onto the patio, dumped a load of charcoal into it, squirted a stream of starter fluid onto the lumps, and ignited it. I went into the kitchen and took a slab of steak and a stick of butter front the re-frigerator, greased the steak, salted and peppered it liberally, and slid it onto a platter. Then I carried it back out to the patio to wait until my charcoal was ready. It was dark enough then, so I turned on the patio lights. The back edge of my property ran through to the next street, and recently I'd rearranged my outside lights so that they would illumine the outer edges of the patio and the walk beyond and leave the near side of the house itself in comparative darkness. I'd considered installing a spotlight whose beam would have reached to the back gate, but decided against it. The neighbors had enough to talk about now.

I lit a cigarette and settled down in the wickerwork chair. The houses on both sides of mine were quiet. Although the patio was almost dark, a faint glow of sunset remained in the western sky. The silence was broken by a metallic ping, a sound I recognized as the aluminum gate on the back street side of my Anchor fence being opened. I rolled out of my chair and crouched behind the grill, wishing I were in the bedroom, where my .38 was.

A slim figure in a white sport shirt moved leisurely up the path. It stopped just outside the bright limits of my patio lights, and I strained my eyes trying to see who it was. "Wilson!" a voice called softly.

I didn't say anything.

"Wilson!" the voice repeated. The voice had an urgent sound. "I'm goin' to walk into the light an' turn around so you can see I'm clean." After a deliberate pause, the blurred figure did so. I still didn't recognize the man clad as he was in nearly form-fitting slacks and shirt, it was obvious he carried no armament. I came out from behind the grill. "Glad I caught you at home," the man continued. "Satisfied with my looks?"

"I'm satisfied."

He covered the remainder of the distance between us in a deliberate manner and held out his hand. "Sam Carstens," he said, introducing himself. His handshake was muscular. "Richie Hoey thought it might be a good idea if I dropped in an' said hello."

"By the back gate?"

Carstens grinned. "Richie don't favor publicity none."

Richie Hoey was the chief of a county fief two hundred miles from Moline, where he operated very much as Tom Harrington had locally. Carstens was sandy-haired, and had a scattering of freckles. There was a reckless tinge to his grin. His name rang a faint bell; it seemed to me I should remember something about a Sam Carstens, but it didn't come to mind. I glanced at the gill; the charcoal was a glowing red. "I was just about to drop a steak on that," I said. "Join me?"

"Don't mind 'f I do, Wilson."

I slid the steak from the platter onto the grill above the coals, and it began sizzling immediately. I turned back to Carstens. "Drink?"

"Fine."

"Gin?"

"Or whatever."

"Bourbon?"

"Reckoned you'd get around to it," the sandy-haired man said comfortably. He settled down in a leisurely manner in the next chair to mine. I went into the kitchen again to make the drinks. After carrying them out to the patio, I made another round trip for plates, knives, and forks. When handing Carstens his bourbon-and-branch, I'd noticed a tracery of fine, white-ridged scars on his left forearm. Back at the grill, I turned the steak over and poured the drippings from the catch-pan back over the meal. "How d'you like yours, Sam?"

"Anyway a-tall when I get it like this." He grinned.

"Rare?"

"Suits fine."

I tested the steak by slicing a corner, then I forked it onto the platter. After carrying it to the table, I cut it through the center and ripped each half onto the plates. I pushed a plate and half of the silverware over to Carstens' side of the table. "Eat up, Sam."

"Right nice of you, Wilson," he replied, pulling his chair closer.

The conversation lapsed. I was half a dozen bites into my own steak before I noticed that Carstens had ignored the knife I'd brought out from the kitchen for him. He was using a bone-handled, long-bladed pocketknife to cut his steak. As I watched him slice the red meat effortlessly, it came to me where I'd heard his name before. Sam Carstens was a knife fighter, and one with a reputation. The network of scars on his left, or guard, forearm should have indicated it to me. Rumor had it that Carstens had killed at least one man with the knife he now used so tranquilly to slice his steak.

Finished, he leaned back it his chair with a repleted sigh and went to work on his front teeth with a soiled toothpick from a shirt pocket. "Nothin' personal in anything I bring up now," he began when the tooth cleaning ritual had been completed to his satisfaction. "What I got to say is strictly business." He was cleaning his knife very carefully with a corner of his handkerchief; I had forgotten to supply napkins. He folded the knife and slipped it into his pocket, eyeing me appraisingly. "Richie thinks you come outta the motel deal smellin' like a rose when you had every chance to come out of it smellin' like the backside of the cowshed. Or smellin' like somethin' that meant good business for the undertaker." He paused just long enough to lend emphasis to the question that followed. "Richie's curious to know if you got somethin' on Harrington?"

It was entirely in character for a shrewd operator like Richie Hoey to sense the ground swell before the first waves appeared. And to send an emissary to take soundings. "Harrington's not as young as he used to be, Sam." I fenced.

Carstens' level stare revealed nothing of his inner thoughts. "Nobody seen no indication of him applyin' for retirement heretofore, Wilson."

"He had an operation recently, too."

"We know about the operation. I'll put it to you plain, Wilson. Was this a one-shot deal, with you gettin' out from under a personal load, or are you makin' a move? You don't need to answer me, but it couldn't hurt you with Richie was you to give him an idea."

I checked the reply I had ready. If Richie Hoey was opposed to my making a move, Carstens wouldn't have appeared in my back yard. Not as a smoker of peace pipes, anyway. If Hoey and others like him weren't opposed to a move against Harrington, I might be able to move a lot faster than I'd dreamed possible. And hard on the heels of that thought came the realization of how I could move fastest of all. I made up my mind. "I'm taking over, Sam," I said flatly.

He nodded. "Richie kind of thought you might have it in mind." There was no expression in his tone. "That's why I'm here, because Richie's not choosin' up sides. He's worked with Tom Harrington a long time, but Richie's a businessman. If Harrington's through, Richie'd like to see you 'n him do business along the same general lines. *If* Harrington's through."

"He's through."

"I hear you sayin' so."

"I'm still walking around, Sam."

"People do be wonderin' 'bout that," Carstens admitted. "What you got in mind, Wilson? Partic'larly?"

"For Harrington?"

"For you."

I'd never met Richie Hoey, but I knew his reputation. He wasn't an easy man to impress, but if I impressed him sufficiently, it could keep him from coming to Harrington's aid in the squeeze play that was bound to follow. "I think Harrington's a piker, Sam," I said.

Still his expression didn't change. "He done piked his way along for a right smart number of years."

I hit him with the second barrel. "I'm marrying Ludmilla Pierson, Sam."

Sam Carstens was not an easy man to impress, either, but that one really fetched him. His eyes widened, then narrowed, while his thin lips pursed in a soundless whistle. Twice he started to speak, and twice he stopped. "Reckon ol' Richie knew what he was doin' when he aimed me this way this evenin'," he finally said drily. "He'll be right interested in hearin' that. Right interested. Gonna be soon?"

"As soon as we figure the noise won't blow the roof off."

His grin was wry. "See what you mean. An' then?"

"Business as usual. Ludmilla would like to have Richie and a few of his friends over for dinner some evening soon after the wedding."

Carstens nodded slowly. "You got the program, man. No doubt about it." He hesitated. "If—"

"If my foot doesn't slip? Tell Richie not to worry about it. I've been getting ready for five years."

"I reckon," Carstens said. "D'you think—"

"I've heard a lot of nice things about the job you're doing for Richie, Sam," I interrupted. "And I need a reliable man in your end of the state. Contacts, that sort of thing. Is there any way I could persuade you to go to work for me?"

The usual mask was back in place on his face. "Richie's been right fair with me, Wilson."

"If you say so," I agreed. "The offer's open, though."

"Appreciate it," Carstens said, closing the subject. I didn't especially want to hire him, although he'd have been a handy type to have available. I knew he'd report the offer to Richie, though, if only to prove that a prophet was without honor in his own country, and this gesture, more than any declaration of mine, would convince Richie I meant business. "Can you think of anything else in the line of news I should carry back to Richie?" Carstens continued.

"You don't think you've got enough now to hold him for a while?"

He grinned. "Could be I do, at that."

"You might tell Richie not to expect Harrington to drop out of sight completely. Not right away. People are used to working with him, so why upset things by changing the look of the whole face of nature? If someone else is pulling the strings, there's no need to let the world know about it."

"Richie appreciates that kind of thinkin'," Carstens said. "Business as usual, that's his motto. Well"—he rose to his feet—"thanks for the steak. An' the talk. I'll just mosey out the way I come in. No need for you to walk out with me."

"Tell Richie he's going to like the setup."

"He'll let you know fast enough if he don't." Carstens went down the walk unhurriedly. In seconds I heard the p-p-ping of the closing gate, and a moment later the sound of a car starting up.

I brushed the remains of our steak dinners to one side and rested my elbows on the formica table top. On balance, the unexpected confrontation had gone well. I had impressed Carstens. His whole attitude had changed after the revelation about Ludmilla. In a different way, Richie Hoey's reaction was bound to be the same. And if Harrington tried any smart moves now, before I was ready to oust him altogether, this should spike his guns. I couldn't see how Richie Hoey would choose up sides against me now. And Richie could be depended upon to get the word around where it would do the most good.

There was still a question in my mind whether the percentage gain counterbalanced my hundred-and-eighty degree swing around to embracing the idea of marrying Lud Pierson.

It better had, though. It damn well better had because it was the only aspect of the forthcoming nuptials I could swallow without choking.

Chapter 6

A month slipped by, a month of sixteen-hour workdays. We had a lot to do: hire more men; enlarge the bituminous batching plant to take care of the increased quantities necessary for a job of that size; clean up all the equipment for the changeover from concrete to bituminous; stockpile sand and gravel, since the pits were at a distance; and accumulate quantities of two-and-a-half-inch stone for the roadbed's binder course and three-eighths-inch stone for its wearing course.

I was working hard but enjoying it. Before, I'd always felt frustrated by the small jobs that had come our way, with their consequent lack of opportunity to make full use of what I liked to think was my organizational ability. And most of the time I'd been so busy scrounging around for an additional few dollars to keep us going that it had been difficult to take any real pleasure in the work. I had no problem like that now. Lud had been as good as her word in setting up a financial connection for me after I told her the marriage was on. It was a strange feeling to walk into a bank just twenty-five miles away and be addressed as "Mr. Wilson."

I had plenty of opportunity now for detailed planning. On day-to-day performance, Wing was great, but he was constitutionally unable to see beyond sunset of a given day. Long ago I'd learned to give him performance sheets to keep him on the rails. With a sheet to guide him, he'd keep a crew out on the job site until midnight, if necessary, to finish a specific assignment. And they'd work for him, where they wouldn't have for me.

Wing would gather the whole crew around him in the morning, sheet in hand. "Today we grade an' level the next section, boys. Sand it, gravel it, stone it, an' pour an' roll at least the breakin'-down pass," he'd say. "An' we don't go home 'til we've done it." If they finished an hour early, he let them go an hour early. It wasn't the way I'd have handled it, but it worked for him, and I kept my nose out of that end of it.

He called me at the house on a hot Saturday afternoon. "C'mon out to the cabin, hoss," he said. "I got some stuff out here."

His voice slurred, indicating an early start on the weekend's drinking. I knew what his "stuff" would be: in addition to that in bottles, it would be seventeen years old, platinumed, and already two years experienced. I didn't want to go, but I hesitated to say "No" for two reasons. The first was that I wanted to reestablish the rapport with Wing we'd had formerly. A refusal on the first real social gesture he'd made in weeks was hardly the way to begin bridging the chasm.

The second reason was even more important. I couldn't wait any longer to tell him I was going to marry Lud Pierson. I wanted him to hear it from me before he had even a hint from anyone else. I'd purposely held off on the house calls Lud wanted me to make until I could find a way to break the news to Wing. In a town like Moline, there was bound to be active speculation as soon as I began making the calls. Public opinion in general, I didn't give a damn about, any more than Ludmilla did; but there were a couple of areas that needed more careful handling, and Wing Darlington was one of them.

"I'll be out in an hour," I promised.

"Great, man. Bring hormones," he said. Then he hung up.

I used most of the hour to finish up a wad of paperwork, then drove out to the cabin. The only surprise there was that my seventeen-year-old had black hair instead of silvery blonde. "Gracie an' Dolly," Wing said, introducing them. "This heah is Jim, girls." Mine was Dolly, a plump, olive-skinned girl looking more than a little nervous. Wing's was the usual platinumed job, taller and more slender—Wing liked the greyhound type—with slightly buck teeth distracting from better than average features. In contrast to her friend, Gracie seemed completely at her ease.

Wing handed around a tray of drinks, and I spent the next thirty minutes catching up in that department. There's nothing worse than a party at which you're more sober than everyone else. By the time I felt adjusted, the four of us were on the bed in the large bedroom. "Interestin' differential in the color specifications between this heah area an' your topknot," Wing informed Gracie.

"You quit that!" she yelped. "You hear me? You—oh!"

Wing scooped her up abruptly and marched to the door leading to the other bedroom. When I turned my head Dolly's eyes were on the gun rack in the corner, on which Wing kept his deer rifle. From the expression on her face, I thought it just as well she didn't know there were half a dozen hand guns in the cabinet behind it.

"Afraid of me?" I asked her.

"N-no," she said uncertainly.

I let the dialogue expire. Dolly wasn't much good in harness; at that age they never are. We were taking ten when we heard a patter of bare feet, and Gracie trotted in from the other bedroom. She was in her pelt, and she laughed at Dolly's scrambling efforts to hide her own exposure. Wing came in from the kitchen in a state of nature, carrying a tray of drinks. When we finished them, I took the tray back for refills. After a while I took Gracie into the smaller bedroom. She was eager, if inexpert. When we returned, Wing was sitting on the edge of the bed beside a bemused-looking Dolly. "You really got a yard of ass, honey," he was saying to the plump girl. "Some one of these days you're gonna make a damn fine little mare when you get settled in proper to a stud."

We took time out for a chicken fry with Wing officiating—neither of the girls could boil water—and a load of beer, then readjourned to the bedrooms. The girls had quit on the hard stuff, but Wing went drink for drink with me. He's tried it a few times, with mixed results, but at midnight he was still bright-eyed and bushy-tailed. The girls were in the shower and Wing and I were on the big bed, smoking. "Like old times, huh, hoss?" Wing said lazily.

"Yes. Wing?"

"Yeah?"

I didn't know how to begin. He rolled over to look at me inquiringly. "I'm marrying Ludmilla Pierson," I said at last. "Soon."

He laughed. "You turnin' comedian on me now, ol' salty dog?"

"I'm serious, Wing."

He shook his head, smiling good-humoredly. "You better get you a new gag writer."

"It makes sense, Wing. When you think about it. She can do us a lot of good. She has connections we can't touch otherwise. We'd never have another worry about financing. We could be the biggest outfit in the state. Hell, there'd be something the matter with us if we weren't the biggest."

His smile had gradually disappeared, and he was regarding me with a puzzled expression. "You're serious? I mean you think you're goin' to marry Lud?" He laughed again, but not as loudly as before. "The way you two feel about each other?"

"Wing, I'm going to marry her."

"You done stripped your gears, man," he said positively. "Not to rub yore nose in it, but she'd use your balls for emery paper did she get the chance."

"She's practical, Wing. As practical as I am. She wants to run things, but she needs a man to do it. She's—"

" 'Pears to me the idea of runnin' things has got to *you*, not her, friend. The way you been actin' lately an' all. You're all the time sayin' think big, but the day you think big enough to imagine all you got to do is ask Ludmilla Pierson to marry you an' you got it made around these parts—"

"Wing."

He stopped.

"It's settled. She's marrying me."

Something changed in his eyes; I couldn't decide what it was. "You never lied to me yet, hoss," he said after a pause.

"And I'm not lying to you now. Can't you see that it makes sense? Can't you see what it could mean for both of us? We could have things—"

"She's said she's marryin' you?" he interrupted. "She's said so in so many words?"

"It's signed, sealed, and all but delivered."

He was silent for a full ten seconds. "Hoss, you're just a natural-born loser," he said at last. "Why don't you—oh, Christ, the hell with it. You an' your power complex."

His bitterness surprised me. "The important thing is it's a shortcut to everything we've—hey, what's the matter?"

He had bounded from the bed, a dark flush of anger staining his bronzed features. "Do I call you Mr. Wilson now?" he inquired sarcastically. Then he stalked from the room.

In seconds, I heard a sharp crack and Gracie's startled exclamation. "*Owww!* What was *that* for?"

"Git yore ass into yore clothes." I hardly recognized Wing's voice. "We're leavin'."

I got off the bed and went into the hall and down it to the shower. The area was crowded with naked bodies. "What are you so upset about, Wing? It's not going to make any difference to us, for God's sake. You've seen me use people before when it was to our advantage, haven't you?"

He refused to look at me. "Get dressed," he snapped at Gracie. "Less'n you want to ride home in yore skin."

She ran past me. Dolly followed more slowly, turning to look back at us. I was still trying to guess the reason for Wing's anger. "You don't think I'm turning my back on the partnership? That's the last—"

He pushed past me without a word, following the girls' into the large bedroom. After a moment, I went into the kitchen, opened a bottle of beer, and carried it in to Dolly. She accepted it absentmindedly. Her eyes were on Gracie, half-dressed, and Wing, who was already into his pants. The plump girl set the bottle down abruptly. "I'm going, too," she announced. "I don't want to be left—" She didn't finish it. She scrambled to her feet and began pulling her dress on over her head.

I made one more try at Wing. "When have I ever steered you wrong, man? I tell you this is the way to do it. What are you getting so hot about? I'm not turning my back on my old friends just because of what this can mean. You know me better than that. You know—"

His expression was like an Indian's. "I used to think I knew you—" He bit off and charged toward the door. Gracie followed him, looking back at me curiously. Dolly ran after them, carrying her shoes and underwear in one hand. In seconds, I heard the spatter of gravel against the cabin wall and the roar of Wing's car as he gunned it out of the parking slot into the driveway and out onto the highway. I could hear the squeal of his tires as he accelerated.

I stood for a moment in the bedroom; it had suddenly become quiet. I could hear water dripping in the shower, and I walked down to it and turned the faucets off, hard, then looked at the imprint of the metal in my palm.

Why was Wing so upset? Because he felt he was being deliberately relegated to a position as a minor cog on the wheel? Somehow I was going to have to get through to him that nothing had really changed between us.

I gave it up, went into the kitchen, opened up a fresh bottle of bourbon, and drank myself blind.

I woke late Sunday afternoon with my mouth tasting like a mildewed rubber boot. I stumbled in and out of the shower, then took a quick tour of the cabin. The kitchen was a mess; empty bottles and glasses were everywhere. I'd neglected to open a window, and the air was heavy with the odor of perspiration, chicken grease, and stale beer. I left everything just as it was and drove home. I'd send a cleaning woman out tomorrow.

By the time I reached the house my head was throbbing so fiercely I knew I had to have a drink. I had my hand on the gin bottle on the top shelf in the kitchen when the telephone rang. I debated not answering it, but on the chance it was Wing, I walked into the front hall. "Yes?" I said. I hardly recognized my own voice.

"Jim? Oh, Jim, where h-have you *been!* I've been t-trying to reach you for two wh-whole *days!*" It was Veronica, and she sounded almost hysterical. She burst into noisy tears and talked so fast between sobs that my splitting head couldn't absorb what she was trying to tell me.

"Whoa, whoa," I interrupted. "Take it slower. What's it all about?"

"Mr. Cartwright c-caught me s-searching his private file yesterday," she sniffled. "And he—he *f-fired* me. And a f-friend just called one from city h-hall and s-said two detectives were c-coming here to ar-rest me!" Her voice trailed off in a wail.

"Arrest you? For what, for God's sake?" But even as I said it, I knew. Not arrest her; not really. Just take her in on a Sunday night when she couldn't reach anyone, throw the fear of God into her, and release her quietly on Monday morning. It was a tactic that had Tom Harrington's thumbprint all over it.

"Jim, what am I g-going to *do?*" she whimpered. "They're on their way n-now. I thought I'd *n-never* reach you."

It was difficult to think with my head clanging like dull iron, but on the other hand, there wasn't much to think about. I couldn't afford to let this happen. Harrington's response was aimed at least as much at me as it was at Veronica, and if I couldn't protect anyone associated with me, I was in a bad way. "Don't open the door," I said at last. "Understand? Don't open it." They wouldn't have a warrant, and I didn't think they'd risk forcing the door. They'd try to bull her into going quietly with them.

"H-how can I k-keep them out?" She was crying openly again.

"Keep it locked," I said impatiently. "If they sound nasty, tell them you have a gun and will use it."

"Jim, you're coming over h-here? P-please?"

"I'm coming. But remember, just sit tight. Don't let anyone in until you hear from me. *Anyone.*"

"*Please* h-hurry," she said. She was sobbing as I hung up the phone.

I drove directly to Tom Harrington's big place on Jackson Street. It wouldn't be the first time Chet Dorsey's boys had unofficially roughed up someone who had incurred Tom Harrington's displeasure. Harrington had given the order, I was positive, and he could countermand it. His Cadillac was in the garage, so I wasn't too concerned when half a dozen rings of his doorbell produced no action. I went down the front steps to his driveway, found a good-sized rock, went back up the steps, and threw the rock through the front door glass, which disappeared in a welter of smashing crystal particles. I reached inside and unlocked the door.

I'd been in the house often enough with Mona, and I walked to Harrington's study. The door was closed, and I opened it without knocking. Tom Harrington sat at his old-fashioned rolltop desk with his white head cocked to one side above an ancient .44 in his right hand. Its barrel was half as long as a .30-30. The .44 was poised negligently, aimed halfway between the door and me. "I got ev'ry right in the world to cut loose on you, Wilson," Harrington said harshly. "Bustin' into my house like this."

"If you were going to do it, you wouldn't be talking about it," I said. I didn't make any sudden moves, though. I could see a bullet in each chamber of the rickety-looking old gun; whether there was one under the hammer I couldn't tell, and I wasn't fussy about finding out. At that distance, even a peashooter carries a sting. "There's no need to get excited. Just cut the crap and call your dogs off Veronica Peters."

His yellow-flecked eyes examined me. "She hung her own ass out on the line, sonny. She can wear what she gets."

"If she has to wear anything, you won't enjoy the aftermath, you hear me?" Almost carelessly, the .44 lined itself up on my head. "I s'pose you're tellin' me you'll close my balls up in my own desk drawer, like you did with Fred Hunter a few years back?"

Moving with slow deliberation, I slid a straight-backed chair into position across from Harrington's worn swivel chair and sat down in it. I slid it because picking it up could have been a mistake. "I'm marrying Lud Pierson, Harrington," I said slowly and distinctly. "Next month. If you don't believe me, pick up the phone and ask her."

Harrington was an old man who hadn't too much starch left to begin with or I'd never have got that far inside his study, but I could see whatever he had left oozing out of him. He'd been around a long time, and he didn't need to be kicked by a mule's rear heels to know that they were loaded. Head-to-head, he might have had a chance still to upset a young upstart like me; with Lud on my team he didn't have a prayer, and he knew it. I was counting most on the fact that a man in his position should be asking himself if, after all the years of scrambling, it was worthwhile to go down with the ship.

"'Pears like you're playin' right handy cards, Wilson, if you don't find a joker in the deck," he said at last. His voice was cracked.

The .44 had moved only three inches out of line with my head, but it had moved. Moving slowly and easily, I leaned forward and picked up the telephone on his desk. His yellow-tinged eyes never looked away from me as I dialed. "Veronica? Jim. This is what I want you to do. Go to the door—"

"Oh, Jim! Two men have been knocking on the door for ten minutes! What am I going to do? They keep it up and *keep* it up. I'm—"

"Shut up and listen, will you? And do what I tell you. Go to the door and call out to them that there's a telephone call for them on your line. Then before you unlock the door and remove the chain latch, push every chair in the place over in front of the door. While they're pushing their way in past the chairs, you run into the bathroom and lock yourself in. Have you got that?"

"I th-thought you were coming here, Jim? I-I can't unlock that door. I'm *afraid*. They'll—they'll—"

"Do as I tell you, damn it! Right now!"

For an instant, the sound of her sobbing breath hung in my ear; then it was gone. I could have counted to three hundred while faint, unidentifiable noises emanated from the receiver. Then there was a scrabbling sound and a harsh voice in my ear. "Garvey," it said.

I handed the phone to Harrington. "Who is it?" he asked after clearing his throat.

"Frank Garvey," I could hear Garvey repeat.

"This is Harrington. Pack up and get out of there, Garvey. I've changed my mind."

There was a pause. "But Chet said—"

"To hell with what Chet said!" For an instant, the old snarl was back in Harrington's voice. "I said I've changed my mind!"

There was another pause. Frank Garvey was a shrewd, tough-minded individual who wore no man's collar and had never advanced far in the department because of it. I knew he was mentally reviewing the conversation to decide if there had been a personal affront. "It's your mind," he said laconically at last. "It does seem you'd know it better. Anything else?"

"Nothing," Harrington said. He cradled the receiver without looking at me.

Sometime during the conversation, the .44 had disappeared. I got to my feet. "Thanks for the cooperation, Harrington," I said as I moved toward the door.

His lips came back from his teeth, but he didn't say anything.

I went outside to the station wagon and drove to Veronica's. Across the street from her apartment building, Frank Garvey was seated in his car, alone. Naturally, Garvey would have waited to see who'd put the chain on the dog. I walked across the street to his car. He looked up at me. "You ought to get with a winner," I told him.

"Seems like it might not be a bad idea, after today," he agreed.

I glanced up at the windows of Veronica's apartment. "What was the word that went with the package?"

"Rough it up 'til it hollered. Nothin' she couldn't have lived with afterward."

"Fine work for a grown man, Garvey."

He shook his head. "You ain't needlin' me out've this car, Wilson. An' if I do got to come out, I come out shootin', understand? You ain't workin' off no head of steam on this mother's son."

I changed horses in midstream. "On getting with a winner, why don't you drop around to the back door some night and we'll talk things over?"

"When I make up my mind about you, Wilson, I'll meet you at high noon on Main Street an' talk to you. I ain't hidin' from no one."

"What is there to make up your mind about?"

He squinted up at me. "When a guy like you goes down, Wilson, he takes a lot of people with him. Innocent bystanders, some of 'em like the kid upstairs. I ain't innocent or exactly a bystander, either, an' I got to like your chances a little bit better'n what I do right now."

"Don't miss the boat," I warned him. Then I walked back across the street. Going up in the self-service elevator, I thought about Garvey. I could use him, or someone like him. For weeks now, I'd had the feeling that things had speeded up too much, that they were moving too fast, that there were no longer enough hours in the day. I was so busy on the Edmonds Road job that I didn't have time for other things, important things that needed doing, like finding out who'd tampered with George Pierson's car. Once, I'd had Wing for jobs like that. Now I considered myself lucky that he was still out on the job every day.

I had to knock for a good three minutes before Veronica opened the door just a crack on the chain latch. When she saw who it was, she fumbled the door wide open and collapsed into my arms, crying and shivering and shaking. Two days of tears had left her eyes red-rimmed, and her usually pleasant features looked both puffy and drawn. "Oh, J-Jim!" she choked, holding on to me tightly. "Oh, J-Jim!"

She was almost in a state of shock; the flesh of her arms was chilly to the touch. After closing and locking the door again, I maneuvered her into her bedroom and began getting her out of her clothes. She looked as if she'd slept in them. She seemed to need physical reassurance; every time I removed one of the hands clutching at me, another took its place. I went to her bureau and routed out a nightgown, finished undressing her, and got her into it. Her big, womanly body appeared shrunken, somehow.

I found a hairbrush in the bathroom and brushed out her hair—it looked like wild Aggie's. She sat docilely on the side of the bed. Every time I got up—once for a wet towel to wash her face; once for drops for her swollen eyes—she tried to restrain me with a hand on my arm. When I had her looking semirespectable again, I motioned her to the bed. "Stretch out," I told her. "Relax. You're still tighter than a vestal virgin."

She eased herself down with a tired sigh. "My stomach hurts," she said forlornly.

"That's from tension."

"Sit with me," she pleaded when I started to clean up some of the debris in the bedroom. I sat down with her again. She was crying quietly, big round tears that slid slowly down her cheeks. "You'll n-never s-speak to me again for being s-such a baby," she sobbed.

I knew why she'd been so frantic. Four years ago, a tall, good-looking girl named Jessie Stanley had fallen in love with one of Roy Hargrave's kid reporters. Jessie was working in Tom Harrington's office, and she leaked a story on a contract to her boy friend. *The Clarion* had used the story, and Harrington had blown his stack. He ran the kid reporter out of town for a starter, and then the word went around among the insiders that four of Chet's boys had taken Jessie down into the basement of the jail and whipped her tail with a trunk strap. Hargraves chickened out on backing her up afterward, she couldn't get another job locally, and she'd left town and gone to Charleston. Eighteen months ago, when I'd first begun looking for an angle on Harrington, I'd driven over to Charleston, looked her up, and made her a proposition. She'd heard me out, then shook her head. "It might work, Jim, but I haven't the nerve for it. Not after—after—try me again in another year." In another year I'd had plans that didn't include Jessie Stanley but I still remembered her eyes. She hadn't been over it then.

"You'll hate me for being s-such a s-sissy," Veronica was moaning.

"Don't talk foolishly," I said. I was somewhere between a feeling of pity for her and a feeling of impatience with her. She was at least half right; I'd grown up with girls who in her situation would have bared it to the strap and not only looked the whole town in the eye afterward but had the strap swingers watching where they put their feet down on dark nights. On the other hand Veronica couldn't change her own nature.

"Hold my hand," she whispered.

I held her hand. Sitting there, listening to the ragged edge leave her breathing, I felt the toll of my own weekend. Twice I felt my eyes closing. I stopped fighting it, finally. I kicked off my shoes, took off my shirt, and stretched out beside Veronica. She put her arms around me at once. She still wanted to talk. To explain herself. "Hush," I said when she started to say something, and it was the last thing I remembered for a while.

When I opened my eyes again, it was almost dark. A single lamp was on in the bedroom, and Veronica was floating around in a fresh nightie. She appeared normal except for her reddened eyes. Evidently she'd put some time on her face at the boudoir mirror. She saw me watching her and came over to the bed smiling kittenishly. Great, I thought. She felt kittenish; I didn't. I spoke before she could. "I've been screwing all weekend, Veronica, and I've got to get back to the house and get things sorted out."

He smile froze grotesquely. "Oh," she said weakly. For once the English language seemed to have dried up on her.

I got up from her bed. "Do you want to go back to the office in the morning?"

She stared at me, unable, for an instant, to make the transition. "Do I want—you mean the Cartwright office? I can't. Mr. Cartwright f-fired me." Quick tears of self pity filled her eyes.

"He'll unfire you if you want to go back."

"Well," she said uncertainly. "I'm not—I don't—it's a good job."

I went to her telephone and dialed Cartwright's house. "Wilson, Vic. Veronica will be in at the usual time in the morning."

He'd already had the word but he was prepared to argue. "I don't think it's wise, Jim. There can only be embarrassment on both sides. Another arrangement—"

"You just heard the arrangement. And if I get any echoes I don't like, it won't be Veronica who's embarrassed. Understand?"

His tone changed to one of resignation. "I'll be expecting her, then."

"No problem," I said to Veronica as I hung up the phone. I walked to the door and she followed me out into the hall. "I'll call you," I added as an afterthought. I was almost out the door before I remembered what all the shooting had been about. I turned back to her. "What did you find in the file?"

"Nothing worth all the trouble I got into," she said resentfully. "All that Mr. Cartwright's notes said were that he was trying to get a statement from a man named Roger Manton, who didn't want to make one."

Roger Manton had driven the dead blackmailer from Spartanburg to Moline. Had in fact driven him to my back door. I'd traced Manton's name through the license number of his car as he circled the block waiting for his partner, who never reappeared. It seemed I was going to have to take a trip to Spartanburg. Although with no body, what could they do?

"I'll call you," I repeated to Veronica. She seemed to be waiting to hear something else, but I had nothing else to say. I went out the door.

It was probably true, I reflected as I walked down the hall. Almost certainly I would call her again. She was good in bed, she was available, and now she was under obligation.

But somehow, after seeing her go to pieces like that, I knew it was never going to be as good again.

CHAPTER 8

Lud and I were married by a Justice of the Peace at five-thirty on a Friday afternoon, and we left immediately for a long weekend at Nags Head, where Lud had a cottage. There had been no preliminary announcement of the wedding, and the JP and his wife were the only witnesses. Lud wore a pastel blue, knee-length dress with three-quarter-length sleeves; and I had on my only business suit. During the drive to the coast, Lud wasn't exactly bursting with song, but she looked as satisfied as any other woman getting her own way.

We stopped to eat around eight o'clock, and it was a strange sort of wedding feast. We both had steak, medium-rare, with french fries and string beans, coffee, and no dessert. I hoped the utilitarian meat-and-potatoes meal was an omen for the marriage, but I doubted it.

It was a long drive to the cottage, and we didn't arrive until a few minutes before midnight. When I got out of the car, I could smell the salt in the sea breeze and hear the sound of nearby surf. The air was almost chilly. I carried our bags inside while Lud went from room to room switching on lights. The bedroom to which she directed me had only one bed in it, a monstrous affair that could have slept six people comfortably. I arranged our bags on folding racks and went back out into the living room.

"A nightcap?" Lud asked brightly. There was a luster about her, not soft and glowing, but hard and shiny. "The liquor's in the cabinet there." She indicated a walnut console in one comer that could have housed a Volkswagen. She produced a key from her handbag and held it out to me.

I shook my head. "I'm ready for bed," I said.

"I'm tired, too," she agreed at once. "You use the bathroom first, Jim. It will take me longer."

I used the bathroom first, then crawled into the enormous bed and turned on my side with my back to the boudoir light that was the room's only illumination. For what seemed like hours, I could hear Lud's slithering bedroom-slippered progress back and forth between her bags and the bathroom. I was legitimately tired, but I forced myself to stay awake. I wanted to be awake when she finally came to bed.

When the springs creaked at last, announcing her arrival, I raised my voice. "Good night," I said.

"Good night," she replied after a five second pause.

Before I fell asleep, I felt her make several cautious readjustments in her position and move close enough to me so that I could feel her body heat;

but she was never quite touching me.

Then I went under completely.

I woke in the gray light of dawn, on my back, staring up at the ceiling of a strange room. I glanced at the adjoining pillow and the sense of disorientation lasted a second longer because Lud was sleeping with an arm over her eyes and the usually firm line of her jaw was so softened in sleep that I hardly recognized her. She was half out of the sheet that was our only covering, and the portion of her nightgown visible to me appeared to consist principally of lace. Porous lace. I eased out of bed without waking her, found a pair of swim trunks in my bag, and let myself out the kitchen door.

The air outside was cold and damp, with feathers of fog blowing about. I followed a steep path two hundred yards down to a sand beach where three foot rollers crashed steadily. I tested the water with a toe. It was nippy, but not as much so as the air. I waded into a breaking wave, paddled my way out beyond the surf, and floated about for a few minutes. When the chill began to get to me, I rode a wave back in.

Walking back up to the cottage, I realized for the first time how isolated it was. Although we had passed other cottages on the way in the previous night, I couldn't see any of them. Ten yards from the kitchen door there was an outside shower connected to a water tank, and I stripped off my trunks and stepped under it to sluice the salt water off me. The water of the shower was chillier than that of the ocean. From the comer of my eye I caught a flash of pink at a kitchen window. When I went back inside, though, the kitchen was quiet and Lud was in bed, presumably asleep,

I went into the bathroom and shaved, and when I came out, Lud still hadn't moved in the bed. I went into the kitchen and opened the refrigerator and examined its well-stocked contents. I put on the coffee, slung together a mess of bacon and eggs, dropped bread in the toaster, and found a large tray. I filled it with bacon-and-egg-laden plates, cups and saucers, cutlery, buttered toast, jelly, and a coffeepot. I carried the tray into the bedroom. "Breakfast," I announced.

"*Mmmmph*," Lud said, apparently from the depths of slumber. The one eye she opened was suspiciously bright, though. She stretched enthusiastically, straining the froth of lace encompassing her pear-shaped breasts. She bounded from bed energetically. "Got to wash my filthy face," she announced as she went past me, her long legs scissoring beneath the gossamer transparency of her gown. She returned in a moment and propped herself up against doubled-up pillows while I placed the tray on her knees. I pulled up a chair and poured the coffee; we ate heartily. Lud sank back with her hands folded over the bowl of her stomach when I removed the tray. "I see your trunks are wet," she said. "I must take a dip, too. How's the water?"

"Cool. No newspapers out here, I suppose?"

"Only on Sunday. And no television. There's a radio in the living room."

I went in to turn it on and try to catch the news. In a few minutes, Lud emerged from the bedroom in a two-piece bathing suit that was so skimpy it covered perhaps a twelfth of her. "You're not afraid of cramps?" I asked her. "After that meal?"

"I'm not going to swim," she replied. "I'm just going to get wet. I'll be back in a few minutes."

I had turned off the radio and was out in the kitchen doing up the breakfast dishes when she came up the path from the beach. After a quick glance toward the house, she peeled off her suit and stepped under the open shower. The cold water surprised her; she skipped sideways involuntarily, then inched back beneath it cautiously. Seen back to, she had a beautifully even tan, with the exception of a narrow band of flesh marking the bra strap of her swim suit, plus a not-much-wider splash of white across her buttocks, which were slim and springy-looking, not quite boyish, but with no customary feminine amplitude. Swathing herself in a huge towel, she walked into the kitchen. "Your domesticity amazes me," she remarked, with a side glance at me in front of the sink, before she disappeared into the bedroom with an artful slippage of her towel that disclosed a single glistening haunch.

The farce continued all day. We didn't go anywhere, and we didn't do anything but eat, yet she changed her clothes four times, each time with a studied casualness that still contrived to reveal an ensemble of flesh that would have brought Simeon Stylites down from his pillar. Or me, except that I had turned my motor off.

I was first into bed again that night, and when the bed creaked under her weight, I spoke my piece. "Good night," I said.

There was a long silence. "Jim," she said finally. I rolled over to look at her. She was kneeling straight up on the edge of the bed, and she had dispensed with the lace. "I want a husband, Jim. Can I put it more plainly?"

"You can, and I have no doubt you will, but that's beside the point. You don't have a husband. You have a business partner."

"There's no reason we can't get along," she said coaxingly.

"We will get along, but not in bed."

"But why? Will you please tell me why?"

"Because I'm all through letting women like you emasculate me. That's why."

She started to bend down over me, then reconsidered. "Once and for all, Jim, I'm not like that. Can't you understand? I'm simply not like that. Mona and I in college—that doesn't count, Jim. Where were the men? And I was merely the one she returned to when her crushes broke up, anyway." She was choosing her words carefully. "There's more than one kind of pleasure in the world, you know. Let's face it. Mona didn't have much fun. You can argue 'til you're blue in the face whether it was her fault or not, but the fact remains that she *didn't* have much fun. When she kept after me to return to—to—well, sometimes I accommodated her. What did it cost me? But what you're accusing me of—no."

"I don't believe you, Lud. Mona was all right when I married her."

"Mona was never all right, and one of these days you'll admit it. I couldn't believe it when you married her. *You*, of all people. I could understand why she did it easily enough—it represented one last try at escaping from herself. I *liked* Mona, but as a man's wife—" She didn't finish.

"How did you get sucked into that movie deal?"

She was silent for a moment. "I suppose that's the thing you're never going to forgive," she said at last. "There were four women partying in a cabin up at the lake, and we kept egging each other on. What I didn't realize was that the partying had been going on all summer with different groups, and the cabin had a reputation. Sometime during the week, when no one was there, that sonofabitch of a blackmailer bored a hole in the outside wall for his camera lens, and there we were. I think I'd have killed him myself if I'd been alone when he first approached me. But he was too smart for that; he walked up to me on the street in broad daylight, and I had to smile sweetly and pretend everything was all right." Her voice changed. "He must have given you a far better opportunity."

"When I bought the film from him, you mean?" I said.

"That's not what I mean. You—"

I rolled away from her again. "Good night, Lud."

She placed a hand on my shoulder. "I can prove every word I've said to you just now, but not by myself."

I spoke to the wall. "I don't want you, Lud. Do I have to take an ad in the *Clarion?*"

She snatched her hand away. "You damned prig! I had better men than you before I was fifteen!"

"Then go round up a few. You obviously don't need me."

She flounced angrily from the bed, and I must have been asleep when she returned because I didn't hear her.

She sulked all the next morning while I read the Sunday paper, but in the afternoon she snapped out of it far enough to prove to me that she hadn't taken her eye off the main chance. She went out to the car and took a heavy briefcase from its trunk. When I saw what she was doing, I set up two card tables in the living room. She sat down across from me at one table, put on her glasses, and began unloading the briefcase. "Do you know what your biggest problem is going to be in Moline now?" she asked. Her tone was strictly business.

"What's that?"

"You've always been the underdog around town before now, and despite certain tactics you've employed, that fact has earned you a certain amount of sympathy. That won't hold true any longer. In the eyes of the towns-people, you've crossed over from the have-nots to the haves."

"I don't see any problem."

"You can't expect the same laissez-faire attitude in the future toward your strong-arm methods. People will resent it. You're going to have to change your approach."

"I'll worry about it when I run into it."

She shrugged. "Hardheaded. All right. See what you think of this."

She handed me the top paper on the pile, and for four hours we went through the contents of the briefcase. At the end of this period I found myself admiring Ludmilla Pierson-Wilson more than I would have thought possible. She had both a sharp eye for a column of figures and a pragmatic ability at character assessment. We talked over people and situations on the most realistic level, and not once could I fault her judgement. "And I thought I was hard-boiled," I said finally.

"Take a look at this," was her only reply. She laid out on the table what proved to be the master plan in a step-by-step campaign by which we would be able to take over control in the state. Phase One was so detailed and so thoroughly documented I could only shake my head. Another hour's discussion and we had hammered the occasional rough spot out of it.

At the conference table we got on well, but we went to bed that night without a word being spoken on either side.

Monday we put in another session at the card tables.

"I'd intended to begin socially with a number of small dinner parties," Lud started off that morning. "As per these lists. Just for the people that matter; not in Moline, but from around the state. But now I believe that one large dinner is a better idea as an entering wedge; have them all in at once to absorb the atmosphere of the change. How about two weeks from Saturday?"

"Fine with me."

"We'll invite Tom Harrington."

I looked at her. She was looking down at her lists. "What the hell's new about that?"

She took off her glasses to examine me. "I'd have thought your rough-neck activities would have taught you never to push a man into a corner from which he can't retreat. That's when he's likely to do something des-perate, not counting the cost. The people we invite will know that Harrington is harmless now, but he can still be useful as a showpiece."

Essentially it was the same thing I'd told Sam Carstens to carry back to Richie Hoey, but I didn't like it coming from Lud. I didn't say anything, though. I wanted to take a better look at my hole card before I started raising the pot.

She was watching my face. "Any objections?"

"When there are, you won't have to ask me."

"Good enough. Let's consolidate the major elements of these lists." She bent over the card table again and printed rapidly in a strong, square-looking script.

Tuesday morning we drove back to Moline. "Since we've arrived at a truce," she said to me as I was putting the bags in the trunk of the car, "let me tell you an essential condition of maintaining it. No tomcatting in Moline. I have my pride."

I turned halfway around to face her fully. "You can shove your pride, Lud. You're not running my private life. Not now and not ever. You've got a business arrangement, and that's all you've got."

She clouded up like a thunderstorm in the Rockies. "I won't have people thinking—"

"If it bothers you, hire a hall and we'll give them an exhibition"—I cut her off—"once. Just once."

She climbed into the car and slammed the door.

But five miles down the road she was speaking to me again, making further plans for the dinner party for Richie Hoey and the state's other wheelers and dealers.

That was the thing about Lud: business was business and it always came first. It was an attitude I appreciated.

CHAPTER 9

I knew I'd had it with Mona fifteen months before the end. I'd had more than my fill of suddenly averted glances and abrupt changes of conversation when I walked up to different groups in the country club locker room. The convincer, if I needed one, occurred when Wing and a couple of other good friends stopped coming to the house altogether. The cuckolded husband is always supposed to be the last to know. Sometimes it doesn't work that way.

It's one thing not to be making it with your wife, but it's another shade of red-winged blackbird to have her laying your friends and business acquaintances. Not because she wanted it but—as nearly as I was ever able to figure it out—for spite. It was never easy for me to try to talk to Mona because she'd been Mona Harrington and had a goddess complex that made communication with a peasant like me difficult for her. My own attempts seemed to irritate her, and interchange was at a low level.

We came in one evening from a dinner party, during which she'd been in a particularly foul mood, snapping peoples' heads off without provocation. It was in the spring of the year and the night temperatures were still in the fifties. It had been a nippy ride home in the bucket seats of the MG that was Mona's car that season. She would never ride in my car. Before we'd left home, I'd built a fire in the twelve-foot fireplace, and the oak log was still burning briskly when we returned. Mona went directly to the fireplace and stood back-to, to the fire with her skirt pulled up behind her, toasting the seat of her pants in an unconscious burlesque of the old print of a red-jacketed British rider-to-hounds warming himself by parting the tails of his jacket before a roaring fire.

I don't know why I picked that particular moment to bring things to a head. Certainly the evening had produced nothing new or unusual in her recent behavior pattern. It could have been that the ferment within me boiled up and took charge by itself. "Good show tonight," I said from the liquor cabinet, where I was pouring myself a drink. "I gave you four stars for bitchiness. Of course you could have done better if you'd been trying."

She stared at me suspiciously. Ordinarily I avoided head-on collisions with her. "Those stinking dinner parties," she said at last. "All that smug chitter-chatter simply infuriates me."

"This afternoon, too?" I said. "I didn't know Fred Wilkinson talked in bed."

Her expression hardened. It never occurred to her to take a backward verbal step. She was Mona Harrington. The fact that she was also Mona Wilson I had long since become convinced meant nothing to her. "If it's any comfort to your ego, dear, Fred's no better a performer than you are," she said bitingly. "Or any other of you insipid males."

I admired the steady hand with which I raised my glass to lower the level of its contents. "This insipid male wonders if you mightn't like a divorce, Mona?"

"Divorce?" she said sharply. "I should say not. What would I want with a divorce? I'd simply have to get another escort, wouldn't I?"

"There's that about it," I agreed. "But let's take it from a personal point of view. Mine, for a change. I've had it, Mona. I'm tired of having my wife referred to behind my back as the town pump. In fact, I'm through. I want the divorce."

She laughed, a brittle sound. "You'll never get it," she stated positively. She moved away from the fire, releasing the skirt that had been bunched up around her waist, only to pick it up again immediately by its hem and draw it off over her head. Every time we had an argument, Mona took off her clothes. It seemed to be a compulsion with her. "You'll never get any-one to testify for you. My father will see to that. If you make just the first little move toward obtaining a divorce, he'll get rid of you like used toilet paper."

I tried to hold myself down. "You don't feel that the state of our marriage could be improved?"

"When I want it improved, I'll improve it," she snapped. "What are you complaining about?" She swept an arm around the comfortably furnished room. "You don't have it so bad. You get out of line, though, and you'll be digging ditches for the rest of your life." She was taking off her bra. "I like things the way they are, and that's the way they're going to stay."

"I'm trying to understand you," I said as she stepped out of her panties. She tossed them aside and went back to the fireplace and posed in front of the mantel.

"You egotistical fools!" she burst out. "I'll *never* understand what it is that gives any of you men a license to think he can satisfy a woman!"

"The operative word is 'woman,' " I said. "Basically, you like girls better than boys, Mona. Like Ludmilla Pierson. You—"

"You leave Ludmilla out of this!"

"Do you deny it?"

"My, how observant we are!" she jeered.

"How about going to a psychiatrist with me, Mona? I don't know if it would do any good, but it's just barely possible we might—"

I stopped. A dark red flush of anger had flooded her features. She left the fireplace, marched to where I was standing, and planted herself squarely in front of me, naked from her eyebrows to her stocking tops. "If I ever learn that you've been discussing me with a psychiatrist, Jim Wilson, it will be the sorriest day of your life. I'll live my own life and you'll keep your nose out of my affairs. It's none of your damn business what I do!" Her voice had turned both harsh and shrill.

"I'm married to you, and it's none of my business?"

"You heard me! If I take the notion, I'll screw every man in this stinking goddam town!"

I came awfully close to going over the dam right that second, but I pulled myself back from the brink. "Husbands and wives have agreed to disagree before, Mona," I said when I could speak. "They stay married, and they party around separately, but they do it discreetly."

"That's not my way," she announced flatly. "And my way is the way we do it, dear." The smile she gave me I carried in my memory for a long time. "Good night."

When she switched her bare ass out of the room and upstairs, I went back to the bottle. I marveled that she thought I was going to let her get away with it.

Three days later, I called Andy Martin to make arrangements to get the evidence I didn't need. Andy knew Tom Harrington, and he didn't want to take it on, but money talks, and when I reached three times his usual fee, he agreed to do it—provided his own testimony wasn't needed.

I'd already made up my mind that no one's testimony would be needed. If Mona was going to plead her case to her father, she'd have to do it from her grave. The details took time to refine, but I had plenty of time.

Ten days after Lud and I came back from Nags Head, Wing drove in from the Edmonds Road job in the morning and we went office hunting together. Lud had been insistent that we had to get out of the office-in-a-hatband stage immediately. Actually, I had an office of sorts at home, but it wasn't the type of setup to impress anyone, and the house was up for sale, anyhow, since I was living at Lud's. When I'd asked Wing on the phone to come in that morning and told him why, he'd sounded glum but had raised no objection.

In a town like Moline there's never too much choice in the way of available office space, and by ten o'clock Wing and I were signing the lease. He had almost nothing to say during the proceedings. I noticed that his eyes were bloodshot and that his handsome features looked drawn. "Are you hitting the bottle?" I asked him us we left the realtor's office.

"I reckon I'm of age," he retorted. "But if you got to know, the answer is no, I'm not." He passed a hand over a blond shadow of beard stubble. "We got us a joker sprayin' our newly laid bituminous nights with kerosene, an' I been layin' out in the brush tryin' to ketch him at it."

Kerosene or gasoline on freshly laid bituminous asphalt cuts it to a point where the binding disintegrates completely. All kerosened sections would have to be done over. "Why the hell haven't you said something about it before?"

"Oh, I thought you'd be all taken up with your bride," he drawled. He waited to see if I would react; when I didn't, he went on again. "It's a penny-ante performance, more of a nuisance 'n anything else. So far, anyway. Type of thing that looks like somebody I fired is tryin' to get in a lick in return. I had a look through the payroll records at the names of those I had to let go recently, but none of 'em look like they got the moxie for this kind of thing."

"You don't think it's more serious than that?"

"More nuisance than anything," he repeated. "Havin' to go back an' patch and send the rollers over it again. The way he operates, the feller seems to know a little bit about bituminous. Mostly he picks sections the rubber-tired rollers have been over but before the steel rollers get the better compaction that would give us a more solid bind."

"Where's the watchman while all this is going on?"

"That's a powerful piece of country to cover in the dark. Even with me out there with him, an' us split up, the Kerosene Kid has slipped in on us twice. I figger he's got a tank slung on the back of his car an' darts in an' out on the fresh-laid sections from the mess of side roads out there. I been tempted to shut down one spreader an' limit his action, but I hate to do it."

"How bad has it been?"

"Oh, not bad. Prob'ly cost us half a day in man-hours fixin' up after the bastard. No real problem yet. Not that I wouldn't like to catch him at it."

"I'll meet you out there tonight and we'll try it again." Wing nodded. "No sense in your spreading yourself too thin trying to corral him by yourself. And speaking of being spread too thin—" I seized the opportunity to move into an area where I expected to have difficulty with Wing—"I'm wondering if that might not be true in other areas. We're carrying quite a load between us, and I've got bids in now on two more jobs I'm reasonably certain we're going to get." Wing smiled. "If we get even one of them, you and I won't be able to handle all the details alone. What would you think about bringing in a couple of people at the supervisory level? I talked to a boy the other day who's working for Lumenti, and I think he'd make us a good man. I'd like to have you talk to him, too, and see if you agree."

"Go ahead an' hire him," Wing said. He sounded dispirited. "I don't need to talk to him. What would I talk to him about? What do I know about an engineer's qualifications these days? I don't even talk the language of these kids comin' out've school." He had been staring moodily into space; he turned to look directly at me. "I've seen it comin'. Expand an' expand an' keep on expandin'. Bring in the young hotshots an' keep ol' Wing out in the weeds where he don't smell up the fancy office we just rented. D'you realize, Jim, that it's not so long ago our weekly payroll didn't match what we're payin' a month for that office?"

He said it with no anger but with a kind of despondent acceptance, and I didn't know what to say to him in reply. "Are you saying you'd prefer us to scratch along as a jerkwater outfit without two 'dozers to rub together and not knowing where its next job is coming from?" I asked finally.

"I don't know what I'm sayin'," he replied. "Or what I'd prefer." He sounded honestly troubled. "I liked it the way we had it, 'fore all this—all this big push. 'Course, I want the company to grow, too." He grinned half-heartedly. "Progress is a bitch, ain't she?"

"It's only the changeover period that's difficult." I tried to soothe him. "In three months you'll think we've always been doing it the new way."

"Yeah, mebbe so. I hope you're right. Well, anyway, no need for you to lose any sleep over this kerosene deal. I'll catch the booger."

"Never mind about my losing sleep. I may be late but I'll meet you there tonight. And if you get there first, look before you jump because I won't be wearing a sign."

He smiled, his first real smile since he'd driven into town. "You do the same, hoss. I'll be seein' you."

He climbed into his rattling Galaxie to drive back out to the job. I watched him go, and I was concerned. It wasn't the same, and we both knew it. The hell of it was I didn't know what it was going to take to make it the same. There didn't seem to be any easily-arrived-at solution.

I spent the next three nights staked out in the roadside brush on Edmonds Road. Wing and I were at opposite ends of a freshly paved section, and we changed our positions each night to correspond with the progress of the job. In the moonless dark, the silent earthmoving machinery bulked around us like prehistoric monsters. Not even an owl hooted the whole three nights. The fourth night I couldn't be there, and Wing called me the next morning to report that the marauder had sprayed kerosene in an irregular pattern over a quarter mile of asphalt.

"I'll get him," Wing promised grimly when I drove out to look at it. As he had said, it wasn't a major problem, but it was certainly a major annoyance. "An' when I do, he'll remember it awhile."

"I wish I could spend more time out here with you, Wing—"

"You got enough to do," he said shortly. "I'll get him."

I drove back to town trying to concentrate on more important problems, but the image of a kerosene-spraying unknown kept breaking up my chain of thought.

I promised myself I'd get back out there to give Wing a hand.

Lud's dinner party eventually expanded to include twenty-eight people, fourteen husbands and their wives, and it got off to a funereal start. We met the group in the formal drawing room, a large room unused except for special occasions. The conversation was stilted and there wasn't much of it. I was uncomfortable in a new suit that Lud had bulldozed the tailor into completing in time for the affair. Most of the men and their women ran to a pattern: large, sleek, whitehaired, and jowly. Lud and I were the youngest persons in the room.

Tom Harrington was there, standing a little apart. Lud had extended the invitation to him in person. She had reported that he hadn't seemed much impressed. I was pleased to see that none of the guests seemed impressed by him, an indication of how quickly it became noised about in circles like this that there was a new snout in the trough.

Lud was looking her best for the occasion, and her best was considerable. She had on a shimmering gown of some kind of gold froth, and her hair-dresser had perspired over her for two hours that afternoon in the master bedroom. She had brought in two men to serve drinks and, whether it was the drinks or her own artful circulating, she had considerably raised the group temperature from its low, low point before we were summoned in to the catered dinner.

She had made her table arrangements carefully, too, after preparing a detailed scouting report on the invitees. She placed the dimmest social bulbs closest to herself at the table, thus assuring herself they'd receive the proper attention. At judicious intervals around the large oval table, she'd placed the more roguish gentlemen next to the liveliest ladies the group afforded. The talk and laughter emanating from these areas of vivacity eventually thawed the protective permafrost of the others, and by the time the second wine was served, everyone was contributing to the conversation. I watched Lud's sharp-eyed glances darting around the table as she stirred up the occasional dead spot with a smile and a query. She was working like a stevedore while still contriving to look like a Botticelli angel.

I had been placed between two of the older women, and I had been given my orders, which were to keep talking. "College is always a good subject," Lud had said. "Most of them have children and grandchildren in college, although the majority of them never went themselves."

"Too busy making money from the age of ten. What am I supposed to talk about? Nothing ever happened to me in college that you could print in a family newspaper."

"Make it up. Tell them about the time you disassembled a Model-T' and lugged it up into the belfry of the chapel and reassembled it there. Tell them anything. They won't know the difference. I don't know why it is that politicians seem to flourish in inverse ratio to the amount of time they spent in school."

"Not politicians," I pointed out. "The men behind the politicians."

"Have it your way. But you keep talking. If I see your jaws stop wagging, I'll throw a biscuit at you."

I kept talking, but it was uphill work, one of the hardest day's work of my life. Both corseted old biddies had surveyed me glacially when I gallantly seated them at the opening of the meal. Neither touched her wine. Their whole attitude proclaimed forcefully that *they* were associating with a wife-murderer and political upstart under protest and only at the urgent behest of their spouses. I didn't break them down exactly, but at the cost of a wilted collar and a moist backbone I had them listening and contributing an occasional remark by the time we reached the dessert course. Just before it was served, Lud awarded me the Croix de Guerre with palms via a quick nod. I had already made up my mind that I was going to have a serious talk with her about this sort of affair, though. It just wasn't my line of work.

Lud signaled for the group's dispersal by rising. She shepherded the women back into the drawing room while I led the men into the library. One of the hired bartenders was dispensing brandy and cigars. "Damn fine dinner, Wilson," a redfaced giant I remembered from the drawing room as Ken Stackpole said to me as soon as the library doors closed. "Your wife's a real organizer. An' that pineapple upside-down cake was great. I'm s'posed to be on a diet"—he patted his gross stomach—"but you reckon yore man here could rustle me up an extra portion now my wife's out of sight?" He laughed heartily.

I turned to look for Lud's butler-bartender, but he had overheard and already anticipated me. He went to a side door and spoke briefly to someone outside it. In minutes, a tray was handed in to him with a dozen of the gooey desserts on it. They disappeared amidst the men, who were circling him like snow in the desert.

"Talk to you a minute, Wilson," Richie Hoey said at my elbow. "'Fore this gang gets the sugar off its teeth."

He was a roly-poly little baldy who had a trick of bouncing up and down on his toes as he spoke. "You really got somethin' goin' for you here," he went on, glancing around the large room and running a gift cigar appreciatively under his nose. "How 'bout you drivin' over to my place some night soon an' meetin' with a few of us? Wouldn't tie you up long. Strictly business." He chuckled.

My interest rose. The few would be an important few. "Any time you say," I replied.

"Week from tonight? Only be three, four of us," he said deprecatingly.

"I'll be there."

"We'll count on it." Shrewd eyes studied me as I held a match for his cigar. "You seem better organized 'n most men your age, Wilson." He turned away without waiting for a reply.

Two different men had mentioned organization just minutes apart. I'd always prided myself on my own ability to coordinate things properly, and Lud seemed just as capable in her own domain. It put a different picture on the situation. I was going to have to revise my objections to the stuffiness of the atmosphere at dinner if that was what it took to reach the business-as-usual stage with Richie Hoey and his friends during the brandy-and-cigars aftermath. I was just going to have to learn to put up with it.

I moved through the room putting into practice another bit of Lud's coaching. Three days before, she'd given me a set of pictures of the men who were to be present, together with a brief item on each, regarding spheres of influence and special interests. As per her instructions, I circulated among the clustered groups of men, fitting faces to names, dropping a word here and there about a special interest. When little pockets of discussion flared up, drawing others into the conversation, I moved on to another group. Twice in my progress around the room I saw Tom Harrington standing in a corner, alone. I didn't go near him. I was surprised that he'd come at all. With what I represented to him, I didn't see how he could afford to be there. I made a note to ask Lud how she had persuaded him.

The room became a beehive of animated, arm-waving groups, and the butler-bartender finally had to tell us that the ladies were waiting for us. En route to rejoin them, Richie Hoey winked at me and grinned. I didn't catch his particular meaning if he had one, but it was indication enough that the entire dinner had gone well.

Lud thought so, too, in the post-affair rehash conducted upstairs in my bedroom. I was sitting in a low-slung chair, dressed in T-shirt and trousers, and Lud was perched on the edge of my bed with her legs tucked up beneath her after having kicked her shoes off. "The women liked you," she was saying. "You don't have charm, but you have force, and sometimes it's almost as good. They all came prepared to dislike you, but you brought them at least part way around. How did you make out with the men?"

I told her about Richie Hoey's invitation, and she listened intently. "That's what we need," she declared when I finished, nodding her blonde head vigorously. "We're on our way, no doubt about it. Next Saturday? I must remember to cancel our table at the country club dance. Too bad in a way; I was going to use it as an opportunity to test the climate of public opinion locally. But first things first. By the way, how did Tom make out?"

"He'll be a week thawing out."

"He's been an intimate friend of those men for years," she protested.

"Maybe it's a case of 'What have you done for me lately?' " I said. "Anyway, they froze him. I don't see why he came at all. What kind of arm-twisting did you have to use to get him to agree? With me at the head of the table, his position was impossible."

Her brows were knitted in a frown. "It wasn't too difficult," she said absently. The frown disappeared, and she leaned back on her elbows, relaxed, looking as soft and appealing as I'd ever seen her look. Before I could press for an explanation, she rose from the bed suddenly and padded over to me in her stockinged feet. "Jim—"

"No," I cut her off instantly.

"No? No what?"

"No snuggling."

The comers of her mouth drew down, then lifted in a conscious effort at a smile. "You'd make a poor shopper at a bargain sale, Jim. How do you know the merchandise is no good until you've tried it?"

"The merchandise doesn't do anything for me."

"No?" She arched herself up on her toes and began a slow pirouette, her breasts jutting boldly. "Perhaps if I—"

"No. Rack it up and drag it out of here, Lud."

She came down off her toes. For a long, silent moment she stared at me, then whirled and stalked from the room, slamming the door so viciously the bureau mirror vibrated, and five seconds later a picture slowly slid down the opposite wall.

I left my chair, picked up her forgotten shoes, and put them outside in the hall.

CHAPTER 10

Three nights later, I stopped in at Veronica's apartment. She seemed surprised to see me. "Let's go out to the cabin," she suggested when it got through to her what I wanted.

"I don't have time," I said.

We went to bed, and while it was good for me, I'd have had to be a wooden Indian not to know that it hadn't been for her. She threw on a robe and followed me out to the door when I was dressed. "Do me a favor, Jim," she said. "Don't come back again."

I had the door open already; I closed it. "What the hell do you mean 'Don't come back again'?"

"What I said." She was pale but her voice was under control. "I'm not a whore, and I won't be used like one."

"Just because I'm busy now—"

"You're going to be busy from now on. And you're m-married, and everything—everything's different." She was crying, her face all twisted.

I stood there thinking of fifteen different things to say, and wound up saying none of them. I opened the door again and left the apartment. I stormed down the corridor and, ignoring the elevator, ran down the stairs to the sidewalk. I'd just turned toward the station wagon, which was parked half a dozen cars from the building entrance, when I saw a man step backward quickly into the shadows of a doorway across the street. It was so dark I couldn't get much of an indication of size or shape, let alone individuality, but I had an impression that he limped. As I took my first steps away from the entrance, I turned my head and watched from the corner of my eye. The man emerged from the doorway and began paralleling my progress, across the street and a few yards behind me, and he was definitely limping. I walked past the station wagon without even looking toward it. In my present mood, I welcomed the opportunity to come to grips with something I could hook my hands into.

Half a block farther on, the shadower crossed the street and took up the pursuit directly behind me but still some distance away. I turned right at the first corner and stepped into the interior of the first doorway. If it was Garvey following me, as I halfway thought it might be, I knew he was too cute to be caught hugging the building wall in his tailing. I was prepared to go out into the middle of the street after him if necessary, but the shadow hurrying past my doorway was so close that I could have touched him. I still couldn't see his face. I caught him in ten yards and neck-chopped him.

He heard me coming but couldn't turn around in time. He went so sprad-
dle-legged that I was sure it wasn't Garvey. I grabbed him as he started to
fall and muscled him back up the street into the doorway. The diffused light
from a window display illuminated the pale, startled features of Whit
Bailey, Mona's inamorata the day I'd killed her. I hadn't set eyes on him
since. I didn't know who was the more surprised, Bailey or me. "What are
you doing following me?" I yelled at him, holding him up by his lapels.

"Noth—nothing." He got it out around a bobbing Adam's apple. He lifted a hand to rub the back of his neck gingerly. "You—you're imagining
things."

"The hell I'm imagining things. What's the idea, Bailey?"

His weak, good-looking features seemed shriveled. "You're—you're mistaken, that's all. You're—"

I backhanded him across the face, left-right, left-right. "Tell me again I'm
mistaken," I challenged. He shrank back against the store window looking
so much like a frightened rabbit that I felt disgusted. "This was never your
idea, Bailey. What are you doing here and who put you up to it?"

He moistened his lips with a quick flirt of his tongue. "I—no one put me
up to it. I tell you you're mistaken—" I raised my hand again, and he
flinched. "Ludmilla!" he blurted out.

"*Ludmilla?*" I echoed incredulously. "You mean she—oh, yes, I begin to
see." In view of her ultimatum to me about tomcatting, Ludmilla obviously had decided to keep herself informed. But Whit Bailey, for God's sake?
"You silly bastard, how did you think you were going to get away with it?
You couldn't shadow a blind—" I stopped abruptly as something occurred
to me. I took another look at Whit Bailey. "Say, are you the one spraying
kerosene on unset asphalt out at Edmonds Road?"

"Of—of course not," he said too quickly.

"You're not a silly bastard, you're a damn fool idiot, Bailey," I said with
conviction. "If Wing Darlington ever catches you at it, he'll pour so much
of your own kerosene up your ass you'll need a plastic rectum." I shook
him until his head bobbed and his shoulders bounced off the door frame.
"Now what's all this about Lud?"

"She—she came to me and said she—she wanted to know what you
were up to nights," he mumbled.

"And you didn't have any better sense than to try to find out. What made
you listen to her?"

"Ludmilla has always been a good friend of mine." He tried to make it
sound dignified, but it came out as a pathetic little whimper.

The more I thought of it, the less possible it sounded. After his run-in
with me at the motel, Bailey shouldn't have wanted any part of me. There
was something very much out of line in his protestations. "How does Lud
happen to be such a friend of yours?"

Despite my grip on him, he had one hand free enough to wave it help-lessly. "She's—just a good friend."

"The hell she is. Friendship would never send you on this errand, man. I could have killed you that day and been justified, and you know it, but here you are, sucking around. Why?"

"She said—she insisted you wouldn't dare do anything to me now, even if you—even if you caught me at it."

"She did, did she?" Lud thought that I'd feel I had too much to lose. "Let me tell you something, Bailey—" I stopped and reconsidered. This type at the end of my arm wasn't much excuse for a man, but he was demonstrably available and there ought to be some way I could make use of him. I groped for an instant, and then the germ of an idea came to me. "Since you're already a secret agent, why don't we take the logical step and make a double agent out of you? I've got a little job you can do for me."

"Oh, I couldn't! I mean—well, Ludmilla wouldn't like it at all!"

I shook him, and he gasped.

"What was that again?"

"Please! I'd be—I'd be no good at it, anyway."

He was certainly right about that. And with him in Ludmilla's pocket anyhow, too great a risk would be involved. It was still nagging at me that I'd never had the time to do anything about finding out who had tampered with George Pierson's car. For a second I'd considered impressing Bailey into service in that connection, but if he even mentioned it to Lud, the lid would be off for fair. And using Bailey would be the equivalent of a halfway measure or less. It was time I got on the stick and did something about it myself, instead of making excuses that I didn't have the time.

I could feel Bailey trembling in my hands. It was a funny thing, but even with the kerosene and all, I couldn't really seem to get mad at the guy. He might have been hell on wheels in bed with a woman, but in every other way that mattered, he was such a no-count type as a man that he was almost pitiful. About to turn him loose, I thought of something else. Lud must have a powerful grip on this one where it hurt to have him risk following me. "What does Lud have on you, Bailey?"

"N-nothing." He wet his lips again. "She's—she's just a good friend." I moved my right hand slightly, and he jerked backward involuntarily. The words popped out of him like seeds from a crushed watermelon. "There was a slight—ah—problem with one of the secretaries at the bank. She—she had a baby. Ludmilla handled everything and—and kept it quiet."

The classic squeeze, I thought. I let go of Bailey, and his hands went automatically to his clothes, smoothing out the bunched-up fabric where I'd been holding him. He looked at me hopefully. "You can run along," I decided. "But if I hear of another drop of kerosene being spread around out on Edmonds Road, I'm coming looking for you. Understand?" He nodded fearfully. "All right. Blow."

He limped three steps in the direction from which he'd come.

"Bailey!" I called. He stopped instantly. "What about this limp? Is it from the bullets I put in your butt?"

He spoke without turning around. "The doctor says it's a muscle pull that will ease in time as it heals thoroughly."

"Glad to hear it. I wouldn't want to have marred your beauty." He probably thought I was being facetious, and on one level I certainly was, but I really meant it. The Baileys of the world had enough of a load to carry without an additional contribution from me. I'd used him as an instrument to bring down Mona, but I actually had nothing against him personally. If it hadn't been him, it would have been someone else.

He started to walk away from me again, slowly, as if afraid I'd call him back. I didn't say anything, and he speeded up. I watched him hurry around the comer and disappear from view. It might have turned out to be a profitable evening, I decided. At the very least, Bailey was a stick to beat Ludmilla with. And, even indebted to her as he was, I had no real fear of his following me again.

I walked back to the station wagon, intending to drive straight home and have it out with her. I might not be able to get mad at Bailey, but I had no difficulty at all in getting mad at her. If she thought she was going to regulate my private life, she had another think coming, and the sooner she found it out, the better.

Three blocks from the house, I passed Mueller's Service Station, where all the Pierson cars were serviced, and it reminded me again of George Pierson's Thunderbird. On impulse, I wheeled in to the gas pumps. It was late enough so that only a single attendant was on duty. I knew that the place was busy enough in the daytime to keep three men employed. It wasn't impossible that one of them knew something about the Thunderbird that he wasn't talking about. In Moline, people grew up learning not to talk about things unless there was a reason for talk.

"Evenin', Mr. Wilson." The young fellow who came out of the office greeted me cheerfully. "Fill it up?"

"Yes," I said. I didn't know the young fellow, but he knew me. It made my question easier when he finished filling the tank and handed me a credit card ticket to sign. "I imagine you had a run of people checking their cars to make sure they weren't going to run off the road," I said casually. "After the accident a while back." He nodded. "I've been meaning to have the wagon checked, as a matter of fact. D'you have a minute to do it now?"

"Sure thing, Mr. Wilson. Pull in on the hoist and I'll have a look."

I backed up, swung around, and drove up on the metal tracks. When I got out of the ear, the attendant gave it the air and the wagon rose to shoulder height. He stepped under it and at once began checking the steering mechanism. I purposely hadn't mentioned steering mechanism to him, but he'd gone directly to it. Evidently it was no secret what had sent the Pierson car off the road that night. No secret around the Mueller Service Station, anyway. What I needed, I thought, was an attendant who showed reluctance to admit that he had such knowledge, which could be an indication that he had knowledge he was afraid to talk about. I'd have to keep trying with the other attendants at the station and see what I drew.

"Looks fine, Mr. Wilson," the boy said at last, emerging from under the wagon.

"Fine," I echoed. He lowered the hoist and I got back into the wagon and drove home. Or more correctly, drove to Ludmilla's. It never felt like a home to me, and I doubted that it ever would. I parked in the double garage and went into the house. When I entered her bedroom, Lud was sound asleep. I turned on her bedside table lamp, and at the onslaught of light, she stirred and flung an arm across her eyes, then removed it and looked up at me. She looked cool and fresh. "What is it?" she asked, sitting up quickly. "What's happened?" Her nightgown appeared to be the same lacy confection she'd worn on our wedding night or its twin.

"I caught Whit Bailey following me tonight," I said. "If I catch him again, I'll tie you down over the end of this bed and take a yard of skin off you with my belt."

She swung herself up from the bed and onto her feet after throwing back the sheet. "Any time you think you can intimidate—"

"I don't know why you took the trouble," I interposed. "I'd have told you if you asked me."

"I assume he found you in the bed of Cartwright's fat secretary," she said calmly.

I wasn't going to give her the satisfaction of knowing that that was over. "He found me where I wanted to be, Lud. And where I intend to be whenever I feel like it."

She shook her head. "No, Jim. No. Your freewheeling days are over. You've got an image to build. There'll be no more of that sort of thing."

The sight of her standing there imperiously cool, handing out dictums, infuriated me. "Damn you, I'll do as I please! I told you beforehand—"

"We both want the same thing, and conduct of that nature jeopardizes it," she said coldly. "I can't permit it. If I—"

"You can't permit it," I snorted. "I suppose the next step is for you to tell Veronica to get out of town?"

"If necessary."

The full-armed facial slap I dealt her sent her reeling backward until she sprawled ungracefully on the bed. She rebounded from it while the sharp sound was still in the air, and came after me like a lynx after a snowshoe rabbit, her long fingernails hooked like claws. I left-hooked her to the ribcage, grabbed her by an arm and a leg as she sagged, picked her up, and threw her at the bed. She landed on her back, gasping, the lace covering a third of her. I took hold of its trailing edges and drew it all the way up her body, bagging her head in its loose folds. I ignored her kicking as I flattened her out, nude from her throat to her painted toenails. Starting with rape, I intended to use and abuse her deliberately in every way known to man. This one needed to be shown who was in charge.

Holding her down with one hand, I ripped off my clothes with the other. I climbed onto the bed with her and had no sooner forcefully split her flesh than I received the first of a series of shocks. She wasn't fighting me. The muffled sounds emanating from beneath the enveloping nightgown were not protests. Instead of the limp, inanimate flesh to which Mona had accustomed me, I was riding a furious, totally knowledgeable pinwheel whose surging, fiery reaction instantly deflected my purpose. How do you beat down a woman who welcomes your assault? Several times, the frenetically savage conflict teetered us on the edge of the bed. When I finally exploded in a draining burst that restored me to some semblance of sanity, I withdrew slowly and rose to my feet. Lud was sprawled loosely, her friction-marked thighs still twitching, and her breasts rising and falling rapidly. In a moment both her hands went up and swept the confining folds of her nightgown from her head. "I *told* you—Mona was—the lesbian," she panted.

I left her bedroom without saying a word.

The experience had shaken all my deep-seated convictions. Ludmilla Pierson-Wilson represented a clear and present danger of a type other than I'd imagined. A man could get altogether too fond of what I'd just had, and I couldn't afford to give the woman another hold on me.

In my own room, I made up my mind. I'd never get back into bed with her again.

Late Saturday afternoon I drove the two hundred miles to Richie Hoey's home and arrived in the early evening. His house, a large but unpretentious white frame dwelling with green gables, was almost in the center of town. It had a postage-stamp-sized lawn in front. Sam Carstens answered the chime at the door, and we exchanged greetings. "Meetin's in the front room," he announced.

I followed him into an old-fashioned "front room" that reminded me of my uncle's house. The wallpaper looked as if it had been in place for fifty years. Ugly, rust-colored draperies closed out most of the light from the small-paned windows, and the fireplace andirons were black, wrought-iron barking dogs. Four heavy armchairs were drawn up in a hollow square, and in front of each was a collapsible television tray. To one side, a tea caddy had been pressed into service as a portable bar.

"Drink?" Sam asked me.

"I believe I'll wait for the others, Sam."

"Here's the boss now," Sam said.

Richie bustled in behind a ten-inch cigar, and Sam left the room. The little round man shook hands energetically, motioned me to one of the chairs, and perched his own fat rump on the edge of another. "Well, now, how's things at your end of the state?" he began, in what was apparently a familiar opening gambit.

"If the goose hung any higher, my only worry would be about someone removing the rope."

He chuckled agreeably and took a drag on his cigar. "I asked you to come a half hour earlier 'n the others, Wilson, because I thought it was time for a little talk between you an' me. Plain talk." He waved the cigar at me. "There's items you haven't taken sufficiently into consideration, so to speak, some of 'em in your own backyard. Most of 'em going back to the fact that of the group at your wife's dinner party the other night, while none of us were politicians in the strict sense of the word, we tell the politicians what to do." He chuckled again, but at once turned serious.

"Now you're a maverick to a lot of the people I talk to, Wilson. You didn't come up through the ranks, an' you're askin' to step in at the top level. I know you done some right smart pushin' an' bangin' in your area to shape things up the way you think they ought to be, but ordinarily you wouldn't have the chance of a crystal ball in a hailstorm. It's a combination of circumstances, plus you bein' the right man—the available man— at the right time, at least to my way of thinkin', that's got you this far. But to get down to cases, there's a missin' link in your operation."

He paused as if awaiting a comment, so I supplied it. "I wasn't aware of it."

"I figgered you wasn't," he said, nodding his bald head emphatically. "Now I been helpin' things to happen' the way I want 'em to happen in this county for a good long time, an' I know that power flows to the man gutsy enough to step in an' grab its tail. You've done that, but out've channels. We may not be politicians, but we work with politicians. An' there's no lone wolves; we work together."

He took another drag on the cigar, whose ash whitened an additional quarter inch. "At the county level, Wilson," he resumed, "when all's said an' done, *everything* traces to politics, all up an' down the line. Tom Harrington was wired in politically all over the state, which was the reason the boys went along with him even after they begun to look a little cross-eyed at some of his goin's-on. Up to now, at least, you don't seem to have paid any attention to the grass roots of the political situation in your county, an' I didn't get the impression the other night that even that whip-smart wife of yours had given it a thought." He paused. "Scares me a little, that wife of yours," he confided. "Glad it ain't me has to ride herd on her. Although from the shape of your saddle horn, you're the man for the job. I think." His pause this time was for effect. "Men in these parts don't take kindly to pushy women. But then I'm not givin' you any news."

"There'll be no problem," I replied to the implied warning. I steered him back to what I considered to be the main point. "Now this political situation—"

"Yeah." He leaned back in his chair and crossed his short legs. "In Albermarle County, Harrington had split off from the organization, so to speak, an' there was some feelin' about it. We'd like to see you work with the organization."

"I've always voted—"

"Sure you've always voted the ticket. I'm not talkin' about that, or about contributions. I'm talkin' about sittin' down with the people in Albermarle County who count an' workin' closely enough with them an' with us so there's no chance of cross-purposes bobbin' up at embarrassin' times." He peered at me through a thin haze of blue cigar smoke. "When you get back to Moline, I'd call it a personal favor if you'd sit down like you are here with me an' talk to a man I believe you'd find right congenial in a lot of respects."

"In Moline? Who's the man?"

"Sig Jacobus."

"I know Sig," I said slowly. A number of things came into focus more sharply at the sound of the name: the coolness between Harrington and Jacobus, an item or two of gossip around town that I'd never tied together, and the lack of cooperation between Sig and Harrington's pet prosecutor at the coroner's hearing after Mona's death. I'd always known that Sig dabbled in politics, of course, but never to what extent. The big question in my mind bore on one fact: if I sat down with him, who would be telling whom? "Not well, but I know him," I went on. "He and Harrington had a difference of opinion a couple of years ago."

"They did that," Richie agreed. "An' affairs in Albermarle County been goin' to hell in a handbasket ever since. We been hurtin' there. Even in his best days, Harrington was always bullheaded, an' when a man been on top as long as he has, he's made enough enemies so some chickens got to come home to roost." He pointed the half-smoked cigar at me. "You got a lot of gumph, Wilson, an' you ain't put a foot down wrong yet, but you couldn't have done what you have in Albermarle County if Harrington'd been able to call on the backin' he'd have had as recently as a year ago. His attitude lately done cancelled all promissory notes."

"I'll be glad to talk to Sig," I said. I wasn't sure that I would be, but it was obviously the thing to say. "I've never been a politically-minded type, and I don't know what I could contribute, specifically. I'm not—"

"You don't need to worry about contributin'," Richie interrupted. "Sig'll just want to know you're on the team. He calls a meetin' every little while, an' you'll sit in an' catch up on the facts of life in your area." He grinned at me. "Just like we'll do for the state here this evenin'. With you, the cart comes before the horse, boy, because you happened to come along at a time when a few people could take an interest in you. Another time it could've been a whole hell of a lot different, I can tell you. Why, it took me—"

He stopped as the chimes sounded at the front door. In a moment Sam Carstens ushered in the dessert-loving big man of Lud's dinner party. I groped for his name and then it came to me: Ken Stackpole. We shook hands. "Glad to see you again, Wilson," Stackpole boomed.

"Didn't happen to bring along any of that pineapple upside-down cake with you, did you?"

"Sam'll bring you in a wedge of apple pie my youngest daughter, Nina, made," Richie promised him. "It'll run your blood pressure up to where Doc Sanders'll rule you off the track."

"He's had me on a diet for fifteen years," Stackpole laughed. He glanced around. "Where's—ah, here he is," he said as the chimes sounded again. Another man I'd seen at Lud's party but to whom I hadn't paid much attention entered behind Sam. The newcomer was a stringy, attenuated individual with wispy gray hair and obvious false teeth. "Bob Jessup, Jim Wilson," said Richie, reintroducing us. "Let's sit down an' get to work, boys. Sam, you can bring in the trays now."

We were barely in our chairs when Sam wheeled in a cart with four large trays on it. In quick succession, he placed each on one of the folding tables beside our chairs. Each tray contained two massive roast beef sandwiches, a huge section of apple pie with a slice of cheese aboard it, and a pot of coffee. Richie did all the talking as we ate, but somehow he managed to clean up his own tray as quickly as the rest of us who had been eating in silence.

Carstens returned and removed everything except the coffee pots, then set up a gateleg table in the center of the hollow square around which we were sitting. When he left the room that time, I heard the click of a lock in the door. Richie went to a desk and unlocked its center drawer, removed a map, which he brought back to the table, and spread it out carefully, smoothing out its creases. I leaned forward to see better, and despite my background, it took me a couple of minutes to recognize what I was looking at.

On a detailed map that featured the road networks of the state, lines had been drawn in various colors. Red, blue, and green lines predominated in the color scheme, with the red lines representing past highway construction projects and the blue lines representing current ones. That left the green lines to represent future projects, and my eyes automatically sought out the location of Albemarle County. I could see highway routes marked in, that I knew as a practical measure couldn't exist for five years. This planning board certainly took the long-range view.

"This is for your benefit, Jim," Richie said to me, picking up a black marking crayon. With practiced ease, he sketched bold lines onto the map, dividing the state into four roughly equal sectors. "This is the way we been operatin'," he continued, whirling the map until it faced me squarely. "As a practical thing, we don't have but so much influence at the capitol, but since there's always good ol' boys up there whose interests coincide with some of ours, there's a general unanimity in the backscratchin' that goes on. Even on state jobs we can usually count on bein' consulted. Unofficially, of course. The county jobs don't always come out even, of course, so once in a while we cross borders accordin' to who's had the latest slice of pie." He winked heavily. "We ration out the jobs amongst the boys you saw at the dinner party plus a few others, an' we try to have a couple of jobs a year go to an 'outside' construction firm in our own counties to keep some sharp newspaper editor from hollerin' 'monopoly.' "

I could see from the black-lined map that Richie's slice of pie was the largest, while Albermarle County and its surrounding area was the smallest, and I suspected there had been some readjustments since the last map-drawing, but I didn't say anything. A man has to walk before he can run. I didn't say much of anything for the balance of the meeting, which lasted an hour and a half. I listened while Richie skillfully dictated the assignment of county construction projects budgeted for the next twelve-month period. There was no disagreement; an occasional question was always speedily and satisfactorily disposed of. The aggregate figures were enough to make my head swim. Accustomed as I was to dealing with a job at a time, and never the largest job, it seemed to me at times that Richie was dealing with the national budget.

"None of us are foolish enough or hungry enough to want *all* the jobs in our territories," Richie explained to me at one point. "But we keep our crews busy, an' when somethin' with a little extra cream in it comes along, we usually ain't behind the door when it gets handed out."

By the time the meeting broke up, I had an increased ration of respect for the other members of the little group. Despite his verbosity and general air of country bumpkinship, Richie was a remarkably sharp man with a pencil. Ken Stackpole, drinking coffee steadily and burping just as steadily, raised only an occasional point, but each one cut to the bone. Jessup contributed almost nothing verbally, but sat back almost as if he was a spectator, rather than a participant.

Richie detained me at the front door as the others departed. "Well?" he demanded. "Learn anything?"

"I'm going to have to go back to school," I said. "A lot of it came too fast." He nodded. "You'll catch up. You've got a good solid foundation. I checked out a couple of your jobs, from bids to completion, before I drove over to your wife's dinner party." He grinned. "Nothin' that could pull the roof down on us quicker than a man in the combine doin' shoddy work that could get us investigated by the legislature." He jerked a thumb at Jessup's lean figure getting into a car that was anything but a late model. "What'd you think of him?"

"He didn't seem to have much to say."

"He don't need to," Richie smiled. "Man could buy an' sell all of us with his loose change. Well—I'm plannin' on bein' over your way again in a week or ten days, Wilson. What would you think of us droppin' in on Sig together over a cup of coffee?"

"Fine," I said. "An hour's notice is all I'll need."

He walked with me out to my car. "Don't worry about nothin' meantime," he said.

"I'm not a worrier, Richie."

He cackled. "I did have that notion," he admitted.

We shook hands, and I drove back to Moline and Lud's house. It was two in the morning when I arrived, but she was waiting up for me. When I came in, she was in the downstairs sitting room in a lime green negligee. "How did it go?" she asked before I was well inside the door.

"It was an eye-opener," I said. "I thought I was doing it all by myself around here, but I found out tonight I was doing a great deal of it on sufferance. The boys had become disenchanted with Harrington. Six months earlier or six months later and they might have squashed me like a mosquito. These people think BIG. We've got to adjust our sights upward."

"I *knew* it would be like that," she said with satisfaction. "Tom Harrington was always so close-mouthed about it, but I was positive there must be a small executive group that made the decisions. Tell me all about it."

"I want to take a shower," I protested.

"Then come ahead and take it. You can talk at the same time." She led the way upstairs and carried a straight-backed chair into the bathroom in my bedroom. "Go ahead," she repeated, seating herself.

I began the story while stripping off my clothes. In the shower I raised my voice above the hiss of the water as I continued to give her the details. "So Richie will be over soon and we'll sit down with Sig," I concluded, shutting off the water and reaching for a towel.

There was a silence. "I don't think I like that," Lud said at last. I leaned out of the shower stall to take a look at her, and she was frowning. "Why do we need Sig Jacobus?"

"Because that's the way the system works," I said. "If Harrington couldn't buck it, do you think we can?"

"Yes, I do," she said confidently. "Perhaps not tomorrow, but in time. We won't work outside the organization; we'll *be* the organization. I never thought Sig Jacobus was overly endowed with brains, anyhow."

Here was a prime example of what Richie had indirectly been warning me against. "Don't get the bit in your teeth, Lud. These men don't care for assertive females."

"Do you think I don't know it? Those old fuddyduddies exasperate me. Why do you think I needed you at all?" She hurried on past that point. "But if we manage it properly, we'll be dictating to Richie Hoey in a couple of years, and not the other way around."

I made no reply to that piece of bombast. For a species supposed to be practical, women show damn little evidence of it at times. Lud was clever enough—every question she'd asked about the meeting had been of a penetrating nature—but she still really had no idea of what made the wheels go around in the state.

When I stepped out of the shower stall, the bathroom was empty. She must have left it only seconds before I did, but when I walked into the bedroom, she was stretched out on the bed and the lime-green negligee and anything that had been beneath it had disappeared. Despite a coating of powder, dull-looking blue bruises still mottled her thighs. I walked over and looked down at her as she stared up at me with an expression I couldn't define. "No," I said.

She came up off the bed like a panther, first to her knees in the middle of it, and then in a follow-through that was all one smooth-flowing motion off the bed onto her feet. "What do you mean, 'No'?"

"What I said. No more of that."

"Why not? What's the matter with you?"

"I'm afraid of you."

"A likely story!" She put her hand on my biceps. "Come on, Jim. This is the frosting on the cake. Let's not throw it away. We're partners, aren't we? Let's *be* partners." She made an impatient gesture when I didn't move. "Don't you trust me?"

"Since you mention it, no."

"That's ridiculous. You're in control and you know it. And I'm the best you ever had in bed and you know that, too." All the old arrogance was back in her voice.

"You're close, anyway, and that's part of the point. Suppose I got to like it too well? It might affect my judgement in regard to you. I'm not sure I could afford to have that happen."

"Of all the childish—!" She snatched my right hand in hers and drew it down her naked body. "Can you tell me you don't want to?"

"No, but I can tell you I'm not going to."

She smothered all but the first syllable of the acid-tipped retort that sprang to her lips, then almost ran from the bedroom.

In the morning I found her nightgown and the lime-green negligee balled up in the corner where she'd pitched them.

It irked me that she had been so coolly confident that I'd return to her bed at the snap of her fingers. But even more, it disturbed me to find out during the dialogue how much I wanted to.

Chapter 11

And so, for ninety days, peace and progress reigned on all fronts. There was no more trouble out on the job, and there was no more trouble with Ludmilla. She still showed flashes of her customary imperiousness, but as if realizing how much it irritated me, she quickly turned it off. Together we planned and saw through several social gatherings, which we arranged to best promote our interests with the right people. Richie Hoey came over to Moline, and he and I called on Sig Jacobus, who seemed satisfied. Even Richie seemed satisfied, although he once more found occasion to mention strong-minded wives.

I had run through the car-on-the-hoist gimmick with all the attendants at Mueller's. Only one of them had given me a blank stare and asked for specifics on what I wanted. He was a part-timer, a moonlighting school teacher named Graham Sawyer, and I didn't know if he honestly wasn't around the station enough to hear what was going on, or if he had a reason for playing dumb. Being a part-timer, he had irregular hours, and although I took to dropping by the station nights trying to catch him on alone, it hadn't worked out.

Harrington was still in the wings, but scarcely a menace, I felt. At another meeting of the brain trust, Richie and his friends had tossed us a substantial bone in the way of a job I hadn't expected to get, one on which we stood to make a real dollar. Wing was still acting standoffish with me, but the situation with him at least was no worse.

And that was how things stood on the evening Veronica telephoned me at Lud's house.

CHAPTER 12

It was a Friday evening, and I'd returned to the house after a gruelling day spent out on the Edmonds Road site with Wing. On the way in, I'd stopped at Mueller's and left the station wagon to be serviced. I asked to have it brought to the house when it was ready, since I had to go out again. Sig Jacobus had asked me to stop in at his place for a few minutes. I walked the three blocks from Mueller's to Lud's place. I'd noticed her car at the service station, too, but she wasn't at home. The housekeeper, Margaret, didn't seem to be around, either. There was no message from Lud, but that wasn't unusual.

The Edmonds Road job was in its final stages, and I'd been working out with Wing the logistics for the transfer of our heavy equipment to the next job, which was to be half again as big. Whether it was from absorbing more sun than I'd been used to recently or from neglecting to eat, I arrived at the house with a headache. In the kitchen, I looked over the contents of the refrigerator, sliced off a couple of pieces of ham and made a sandwich, opened up a bottle of beer and a can of peaches, and made a standing-up meal. The whole house was quiet as I ate.

While waiting for the station wagon to be delivered, I went upstairs and began rechecking a set of figures at a makeshift desk I'd set up in a corner of my bedroom. The headache grew worse, and I stretched out on the bed for a few minutes to see if that would help. It didn't, and I decided that if my head was going to ache it might as well have a reason. I went back downstairs to the kitchen and opened up another bottle of beer.

As I turned away from the refrigerator I saw through the kitchen window Lud's car backing into our driveway. A white-coveralled attendant in a long-billed work cap got out and walked toward the house, the car keys in his hand. It was customary for attendants delivering the cars to drop the keys just inside the back door. I opened the door just as he reached the top step. "Is the station wagon nearly ready?" I asked, realizing for the first time that the attendant was Graham Sawyer, the moonlighting school teacher.

He looked disconcerted at the sight of me standing there. "Mrs. Wilson came in, in a big hurry a few moments ago, sir," he said. "Her car wasn't ready right then, but the station wagon was, so she took it instead."

That was like Lud, too. If she had someplace to go and no transportation at hand, she was perfectly capable of walking out into the middle of the street and stopping the first car that came along and asking—demanding, rather—that it take her to her destination. I held out my hand for the keys. Sawyer gave them to me and turned to leave. "Come inside a minute," I said to him. "I want to talk to you."

The way my head felt, the statement was less true than it had been any time in the past four months, probably, but the combination of the empty house and his arrival alone seemed too good to pass up. It certainly gave me a chance at him that I hadn't been able to contrive at the station.

He hesitated before entering with obvious reluctance as I held the door for him. "I'll get grease on everything," he muttered as I closed the door. He was a mousy little man, and he had taken off his long-billed cap upon entering and stood turning it around and around in his hands.

"Don't worry about it, Sawyer. Have a beer?"

"No, thanks, Mr. Wilson."

"Sit down."

He sat stiffly, plainly wishing he were elsewhere. I sat down opposite him. I couldn't see any point in beating about the bush. If there was nothing to be learned from this man about George Pierson's car, then there was nothing to be learned from anyone at Mueller's. I was convinced of that. Actually, the situation in general made the whole matter seem a lot less pressing than it had been originally, but with the opportunity squarely in hand—

"I asked you a question indirectly before," I began, "and you evaded a direct answer. I'll ask it plainly now, and I expect an answer. Did you ever see or hear of anyone tampering with George Pierson's car prior to his accident? Before you answer, I want you to know I've done some investigating since I talked to you last."

"No, sir, I never saw or heard of anything like that."

He said it so promptly and so positively that I was almost convinced. He sensed my mood; he had his cap halfway to his head and was rising from his chair when I spoke again. "The subject bothers you though, doesn't it, Sawyer? Why?"

"No reason, sir. I mean, it doesn't bother me."

But it did. My next question seemed to frame itself. "Did you ever see anything out of the ordinary take place in connection with that car?"

And he hesitated. He didn't know how much I knew. I waited while he made two false starts and began over again. "Not really," he said at last.

"Tell me about this business that was not really out of the ordinary, Sawyer."

He had settled back in his chair at my renewed questioning of him. He leaned forward in it, blinking at me. He wasn't wearing glasses, but he had a myopic look, as if he needed them. "I don't think you appreciate my position, Mr. Wilson," he said earnestly. There was a note of harried apprehension in his voice. "I have a wife and family, and I'm trying to get along.

Anything I say to you—a wild guess, *anything*—if you act on it, depending upon the outcome, I'm going to have you or the other man mad at me and I can't afford that. It isn't as if I saw anything."

I had listened to this with growing impatience. I rose to my feet. "Cut the crap, Sawyer. Talk."

He gulped, then spoke hurriedly. "I saw the man who drove the Thunderbird away from the station that night. And that's all I saw."

"You mean it wasn't George Pierson?"

"That's right. The car had been in for servicing, and it was supposed to be delivered, but I was on duty alone. The telephone rang, and I had to take it inside. I heard a car start up, and by leaning around a corner of the desk, I could see the T-bird moving out." He paused. "Except for what happened afterward, I wouldn't have thought anything about it. Someone's always coming in for a car if we're late with it, like Mrs. Wilson did tonight."

"Who took the car, Sawyer?"

I expected him to say Lud, but for a second I thought he wasn't going to answer at all. "Mr. Darlington," he said finally.

"Mr.—Darlington? You mean Wing Darlington?" He nodded. I started to laugh; I couldn't help it. "And that's what you were afraid to tell me?" He nodded again, grinning in relief at my reaction. "When bigger jackasses are made, Sawyer, be sure you're standing in line. Wing Darlington could no more have—"

The telephone rang shrilly, and I moved automatically toward the hall to answer it. "Can I go now?" Sawyer asked from behind me.

"Sure," I said absently. "See you later." I hesitated before picking up the phone. What could Wing have been doing with George's car? It was an unlikely combination. But Wing Darlington kill George Pierson? They'd been best friends in school. It was ridiculous. Absurd. Totally—

The phone shrilled insistently, and I reached for it. "Yes?"

"I'm calling from a pay station, Jim." It was Veronica Peters. I hadn't heard her voice in weeks. Her speech was slurred breathlessly, as if she'd been running. "I've just slipped out of Mr. Cartwright's office for a moment. They've brought that man over from Spartanburg to make a statement under a promise of immunity, Jim, and they're issuing a warrant for your arrest."

"Arrest? What the hell for? They've got a man's unsupported statement—" I didn't finish it. They had a man's unsupported statement about what he suspected had taken place, and no body. They'd never have a body.

Veronica was still talking. I heard what she was saying, but I couldn't concentrate on it. I was wishing I hadn't turned Graham Sawyer loose so soon. Wing Darlington? Wing had killed George Pierson? But that would mean—could mean—

"And Mr. Harrington called Frank Garvey and told him to get a group together to arrest you," Veronica concluded.

That roused me. "Group? What do you mean, a group?" I thought of something else. "Listen, they let you walk right out of the office to make this phone call to me?"

"I don't know, Jim. No one tried to stop me when I said I had to step out of the office for a minute."

I didn't like it. Were Harrington and his people so cocksure that they didn't care if she called me? Of course, they could be counting on the fact that we'd stopped seeing each other. Considering our parting, it was surprising she'd bothered to call. "Thanks for phoning, Veronica. I'll get this straightened out. You get back to the office before they miss you."

"You'll be careful, Jim?"

"Careful?" I knew I wasn't keeping the irritation out of my voice, but I couldn't help it. "What is there to be careful about? It doesn't amount to a thing. I appreciate your calling, though," I added hastily. "*You* be careful, and I'll be in touch. Good-bye now." I hung up while she was still trying to say something.

I stood there staring down at the phone. I knew I should be thinking about moving in on Harrington in a way that would cut his water off permanently. Sending Frank Garvey to arrest me—what kind of cards did he think he was playing? They had nothing at all they could make stick.

But I couldn't focus on Harrington. Wing Darlington kept crowding him out of my mind: laughing, roughhousing, whoring, debonair, devil-may-care Wing. If Wing Darlington had killed George Pierson, what did it *mean?* I beat my brain around trying to find an answer and came up with nothing.

I left the phone and walked rapidly to the front door. The sight of Lud's car in the driveway slowed me; I'd forgotten that she had the station wagon. Well, this wouldn't wait. I'd take her car. I had trouble getting it started. Even after it caught, the motor banged and bucked on half its cylinders. Whoever washed it had sloshed water under the hood, I thought. I eased out of the driveway and headed for Wing's place.

The car jerked along, pooping and farting. I kept expecting it to dry out, but it didn't. It got worse. I pulled over to the curb under a streetlight, and got out and raised the hood. In the half-darkness, I felt around the spark plugs. They seemed dry, and the engine was definitely getting gas; it was just misfiring consistently. I removed a plug and tried to measure the spark gap by eye. It looked a bit wide. I gave it an experimental squeeze between thumb and forefinger and replaced it. There was no noticeable improvement. I got back into the car anyway and started off again. It backjumped every little bit, but it ran.

Wing's place was dark when I reached it, and I pulled into the curb and sat staring at it. My headache had reached boiler plate-factory proportions. I couldn't make up my mind whether I thought there was even a slight chance that Wing had killed George. *Could* he have done it? That was easier; if he ever decided to do it, he had nerve and to spare for the job. But *why?* I definitely wanted to talk to him. Where could I find him at this hour on a Friday night? The answer to that came as automatically as the response about his nerve: I'd find him at the cabin.

Since the car was so hard to start, I'd kept the motor running. As I started off again, a police cruiser passed me going the other way. It was probably my state of mental upset, but I thought the uniformed patrolman driving it turned for a quick look. It reminded me that I wanted no interruptions until I'd talked to Wing. I skirted the center of town and got out on the highway. With the motor wide open, the car ran better. Not good, but better. There was a serious loss of power, and at any other time I'd have done something about it at once.

It took me twenty-five minutes to reach the cabin. I couldn't see lights anywhere as I drove in, but I cut the engine and coasted the final seventy yards. I was glad I did because Wing's Galaxie was parked in the slot. I braked to a stop before I got close enough for the noise of the car's wheels on the gravel to be heard. That close, I could see a chink of light at a drawn side curtain. I got out of Lud's car and circled it to stay off the gravel, then walked on a soft cushion of pine needles. My route brought me almost to the rear of the cabin. Then I saw the silhouette of another car parked there. Its familiar outline brought me up short. Still not really believing it, I went over and put my hand on my own station wagon.

I turned and looked at the silent cabin. I started around it to the front, then walked back and reached through the station wagon's open front window and took from the glove compartment the Smith & Wesson .38 I'd carried there ever since the night I'd run into Whit Bailey in front of Veronica's apartment. I approached the front of the cabin noiselessly, dropped the gun in my jacket pocket, and took out my key. There wasn't a whisper of sound from inside. I inserted the key into the lock and turned it a hair at a time. There was the faintest of clicks; then the door opened. I waited another moment before widening the aperture sufficiently for me to slip inside.

They were in the large bedroom, and Lud was speaking. "—changes made," she was saying. "Sooner than you think."

"You're makin' heap powerful talk all of a sudden," I heard Wing's drawl. "For a gal who's been walkin' the chalk line you have lately. You still goin' to lie to me that Jim don't have nothin' on you?"

"I'll change the story slightly." Lud sounded pleased with herself. "What he had, he no longer has. And since he's unmanageable, and I no longer have need for him, he's at the end of the line. That's why I've kept

Harrington on the sidelines. I can use him until we get your rough edges knocked off and I can present you to society and we can get married."

"You got me with that marriage bit once, sexy," Wing said. "You don't git me with it again."

"The hardest thing I've had to do was keep Tom from using this Manton until I was ready to have Tom pull the trigger," Lud continued. "When I get rid of Jim, the people who matter will go along with Harrington because there'll be no one else available. And I'll control him."

"Lord, you're mouthy tonight, woman," Wing said lazily. "Who's this Manton you're yammerin' about? An' get rid of ol' Jim? You could break all your pearly little teeth on *that* project, now you better believe it."

"I'm rid of him, Wing."

His voice altered as if he had changed position to look at her. "You're *rid* of him? What the hell you talkin' about?"

"He'll be picked up tonight on an investigation-of-murder charge and killed while resisting arrest."

"He'll be—what?" The bed creaked, and I heard the splat of Wing's bare feet hitting the floor. I moved silently toward the bedroom. "Now lissen here, Lud, have you gone crazy altogether?"

She laughed. "I'll tell you how sane I am. I've left him with a car that doesn't run properly so there's no chance of his outrunning a cruiser. If he should get to the car, which I doubt." Her tone changed. "Where do you think you're going?"

"To Jim, to straighten out this infernal mess you've cooked up. You must be out of your damn mind."

"Take your hand off those clothes!" Her voice had an edge like a factory whistle. "Unless you'd like to end up trying to answer some unanswerable questions about George's death." Her voice changed again. "What are you upset about? You should be thanking me. You're his heir, you know, although I imagine I'll be entitled to a widow's third."

"Why, goddam you, Lud, he's my *partner!* I'll—"

"Hi, kids," I said from the doorway. Wing whirled from his standing position beside the beds; he hadn't a stitch on. Lud, on the bed, was wearing the same. It was like seeing the same movie twice. "Happy to see you making it with all my wives," I said to Wing. "It must save you a lot of time you'd otherwise spend chasing less available whores."

Lud spoke before Wing could. "What kick do you think you have coming?" she demanded. There was no fear in her voice. "You wouldn't touch me."

"There's that," I agreed. "But what about the interesting little conversation I just tuned in on?"

She was silent. I put my hand in my jacket pocket, and she started to get up. I took out the Smith & Wesson, and she shrank back upon the bed.

Wing was watching me like a kingfisher over a pool. "I can understand your having me x'd out from the start, Lud," I said conversationally. "Considering the circumstances. But how do you think you're going to beat the angle of the movie film?"

"Put that gun away," she ordered. "You're not scaring anyone with it." Her eyes said differently, though.

"Let's hear how cleverly you outmaneuvered me on the film deal," I suggested. "And I'd recommend that you talk fast. You might run out of breath."

She wet her lips. "After I'd exhausted all other possibilities, I sent Andy Martin to every bank in this end of the state with a sample of your handwriting, looking for a safe deposit box in an assumed name." She was gathering confidence from the sound of her own voice. "When he finally located Mr. Joseph Winters' box over in Palmetto, I brought a man down from New York City to pose as an Internal Revenue field agent for those hick bank officials over there." She stopped.

"And the film's no longer in the box?"

"That's right," she said defiantly. "I burned it."

"So it comes down to this." I waved the gun at her.

"You're not going to use it."

I couldn't make up my mind. I couldn't kill her and salvage anything from the operation. But I couldn't do anything else, either. She'd boxed me in neatly from every point of the compass. She'd taken every single bit of initiative right out of my hands.

My frustration got through to her and inexplicably bolstered her confidence. "Look at the big man," she said to Wing. "Look at the giant intellect turning over." She turned to me. "I gave you every chance. *Every* chance. Didn't I?" She turned back to the silently watching Wing. "Look at him. Just look at his expression." It could have been hysteria, but she started to laugh. "He's—been planning for years—and now—he's run out of plans!" she got out between choking bursts of merriment.

A bright red flare went off inside my skull. "No!" she gasped as I walked to the bed. "NO!" She screamed it that time while trying to scramble off the bed. The gun went off by itself, five times. It polka-dotted her from her Adam's apple to her navel, knocking her onto her back. Her mouth opened as wide as her staring eyes; she made one deep whistling sound, and then her mouth went slack.

Wing hit me from my blind side like a runaway truck. The gun popped out of my hand into the air, and we both lunged for it. He caught it before it hit the floor. "My name ain't Bailey, hoss," he said softly.

I went after him, and he popped me on the side of the head with the gun. The room grew dark as I staggered up against a wall. I was just peeling myself off it to go after him again when we both heard it at the same time: sirens in the distance.

"Knock it off on the muscles," he ordered. He looked from me to Lud on the bed and back again. "Well, man, you just bought *all* the action," he continued bitterly. "Not even in this county do they issue licenses to kill *two* wives. Your ass has had the course, son."

"You sonofabitch, Wing—"

"*Aaahhh,* set it to music, hoss," he said wearily. "She did it to us both. 'Kill George for me, Wing, dear, an' we'll be married.' " He grinned mirthlessly. "So I was gonna show you who was goin' to be the real big shot around town." He gestured with the gun at the bed. "I been pluggin' that twice a week reg'lar since high school, but what the hell could I say to you the night out here you told me you were gonna marry her? We were partners, for God's sake! How do you think I felt? An' where did it leave me to go? After gettin' rid of George for her, she had me in her pocket."

I could see it all. Now that it was far too late, I could see every shade and nuance of Lud's skillful scheming.

The sirens were getting louder. I looked once more at her body, sprawled on the bed. "Get out of here, Wing," I said. "Cut out through the woods. They haven't got anything on you. She's the only other one who knows about George, and she's dead."

He shook his head. "They'd fetch it up soon's they started nosin' around. It makes too pretty a package for them to miss." He cocked an ear in the direction of the sirens. "You reckon that's the war party comin' after you?"

"I passed a cruiser on the way out here," I remembered. "He could have followed me."

"You goin' peaceable?" Wing asked me. He sounded honestly curious.

I thought about it for a minute. "I think not."

"So we play the hand," he said briskly. Naked, he walked to the gun rack and took down the deer rifle. "Better reload that thing," he said, tossing me the Smith & Wesson. Then he went around and turned off all the lights.

I went to the cabinet and reloaded the .38, then picked up a Colt Ace automatic and stuck it in my belt. "You could still make it into the woods," I was saying when a blinding sheet of light illuminated the interior of the cabin. A bullhorn blared shatteringly.

"Come on out of there, Wilson!" it blatted. "We know you're in there! Come out with your hands in the air!"

"You take this room an' I'll take the other," Wing said quickly. "Keep 'em amused longer that way." He strode to the window in the smaller bedroom across the hall, smashed the glass with the butt of the deer rifle, reversed the rifle while he was leaning out, and took out the spotlight with one shot. It went out in sections, and the room gradually darkened again. Wing pivoted quickly and fired to his right. "Someone slitherin' around out there," he explained. "See anything?"

"Nothing."

A ragged volley of shots ripped through the cabin, and a bullet pinged off a pipe. I knocked out the glass in the window in front of me, and when the crash died out, a voice drifted in to me clearly. "What're the *two* Wilson cars doin' out here?" it complained.

"Never mind," another voice said harshly. "Get out'n my way an' give me workin' room."

There was a staccato brrrtt-t-t-t, and a beehive of bullets went through the wall over my head. I heard the sound of Wing hitting the floor across the hall before I hit it myself. Plaster showered down from the wall in a fine spray. "Short party tonight, hoss," Wing called across to me. "That's Garvey. He's chopper-happy."

I fired quickly at moving shadows outside my window—whether men or not I couldn't be sure. "Move out into the hall, Wing," I said as softly as I could. Revolvers were popping all around us in the night. "That thing will take us out of here in one punch if we stay close to the walls."

Another spotlight came on and again illuminated the cabin's interior. I could see Wing's grin as he inched his way out on his belly to join me. "Make me a reservation if you get there 'fore I do," he said as he fired through the front door. "For luck," he explained. "Shame not to get one or two of 'em first."

The machine gun started up again, this time on Wing's side of the cabin. His lips were still moving, but I couldn't hear what he was saying above the noise. Plaster spurted from the wall, baseboard-high. There was a loud *Spaaaang!* followed by a shrieking roar as a slug ricocheted from the air conditioner. I heard Wing grunt, and I turned my head. He was limp on the floor. The battered slug had caught him in the forehead, laying it open an inch. I couldn't tell if it had killed him or not, but in another second it didn't make any difference because in his next pass, Garvey's creeping barrage laced into Wing's body from end to end. He jerked and twitched as the slugs bit into him, but there was no sign of life.

There was no future where I was. As soon as Garvey rounded the cabin again, I faced the same dose. If tear gas didn't arrive first. I got to my feet, picked up Wing's naked body, and cradled it in my left arm. Discarding the empty .38, I snatched the Colt from my belt. Something slapped my arm, which immediately began to burn. I ran into the other bedroom. A bullet in the fleshy part of the thigh almost brought me down, but I kept going. I went out through the window, jumping as high and as far as I could, still carrying Wing. If I could just make it to the pine trees—

I was still in the air when I saw Garvey rounding the corner of the cabin, his machine gun on his hip. I twisted to try to bring the Colt to bear on him, but my momentum was turning me the other way. He was good with his damn cornpopper; he picked me up with it in midair. For a second I felt the bullets ripping into Wing again, and then as I continued my helpless turning a sheet of flame ran down my back.

I never remembered hitting the ground.

The trial is almost over now. The verdict will be automatic, and so will the sentence.

I've attended the trial on a stretcher, since the machine gun bullets fused my spine, and I'm curious to know how they're going to manage getting me into the chair.

Nights, when there's time to think, I go back over the whole thing in my mind, wondering what I might have done differently that would have ensured a changed result. But it's history now.

I have only one worry left now, one fear.

If a softhearted politician should commute the sentence to life imprisonment, I don't know what I'd do.

Or perhaps I mean that I know all too well what I'd have to do.

THE END

Fletcher Flora
BY CHARLES KELLY

Fletcher Flora, an intellectual Kansan with a wry, almost British sense of humor, once wrote a serial for *Cosmopolitan* magazine called "The Gimlet Brief." It was racy enough to be cited in an October 1957 *Playboy* article called "The Pious Pornographers: Sex and Sanctimony in the Ladies' Home Jungle," which said Flora's piece was an example of how some women's magazines took moralistic stands while being obsessed with sex themselves. Flora found the comment amusing. While Flora's books and stories often did deal with sexual matters in a sophisticated way, he himself was a quiet family man and educator never tempted by the bright lights of New York or Hollywood.

A well-read man who enjoyed the works of Sinclair Lewis and H. L. Mencken, Flora was a pipe smoker and a tennis player supple enough as a young man to do a back flip from a standing start. He was also a combat veteran and a classical music lover (Beethoven and Tchaikovsky were favorites) who enjoyed the occasional glass of bourbon. His loved to laugh and tell jokes, his chuckles bubbling over before he reached the punch line. And he was very amused by one British reviewer's remark that the name Fletcher Floyd Flora "had to be a pen name." In fact, its origins were English. The writer was descended from a Flora exiled to the New World from England for stealing a handkerchief.

Born in Parsons, Kansas, in 1914, Flora took at associate's degree at Parson's Junior College when he was 20, a bachelor's degree at Kansas State College four years later, then studied at the University of Kansas for the next two years. In 1940, he married Betty Ogden, who went on to become a librarian. After they moved to St. Louis, he taught English and high school history in two Missouri communities, Golden City and Fairview, and also coached basketball and track. Afterwards, he served a period as the assistant county clerk in Fulton County, Missouri.

Flora was drafted into the U.S. Army in 1943 at the age of 29, with World War II well under way. As a married man with an infant son, Flora joined the war effort reluctantly (he was something of a "lone wolf" and no respecter of authority), but rose to the rank of staff sergeant and served as an infantry squad leader. As a member of the 127th Infantry Regiment, Flora saw combat in New Guinea and in the landings at Leyte and Luzon.

Because of his governmental experience, he also served as a liaison responsible for setting up civil governments in Philippine villages as they were liberated.

Flora was badly wounded by mortar fire in the fight for Luzon. He said later the mortar attack blew up the field hospital, so he had to be taken to a mess tent and operated on with flatware. He spent months in the hospital recovering from shrapnel wounds in both legs and his right arm and never again regained full mobility in his right arm.

Released from service, Flora returned to Kansas and took a job as an education adviser at the U.S. Army Disciplinary Barracks in Leavenworth, helping inmates get their high school and college diplomas. He and his wife had three children, Harrison, Timothy and Susan. His daughter says the household had a bohemian flavor. A lifelong Democrat with a liberal bent, Flora had no use for restrictive social conventions, racism, or organized religion, though his children attended the Methodist Church and were allowed to decide about religion on their own.

Flora devoted his life to them, and to writing. His daughter recalls him as being a quiet, introspective man, often sitting at the end of their living room gazing at the night sky with his typewriter in front of him. He wore a felt hat and smoked a pipe, loved listening to baseball games on the radio, and sometimes took his kids to Kansas City, Missouri, to cheer on the then-Kansas City Athletics. He also took them to Kansas City to a sprawling multi-story bookstore where they could wander the stacks and select books for themselves.

Flora began writing for detective pulp magazines in the early 1950s, and quickly moved on to *Ellery Queen's Mystery Magazine*, *Alfred Hitchcock's Mystery Magazine* and similar publications. The two cousins who wrote under the name "Ellery Queen"—Fred Dannay and Manfred B. Lee—were fans of Flora's style, encouraged him and aided him in his writing efforts. His widow says the trick endings he often put on his short stories worked well in the context of *Alfred Hitchcock's Mystery Magazine*, and Alfred Hitchcock often sent the family elaborate cards at Christmas.

A number of Flora's contemporary writers took the blood-and-thunder approach, but Flora's style was "literate, urbane and sometimes lyrical," mystery novelist Bill Pronzini said in recapping the writer's career in *Twentieth-Century Crime and Mystery Writers*. Flora had a fondness for odd characters, according to an entry in *Library Journal*, and the writer pleaded guilty to the indictment: "(I) have been accused of spending too much time in left field," he said. "I met such a writer as Nathanael West [author of *The Day of the Locust* and *Miss Lonelyhearts*] out there, however, and feel that the company is pretty good." Flora's off-kilter approach is on display in his novel *Killing Cousins*, for which he received a Cock Robin Mystery Award. In it, Flora treats murder lightly, as "a sort of minor peccadillo," and satirizes the public's enthusiastic embrace of a juicy homicide.

In addition to writing books under his own name, Flora wrote at least one novel under the Ellery Queen pen name, his widow says [Editor's note: three novels, actually]. And he also finished a book begun by the novelist Stuart Palmer, creator of the spinster sleuth Hildegarde Withers. After Palmer died in 1968, Flora completed the Palmer novel called *Hildegarde Withers Makes the Scene* and shared authorial credit with Palmer. That book was made into a TV movie called "A Very Missing Person."

Physical difficulties, including the aftereffects of his war wounds, caught up with Flora early. When he was 48 years old, he suffered a stroke that partially paralyzed his right side. He had to give up his job, but continued to write and to keep up his family obligations, even doing the cooking. He died in 1969 of a heart attack.

In *Crime and Mystery Writers*, Pronzini said Flora was "a talented writer whose work received regrettably little attention in his lifetime." To some degree, Pronzini attributed that to Flora's emphasis on style and characterization rather than intricate plotting. More than that, Pronzini said Flora fell victim to indifferent agents and publishers and poor advice. Flora's widow Betty praises the writer's long-time agent, Scott Meredith, for working hard for him, but believes Flora's offbeat stories simply had a hard time securing a place in the popular market. Since his death, Flora's writing has developed a small cult following.

Park Avenue Tramp is an excellent example of the wry attitude often expressed in Flora's fiction. In manuscript form, it was called *Girl from Park Avenue*, and it's not clear whether we have an editor or Flora to thank for the more evocative title. It's a story of people doomed by their own natures—Charity McAdams Farnese, the "tramp," Joe Doyle, the terminal piano player, Oliver Alton Farnese, Charity's cruel, vacuous husband, Sweeney, his tormented private investigator. The story unfolds with almost Biblical inevitability. It's compulsively readable, not because of the plot, but because the reader is drawn further and further into each character, hoping for salvation for at least some of them. Flora keeps the reader glued to page, never lets him or her off the hook. Don't start it if you've got something pressing to do, because it's a one-sitting book.

—Scottsdale, AZ
November 2006

Park Avenue Tramp

BY FLETCHER FLORA

CHAPTER 1

She had been somewhere with someone, but she couldn't quite remember the place or the person. As a matter of fact she had a feeling that she had been a number of places with a number of persons, but she couldn't quite remember that for certain either. Anyhow, wherever she had been and with whomever, it was now certain that she was alone and walking down a narrow street that was dark and dirty and probably not a street that a woman should walk down alone at this hour, which was either very late or very early, depending on which way it happened to be from midnight, but none of this seemed particularly important. What seemed important was to find a place to sit down and have a drink and think calmly about where she had been and where she probably ought to go. Where she had been was surely not far, after all, for she was walking in sandals that were practically nothing but very high heels, and it would be a simple matter, if she could sit down and have a drink and think calmly, to work back to it in her mind.

A place where you could sit down and have a drink and think calmly was a bar, and a bar always had the added advantage of having a bartender, and bartenders were almost always informed, intelligent persons who were just exactly the persons to ask for advice or information on such matters as where you'd been and come from and ought to go. She had had a great deal of experience with bartenders, and on the whole, with very few exceptions, she had found them much superior to psychiatrists, and much less expensive. Perhaps that wasn't fair, however, for she hadn't actually been to a psychiatrist that she could remember at the moment, although it was entirely possible that a person who had forgotten where she had been could also forget having gone to a psychiatrist some time or other. But it didn't make any difference, really, whether she had personally been to a psychiatrist or not, for she was sure that she must have friends who had gone and told her about it, just for the experience if nothing else, and this was also something that she would probably remember after a while, if only she could find a bar with a bartender. And there between two shops, if she was not mistaken, one was.

Yes. Yes, it was. It was certainly a bar. It wasn't very big or very bright, although there was a small neon identification that she couldn't quite make out for some odd reason, and it didn't seem to be a bar that was trying to impose itself on anyone, but just a bar that was only trying in a quiet way to get along and earn a living. She liked that about it. Already she was feeling very compatible with this particular bar. It was extremely refreshing after so many places that were always trying to be impressive, and her compatibility achieved a quality of tenderness that prompted her to stroke its brick face gently with one hand and make a soft crooning sound in her throat that was like a little impromptu lullaby. Opening the door, she went inside and got onto a stool and started to tell the bartender what she wanted, but she couldn't think what she wanted was, which ought to be whatever she had been having, and she felt rather embarrassed about it.

"I'm sorry," she said, "but I've forgotten what I've been drinking. Isn't that silly?"

"Lots of people forget," the bartender said.

"It's nice of you to say that," she said. "It's very comforting."

"That's all right, lady," he said. "It's my pleasure."

She looked at him gravely and decided that he was undoubtedly a superior bartender, which would make him very superior indeed. It might seem unlikely on first thought that a superior bartender would be working in a little unassuming bar that was only trying to get along, but on second thought it didn't seem unlikely at all, for it was often the little unassuming places that had genuine quality and character and were perfectly what they were supposed to be, which was rare, and it was exactly such a place in which a superior bartender would want to work, even at some material sacrifice. She felt a great deal of respect for this honest and dedicated bartender. She was certain that she could rely on him implicitly.

"Perhaps you can help me," she said. "In your opinion, what have I been drinking?"

"You look like a Martini to me," he said.

"Really? A Martini?"

"That's right. The second you came in I said to myself that you were a Martini."

"Is that possible? To look at a person and tell that she's a Martini or a Manhattan or something or other?"

"Just with the specialists. Some people are slobs who'll drink anything. You can't tell with them."

"Can you tell just by looking whether a person's a specialist or not?"

"Oh, sure. Sure. Almost always."

"That's remarkable. How can you tell?"

"A specialist's got distinction. Something about him. Once you learn to recognize it, you can't miss."

"Never?"

"Well, almost never. If you can't tell by looking, you can tell by smelling."

"Oh, now. That's too much."

"It's a fact. I can tell you're a Martini just by looking, but if I were blind I could tell by smelling."

"How does a Martini smell?"

"Like a Martini," he said.

She laughed with pleasure at this clever and delightful bartender. Pushing at her pale blonde hair, which had a low part and a tendency to fall forward over her eye on the heavy side, she watched him mix her Martini and tried to guess how old he was. She had made quite a study of the ages of bartenders, and she had discovered that the mean age of all the bartenders she had studied was about forty, but the median age was quite a bit lower, and she thought that the age of this one was about the median, but she couldn't be sure. That was another thing she had discovered. It was almost impossible to tell the age of a bartender by looking, contrary to what was possible to bartenders with regard to specialists, and she had a theory that this was because they were compelled by their profession to assume certain expressions and attitudes that neutralized the effects of falling hair and dental plates and things of that sort.

She wondered if bartenders away from their bars did the same kinds of things that lawyers and doctors and stock brokers and executives and men in general were inclined to do. She wondered if they were vulnerable to the compelling drives and appetites and incredible caprices that were always complicating things and making them difficult and getting one into trouble that was sometimes serious. She wondered, for instance, if they made love. It was only natural to assume that they did, but somehow what was natural seemed in this instance unnatural. Bartenders were so invariably detached and almost clinical, although attentive and compassionate, that it was as impossible to imagine their being glandular as it was to guess accurately their ages. This one, for example, this clever and delightful bartender who was probably below the mean and about the median and really much better-looking than quite a few men she had made love with willingly—did he ever take off his starched white jacket and do interesting and exciting physical things? She thought it would he amusing to find out, but it was only something that she thought incidentally, and not something that she thought deliberately, or with intention.

"One Martini," the bartender said. "Very dry."

"How did you know very dry?" she said. "I distinctly remember not saying anything about very dry. It's one of the few things I remember."

"You look very dry," he said.

"Do I smell very dry also?"

"Naturally. You naturally smell like you look."

"Tell me something honestly. What is the very dry Martini look and smell like?"

"Very good. Lots of class."

"Thank you. You're sweet and comforting. I've never been seen and smelled by a sweeter or more comforting bartender."

"Besides that, I'm helpful."

"Yes, you are. You were helpful in telling me what I've been drinking, and it would be even more helpful if you'd tell me where I've been."

"Don't you know?"

"I don't seem to."

"Did you walk here from wherever it was?"

"Yes. I don't remember walking all the way, but suddenly I knew I was walking and remember walking from were I knew."

"Well, chances are it's close. It isn't likely you walked very far."

"I know. I thought of that myself."

She said this proudly, as if it were a considerable accomplishment, and he looked at her closely across the bar with a kind of skeptical wariness.

"Do you do this often?" he said.

"Forget where I've been and how I got where I am? I wouldn't say often. Once in a while is more like it. What happens is that I go somewhere with someone and get to drinking quite a bit, and then I apparently just walk off by myself and later have to remember where I was. It's nothing to be disturbed about. I'll just sit here and drink my Martini and think about it calmly, and pretty soon it'll come to me."

"While you're thinking, try to think where you live in case it becomes necessary to see that you get home. Will you do that?"

"I don't have to think about that, because I already know. I live in an apartment house on Park Avenue. I remember that clearly. Would you be interested in the address exactly?"

"No."

"I'm sorry. You've been so comforting and helpful that I thought you might come and see me there and mix very dry Martinis for us."

"I never go see people who live on Park Avenue. Thanks just the same."

"Why don't you ever go see people who live on Park Avenue? What's wrong with us?'

"Nothing's wrong with you. You're out of my class, that's all."

"Oh, nonsense. Do you know what Park Avenue is? It's a super-slum. I read that about it in a book, but I don't remember what book it was or who wrote it."

"There seems to be a lot you don't remember, and what I don't understand about it is how you remember leaving where you live and know where you are but don't remember where you were in the meanwhile."

"That's just the way it is. The beginning's all right, and the end's usually all right, but now and then there's something in the middle that gets lost."

"All right. You sit here and try to remember the middle, and if there's any way I can help, like fixing another Martini or something, you let me know."

He moved away and got very busy catching up with what he'd neglected while talking with her, and she took a drink of her Martini and spun herself slowly half around on her stool and looked at the room and what was going on in it. The room was quite narrow and rather long, dimly lit by lamps in brackets on opposite walls, and it was littered with small tables and chairs and people of various sizes. About half the people were men, and the other half were women, and this was an ideal arrangement. The men were dressed every which way in almost anything, and so were the women, and the clearest difference between them was that the women had tried a little harder to make it look like a night out.

Some of the women were older than others, and some were prettier, and this was, she thought, a condition that prevailed practically everywhere you went, even on Park Avenue, and she conceded gladly that the only immediately apparent distinction of any significance between these women and her, as a representative of Park Avenue, was that none of them was wearing, like her, a gown that cost $750 and sandals that cost $50 and panties that cost about $25, as nearly as she could remember. The last item was not an immediately apparent distinction, of course, but it was at least a fair assumption.

Actually, she didn't think of this difference of expense as proving any difference of quality, one way or the other. As a matter of fact, she hardly ever thought of money, except amusing ways to spend it or how terrible it would be not to have it, and now, after thinking briefly of clothes and the cost of them, she abandoned this line of thought as being a bore and of less significance than it had at first seemed to be. Down the room, she noticed, was a small cleared space that must have been intended for dancing, which signified music, but she could not remember having heard any music of any kind since her arrival from wherever she'd been. Beyond the cleared space, however, was a little platform, an elevation of about a foot, and on the platform was a piano and a snare drum on a stand. Nothing else, unless you counted the piano bench and a single chair. Except the bench and the chair, just the piano and the drum. She thought they looked deserted and sad and strangely static on the small platform, like a still life painted a hundred years ago by an unhappy artist with too little to eat, and she wanted suddenly to put her head on her arms on the bar and cry.

It wouldn't do, however. It would only make her look like a hag and would accomplish nothing. What she had to do was have another drink of Martini and try calmly to think of where she'd come from. She revolved slowly on the stool and drank from her glass and began to think. To begin with, she started from where she now was and attempted to go back carefully from there, but the moment she reached the place on the narrow street where she'd become aware of herself and part of her surroundings, the street ended, the buildings dissolved, and she herself became a kind of black hiatus between then and there and another place at an earlier time. It was very discouraging and rather exhausting, but she tried patiently several times before she conceded that it was simply no use. She didn't really care where she'd been, so far as that went, but it was possible that there were obligations or effects associated with it that she ought to know about and so she reversed her procedure and began trying to reach her present time from the other end, the beginning.

She had left her Park Avenue apartment a little after five and had gone to another Park Avenue apartment where there was a cocktail party. This apartment was the apartment of Samantha Cox, who believed that having lots of money did not excuse one from doing something substantial and making a personal contribution to Life with a capital L. Samantha's contribution was taking lessons in acting and doing small parts in television shows, nothing yet by Paddy Chayefsky, and how substantial this was as a contribution to Life was something that could be argued. She had met a lot of people at Samantha's party, and had drunk quite a few Martinis, and after a while several of the people, including her, had decided that it would be a good idea to go somewhere and eat, and someone had said he was feeling a violent urge for some of the marvelous Italian food they served at a place on West 10th Street in Greenwich Village, and that's where they'd gone.

She hadn't eaten much of the Italian food, however marvelous, but she had, as she recalled, drunk two or three more Martinis, and afterward they had gone to another place where she had drunk two or three more than that, and still afterward to still another place where there had been a comedian who told dirty jokes that weren't very funny and several very tall girls in G-strings. She must have switched parties at this place, for she distinctly remembered for the first time riding in the front seat of a white Mark II, and this must mean that she had met and gone away with Milton Crawford, for Milton was the only man she could think of among her fairly close associates who drove a white Mark II.

Yes, it had been Milton. She was certain now. Going from the place they had met to the next place, he had kept patting her thigh, and she had let him, not considering it very important, and at the next place, which was noisy and uninhibited and very crowded, he had asked her if she would stay with him in his apartment, and she had said that she didn't really feel much like it but might feel more like it later. She didn't like Milton very much, although she didn't make a cardinal issue of it, and it was more difficult to feel like it with him than with some others. Anyhow, after making it indefinite about staying with him, she had excused herself and gone to the ladies' room, and it had been very hot in there and a long way from clean, and she remembered thinking that she wouldn't use the toilet even if she were saturated with penicillin, and this thought had made her feel even less like staying for what would be left of the night with Milton. She had gone out of the room and out of the larger room with all the noise and people and had stood outside leaning against the building and had taken several deep breaths of air.

There. There, there, there. That was when and where she'd become a dark hiatus. The precise place and time. There was no telling how long exactly the hiatus had lasted, but probably not very long, and it would be an absolute waste of time and effort to try to remember what had been done in it, for she knew from experience that it was no use. Besides, at that moment, the drum and the piano began to talk to each other, and she quit remembering and began listening. She listened for a while without turning, and she thought that it was good dialogue, very clever. Whoever was making the drum talk was doing it lightly with a brush, and whoever was making the piano talk was doing it also lightly with a brush of fingers, and the effect was a delicacy, an intimacy, like lovers whispering. Pretty soon, in the first pause in the dialogue, she revolved half around on the stool and looked over tables and chairs and heads to the platform beyond the small area for dancing.

The young man who was brushing the drum had a round, absorbed face and round, bewitched eyes and little brown curls coiled so tightly all over his head that she was immediately inclined to discount them as being very unlikely.

The young man who was playing the piano was about medium height with slightly stooped shoulders, and if he had been naked she could have counted far too many of his bones, and he had black hair and an ugly, thin, dark face with a slightly twisted nose and twisted mouth. She thought with a kind of strange despair that he was the most beautiful man she had ever seen in all her life.

CHAPTER 2

Piano and the drum were lovers. After giving thanks to a dark psychotic god, they laughed and wept and made erotic love. What had been in the beginning a jam-session psalm became, in an instant, jazz pornography. The young man with bewitched eyes leaned above the drum, and the young man with the beautiful ugly face leaned above the piano, and the girl from Park Avenue leaned above the bar and listened and held an empty Martini glass, and the superior bartender leaned against the backbar opposite her and felt in his heart a rare and reluctant bitterness.

For a while she had sat sidewise to the bar with her eyes fixed on the piano player, but then she had turned slowly back to face the bar squarely, and that's the way she was sitting now, in a posture of intent listening, with her shoulders folded slightly forward and her pale hair falling down over her eye on the heavy side. The bartender from his position could see directly past pale hair and short nose and soft mouth into the cleft between her resilient breasts that were half exposed, even when she sat erect, by the décolleté gown that had probably cost more than he made in two long months of mixing drinks and drawing beer. Watching her, he was aware of an exorbitant emotional reaction, but it was not the view of her breasts that stimulated it. He was used to nudity, resistant if not immune, and he was no longer subject as he had once been in his youth, to the hard thrust of instant desire at the sight of suggestive flesh. It was her face that disturbed him and made him feel the reluctant bitterness, for it was a small, sad, lovely face of fine structure in which sadness and loveliness would survive as a shadow of themselves after the erosions of gin and promiscuous love and nervous breakdowns. It was a face, in fact, which he would surely remember, and remembering was almost always the worst kind of mistake. This was something he had learned from a long time of tending bar. A man was a fool to take anything home in his head.

Well, he had learned a lot tending bar, and it had been, on the whole, a good and satisfying kind of life. Maybe it wasn't the thing he would have done if he could have done what he wanted most to do, but just the same it was far from being the worst thing he might have done, and he had no complaints, no bellyaches, no futile regrets for not having become something more than he was. The only thing he wished: he wished he were not so vulnerable to the faces. Not specific faces. Not the face of this person or that person as distinguished from all other faces that had stared at themselves in the mirror behind the backbar. Composite faces. Type faces. The face of the old man who sat nursing his bourbon and water in the silence of his own dissolution as be listened to the relentless ticking of the metronome of God. The adjusted face of the pro whore who exploited love, and the sick face of the amateur whore that love exploited. The faces of the lost and the tired and the damned. And now, to disturb his peace for an hour or two, the specific, haunting face of a Park Avenue tramp who had stopped in to find out where she'd been. The rare face of a dissolute child.

She was holding the brittle bulb of her glass in the palms of her cupped hands, and pretty soon she looked up with an odd expression of supplication, as if she wanted desperately to have the bulb filled but somehow did not think it would be proper to ask. The bartender moved across the narrow space between the back and front bars.

"Another Martini, lady?" be said.

"Yes, please."

She pushed the glass toward him and continued to sit in the posture of intent listening while he measured and mixed gin and vermouth. The drum and the piano were now angry with each other. The piano was speaking with censurable profanity.

"Have you remembered where you were?" the bartender said.

"Yes, thank you," she said. "Not exactly, that is, but in a general way. It was a very noisy place with a band that was much too big and a dirty ladies' room. I went there with this particular man I know who wanted me to go home with him, but I decided that I wouldn't. I went outside and leaned against the front of the building and took several deep breaths of air, and that's all I remember until I was suddenly walking along the street. Do you have any idea what place it was?"

"It could be one of several. Anyhow, it must be near. I can have someone help you look for it, if you like."

"No. That won't be necessary. I don't care to go back. If I did, I would have to explain to Milton why I don't want to stay with him, and he would probably be difficult. Besides, to tell the truth, I'm not quite sure myself why I don't."

"I see. How do you propose to get home?"

"I'll take a taxi or something. It's entirely possible that I may not bother to go home at all."

"Well, you'll have to go somewhere."

"That's true. It's always necessary to go somewhere. I wonder why."

"I don't know, lady. It's just expected of us, I guess."

"Yes. You're right, as usual. We're always doing what's expected of us. The trouble is, however, I'm not. I get into quite a bit of trouble that way."

"I can imagine."

"You're very understanding. I can see that. Don't worry about me, though. I'll go somewhere else when it becomes necessary, but right now I'm happy to be exactly where I am. I like this place very much. We're compatible. I believe that I was guided here. After all, I didn't have the least idea where I was coming, and here I came. Isn't that logical?"

"You blacked out, lady. You might have wound up anywhere, and you ought to be careful. Something might happen to you some time."

"Something's always happening to me. I seem to be the sort of person that things just happen to. Can you believe it?"

"Yes, I can. I believe it."

The piano was now contrite. It was filled with guilt and sorrow for having been profane. It wept softly, and the drum consoled it, and the sad lovely face of the girl to whom things happened was the compassionate mourner for all the troubled drums and pianos in the world.

"Who is that beautiful guy?" she said.

"What beautiful guy?" the bartender said.

"The one on the platform."

"There's no beautiful guy on the platform, lady. There's only Chester Lewis on the drum and Joe Doyle on the piano."

"That's the one. The piano."

"Joe's not beautiful, lady. He's only a so-so piano thumper with a twisted nose and a bum pump."

She lifted her glass in both hands and drank from it and stared at him sadly over the edge. In sadness and disappointment she shook her head slowly from side to side, the pale hair moving back and forth with the motion over the eye on the heavy side.

"I thought you were an understanding and perceptive bartender," she said, "and I still think so. But now you are being disappointing. The piano is easily the most beautiful guy I've ever seen in all my life."

"Excuse me, lady. Everyone to his own taste."

"Are you being tolerant? I'm not sure I like that. It means I'm being tolerated, which is not particularly pleasant."

"All right, lady. Joe's beautiful. He's the most beautiful guy in the world."

"Well, you don't have to be *too* agreeable. I admit that the piano has a twisted nose, and I admit that he might even be considered ugly by many people, but that's because many people are not perceptive, which I was inclined to believe you were. What I mean is, he's beautiful because he's so ugly. Do you understand that?"

"Sorry. Explain it to me,"

"At first it may seem paradoxical, but a little thought will show you that it isn't paradoxical at all. What you must realize is that everything goes in circles by degrees. The moon and the sun and the earth and all the planets. This has been demonstrated. I've thought a great deal about this, and I'm certain that everything else goes the same way. Every single thing.

Ugliness and beauty, for example. If one becomes too beautiful, he has gone too far around the circle and becomes ugly. If one becomes too ugly, he has gone far enough around the circle to become beautiful. Isn't that reasonable? Don't you agree?"

"Sure, sure. I get it. Joe's so damn ugly he's come around to being beautiful. It's simple."

"That's right. Now you are being the perceptive person I thought you were."

He looked at her, at her fine grave face and nearly bare breasts, and he thought tiredly that this one was surely gone. If not gone, going, going. All her life, he thought, she had been doing by compulsion in desperation all the significant things that required the sacrifice of herself, some part of herself, and after they were done, after the sacrifice, she had tried to explain and justify, by circles or squares or Omar Khayyam or almost any too-late God-damned rationalization, whatever she had done, whatever sacrifice made, and in the future she would go on drinking too much gin and sleeping in too many beds and blacking out between bed and bottle, and in the end, if she was lucky, she would wind up jumping off a high place, or taking too many soporifics, or having shock treatments and lying on a couch in an expensive sanitarium trying to remember where she'd been and how she'd got where she was, and weaving bright little rugs on a hand-loom for therapy. The worst of it was, she hit him in his vulnerability; she had a face he would remember, and he would see it in the darkness above his bed, tonight and possibly nights afterward, and a long time from now, between a beer and a bourbon, he would wonder suddenly if she were dead or alive and what the diagnosis had been.

"What did you mean by bum pump?" she said.

"Nothing," he said. "Forget it."

"You meant something. Of course you meant something."

"All right. A pump's a heart."

"I know a pump's a heart. I know all sorts of slang. Once, just for fun, I took two tests. You know. These multiple choice things that you get in school and places. One of them was about highbrow words, and the other was about lowbrow words, to find out which ones you knew best, and I came out knowing a lot more about lowbrow. Would you believe it?"

"And you from Park Avenue? Not quite."

"It's true. I came out a much better lowbrow. I was quite proud of myself."

"Congratulations."

"Thank you. You're very kind. Tell me, however. Why does this beautiful piano have a bad heart?"

"It started as a kid, I guess. Rheumatic fever. I don't know, really. It's just something I heard about"

"What's rheumatic fever?"

"It's something you get as a kid that gives you a bad heart."

"I don't know about this. Is it serious?"

"Anything that gives you a bad heart is serious."

"I mean the heart. Is the heart serious?"

"Not so much. He may live another year or two."

She drank what was left of her Martini and looked at the empty glass as if it had somehow deserted her when she needed it most. He thought for a moment that she was going to cry, but she didn't. She hadn't cried for a long, long time. Not since crying for a reason that he couldn't know and she wished to forget. It wasn't likely that she would ever cry again.

"I love him," she said.

"Sure," he said

"It's true. I thought I loved him because he was so beautiful by being ugly, and now I know I love him, because he has a bum heart from having rheumatic fever as a small boy. Do you honestly think he will die soon?"

"Not before tomorrow. It'll be long enough if you love him until tomorrow."

"Maybe I could give him a little happiness in the end."

"I doubt it."

"Why? I've given several people a little happiness, I believe. It's not impossible."

"Leave him alone. You'd probably only make him more aware of what he's about to be missing."

"I feel compelled to try. At least, he should be allowed to accept or reject the proposition for himself. We have no right to make the decision."

At that moment, the drum and the piano became silent, and she sat silently listening to the silence of the drum and piano that was like an empty space in the sound that continued, and then, after a minute or two, the piano began playing again by itself, and she revolved the half-turn on the stool and looked that way. The drum, whose name was Chester Lewis, was gone. Only Joe Doyle, the piano, remained. Joe Doyle, the piano, was not now playing the clever stuff, the jam stuff. He was playing tunes, the little melodies that reminded people of things that had happened. At the moment of her looking, he was playing something that she remembered by sound but not by name. It had no particular associations.

"What's he doing?" she said.

"He's winding it up," the bartender said. "It's the routine. Every night, last thing before closing, he plays a few of the little tunes. Requests. It sets people up for whatever they have in mind."

"Is anyone allowed to make a request?"

"Sure. Anyone. It's free."

"In that case, I must make one."

"I'll deliver it, if you like. Just name the tune."

"No. I don't think so." She lifted her glass and tipped it, and the olive rolled out onto the bar with two amber drops. "Thank you very much, but I think it would be better if I delivered it myself."

CHAPTER 3

Slipping off the stool to the floor, she stood for a few seconds in precarious balance. Then she walked back carefully among the tables to the small platform and took the enormous twelve-inch step upward with elaborate caution and leaned against the piano with a vast feeling of relief and pride in having arrived safely. She looked down at Joe Doyle and smiled, and he looked up and grinned a professional grin in which there was the slightest touch of bitterness.

"Hello, Joe Doyle," she said.

"Hello, baby," he said.

"Do you know something? You're wonderful."

"Do you know something else? You're drunk."

"No. I've drunk a number of Martinis in a number of places, and for a little while I was drunk, or at least blacked out, but now I've recovered and become perfectly sober."

"You're drunk, baby. If you weren't drunk, you wouldn't think I was wonderful."

They were always drunk, he thought, always drunk. That was the way he got them, when the night was running out. Out of a glass in the tail of the night to lean against his piano and ask for the slight and shabby little tunes that had achieved permanence and an exorbitant importance in their minds because they were associated with something that had happened or had not happened or might yet happen, with good luck or bad, some place and time. Mostly they were just women with faces you never saw and names you never heard, and they came and went and in effect had never been, no strain whatever on even a bum heart, but once in a great, great while, a time or two in a couple of thousand nights, there was one with a face and a name who left a memory, and you looked up and saw her leaning over the piano in her expensive gown with her pale hair over her eye on the heavy side, and you felt it suddenly in the bum heart, and you wished it were possible for you to live a little longer than the prognosis, at least long enough to learn in your own way that it would have been better if you hadn't lived so long.

"If it embarrasses you to be called wonderful," she said, "I apologize. You're good. Do you object to that? You're very good."

"No, baby. Not even good. Jelly Roll Morton was good. Fats Waller was good. The Duke's good. Not me. I'm just a thumper."

"I can see that you're determined to belittle yourself, and I don't want to hear it. You'd be surprised to know how sad it makes me to hear it. What I want to hear instead is a particular tune. Will you play me a particular tune, Joe Doyle?"

Sure, he thought, sure. Play me something, Joe. Play me something for me alone. They all came out of a glass in the tail of the night to hear the particular little tunes that stood for a time or a place or a man, and afterward they went away with someone or anyone to someplace or anyplace, and you let them go and remembered them at most for a minute. Even this one who had a face and was felt in the heart and had come, from the looks of her, down into the mean streets from a steel and stone tower, for kicks. Even this one? Especially this one. She was a tramp at best and a nut at worst and probably a lush in either case, and nothing could come of her but trouble in the unlikely event that anything could come of her at all, and whatever she made you feel in the heart in a minute or two of the tail of the night, you had better play her a tune and let her go if you had any concern for what was left of your life.

You name it, baby," he said, "I'll play it."

" 'Rippling Waters,' " she said. "I want particularly to hear 'Rippling Waters.' "

He looked down at his fingers that had gone on playing softly the tune they had been playing and were now lightly running scales between the last tune and the next one.

"That's Willie Smith," he said. "What do you know about Willie Smith?"

"I know lots of surprising things," she said.

"I'll bet you do."

"It's the truth. You may ask any of my friends, if you care to. I'm always surprising them with things I know."

"I don't know any of your friends, baby. It isn't like that I ever will."

"That's all right. I don't think you'd like them much, anyhow. Most of the time I don't like them very much myself."

"That's rough. Real rough. What do you do when you don't like even your friends?"

"I don't know. It's a problem that I've often thought about myself. When you stop to think seriously about it, it doesn't seem quite natural, does it? Do you suppose there's something wrong with me?"

"I suppose there's something wrong with all of us in one way or another."

"That's exactly the conclusion I've come to all the times I've thought about it. There just doesn't seem to be any other conclusion to come to. Anyhow, there's probably no use in thinking about it at all, especially now that I'm waiting for you to play 'Rippling Waters' if you happen to know it"

"I happen to," he said.

His fingers broke out of the scale and into the tune, and she leaned over the piano and listened, and closed her eyes with the intensity of her listening. Looking up at her, at the small breasts exposed almost entirely by her position and the small face suddenly at peace under the shadow of her lashes, he thought that she looked like a perverse child who played in perversity at being a whore and had gone to sleep in the middle of the game, but he knew that she was no child, and he suspected that she had never in her life been a child truly. Anyhow, what she was or wasn't or had never been was something that was no concern of his, and all he really knew or wanted to know was that the night had gone on long enough. He stopped playing and dropped his hands from the keys, and she opened her eyes and nodded her head with a kind of grave suggestion of approval and gratitude.

"Thank you very much," she said. "And now I must buy you a drink for being so kind."

"That isn't necessary, baby. It's part of the routine."

"Do you refuse to have a drink with me?"

"I didn't say that. I just said it isn't necessary to buy me one."

"I see that I have made a wrong impression, and it's all my fault because I'm so used to tipping people for everything. What I mean is, will you please give me the pleasure of having a drink with me?"

"Sorry. I don't drink much."

"Really? I was always under the impression that musicians drank a great deal. Is it because of having had rheumatic fever as a small boy that you don't drink much?"

"When you said you knew lots of surprising things, you weren't fooling, were you? Do you mind telling me how the hell you know what I had as a small boy?"

"It's simple. The bartender told me. You mustn't blame him, in case you didn't want me to know, because it just came out incidentally when I said you were beautiful and he said you weren't."

"All right." He stood up and touched her suddenly and lightly on one arm, as if he somehow doubted she was really there. "I'm wonderful and beautiful, baby, and the last thing you need tonight is another drink, but I'm needing one more and more all the time. Shall we sit at the bar?"

"Yes. I always prefer sitting at the bar, if possible. It's much more convenient and gives you a chance to talk with the bartender. I'm making a study of bartenders, you know."

"I should have guessed," he said.

They went to the bar and sat on stools and waited for the attention of the superior bartender, who was busy at the moment at the far end of the bar with a woman with very bright red hair and a man with hardly any hair at all.

"If we're going to have a drink together," she said, "perhaps I'd better introduce myself. My name is Charity Farnese. I'm a very dry Martini."

"How do you do."

"If I hadn't told you, would you have known from looking that I'm a Martini?"

"Sure. Anyone could tell."

"Honestly? When I first came in here some time ago, I'd forgotten what I'd been drinking, and the bartender told me I looked like a Martini, which is what I actually am, and I thought then that it was something exceptional, his being able to tell just by looking, but perhaps it wasn't so clever as I thought."

"What do you mean, you couldn't remember what you'd been drinking?"

"Well, it was Martinis, of course, because that's what it always is, but I couldn't remember right at the moment. When I have one of these times of blacking out, it's difficult to remember afterward what happened before. I need to think calmly about it for a while before I can remember."

"Is blacking out a habit of yours?"

"Not a habit. It only happens sometimes."

"I see. Nothing to worry about, of course. Did you black out tonight?"

"Yes. That's what I did. I'd been to all these places with some people, and then I met a man I know named Milton Crawford, and we went to another place that was crowded and noisy. I remember that about it, although I don't remember its name or where it was exactly. Milton wanted me to go to his apartment and spend the rest of the night with him, but I wasn't very interested because I really don't like him very much. I went to the ladies' room and then outside, and it must have been right then that I blacked out, because I was walking down this street alone when I next knew what I was doing, and I came in here."

He looked down at his hands, which were lying on the bar. He clenched the fingers and spread them and clenched them again.

"Jesus," he said.

"What's the matter?" she said. "Why did you say that?"

"Oh, nothing. Nothing's the matter. Tell me, baby. Doesn't having these blackouts ever bother you a little?"

"Well, they're curious and sometimes inconvenient, I admit, but I don't see any use in worrying about them in particular."

"I suppose not. No use whatsoever. Do you ever remember afterward what happened during one of them?"

"No. Not during. Just the last thing before and the first thing after. Of course I'm able to get a pretty good idea sometimes from whatever situation I happen to be in when I become aware of things again."

"Sure, sure. I should imagine."

"It's rather depressing when I seem to have been doing something that I wouldn't ordinarily have done."

"It must be. It must be real depressing."

Joe looked down at his hands again, clenching and unclenching the fingers, apparently trying to think of something appropriate to say, and what he was actually thinking was that this one was a real nut, a psycho, and the only thing he ought to say was a quick good-by, and he couldn't understand why he didn't. Well, anyhow, he would have the drink that he'd been invited to have, and that would be all of it. After having the drink, he would say the good-by that he ought to say now, and no harm would be done, nothing lost, and he would go home and to bed, and maybe listen before sleeping to Gieseking playing the "Emperor Concerto" the way Joe Doyle would give his soul to play it if you could trade your soul for genius. It was good to lie in the darkness and listen to Beethoven out of Gieseking or Chopin out of Brailowsky. It kept you from wanting what you didn't have, or missing abortively what you couldn't.

The superior bartender, who had finished his business with the woman with red hair and the man with practically none, came down along the bar and stopped opposite them, Without asking, he poured rye and water and mixed a Martini, which he also poured. He moved along to two empty masculine beers a couple of stools beyond. Besides Joe and Charity and the redhead and the baldhead, the two beers, who seemed rather despondent, were the only customers now left at the bar. The tables in the room behind were becoming more and more vacant. Joe swallowed his rye quickly and washed it with some of the water.

"Look, baby," he said, "won't this friend of yours be wondering what's happened to you?"

"Milton? He's not a friend exactly. He's just a man I happen to know."

"Won't he be wondering?"

"I don't think so. Not seriously, anyhow. Milton's not very reliable, to be honest, and besides, he knows that I'm apt to go away from anyplace if I take the notion. That's the way I happened to be with Milton, as a matter of fact. I was somewhere with some other people, and I took the notion to go away with Milton, and I did."

"Do you have a car?"

"Not here. I have one, of course, but I left it somewhere."

"How do you expect to get home?"

"Home? I don't know. I hadn't thought much about it. I suppose it's something that has to be considered eventually, but I don't see the need for being in any hurry about it."

"It's late, baby. It's very late, and there's another night coming to get ready for. I ought to go home, and so had you, and I'll tell you what I'll do. You try real hard to remember this last place you were, and I'll take you there. Maybe Milton's still waiting."

"I'm not sure that I want to find Milton, even if I could remember where

it was I left him. He wanted me to stay with him, as I said, and he's sure
to be unpleasant if I refuse."

"I'm sure you can handle him."

"You're right about that. Milton's rather a weak character. He's not at all
hard to handle."

"Try to remember the place."

"It's no use; I can tell you that without trying. I can remember something
about it, but not its name or where it was."

"All right. Finish your Martini. It can't be very far if you walked here.
We'll look for it."

"I'd much rather not. I'm not at all interested in finding Milton or going
home. I'd much rather stay with you."

"Never mind. Finish your Martini and come along."

He stood up beside her, and when she saw that he was determined, she
finished her Martini and stood up also, and they walked back among the
tables, which had become almost entirely unoccupied, and down a short
hall in the rear to the alley. His car was parked there in a small space that
had room for only one more. It wasn't a Mark II by a long way, but it started and ran, and they went to several places in it in the hour that followed
and would have gone to several others if they had not been closed. The
ones that were open might have been crowded and noisy earlier, but they
were becoming empty and quiet and somehow depressing now, and it
seemed helpful in each one to have another drink. Finally he was forced
to concede what she had predicted in the beginning, that it was no use.
Milton was gone from wherever he'd been, and as far as she could remember it might have been any one or none of the places they went.

"All right," he said. "To hell with Milton. Tell me where you live, baby,
and I'll take you there myself, which is what I should have done an hour
ago."

She had drunk an incredible number of Martinis before and after the
blackout, but she had achieved by the very enormity of excess an illogical
reaction with which she was familiar and in which she was able to think
with errant clarity and a vast and dangerous indifference to consequences.
She remembered perfectly where she lived, the exact address, and she
understood that not going there now would result in something unpleasant, or worse, but this did not seem at all important as compared with the
experience to which she was committed. She had never had an experience
with a beautiful ugly piano player with a rheumatic heart before, and it
would surely be a great shame if it were simply to end before coming to
anything significant.

"I'm sorry," she said, "but I seem to have forgotten."

"Come off, baby." They were sitting in his car in the street outside the last place they had been, and he turned and stared at her in the dim light that barely reached them from the nearest lamp. "You trying to say you don't even know where you live?"

"It's only temporary, of course. As I said, I forget things for a while, and then later, after thinking calmly, I remember again."

"Well, start thinking."

"It won't do any good immediately. I can tell you that from experience. In the morning it will come to me clearly, but it isn't at all likely to come before."

Lifting his hands, he let them drop in a little gesture of despair.

"Oh, Jesus," he said. "Jesus, Jesus."

"Please don't be angry with me," she said. "I'd hate for you to be angry with me."

"I'm not angry."

"You were kind to help me look for Milton, even though I didn't want to, and now I'm only making trouble for you, and what I really want to do is make you happy. It's very odd. Since the moment I saw you and the bartender told me about your heart and all, I've felt a great wish to make you happy."

"Never mind. Just tell me where the hell you want to go."

"Well, I could go to a hotel or someplace, of course, but it would be much more pleasant if I could stay with you."

He closed his eyes to shut out the sight of her, but all he did was trap her image behind his lids, and he cursed himself for the fool he was going to be. However she looked, however sad and lost and lovely, she was a tramp and trouble and not for him, a dipsomaniac and probably a nymphomaniac and God only knew what other kinds of maniac all told. What he ought to do, he knew very well, was take her at once to the nearest hotel, but what he wanted to do was take her home, and in the end he did what he wanted. He opened his eyes and started the car and drove to the place in which he lived, which was a large room on the third floor of a house not far from Washington Square.

As for her, she didn't know precisely where she went or how she got there, but her senses had the extraordinary sensitivity they sometimes had in dreams, and she seemed to see and feel and hear with exaggerated intensity and excitement. She was aware of the house and the room and a bed in the room and of a sonata played softly again and again in darkness by someone on a record. Most of all, in the bed, she was aware of his thin body with its bad heart.

CHAPTER 4

She awoke naked in bed and opened her eyes and was warned at once by a faded pattern of paper on the ceiling that it was not her own bed in her own room in her own apartment. Closing her eyes again, she said to herself in the simple, primer-like sentences that one might use in speaking to a child: "I am Charity McAdams Farnese. I am married to Oliver Alton Farnese. I live in an apartment on Park Avenue, and I didn't go home last night."

There was nothing new about this, for she had wakened many times in strange places to repeat the little formula of identification, but this time, though it was nothing new, there was something different. All the other times, it had required several minutes of thinking before she could remember where she had been and was, whom she had been with and was with, but now, this time in this bed, she knew at once what had happened and who was lying beside her. There was another difference, too. The other times, at least most of the other times recently, she had been assailed by regret and suicidal despair, but this time, knowing everything instantly, she felt no regret at all and was almost happy. It was remarkable, really, how *well* she felt.

Except for her head, of course. It was impossible to feel entirely well when every throb of the tiny pulses in her temples was like a detonation. Besides the detonations, she could hear another sound, to which she listened., and after a few moments she realized that it was the soft, measured sound of the breathing of Joe Doyle. Opening her eyes for the second time since waking, she turned her head slowly on its pillow and looked at him. He was lying on his back, and his eyes were closed, and on his face was an expression of intense concentration, as if sleep were achieved only by the greatest effort under constant tension. He was covered by a sheet to the waist, but the upper part of his body was exposed, and she could see clearly, in the lateral wall of the side nearer her, every one of his seven true ribs. She counted them slowly, forming the shape of the numbers silently with her lips and pointing with a finger at each rib, moving the finger slowly with the counting across the intercostal spaces. She felt, for his ribs and his entire thorax, a passionate tenderness, and this was still another difference between the way she was at this awakening and the way she had been at other awakenings for a long time, for neither passion nor tenderness were emotions she ordinarily was capable of feeling until after quite a long period of adjustment to another day. He looked so very spare, his skin so thinly spread upon his bones, that she had the notion that it would be possible, if she kept staring steadily long enough, to see deeply into him, through skin and beyond bones to the heart that throbbed like a poisonous monster in its dark pericardial cavity. Examining him so, with the extraordinary passionate tenderness in which there was beginning to be a stirring of excitement, she wanted to roll over facing him on her side and take him into her arms, but she didn't do it, in spite of wanting to very much, because be would surely awaken if she did, and she had already decided that it would be better if he did not waken until after she was gone.

Last night she had thought that she would never want to leave him, at least not permanently, and today she actually didn't want to leave him, at least not yet, but anyone with any experience knew that what one wanted and what was practical were often entirely different things, and this difference was especially apparent the day after the night. Perhaps she would go on wanting him after leaving him, and if this turned out to be so, she might possibly come back to find him, but it wasn't probable, and it was exceptional that she wanted him even now, having wakened beside him in the bed. Usually, when she got to drinking and going places, she would also get to wanting a man, and then she would find one and have him, and afterward, the next morning or even the same night, she would be filled with loathing for the man, whoever he was, and it was impossible for her ever to want that particular man again.

There had been two previous exceptions to this since she became Charity McAdams Farnese instead of just Charity McAdams, and they had both turned out badly, and the way they had turned out badly was very odd. She had met these men at different times in different places, and later, after she had been with each of them the first time, she discovered that she wanted to be with them again, and she had gone back and been with them, several times with each, and in both cases they had been severely beaten by someone, without apparent reason. Not just beaten up in the ordinary way that men sometimes came out of fights, but really severely beaten with their jaws and noses broken and their teeth knocked out almost entirely.

This was very odd. If it had happened to only one of them, it would not have seemed significant in relation to her having been with them several times, but its happening to both the way it did was enough to make her wonder if she were not to blame through some kind of strange influence that brought misfortune to anyone she wanted and was with more than once. So far as she knew, it had never happened to anyone she had loathed and left permanently afterward, and this was one reason why it was not probable that she would come back to be with Joe Doyle again, even though it seemed now that she might want to. The two men who had been beaten had been athletic types who played tennis and handball and polo and other physical games, and they had survived without permanent damage, except that their faces were ruined, but Joe was so frail that he would surely suffer more, and there was a chance, his heart being bad, that he might not survive at all. She felt for him far too much passionate tenderness to want that to happen.

She wondered what time it was. She looked around the room for a clock, but she couldn't see one, and then she thought of Joe's watch, which he was wearing, but she couldn't read the dial from her position. Very slowly and carefully so as not to rock the bed or make the springs creak, she got up onto her knees and leaned down in what looked like an exaggerated salaam, her eyes about three inches from the watch on his wrist, and then she could see that it was almost one o'clock of what must be an afternoon.

Oh, God, she thought. *Oh, God.*

By the simple reading of the time, she was shocked into a realistic consideration of her position, and the despair which she had not felt so far this time came suddenly to claim her. Even in her despair, however, she was able to plan what she would say and do to explain where she had been all night and why she had not come home. It would be necessary not only to tell her husband a lie, but also to get someone reliable to support her in it if necessary. She had told her husband so many lies that she had become expert at it and did not consider it a great problem, and what she usually told him was that she had spent the night with a friend, but the precarious part was to find a friend that you could trust with the knowledge that you had been doing something that needed lying about.

There were a number of friends who were willing to do this once, or even now and then, but no one wanted to do it frequently, and she knelt on the bed, sitting back on her heels, and tried to think of someone she had not used before or not for a long time. She thought first of Samantha Cox, at whose apartment this particular experience had begun, but she was not sure that Samantha would help her, and she was not sure that she wanted to trust Samantha with her confidence, for Samantha was the kind who might use the knowledge against her out of pure spite. She continued to consider various prospects, and finally she decided on a friend named Bernardine DeWitt, who had helped her once before long enough ago that she might be willing to do it again. Besides, now that she thought about it, Bernardine had been in the group that she, Charity, had been in before going off with Milton Crawford, and Bernardine was probably already pretty sure, anyhow, that Charity had done something that would require deception.

Having decided on Bernardine, she lay back and lifted her legs and swung them around and off the bed. Slowly and quietly, avoiding squeaks and bumps, she stood up in anguish and a brief engulfing darkness. Her head was bursting, simply bursting. She stood rigidly in anguish until darkness passed, and then she became aware of the obtrusion of another part of her body, an urgent need to relieve herself, and she wondered if the room had a private bathroom or if it was one of these places where you had to go down the hall to one that was shared. Looking around the four walls of the room, she saw three doors, one of which would be the door to the hall. This, she was sure, was the one that stood alone in the wall directly across from the bed, and one of the other two, standing as a pair in another wall, might be, with luck, a bathroom, and in the bathroom, with more luck, she might even find some aspirin.

Moving carefully to the closer door, she opened it and found a closet behind. On a rod running across the closet were hanging three suits and a topcoat and a raincoat, and on the floor were three pairs of shoes. In spite of her urgency, she took time to stand for a moment and look at the articles of clothing, which seemed inadequate and filled with pathos as compared with the quantity and quality of clothing that you would find in one of the closets of someone like Milton Crawford, for instance. She felt for Joe Doyle's clothes the same passionate tenderness that she had felt for his thorax.

Closing this door, she moved over a few steps and opened the other. Behind this one was actually a bathroom, and she went in and closed the door after her and relieved herself, and then she looked in a little medicine cabinet above the lavatory and found some aspirin and swallowed two. She would have liked to take a shower, but the running water would have made far too much noise, and so she only turned on the tap a little bit and rinsed her face with cold water that she gathered in her cupped bands. Returning to the other room, she saw her $25 panties and $750 gown lying neatly on a chair, which surprised her, for she never put anything neatly anywhere, not even at home, and she definitely remembered dropping them on the floor last night when she took them off.

Joe Doyle bad picked them up and put them neatly where they were, probably when he'd got up afterward, and this seemed to her extremely thoughtful and considerate.

Filled with gratitude, she walked silently to the bed and looked down at him, feeling with the gratitude a slowly rising sense of excitement. He stirred a little and took a breath that broke the rhythm of his normal breathing and was like a gasp of pain in his throat, and she took three steps backward quickly. She hoped he wouldn't waken and see her the way she was, without anything on, for that would probably get something started that would go on for quite a long time, and she absolutely had to get home as quickly as possible. Acutely conscious now of the need to hurry, she dressed in a matter off seconds and walked to the hall door. She hesitated there, starting to turn to look once more at Joe Doyle lying on the bed, but then she decided that it would be much better and easier if she didn't look at him again, and so she went out of the room and down three flights of stairs to the street.

She didn't know immediately where she was and which way she ought to start walking, but then she was able to relate herself to Washington Square and started walking in that direction. She felt very conspicuous, dressed as she was, and the shoes that were practically nothing but high heels were hard to walk in, and her ankles kept turning. It was essential to find a taxi to take her home, and the thought of the taxi reminded her of the need for money, and she had a moment's sinking feeling before she realized that she was clutching unconsciously the small jeweled purse that she had somehow kept and carried from place to place through everything that had happened. She continued to walk and watch for a taxi, and after a while she saw one and flagged it and got in with an enormous but short-lived sense of relief and security.

She began to think about her husband. About Oliver Alton Farnese. She didn't like to think about him and didn't do it any oftener than was necessary, but sometimes it couldn't be helped, and one of the times it couldn't be helped was when she had to deceive him about something. What she had to decide now was whether to go to Bernardine's and arrange the lie and then home, or to go home directly. She needed Bernardine and wanted to make use of her, but she didn't feel up to seeing her or talking with her face to face. She preferred to go home, and told the taxi driver to take her there. She was certain that Oliver would not be there at this time of day.

Oliver was a creature of routine. It seemed essential to his survival to do things over and over in the same way at the same time. It was simply pathological the way he did it, and she knew from experience that he would not break his pattern just because his wife had not come home one night, which he was rather used to. Perhaps he would break it if she stayed missing too long or turned up dead somewhere, something like that, but even if she turned up dead he would break it only long enough to bury her and settle the affairs that would arise as a result of her dying. Oliver was peculiar. Sometimes she was afraid of him, and after the two men she had been with several times had been beaten, she had wondered if perhaps Oliver had had something to do with it, but this was an explanation she refused even to consider simply because it was far too frightening.

Thinking, she lost contact with the city and her position in it, not even knowing when they came onto Park Avenue, and the next contact she established was when the taxi stopped in front of her apartment building. She got out of the taxi and paid her fare and went in through the lobby to the elevator. The operator said good afternoon with functional courtesy and did not show the least interest in her appearance, which was not right for the time of day. Riding up in the elevator, in the silent steel car with the world closed out, she again had briefly a deep sense of having achieved security and even peace, but it didn't last, of course, as it never lasted, and she was faced on her floor with the necessity of walking all the way down to the entrance to her apartment and probably having to cope with Edith, the maid, whom she hated. She might be able to avoid Edith if she had brought or had not lost her key to the door, but there was no such luck. The key was not in her purse, and she was compelled to ring.

Edith opened the door and said, "Good afternoon, Madam," and Charity answered civilly with an effort and went past Edith and through the foyer and into the living room. Edith always addressed her as Madam, and Charity didn't like it. It made her feel like the manager of a whore house, and the way Edith said it, in that snotty voice, it was probably exactly what she was meant to feel, or at least like one of the whores.

"I spent the night with a friend," she said.

She was immediately ashamed and angry that she had felt it necessary to explain anything to a bitch of a maid. It was not that she felt snobbish about servants, for she didn't, but it was just that Edith was so Goddamned supercilious, an absolute bitch, and she was, besides, a dirty spy who carried stories to Oliver Alton Farnese. That was why Oliver wouldn't get rid of her, or let Charity get rid of her, saying always when Charity brought up the matter that Edith was a perfectly good servant and would be kept as long as she remained one.

"Yes, Madam," Edith said.

Charity stopped and turned and looked at her. "What do you mean by saying that in that way?" she said.

"Nothing, Madam. I only meant that I understand that you spent the night with a friend."

"The hell you did! You meant something else entirely. Perhaps you were thinking that a friend might include almost anyone of either sex. Is that it?"

"No, Madam."

"Why are you staring at me that way?"

"I'm sorry, Madam. I didn't intend to stare."

"Of course you intended to stare. It's ridiculous to say that you can stand there staring without intending to. I consider you a dirty, spying bitch, Edith, and I'd fire you instantly if only my husband would permit it. Is that perfectly clear?"

"Yes, Madam."

"All right. Because you're such a bitch and would like to think the worst possible things about me, I'll tell you that I spent the night with my friend

Bernardine DeWitt. Do you understand that, Edith? Do you understand that clearly?"

"Yes, Madam. With Mrs. DeWitt."

Turning, Charity went on through the apartment to her own room. She took off all her clothes, and lay down on her back across the bed and closed her eyes and pressed the eyeballs with the tips of her fingers until the pain became intense. She felt shaken and sickened by the scene with Edith, and every time one occurred, which was frequently, she swore that one would never happen again, but one always did, and the worst of it was that the mistress always seemed to come out of it in the wrong position, Charity the bitch, instead of Edith. Well, this time she had made what might turn out to be a bad mistake, which was what came of losing your temper and saying things without thinking. She had said that she spent the night with Bernardine, had committed herself to the lie before it was secured, and now Bernardine would simply have to help her or she would be in more trouble than she could handle. She would have to call Bernardine without delay, this instant, and secure the lie.

Sitting up on the edge of the bed, she picked up her telephone, which was a private line, not an extension, and held it in her hands and tried to think of Bernardine's private number, the one to the phone in her bedroom, not the one to the apartment that a servant would answer. After an effort, she remembered the number and dialed it, and fortunately Bernardine was there and answered.

"Hello, Bernie," Charity said. "This is Charity."

"Charity!" Bernardine's voice, which had sounded sleepy when she answered the telephone, became suddenly lively. "My God, darling, whatever in the world became of you?"

"Well, that's why I called. I want to talk to you about it. I seemed to remember that you were in the group last night that I went several places with, but I wasn't absolutely sure."

"I was there all right, darling, but where the hell were you? After a while, I mean. We looked and looked for you, but you had simply disappeared."

"I met Milton Crawford in that place where we were, the last place, and he wanted me to go away with him to another place, and I did."

She hesitated, wondering how much she ought to tell Bernardine, but she knew that she might as well tell it all, only leaving out names, for Bernardine was no fool, and a lie that she would know was a lie might just annoy her sufficiently to make her refuse to help. You could tell from the very quality of the silence on the wire that Bernardine was waiting for Charity to ask whatever favor she'd called to ask and was prepared to be contrary about it if there was the least bit of nonsense.

"Well," Charity said, "I went on to this other place with Milton, and he got to be a bore by patting my leg constantly and urging me to go to his apartment with him, and finally I left by myself and blacked out and ended up in this place where there was a beautiful piano player who tried to help me find Milton, but we couldn't. That's about all there is to it, Bernie, except I didn't come home, and Oliver will want to know where I was."

"So do I, darling. Where were you?"

"I told you, Bernie. I was with this piano player."

"Imagine! With a piano player! Darling, how was he?"

"Look, Bernie, I know it's very amusing and all that, but I'm feeling pretty desperate about it, and what I need is help. You being divorced and all, not having a husband to say anything different to Oliver, I thought maybe you'd be willing to let me tell him I spent the night with you."

"And to lie for you, of course, if he asks me about it."

"Obviously it wouldn't do any good for me to say I had if you said I hadn't."

"Obviously. Darling, I don't want to make a big issue out of a little lie, but I remember doing this for you once before, and I wouldn't want it to become a habit."

"I'll never ask you again, Bernie. Honestly, I won't."

"All right, darling. I'll lie to Oliver for you if it becomes necessary. Sometime you must tell me how it is with a piano player."

Bernardine laughed as if it were the greatest of jokes, and Charity said thanks and good-by. After replacing the telephone in its cradle, she lay back across the bed and pressed again on her closed eyes with the tips of her fingers. She was pretty sure she could trust Bernardine, so she could quit worrying about that part of it now. What she needed to do was take a hot shower and get into bed properly for a couple of hours, but she was suddenly too exhausted to move.

She wondered if Joe Doyle were still asleep in the room in the house not far from Washington Square, or if he had awakened by now and found her gone.

CHAPTER 5

He was awake. He had wakened, as a matter of fact, before she left. Waking instantly, he did not instantly open his eyes. When he did open them, he thought for a moment that he was not awake after all, but had only drifted on the verge of waking into a dream, for the first thing he saw was a naked girl who seemed to be performing the second duty of Islam. He closed his eyes and opened them again, and the girl was still there, but now she was erect on her knees, her buttocks resting on her heels, and she was apparently thinking intently about something important.

He was not having hallucinations. Neither had he died in the night and gone to an unlikely paradise with blonde houris. He was Joe Doyle, relatively sane, alive in his own bed, and he was, though not crazy, a fool. In the tag hours, in the recurring span of a man's greatest vulnerability, he had acquired a fancy dame on a dipso prowl, and he had brought her home, and here she was. Charity. Charity Farnese. Here she was in his bed with the taste in her mouth of the night before, and she was probably wondering for the umpteenth desperate time why she had done what she'd done, and how in God's name she would account for it to her friends or husband or confessor or whomever she might, in her need for catharsis or shriving, make her accounting to. Watching her through eyes so narrowly open that her body was blurred by his lashes, he felt, as she had in watching him, a stirring of excitement, but he did not move speak, and the reason he didn't was essentially the same reason she had decided to slip away. Even when it was felt in the heart, there was no percentage in going farther with what had already gone too far because it couldn't go far enough.

In a little while, she eased back and lifted her legs and swung them off the bed, and she did this carefully and quietly with the obvious purpose of not disturbing him. He couldn't see her for several minutes after that, but he heard her open the closet door, and then the door to the bathroom. She want into the bathroom, and everything was completely quiet for the time that she was there, and as a matter of fact he did not hear her come out or know that she was near until she was suddenly standing beside the bed looking down at him. He had not opened his eyes any wider than the slit, and so she didn't know he was awake and had been watching her when she was in sight and listening to her movements when she was not, but now, seeing again so suddenly her slim and nearly perfect body blurred by his lashes, he almost betrayed himself by the minor violence of a reaction that caused his own body to jerk involuntarily and his breath to break off in his throat. Startled, she stepped back and began at once to dress, which was quickly accomplished, and then she walked to the door and hesitated and went out.

After she was gone, he continued to lie in bed, not because there was any possibility of his sleeping again, but because there wasn't anything he could think of that was worth getting up to do, and after a few minutes he began to listen to his heart. He couldn't actually hear it, of course, but by placing his right hand flat on his chest above it, he could feel it beating in his palm. By the beat of it, the feel of it, he achieved a sense of the sound of it. He often did this. It prompted in him a morbid speculation, which had also become a kind of morbid pleasure. The speculation was on how many tens or hundreds or thousands of beats were left to go, and the pleasure was derived from his pride in having learned that he could speculate on this without fear of self-pity. It had occurred to him once that it was rather like testing a car for mileage. You put a certain amount of gas in the tank, and then you ran the car until it quit running, and as the mileage meter came closer and closer to what you thought would be the end, you kept waiting more and more expectantly for the cough, the missed beat, the silence. The analogy was adequate only to that point, however. When the car engine stopped, you just gave it more gas and started it again.

Another thing he often did while listening to his heart was to go back over his life and try to find something, a direction or a pattern, that would convince him that he had been significant or essential to some plan or purpose, but he could never find anything. It was not that he felt that his life was a waste, just time pulled for nothing, but only that the most you could say about any ordinary life was that it had been lived. He was only a fifth-rate piano thumper, of course, but this was not the point, for practically everyone was a fifth-rate something or other, and if there was any plan or purpose, the fifth-raters were as much a part of it as anyone else. He was not especially bitter about anything, he decided. It was better to live a short time than no time, and he was glad to have been what he was, since he couldn't have been anything better.

Once he had tried to be. He had wanted to be a really good pianist, if not concert at least jazz, but he didn't have the big talent that it took, and he had accepted this, once he was convinced of it, as readily as he had accepted the later understanding that he was going to die before he had lived very long, as average lives went. After high school, he had worked his way through three years of fine arts in college, piano especially, and it was then that he had accepted the reality of what he wasn't and would never be, and he had left after the three years and played around the country with a fair dance orchestra that finally got to New York in a small spot. In New York, after a while, he began to feel the pain in his heart, and it reminded him for the first time in many years of the pain he had used to feel in the joints of his arms and legs when he was a boy.

He went to a doctor, who examined him and made an appointment for him at a hospital. At the hospital he was examined more thoroughly and asked detailed questions about the diseases he had had as a boy and as a man, but particularly as a boy, and then he returned to the doctor he had consulted originally. Previously the doctor had been noncommittal, but this time, his tentative diagnosis verified by the hospital, he was as clinically precise and as sympathetic as professional detachment permitted him to be.

"You have rheumatic heart disease," he said. "It's caused by fibrosis and scarring of the valves. Usually the mitral valve is affected. Sometimes the aortic valve is also affected. This is true in your case."

"What does that mean?" Joe said.

"It means that your heart's been working too hard for too long to do its job."

"And now it's wearing out, breaking down. Is that it?"

"That's it."

"How long will it last?"

"That's hard to predict. Cases vary, of course. Average expectancy from the time of the damage is thirteen to fifteen years."

"You mean this was caused by the sickness I had as a boy? The time I had the fever and the aches in my bones?"

"That's right. Rheumatic fever."

"I'd almost forgotten it," Joe said.

He went away and began to think about what he would do. He knew he was not living the right kind of life for a heart cripple; there was too much tension and too little rest. Too many late hours and too little sleep. Too little eating and too much drinking and smoking. Too much of all that was bad for him and far too little of what was good. But playing the piano was about all he knew, the only way he had to earn a living, and he decided deliberately that he might as well go on with it for all the difference in time it would probably make. Not with a dance orchestra that was always moving around, however. He wanted to stay put, to get used to a place to die in, and New York, so far as he could see, was as good a place as any other.

He started off playing for living expenses in a couple of different bars in the Village, and then he met Chester Lewis, who had just come out of a special kind of hospital where he had gone to get a monkey permanently off his back. Chester was a pretty good drummer who needed a job drumming, and they'd got together, mostly just for fun in the beginning, and developed some of the little conversation pieces between the drum and the piano, and they'd been surprised and delighted by the things that could be said in this way. They'd tried it on the customers one night in the bar where Joe was playing, and it had gone well, and later they'd moved to a better job in the club where they now were, which was about as far from Sheridan Square south as Joe's room was from Washington Square north.

This was just the outline, of course, the stripped pattern of his life as he saw it, but it was the pattern that would mean something if anything at all meant anything worth knowing, and nothing seemed to. It gave him a very strange feeling to think that he had been dying since he was twelve years old, when he'd had the fever and the aches, but it wasn't really so strange after all, when you thought about it a while longer, for everyone started dying the instant he was born. The only difference was that Joe Doyle had only been dying a little faster than most others. Anyhow, he had already passed the average that the doctor had mentioned, the thirteen to fifteen years, and this was somehow a monstrous deception, a kind of preternatural con trick to assure him that he was living, from a special point of view, a long life instead of a short one....

And now, lying in bed after the departure of Charity Farnese, he was thinking too much and becoming depressed. Getting up abruptly, he showered and shaved and dressed and went downstairs. He had not eaten since the middle of the afternoon yesterday, and it was past time to eat again, but he was not in the least hungry and knew that the sight and smell of food would only make him sick. What he needed was a couple of ounces of rye, after which he would feel better and possibly able to eat at least a sandwich, and where he might as well go to get both was the club where he worked. Besides, Chester Lewis would probably be there, or would come in later, and they could make a little talk with the piano and the drum before the bar opened at four.

When he reached the club, Chester wasn't there yet, but Yancy Foster, the superior bartender, was. Joe sat down on a stool at the bar, and Yancy looked at him sourly.

"Hello, beautiful," Yancy said.

"That was last night," Joe said.

"You said it, it was last night," Yancy said. "Did you find Milton?"

"Not a trace. I think Milton was someone who happened to her some other night."

"Lots of others have happened to her other nights. Lots of others have been left over."

"Sure, Yancy. Sure."

"Oh, she had something, all right. Something special. I admit that. She drifts in here out of a black fog, looking like a delinquent angel and talking like a schizy intellectual, and you keep watching her and talking with her and wondering what the hell will finally become of her, and you wish that it wouldn't."

"Yeah. That's right, Yancy. You keep wishing that it wouldn't."

"A man's a fool. He thinks he's got his immunity built up, and then some little tramp comes along and starts a fever in him."

"You talking to me or yourself, Yancy?"

"I'm just talking, sonny. Anyone can listen who wants to. Probably nobody will. Not even me."

"I'm listening, Yancy. Hanging on every word."

"I can see you are. I can see you're real interested. Well, what I say is, they're all a little different from each other in one way or another, but the difference isn't important, whatever it is, and what's important is the way they're alike. These fancy, crazy dames! They come here on the prowl from their plush nests on MacDougal Street or Park Avenue or wherever they happen to live, and they may have different faces and answer to different names and have different fancy names for the crazy things wrong with them, but what they all are without exception is more trouble than any man with any brains would ever want"

"You're eloquent, Yancy. You should have been a missionary or something."

"Sure, sure. I know. You mean I should go to hell."

"No, Yancy. What I mean is, I was with you before you started. I don't need the lecture."

"You don't think so? Well maybe not. You need something, though, sonny. You look like the wrath of God."

"I need a couple ounces of rye, Yancy. I've been trying to tell you"

"Like hell you need a couple ounces of rye. What you need is food. How long since you've eaten?"

"I don't remember, Yancy. I eat when I'm hungry"

"There's some good beef. I'll fix you a sandwich."

"All right, Yancy. While you're fixing the sandwich, I'll drink the rye."

Yancey poured the rye and handed it to him, and he sat hunched over the bar with the strong fumes rising into his nostrils. He looked ahead into the mirror at the reflection of the room behind him, the oppressive litter in stale shadows of tables and chairs on a worn tile floor still wet in spots from mopping, and it didn't seem at that moment a particular misfortune that he was going to die before long.

CHAPTER 6

The morning of that day, Oliver Alton Farnese got up at eight o'clock. This could have been predicted by anyone who was aware of his habits. He got up at eight o'clock every day except Saturday, when he got up at nine, and Sunday, when he got up at ten.

After rising, he shaved and bathed and dressed. His clothes had been laid out for him in a particular place in a particular order, and he not only knew exactly what they would be for every change he made during the course of the day, but for every change for every day for the rest of the week, for he composed every Sunday night a detailed list of what he would wear for every occasion of the week following, and this list was deviated from only in emergency, and not even in emergency without specific authorization.

After shaving and bathing and dressing, he went to the dining room. On the way, he stopped in the hall outside the door of the room in which Charity sometimes slept, and he waited for about thirty seconds for the sound or sense of motion or static life in the room beyond the door, but nothing was heard or sensed, as he had suspected nothing would be, and then he went on to the dining room and sat down and had his breakfast of orange juice and bacon and toast and marmalade and coffee, which was served to him by Edith, the maid. He knew that his breakfast this morning would consist of these things, and that breakfast tomorrow would consist of certain other things, and breakfast of the morning of the day after tomorrow of certain others, for he planned his menus, as he planned his wardrobe, precisely and obdurately, every Sunday night, for a week to come.

"Did Mrs. Farnese come home last night?" he said to Edith.

"No, sir."

"Did she leave any word for me?"

"No, sir."

"Did she say where she was going?"

"No, sir. Mrs. Farnese never tells me where she's going."

"That's right. She doesn't. Do you know why, Edith?"

"Yes, sir."

"Of course you do. It's because she despises you. She thinks you're an informer. Are you an informer, Edith?"

"I know where my first obligation is, sir."

"That's nicely put, Edith. Very delicate. You have no idea how much I appreciate your loyalty. You also know where your first advantage is, don't you, Edith?"

"I think so, sir."

"You are never a disappointment to me, Edith, You always say precisely the right thing. You know exactly when to lie and when to tell the truth."

"Thank you, sir."

"Tell me, Edith. Where do you think my wife spent the night?"

"I assume, sir, that she spent it with a friend."

"Precisely, Edith. There is no doubt in the world that she spent the night with a friend. Can you tell me what a friend is, Edith?"

"No, sir."

"Oh, come, now. Surely you can. Is a friend someone you have known well for a long time, or is it possible for a friend to be someone you merely meet in the course of a night and decide to be friendly with?"

"I don't know, sir. I've never had a friend."

"Edith, Edith, I adore you. I really do." He laughed softly, a sibilance with no sound of a vowel. "Go away, Edith. Please do. You have been perfect, absolutely perfect, and if you stay another moment you are liable to say something that will spoil everything."

"Yes, sir. Thank you, sir."

She went away, and he poured himself a second cup of coffee and glanced at a morning paper while he drank it. He was hardly aware, however, of what he saw. He was savoring, instead, the aftermath of Edith, and the aftermath, constantly recurring, was the substance of anticipation. He was a rich man, incredibly rich to the cold and avaricious bitch who served his table and told him tales, and it amused him enormously to see how she served him and cultivated him in the design and expectation of an eventual expression of gratitude. It would be a truly delectable pleasure when he decided to make it plain, in due time, that he had despised her all along as much as she had ever been despised by Charity, or by anyone else.

He allowed himself a half-hour for dressing and a half-hour for breakfast. At nine, he left the table and walked through the living room and the foyer to the door. Edith, who knew his schedule perfectly, was waiting at the door with his hat. He took it and put it on his head while she opened the door to let him out. On the way into the hall, just before the door closed behind him, he said, "Good morning, Edith," and she said, "Good morning, sir," and the last word, the subservient sir, was amputated in the air by the door's closing. It was always this way. This way exactly.

At the elevator, he pushed the button and stood waiting briefly with indiscernible impatience as the car climbed its shaft in response to his summons. He was not impatient because he was in a hurry or had any place to be at a certain time, although it was part of his schedule to be certain places at certain times, but simply because he felt that his waiting was somehow improper and unnecessary, and that the car should have been waiting, instead, for him. He arrived at the elevator at this minute of the hour five mornings a week, give or take thirty seconds at the most, and it was in effect a personal affront, a deliberate indifference to the reservation he had made of time and space, that the operator did not wait with the car as Edith waited with his hat.

When the car arrived, its door slipping open with a soft gasp after its breathless ascent, he stepped inside and said, "Good morning," in the identical tone he always used at this time to greet the operator, and the operator said, "Good morning, Mr. Farnese. Beautiful day outside," and this was an example of another minor irritant that had acquired the cumulative quality of a threat from being repeated so often. The operator always seemed to find it necessary to append a comment to the simple greeting, which would have been tolerable if it had been regularly repeated, but it wasn't. Sometimes it was a comment like this one, pertaining to the kind of day it happened to be, and sometimes it was something altogether different, pertaining to a current event or something of the sort, and it was impossible to anticipate with any accuracy what it would be on any given morning, and this was disturbing. People who performed repeatedly the same services should say repeatedly the same words and should look consistently the same way. When they did not, it was a violation of the order of things and therefore threatening.

Leaving the building with a word for the doorman, he found that his black Imperial had been brought around from the garage as usual. Getting behind the wheel, he drove by a particular route to the office he maintained in a building on Fifth Avenue, and it was, when he got there, a particular time. Crossing the outer room, he said, "Good morning, Miss Carling," to the woman he called his secretary and who was actually nothing necessary at all, and went into the inner room and sat down at his desk, and after that there was nothing especially to do.

He didn't need the office. He didn't need to go there. Except that the office and his going there were necessary to the survival of the flesh and blood and bones and nerves that existed in the unique identity of Oliver Alton Farnese. Some of his mail was directed there, and this he opened and read and disposed of, and sometimes he even dictated to Miss Carling a reply to one or more of the letters. Now and then he made or granted an appointment with someone, and these appointments were scheduled as strictly for definite times as if he had a full agenda. If a person who had an appointment arrived early, he was kept waiting until the scheduled hour, and if he arrived late, he was advised by Miss Carling that he could not be seen and would have to make another appointment, if he wished, for another day.

Much of the time, after and between the mail and the appointments, if there were any of either, Farnese passed in reading selected newspapers and magazines related to investments and industry and certain sports. He did not handle his investments, nor did he engage in industry or games, but some attention to these matters seemed appropriate to his position, and they bored him somewhat less than art and literature and politics and social affairs. The truth was, he could not possibly have survived the pressures and tensions of any competitive activity whatever, and his father had recognized this and had left him the bulk of a huge family fortune so legally restricted and secured that he really had very little to do with it, except to sign documents occasionally and live richly off the income.

He had practically nothing to do that had to be done, and there was practically nothing that could have been done that he wanted to do, but it was essential to his survival to be constantly committed, if not genuinely occupied. All his life he had lived in private terror under the perpetual threat of personal disintegration. He shored himself with the minutiae of a self-imposed and obsessive regimentation. He substituted rigidity for strength, cruelty for courage. In the observation of the infliction of pain, he took an almost orgiastic pleasure. He was monstrously vain.

Miss Carling, who usually did all her day's work in thirty minutes and frequently in no minutes, was expected, nevertheless, to be present for seven hours. She arrived at nine and departed for the day at five and took an hour for lunch between noon and one. Farnese lunched between one and half-past two. He went regularly to his club, where he received from the head-waiter a copy of the planned luncheon menu a week in advance, which enabled him to plan his personal menus in advance also, and so he always knew exactly what he would eat on any day, exactly what he would drink before and after the meal, and almost exactly how long it would require to do it. His schedule was rarely disturbed by the claims of other members on his time, for he was not understood or liked, and he usually drank and ate alone. At any rate, he was inevitably at his desk in the office at two-thirty, and often he sat there for the rest of the afternoon and did nothing at all.

This afternoon, however, he had an appointment at three o'clock with a private detective. The detective arrived six minutes early and was compelled to wait in the outer office. He was a grossly obese man whose swollen body with its narrow shoulders and heavy mammae and broad, tremulous hips and rump gave him, in spite of his size, a womanish appearance. His head was bald, his scalp scored and pocked by some kind of skin infection he had once had, and his face was gray and soggy. His name was Bertram Sweeney, and for more than a year it had been his job to shadow Charity McAdams Farnese and report regularly on her activities to Oliver Alton Farnese, her husband.

At three o'clock, he was told by Miss Carling that be could go into the inner office, and he went in and sat down in the chair from which he always made his reports. He removed a notebook from a sagging side pocket of his coat and opened it to the place where Charity had entered it yesterday afternoon, and then, without speaking, he sat holding the open notebook on one knee and looking at Farnese. He hated the man who had hired him. He hated Farnese for many reasons, some of them valid, but mostly he hated him because it was so much easier to hate anyone than to like him or to be indifferent to him.

Farnese also sat without speaking for quite a long time. He sat erect in his chair with his hands folded on the desk in front of him, and there was in the rigid immobility of his posture a cataleptic quality that was almost frightening. A tall, slender man with blond, graydusted hair and a face like a narrow wedge of stone, he might have been in his withdrawal either psychotic or ascetic, but what he was in the opinion of Sweeney could best be expressed in the language of the gutter, which Sweeney spoke fluently, and now to himself in the merest whisper he called Farnese the name of what he was, forming the word with livid lips. He wasn't fooled, either, by the pose of quietude that Farnese held. He had learned long ago to sense the sickening turbulence beneath the surface of icy reserve, and when he sat and made his reports with quiet malice, he laughed and laughed within himself, the laughter growing and becoming so enormous inside his flabby body that he was sure it would break loose like thunder in the room.

When Farnese spoke at last, his voice, like his face, did not betray his feelings. It was modulated and flat, deviating only slightly from a monotone. His thin lips barely moved to permit the passage of words, and if there was any sign of emotional disturbance at all, it was in the fine line of a scar that followed so precisely for about three inches the line of the mandible that it seemed to have been made deliberately by a scalpel. This scar was ordinarily invisible, but sometimes it turned dead white, as now, and could be seen plainly against darker flesh, and Sweeney found it extremely interesting, and useful as a kind of adrenal barometer. He had thought at first that Farnese was older than he admitted, that the scar was evidence of plastic surgery, but he now knew definitely that this was not so. Farnese was forty-five. He had married Charity McAdams when he was forty-one and she was twenty-five. They had been married, after a fashion, four years. These were vital statistics of which Sweeney was certain.

"All right," Farnese said. "Begin whenever you're ready."

Sweeney began. Using his notes to remind himself of specific times and places, he reported that he had been waiting yesterday afternoon, as per instructions, in the office of the garage in the apartment building on Park

Avenue in which the Farneses lived. At exactly 4:57 be had received a telephone message from the Farnese maid that Mrs. Farnese had just left the
apartment. He, Sweeney, had picked her up at the front entrance and followed her to the apartment of Miss Samantha Coy, who was not new to
Sweeney's notebook. Mrs. Farnese had remained here for nearly two hours,
leaving with a party of six, including herself, at 6:43. The party of six was
evenly composed of men and women in pairs, and they had apparently had
quite a few cocktails, and they drove in one car, a Cadillac, to an Italian
restaurant on Tenth Street. They had arrived at the restaurant at 7:18.

"Never mind the exact timetable," Farnese said. "I've told you before that
it isn't necessary."

"I like to be accurate," Sweeney said.

"Never mind it. When I want to know a time, I'll ask for it. Get on with
the report and omit the details."

Sweeney bowed his head above his notebook and whispered to himself
the name of what Farnese was. He continued his report.

After leaving the Italian restaurant, the party of six had driven in the
Cadillac to Fourth Street, where they visited three nightclubs in about
three hours. While they were in the third of these, Mrs. Farnese had
deserted the party and had gone away with a young man in a white Mark
II. Sweeney did not know the identity of the man, but he had obtained the
license number of the Mark II, and it would be a simple matter from that
to get the identity.

"Don't bother," Farnese said. "I know who he is."

"Oh," Sweeney said.

Mrs. Farnese and the man in the Mark II, he said, had gone to a place in
the area of Sheridan Square. Another night spot. The place was very
crowded and noisy, filled with confusion, but Mrs. Farnese and the man
had sat at a small table not far from the bar, and he, Sweeney, had managed to grab a stool from which he could observe them clearly. After a
while, Mrs. Farnese had got up and gone away alone, presumably to the
ladies' room. Since the man had remained at the table, it was a fair assumption that Mrs. Farnese would return, which was the assumption that
Sweeney made, and this was a mistake, or had almost been one, for she
didn't return after all, and it was only by the sheerest luck that he had
caught a glimpse of her at the last second as she was going out past the
check stand.

When he got outside after her, she was standing on the sidewalk in front
of the building, just standing there very quietly, and there had been, he
thought, an odd expression on her face. Or maybe it had been the absence
of any expression at all. A kind of vacancy. It was pretty hard to describe,
but about the best word he could think of was *gone*. She'd looked gone. Not
there. Nobody home.

Moving suddenly, as if she'd just remembered something, she'd started walking down the street with him behind her, and she'd walked very rapidly for several blocks and had then stopped in front of still another night spot, a crummy little place identified by a few twists of neon tubing as Duo's. She'd patted the bricks by the door as if she were in love with them, and had gone inside and sat at the bar and talked for quite a while with the bartender.

"Is this bartender important?" Farnese said.

"What do you mean?" Sweeney said.

"Did she do anything with him, go away with him, give any indication at all that he was any more to her than a common bartender?"

"No. Nothing like that. She just talked with him and drank the Martinis that he made for her."

"Then why make a point of him? Please get finished."

"Oh. Sorry." Sweeney took a deep breath, held it five seconds, released it slowly. "There was a piano player there. A so-so thumper. Name's Joe Doyle. He's the one she went away with. After quite a while, that was. I was sitting at the bar talking to a redhead who hit me for a drink."

"Did you follow or stay with the redhead?"

"Followed. When I'm on a job, the job comes first"

"I congratulate you on your integrity. Where did they go?"

"They picked up his car in the alley and made a tour of half a dozen places. Didn't stay long in any one of them. They seemed to be looking for someone, and it's a good bet it was the guy in the Mark II."

"Possibly. But they didn't find him, of course."

"No. Finally they drove to the place this other guy lives. The piano thumper. Joe Doyle."

"Where is this?"

"An old residence south of Washington Square. Probably he has a room there. Maybe a small apartment."

"Quite likely. What did they do then?"

"Well, that's a matter for speculation." Watching the stony face of Farnese, Sweeney spoke now with deep, delicious malice. "They went inside together, and they didn't come out. Not before daylight, anyhow. I waited that long, and then I went home for a nap. A guy has to sleep now and then."

Farnese said nothing. He sat rigidly erect in the cataleptic pose, and Sweeney kept his eyes on the fine white line of scar tissue along the mandible, and the thunderous mirth grew in Sweeney's gross body.

"That's all," Sweeney said.

"Very well," Farnese said.

"Shall I continue on the job?"

"Not today. Perhaps tomorrow or the next day. I'll let you know."

"All right," Sweeney said.

He folded his notebook and replaced it carefully in the sagging pocket of his coat. Rising, he walked to the door and let himself out of the room, and Farnese continued to sit unmoving in his chair. He sat with his hands folded and submitted himself to the violations of fury and terror and incongruous desire.

Chapter 7

Bertram Sweeney went directly to his office, which was a small mal-odorous room at the rear of the third floor of a building that was head-quarters for a dozen fringe operations. He stood for a couple of minutes in the center of the room, rubbing his scarred scalp with the palm of his right hand, and then he walked across to a narrow window and stood staring down through dirty glass into the litter of an alley.

The world today, he felt, was even a worse place than it usually was, and this made it intolerably bad. The world was a pustule, and of all the infec-tious organisms that lived in it, there was none more loathsome than Bertram Sweeney. He didn't know how he could possibly stand himself and the world for the rest of the day, and so he began to do what he always did when the gross ugliness of the two, the world and Sweeney, became too oppressive for him to bear. He began to slip softly into fantasy.

Turning away from the window, he sat down in the swivel chair behind his desk and removed an 8x10 photograph of Charity Farnese from the desk's belly drawer. He stood the photograph on the desk and rocked back in the chair and sat staring at the face of Charity with a kind of drugged dreaminess in his eyes and an odd, unpleasant slackness in his mouth. He had got the picture at the beginning of his service to Oliver Alton Farnese, and it had been then much smaller, about the size of an identification photo you could carry in a wallet, but he had taken it to a studio and had it blown up and two copies made. One of the copies he kept at home, the rented room in which he slept, and the other one he kept here, in the office, and so he had a picture of Charity, whichever place he was, to look at and talk to and take with him in dreams to a different world in which there lived a different Bertram Sweeney.

"You lovely," he whispered. "You wanton, prowling little lovely."

Charity looked back at him with an expression compounded of excite-ment and tenderness and ineffable sadness, as if she understood quite well that she was surely going to do something for pleasure that would later cause her pain. Her pale hair fell forward on the heavy side, and in her eyes was a capricious solemnity. He could have sworn that her lips moved in the slightest of smiles and shaped the suggestion of a tender word.

They were lovers, of course. They existed in a detached and intimate devotion to each other in this second world of Bertram Sweeney, and Charity in the second world was precisely as she was in the first, except that in the second her dispersed and wasted self and love were reserved entirely for Sweeney, who was a tall, straight man with heavy hair and a fine, plain face and flat belly and long, strong legs. They were restricted only by the resources of fantasy, and they were at different times in many places, but the best and most recurrent place was a long beach of white sand between lush green growth and a bright blue sea in a hot country.

He was standing suddenly on the beach at the edge of the water, and the water whispered up the sand and broke like a salty caress around his ankles, and his strong brown body gleamed like bronze in the tropical sun. Then he heard her call his name, once and clearly, and she was running toward him from a distance, closer and closer to Bertram Sweeney, her body as bare and bronzed as his, so light and fleet and airily moving that it left no prints at all upon the sand.

Her hands solicited his love. She whispered soft salacities. Now they were quiet in the ebb of desire. Now they were roused in its flux and flow. All day they were lovers in the sun. Night came, and they were lovers in the night. They slept entwined on the white sand beneath enormous stars.

So it was with Bertram Sweeney, who consistently spied upon and betrayed the woman he loved in two worlds and possessed in one, and his ability to do this could be explained only as a miracle of adjustment to a complex situation. He had thought at first, when Farnese hired him, that he was being retained simply to obtain evidence of adultery for a divorce, and this would have been simplicity itself, the matter of a minor effort on any one of many nights, and the only thing he couldn't understand was why Farnese, a man of great wealth, would hire a fringe operator like Bertram Sweeney. Then, as the arrangement continued, he began to understand that Farnese did not want a divorce on grounds of adultery, or any grounds at all, and he had hired a fringe operator because that was the only kind who would serve him in his purpose. What this purpose was precisely, Sweeney did not know, but he knew that it was not pleasant and possibly abnormal. He was no fancy psychiatrist, Sweeney wasn't, but he had sat and sensed the agony of emotions in the man he served and hated, and what he had sensed besides the natural fury of a cuckold was an intense excitement that was not natural at all.

Well, Sweeney could understand that, in a way, although he was only a fat and ugly man in hopeless love, not a husband with certain claims and rights to assert. It was part of the miraculous adjustment to a complexity, as far as Sweeney was concerned, and he had felt many times the same fury and excitement he sensed in Farnese. He felt it when be stood at the end of a night's work outside whatever place Charity had gone with whatever man, and afterward he would go home and look at the picture and go south to the white beach.

Farnese was a stinking sadist, of course, and probably it gave him a charge to be on top of the situation, knowing always the truth and saying nothing, knowing that he could, if he chose, exercise the advantage of an executioner at any time. As he had, in fact, exercised it twice in the cases of two selected men. Sweeney had been the agent in both cases. He had arranged the details and had felt afterward that the revenge was as much his as Farnese's. His conscience did not disturb him appreciably.

Sweeney was certain of Farnese's sadism, and he was also certain of something else. The sadism was not exercised against Charity Farnese for the sake of a more subtle cruelty, but if it ever was, to Sweeney's knowledge, then Sweeney would kill Farnese. He had even decided how he would do it. He would simply walk into Farnese's office, as he had today, and he would sit down in the chair he had sat in today, and he would take from the pocket of his coat, instead of the notebook, a gun. He would look at Farnese and say nothing and shoot him dead, and Farnese would understand clearly in the end why he was dying. There would be a kind of artistry in the simplicity of it, and the necessary sacrifice of Bertram Sweeney would mean nothing much to anyone on earth, not even to Bertram Sweeney.

So he sat at his desk this particular day that followed a particular night. Bertram Sweeney, private detective and consistent betrayer for pay.

He sat at his desk in a fantasy of love at the edge of a whispering sea.

CHAPTER 8

By four o'clock, Charity was needing a Martini very badly. The aspirin she had taken had helped her headache a little, but it was still bad enough, and not even a hot bath and a long time of lying quietly on the bed had reduced it appreciably more. What she needed was a very dry, cold Martini, and she was sure that if she had one it would make her head quit aching immediately.

She lay and thought about the Martini for quite a while, the cold, whitish liquid in a crystal shell, the crystal cold in her fingers. She wished there were a way of getting the Martini without getting up and dressing and going to make it, but the only other way was to have Edith make it and bring it to her, and she didn't want to see Edith or give her the satisfaction of knowing that she, Charity, needed a Martini at four o'clock in the afternoon. She did need the Martini, however, after thinking about it for so long, and so she got up very slowly in deference to her head and put on a robe, which was a compromise with dressing, and went out to the kitchen and got some ice, which she carried into the living room, where she got two bottles and a shaker from a cabinet. She carried the ice and the two bottles and the shaker back to her room, and it seemed to her that it would be very poor economy of effort to mix only one Martini when she could mix two or three with practically the same expenditure, and so she mixed three and poured one and drank it quickly.

Afterward, she poured another and held it in her hands and sat down in a deep chair. This second one she sipped, and she was perfectly right, as she had been before in identical circumstances. Her head began to feel better at once, clearer and less painful, and the only disadvantage to this was that she began to think clearly of Joe Doyle and to want to be with him again. Remembering the night and its excitement, she remembered also his bad heart, and it occurred to her that the excitement had probably not been good for the heart. What if he had died in her arms? This would have been a great shock and a terrible complication, but at the same time there was in the idea a quality of total consummation that was at once thrilling and. terrifying. She did not wish to go on thinking like this about Joe Doyle, and so she began to think instead about her father, who was dead. Thinking about her father always made her feel lost and lonely, even so long after he had died, but thinking about him had at least the comfort of escape, for it was necessary to go away in her mind from this time and place.

When she went away in her mind to think about her father, she seemed always to go to the same place in the beginning, and this place was the street that ran in front of the house in the town in which she used to live, and the time of her arrival there was always evening of a summer day. The street was sad and lovely on summer evenings, and it ran both ways into a kind of eternal bittersweet status quo in which nothing ever changed. Great oaks and elms and maples grew in the parkings on both sides and touched leaves above, and below the overhead arc of limbs and leaves it was cool and shadowed, with just enough filtered light to make things softly visible, and among the leaves were a thousand singing cicadas.

She was standing by the street in front of the house, and she felt very sad and in love with herself, and she turned and walked slowly up the walk from the street to her house, which was one of the finest houses in town, and on the walk coming toward her was her father, whom she loved more than anyone on earth, even including herself. They met on the walk, and her father put his arms around her and held her and stroked her hair. Nothing was said, not a word by either of them, and after a while he released her and went on down the walk, and. she went on in the opposite direction toward the house, and that was the end of the way she seemed always to start thinking about her father. Maybe it was something that had actually happened, but she couldn't remember that it had happened in just such a way at such a time, and it was more likely that it was only an association of imagery that stood together for the way she had felt about him.

James McAdams, her father, was the only man she ever loved with the simple, asexual love of a child, and all loves that followed were corruptions. When she was fourteen, he died suddenly in an automobile accident, and everyone thought at the time that she was very brave and stoical because she did not cry or display her grief, but the reason she didn't was that she was too numbed by pain and too terrified by the realization that she lived in a world where something like this could happen to someone like him, and collaterally to her. After his burial, while her mother in smart black was receiving the sympathy of relatives and friends in the living room, she locked herself in her own room alone and finally cried bitterly for a long time in the terrible emptiness in which he had left her, and after that she never cried again for any reason, although many things happened to her that were worth crying about.

She knew other men, of course, and as she grew older she knew far too many for her own good, but she never quite knew why she did, or why she kept making the complete concessions that she made, the repeated sacrifice of herself. The truth was, having lost the best man of all, she despised all others. Having given to the best man her best love, she was compelled to give a lesser love to all who followed, and the love she gave, although she would never know it, was a necessary expression of her contempt and despair.

At the age of eighteen, she was sent to a good college for young women in New York. She was already becoming a considerable problem, having acquired a limited notoriety at home, and it was felt that college would give her new interests and a new direction, but it didn't. As a matter of fact, it proved to be an almost intolerable burden, so far as she was concerned, and after completing the first year and slightly more than half the second, she was suspended for failure to make satisfactory marks. Her scholastic failure was genuine enough, but it was also a fortunate convenience for the authorities at the school, for there were other matters for which she could have been suspended or expelled, and it was practically certain the punitive action could not have been avoided much longer.

Home again, she was again a problem. She seemed always to be in a fever of excitement or in a paralysis of depression, and in the fever there were far too many affairs with random men and far too much of the drinking that increased steadily as she grew older, and in the paralysis there was also too much drinking, although she did not then see any men or want to see any. Her mother suggested that she consult a doctor, meaning specifically a psychiatrist, but Charity refused. Three times she considered deliberately what it would be like to die, and what would be the most agreeable way to accomplish death, but she never even came to any conclusion, let alone reaching a point of taking any action, and she wondered afterward if she were actually seriously considering death at all, and if she would not be too great a coward to kill herself for any reason whatever.

Then she met Oliver Alton Farnese. There was a local Farnese, a cousin to Oliver and a relatively poor relation, although he was by local standards affluent enough. Oliver had come from New York on a matter which was a combination family-business deal that was not publicized and not generally known but concerned, in fact, a loan that the local Farnese was trying to secure. Oliver usually had nothing much to do with Farnese business, but in this case, since it was a relatively unimportant matter that concerned a cousin, he was allowed to handle it. It gave him something to do and made him feel useful.

Charity met him at a dinner party to which she went reluctantly with her mother, and three weeks later, two weeks after Farnese had planned to return to New York, she married him quietly in the chapel of the Episcopal church. The marriage was considered by Charity's mother as an incredible stroke of the best possible luck. In a way this was so, for it solved for her a serious problem that she was utterly incapable of solving herself. For Charity it really solved nothing, but she at least thought rationally about it and married Farnese deliberately for two good reasons. In the first place, she thought it would be pleasant to live on Park Avenue in New York City and have all the money she could possibly spend. In the second place, she did not love him in the least and therefore felt no emotional commitment to him. If she had loved him, she wouldn't have married him.

Now she had thought herself from Joe Doyle to James McAdams to Oliver Farnese, and she was in danger of coming around the circle to Joe Doyle again, the same way one came by her theory around the circle from good to bad or bad to good, and what she needed to do and had better do was to think constructively about Oliver, how she could most convincingly tell him all necessary lies when he came home, which would be soon. She looked at the little electric clock beside her bed and saw that it would be, in fact, exactly twenty-five minutes from now, at six o'clock, and she knew this definitely because Oliver always knocked on her door at six o'clock if he did not see her first in some other part of the apartment. Of course, she wasn't always in the apartment at all, when he came home, but she was certain that he knocked on the door of her room those times too, for it was part of his schedule.

She couldn't decide whether to be contrite or casual or physically solicitous, which would require an effort but would possibly divert him, and the more she thought about it, the more difficult it became to decide and the more fearful she became, for she was truly afraid of him and often had to exercise the most rigid control in order to hide it. She remembered then that there was still another Martini left in the shaker, which was just the thing to reduce her problem to the most absurd simplicity, and so she got up and poured the Martini and sat down again and began to drink it, and she immediately decided that she would be casual. Drinking slowly, she began to watch the two hands of the clock move toward six o'clock. She couldn't actually see the hands move at all, but nevertheless they constantly came closer and closer to the formation of a straight angle, and her tension kept increasing with the imperceptible movement of the hands, and this meant, of course, that she would be neither contrite nor casual nor solicitous when the time came, but rather coldly courteous, a form of combined hostility and fear that would not make a bad situation better.

Just before six, the hands almost at the point of their farthest separation, she finished her third Martini and got up and carried the shaker and glass and two bottles into the bathroom and set them in the tub. She wished now that she had dressed instead of remaining naked under a robe, which made her feel somehow more vulnerable, but it was too late now, actually six exactly, and while she looked at the clock and wished she were dressed, at fifteen seconds after the hour, Oliver knocked on the door. She went at once and let him in, and he followed her a few steps into the room and stood watching her as if she were some kind of curiosity that interested him mildly. The thin scar along the mandible was livid.

"How are you, my dear?" he said.

He often called her his dear, and it made her uneasy. A long time ago, when she was a child, she had gone to a movie in which there was an evil duke, something like that, and the duke, for a reason she couldn't remember, had kept his little niece locked in a room in a stone tower of his castle, and every time he went to see her, the first thing he said was, "How are you, my dear?" in just the way that Oliver said it. It was something that had stuck in Charity's mind, and often at night after seeing the movie, she had dreamed that the duke was standing by her bed and smiling and saying, "How are you, my dear?" and she had wakened in terror and lain rigidly without opening her eyes in the fear that the evil duke, if she looked, would actually be there.

"I'm perfectly well, thank you," she said.

"Are you?" he said. "It seems to me that you're looking rather tired."

"No, not at all. I'm feeling perfectly well."

"Did yon have an interesting time last night?"

"Not particularly. It was rather dull, as a matter of fact. I went to a cocktail party at Samantha Cox's in the afternoon and to several places afterward."

"If it was so dull, why didn't you come home?"

"Oh, I don't know. You understand how it is when you get started with something. You simply go on and on for no good reason."

"That's very interesting, my dear. I'm always interested to know why you do things you don't want to do. Tell me about it, please."

"Why I do things?"

"No. What you did last night. The several places you went after Samantha's."

"It's hardly worth while. It was nothing at all that would amuse you."

"Nevertheless, I'd like to hear about it. Especially how it happened that you didn't come home. It's true that you didn't come home, isn't it? I was sure that you weren't in your room when I left this morning."

"Yes, it's true that I didn't come home. I stayed all night with Bernardine Dewitt."

"I see. Was Bernardine with you all evening?"

"Yes. She was at Samantha's, and a group of us went to this Italian restaurant because someone said that the food was exceptionally good, but it didn't particularly appeal to me. As you know, I don't especially care for Italian food."

"That's too bad. I'm sorry you didn't enjoy your dinner. Tell me where you went after the restaurant."

"Well, to all those places down in the Village. We all got to drinking quite a bit and going from one place to another, and I don't remember at all clearly what the places were. After a while, Bernardine began to become ill, which isn't unusual, and wanted to go home, and we took her there. She was in a pretty bad condition, really, and I went up to her apartment with her and put her to bed, and she kept asking me to stay, and so I finally did because there was nothing else I could do as a friend."

"Certainly. I understand that. You are very loyal, my dear, if nothing else."

She thought she detected an inflection in his voice that might have been irony, and she looked at him closely from the corners of her eyes to see if there was any sign of it on his face, but she couldn't see any in his expression, which was attentive and sober, and she began to think that she was going to get away with the lie much more easily than she'd hoped.

"The only thing I don't understand," he said, "is why you didn't call and let me know where you were. It would only have been considerate to have called."

"Well, I didn't think you'd worry, and I'm sorry if you did. I thought you would assume that I was staying all night with someone."

"Quite right. That's exactly what I assumed."

"It's all right, then, I wouldn't have wanted you to worry."

"Thank you, my dear. You're very kind. You can't imagine how relieved I am to know that it was Bernardine you spent the night with, for I had the idea it was a cheap little piano player named Joe Doyle."

He said it so quietly that she didn't for a second quite grasp the significance of what he'd said, and then, when she did, she felt instantly and terribly sick to the stomach and in imminent danger of losing her Martinis. She understood that she wasn't going to get away with the lie so easily as she'd begun to think, that she wasn't, in fact, going to get away with it at all, but she couldn't see how Oliver could possibly know already about Joe Doyle. Although it was plainly futile to adhere to the story about staying with Bernardine, it was just as futile to try now to make up another one that would be any better, and what she would have to do would be to take a position of being maliciously persecuted and decline to explain anything whatever.

"I don't know what you mean," she said.

"Of course you do, my dear. I mean that you are, besides other things, a pathological liar."

"Well, I can see that you are angry and determined to accuse me of all sorts of things that aren't true, and I don't believe I feel like listening to it."

"Oh, come, my dear. It's time we were honest with each other. Shall I tell you exactly what you did last night? You went, as you said, to the Italian restaurant, and then you went, as you also said, to several places in the

Village. After that, however, you deviated slightly from the truth. Instead of going to Bernardine's you went off with Milton Crawford to a nightclub in the vicinity of Sheridan Square. You left that place alone and walked down the street to another place named Duo's, and it was there that you picked up the piano player—and I want to compliment you on your good taste and discrimination in picking the piano player instead of the bartender or the porter. Eventually, omitting the details, you went with him to his room or apartment in a residence south of Washington Square, and you stayed there with him for the rest of the night. What did you do while you were there, my dear? Please tell me what you and the piano player did to amuse yourselves."

"I've already told you where I went and what I did, and it's obvious that you have decided not to believe that or anything else I may say, so I don't care to talk about it."

She kept watching him from the corners of her eyes, her fear of him assuming a kind of supernatural quality, for she felt that he must surely be at least a minor malignant deity who was capable of knowing by extrasensory perception everything she did and thought, and every place she went. He was still looking at her as if she were a curiosity, and his voice had not raised or shaken while he was telling her about last night and Joe Doyle, but the thin scar was now dead white against his skin, and there was a bright sheen to his eyes that made him appear to be blind. She knew that he was certainly furious, but she was suddenly aware that he was also feeling something besides fury, a violent ambivalence of some sort, and then immediately she realized what it was he was feeling. He was looking at her and thinking about what he had just asked, what she and Joe Doyle had done together in the room in the house just south of Washington Square, and he was by his thinking excited carnally. Knowing this, she had the oddest notion that her robe had simply disintegrated to leave her naked in front of him, and she was ashamed of her nakedness, which was something she had not been for a long time.

"Surely you'll tell me," he said. "Remember that I'm your husband, my dear. Don't you think that I have earned your confidence?"

She merely shook her head, not answering, and he walked across to her slowly, and she thought with a queer kind of detachment that the sheen of blindness on his eyes was very much like the shimmering intense heat on the surface of the streets on a blistering day.

"Did you do this?" he said. "And this? And this?"

She had not dreamed his hands could be so compelling and strong, nor that they could draw from her imperiously what she did not wish to give, and afterward, long after he was gone, she lay exhausted and immobile in her shame.

CHAPTER 9

She lay and listened and heard Oliver leave at seven. She concentrated for a few minutes on remembering what day it was and what Oliver regularly did in the evening of that day, and pretty soon she remembered that it was the day when he had dinner at his club and played bridge afterward. He would be home again not earlier than ten-thirty and not later than eleven.

A few minutes after Oliver had gone, Edith knocked on the door and asked through it if Madam was dining in, and Charity replied that she was not dining in or out or anywhere, not dining at all, and Edith said, "Very well, Madam," and went off. After that, Charity began to think about how much she hated Edith and to wonder what she could possibly do to make Edith suffer in some way, but there didn't seem to be anything possible that wouldn't take far too much effort.

Thinking of Edith made her feel hot and angry, and feeling hot and angry made her feel thirsty. She wanted another Martini, which surely wouldn't hurt her, and so she got up and went into the bathroom and got the bottles and shaker out of the tub and carried them into the bedroom and set them on the table beside her bed. She had no ice, however, and if she didn't want to drink her Martini warm, which she didn't, it would be necessary to go again to the kitchen for ice. She stood looking at the bottles and shaker, considering the problem, and she decided that it was just as well that she had to go to the kitchen anyhow, for she was simply going to have to eat something, in spite of what she'd told Edith, if she expected to continue having Martinis without unfortunate results, or results even more unfortunate than she frequently had.

Carrying the shaker, she went to the kitchen softly, without encountering Edith. She set the shaker on a table and opened the refrigerator, but there wasn't a thing to eat there that appealed to her, and after considering several things and rejecting them, she got some ice and put it in the shaker and closed the refrigerator door. What she wanted, she thought, was something quite salty. Not caviar; caviar was salty enough, but she didn't much care for it otherwise. Something more like anchovies was what she wanted. Yes, anchovies were just right. They were extremely salty and had, unlike caviar, no objectionable quality besides.

She found a can of anchovies and opened it with difficulty and put the anchovies on a small plate. Then she found a box of cocktail crackers and put several of them on the small plate beside the anchovies. Carrying the shaker in one hand and the plate in the other, she returned to her room, still without encountering Edith. There, she ate one of the anchovies on one of the crackers and then mixed three more Martinis in the shaker and poured one of them into her glass.

This is all, she thought. This is absolutely all. I'll drink these three Martinis slowly during the entire evening, and when they're gone I'll not drink another single one, not even a very last one the last thing before sleeping.

She sipped the first one while she ate all the salty anchovies on the little crackers, after which she began a difficult period of resolutely refusing to drink the second one too soon. Refusing would have been much easier if only she had had something to do to occupy her mind and time, but there wasn't anything she wanted to do, and as a matter of fact almost everything she thought of was something she positively didn't want to do. Television was depressing, and listening to hi-fi would have necessitated leaving her own room, and reading was something she hadn't done for such a long time that it didn't really occur to her as a serious possibility. One of her big problems was occupying her mind and time when she didn't have anywhere to go. Once she had thought that she would occupy herself at such times by writing down her personal story, but she had learned in thinking about it that there was hardly a thing she had ever done for which she could give a credible reason, and it would be incredible to write about herself doing all those things for no reasons at all.

She wished she could dress and go out, but she didn't think it would be wise in the situation that had developed. Not that she was given to doing what was wise in most situations, but sometimes, as now, she was compelled to do what would have been wise if she had done it a little sooner. Anyhow, though she couldn't go, she could at least think about where she would go if it were possible, and the moment she began to think along this line, the place she wanted to go was Duo's, and the reason she wanted to go there was to see Joe Doyle. It had been about twenty hours since she had first seen him, and only about eight since she had last seen him, and now she actually wanted to see him again already, instead of never wanting to see him again, as was usual regarding men in such cases, and this was disturbing. Especially in the situation as it had developed.

How had Oliver learned about last night? And how long, if there were to be another night, would it take him to learn about it too? Her rational mind insisted that he had been informed by a spy, either a hired professional or someone who had seen her and followed her and told Oliver out of pure malice, but she couldn't lose the irrational feeling that there was something super-normal about it, the employment by him of some frightening ability to know things that an ordinary person couldn't possibly know. More disturbing still, now that his information had been secured by whatever means, how many other instances did he know about? How many times, when she had thought him deceived, had he known everything all along? And why had be never before said anything or done anything to her directly?

This line of thinking took her inevitably to the men who had been mysteriously beaten, which was a direction she didn't want to go, and she decided that enough time had lapsed since the last Martini to justify another. She poured it and drank half of it too fast and went on wanting to see Joe Doyle. She didn't want to want to, for she didn't want, incidentally, to get him into trouble and herself into more trouble than she was already in, but the knowledge that it was perilous and unwise to see him again actually made her desire it all the more. Finishing more slowly the second half of the second Martini, she began to see him again with remarkable clarity as she had seen him in various situations from the beginning to the end of their experience, and she was just counting his true ribs when Edith interrupted by knocking on the door.

She wished Edith would go away, and she remained silent in the hope that Edith would, but after a few moments Edith knocked again and called through the door, and Charity went across to the door and opened it. Edith was standing with the expression on her face that managed to be poisonously insulting by being so carefully courteous, and the instant Charity saw her, she began to feel angry and compelled to say something that would make a scene.

"What do you want?" she said.

"Do you have any further use for me, Madam?" Edith said. "If not, I'd like to retire."

"Certainly I have no further use for you, Edith," Charity said. "Surely it's always been perfectly clear that I've never had any use whatever for you at any time."

"Yes, Madam. I understand."

"Furthermore, now that you've brought it up, Edith, why is it that you always retire and never simply go to bed? What, precisely, is the difference between retiring and going to bed? Is there something vulgar in going to bed, Edith? Is it somehow more proper to retire?"

"I'm sorry, Madam. I didn't mean to offend you. May I go to bed?"

"No. I think you'd better retire, after all. Now that you've said it, I can see that going to bed doesn't suit you in the least. I am more the type who goes to bed. Isn't that so, Edith?"

"If you say so, Madam."

"Yes. I was sure you'd agree with me. I simply can't imagine your going to bed, no matter how hard I try, but you, on the other hand, certainly have no difficulty in imagining it of me."

"I have never thought about it at all, Madam."

"Oh, nonsense, Edith. There's no use in trying to be deceitful. You not only have thought of it, but have made innumerable points of suggesting it to my husband. Isn't it true that you discuss such matters with my husband?"

"No, Madam."

"Well, you're a dreadful liar, of course, and I didn't expect you to admit it. Tell me, Edith, how long has my husband been having me followed?"

"I don't know what you mean, Madam."

"Of course you know what I mean. I have no doubt at all that you are somehow mixed up in it."

"I never discuss your personal affairs with your husband, Madam."

"Really? That's very honorable of you, Edith. I'm convinced that you're the most honorable spy and liar and bitch alive."

"Thank you, Madam."

"Not at all. I'm very happy to tell you."

"May I retire now, Madam?"

"Certainly. Retire, Edith. Please do. Perhaps you will never wake up."

Well, she had made another scene, as she had known she would, but this time she did not feel bad about it, not at all ashamed and degraded, and as a matter of fact she felt rather exhilarated. Closing the door, she went back and stood looking at the shaker. She wished that there were something left in it, or at least that she had not resolved to mix no more Martinis tonight, not even a last one before sleeping. It disturbed her when she broke resolutions almost immediately after making them, which she almost always did, and now she tried to think back to what the resolution had been exactly, if it had not possibly been just a random thought instead of a genuine resolution, and while she was thinking she mixed a last, large Martini just in case she was enabled to drink it by finding a loophole in the resolution. The resolution seemed to be impregnable, however, and so she finally acknowledged that she had trapped herself in another unpleasant commitment and would have to avoid it simply by ignoring it. Pouring what she could of the large Martini into her glass, she left the glass sitting on the table beside her bed while she took off her robe and turned out the lights, and then she sat down and picked up the glass and emptied it slowly and lay back on the bed and tried to go to sleep.

Sleeping was always made difficult by thinking. She had often tried to discover a way of making her mind a perfect blank, and she had been told once by a strange little man at a cocktail party that this was actually possible if you could only learn the trick, but he had been unable to tell her how to learn it, although he claimed to know it himself, and she had had no success in discovering it by her own methods or in finding anyone else who knew it and could explain it more clearly than the strange little man. Another thing she had tried was thinking only of pleasant things, and once in a while she was able to accomplish this, but unfortunately thinking was a matter of association, and every pleasant thing she could think of was associated in some way with unpleasant things, or was both pleasant and unpleasant in itself.

Tonight she tried to think of her father, which was something wholly pleasant, except when it came to the time when he had died, and then, to avoid most of everything that had happened since his dying, she jumped all the way in her mind to Joe Doyle, and she still wanted to see him and be with him again, but she couldn't think of him without thinking of Oliver in association, and that was bad. She tried, however, she lay quietly trying for more than an hour before she finally decided that she would absolutely have to have two or three sleeping pills after all. But while she was getting up to go after the pills, she remembered the part of the large Martini that hadn't fitted into the glass, and she thought that maybe it would be just the right amount more to get her to sleep with the soporifics.

She poured it and drank it and tried the sleeping again for a whole half hour, but it was no use. This time she got the pills from the bathroom and swallowed them on top of the Martinis, and eventually, because of one or the other or both, she went to sleep and slept fairly well until after noon of the next day.

She thought instantly of Joe Doyle. His name and image were waiting patiently in her mind for the return of her consciousness, as one might wait all night in a dark room for the coming of light, and it seemed only last night that she had been with him, instead of the night before, as if the time between had never been, although the things that had happened were remembered and real. Considering all the gin and soporifics, she felt remarkably good. She even felt moderately hungry and capable of thinking seriously of food, and she decided that she would dress and go out somewhere for lunch.

She went into the bathroom and bathed and returned to the bedroom and dressed, and then, as she brushed her hair and fixed her face, she tried to decide if it would be a good idea to find someone to go to lunch with, but she came to the conclusion that it wouldn't. It would be too much trouble and take too much time, and it might interfere with what she had better do afterward, which was to go to Bernardine DeWitt's apartment on MacDougal Street and tell her that it would be unnecessary, after all, to lie about the night before last, which seemed like last night. Having arranged these details, she finished her face and called the garage on the telephone.

"This is Mrs. Oliver Alton Farnese," she said crisply. "Have my car brought around immediately. The Jaguar, please."

After saying this, she wondered if the Jaguar was the car she had recently left somewhere that she couldn't recall, but apparently it either wasn't
or had been returned by someone, for the attendant in the garage said he
would have it taken around right away, and when she got downstairs it
was waiting for her. She drove to a restaurant on Fifth Avenue and had
most of a large salad for lunch, and it wasn't until after she had finished
eating that she had a Martini. This was not a record or anything like that,
but at least it was unusual and indicated that this might turn out to be one
of her moderate days. She didn't make any resolution concerning it, however.

After drinking the Martini, she left the restaurant and drove to
Bernardine's on MacDougal Street, and the day began at once to be less
moderate than she had thought it might. It was about three o'clock when
she got there, and several people were drinking cocktails and talking in
groups of two or three about various things, and it had the feel to Charity
of something that had just begun and would go on for a long time and
become quite a lot bigger. Bernardine was being vivacious with a blond
young man with an incredibly perfect profile, and she smiled across the
room at Charity and lifted a hand with a glass in it, and Charity went to
find a glass of her own, which she found on a tray in the hands of a maid.
What she intended to do was have one cocktail, or possibly two, and talk
with Bernardine and go home, and so, with this intention in mind, she
went over to where Bernardine was talking vivaciously to the profile, and
it was apparent that Bernardine didn't particularly like it.

"Hello, darling," Bernardine said. "Do you know Perry Humferdill? I've
only just met him myself, to tell the truth. Someone brought him. Perry,
this is Charity Farnese."

Perry Humferdill took Charity's free hand and held it and exposed a
great many teeth that had the perfection of plates. The day had obviously
not been moderate in his case for several hours at least. His full face was-
n't as good as his profile, but it was superior, nevertheless, if you cared for
beautiful men, which Charity didn't especially, unless they were beautiful
by being exceptionally ugly.

"Really?" she said. "Is your name really Humferdill?"

He released her hand and covered his teeth.

"Yes," he said. "Perry Humferdill. From Dallas."

"Well," she said. "Imagine."

"Never mind Charity," Bernardine said. "She is almost always insulting
until after the third or fourth Martini, and then it's simply amazing how
friendly she becomes with almost anyone. Darling, have you taken any
more piano lessons lately?"

"No," Charity said. "I've decided to give up the piano, as a matter of fact, and I merely dropped in to tell you that it won't be necessary for you to do what we arranged yesterday. I didn't know, of course, that you were having a party."

"Well, I didn't know it myself, actually, but it seems that I am. It's just something that got started as a result of several people coming at almost the same time, and apparently they have been calling other people, who will also call other people, and I'm sure there's no way in the world to stop it even if I wanted to."

"I know. It's remarkable how something can simply get started and keep going and going. It's happened to me a number of times. I'm sure it will be a very good party, anyhow, and I wish I could stay, but I can't. I'll just have one more Martini, if you don't mind, before I go."

Bernardine said she didn't mind, and Charity smiled at Perry Humferdill from Dallas as if she didn't quite believe in either one, and Perry Humferdill uncovered his teeth again and said that it had been a pleasure meeting her, which she knew wasn't true. Moving away, Charity was still feeling fairly resolute and still intended to leave after one more Martini, but the party was growing quite rapidly, and she kept meeting someone else she knew with whom she was compelled to have a cocktail out of politeness, and somehow or other it got to be six o'clock in the sudden way that time has, and at six o'clock she saw Milton Crawford, who had not yet seen her and who was certain to be sullen and difficult about her having deserted him. She didn't feel like making up any lies to explain why she had done it, and so she decided that she had definitely better leave, but it was a little too late and far too early to return home.

She began to think of other places to go, and all the time she knew perfectly well that the only place she wanted to go and was certainly going was the little bar near Sheridan Square in which Joe Doyle played the piano.

CHAPTER 10

Charity crawled onto a stool in the bar near Sheridan Square.

"Well," said Yancy, the superior bartender.

"You remember me," she said, and smiled with delight. "I was afraid you wouldn't."

"Oh, I remember you, all right," Yancy said.

"You can't imagine how pleased I am. Do you customarily remember all your customers?"

"Just the opposite, as a matter of fact. I customarily forget them."

"Really? That makes me rather special, doesn't it?"

"Special's the word, lady."

"Well, as you know, I have great respect for your opinion, and I'm extremely flattered that you think so. Would you be willing to tell me why you have remembered me instead of forgetting me in the customary way?"

"I just told you, lady. You're special."

"How special?"

"You're rich and beautiful."

"Is that special? Surely lots of women are rich and beautiful."

"Not in this place. Sometimes we get beautiful ones, and now and then we get rich ones, but hardly ever anyone who's both."

"Nevertheless, I'm not so flattered as I was. I was hoping for something quite a lot more special than merely being rich and beautiful."

"I can mention other things, if you insist."

"I do. I insist that you mention them."

"Well, let's put it this way, lady. You're nuts. You wander around in blackouts and don't remember where you've been or how you got where you are."

"That's better. Much better. Now you are really getting into the special things."

"Did you have another blackout today?"

"No. Not at all. I went to an unexpected party and had a few Martinis, but not nearly enough to cause a blackout." She pushed at her hair on the heavy side and looked up at him through her lashes. "I've been rather moderate, to tell the truth. You can see that for yourself. You can see that I've been here for several minutes already and haven't even asked for a drink."

"I admit that it struck me. Congratulations on your moderation."

She laughed, bringing her hands together above the bar. "I like that! Congratulations on your moderation. There's a kind of swing to it.

However, now that a drink has been mentioned, I believe I'd like to have one. Do you think having one would be immoderate?"

"Not unless it led to too many more."

"Well, it probably will; unfortunately, that seems to be what happens practically every time. At this party I went to unexpectedly this afternoon, for instance, I was determined to have two Martinis before leaving, but I kept meeting people who brought me more, and I was compelled to drink them out of politeness, naturally."

"Naturally."

She looked at him sharply past the edge of the heavy hair. "Did you say that sarcastically?"

"Not I, lady. I was only being agreeable."

"Yes. Of course you were. You're a superior, agreeable bartender, and I admire you very much. I apologize for my suspicions."

"It's all right, lady. No apologies necessary."

"Looking back, I confess that I wasn't quite so moderate as I thought I was."

"Well, what's moderate for one isn't for another."

"That's true. You're exactly right. I have quite a capacity for drinking Martinis, and I'm positive it would do me no harm to have another now."

"Sure, lady. Very dry."

He mixed it and poured it and went away to wait on another customer who had arrived a minute or two before. The new customer was a grossly fat and ugly man with a scarred hairless scalp. He ordered a beer and sat looking into it with a slack, transported expression, as if he saw in the brew a vision of another place—a white sand beach, perhaps, in a far, hot country. Yancy, after drawing the beer and ringing up the price, returned to Charity. She had drunk half the Martini and was waiting to mention something she had just thought of and was concentrating on until it could be mentioned.

"Why did you ask me if I'd had another blackout?" she said.

"Because you came back here. I thought maybe you repeated yourself in them."

"Oh. I see. I don't, however. I never do exactly the same thing over. I'm perfectly aware of where I've been and how I got where I am now and why I came from there to here." She revolved half around on the stool, looked down the room, revolved back. "Where's that beautiful Joe Doyle who plays the piano?"

"He's not here,"

"I can see that he's not here. That's apparent. I want to know where he is, not where he's not."

"He's home, I guess. That's where he's supposed to be, anyhow."

"Will he be here later?"

"No."

"Why not? Is it his night off or something?"

"He's sick."

"Sick? What do you mean, sick? I wish you wouldn't just answer each question one at a time. Can't you simply tell me everything at once?"

"He's sick, lady. A real sick guy. I told you that before. He was here last night, playing piano to Chester Lewis's drum as usual, and about eleven, a little after, he fainted. Went out like a light and fell over on the keys."

"Is this true? Are you only trying to make me feel bad?"

"I've got no reason to want to make you feel bad."

"That's right. You haven't. And even if you had, you probably wouldn't do it. Do you think it was a heart attack?"

"No. I don't think so. He just fainted."

"Isn't it rather odd and unusual for a man to faint? What do you think could have caused it?"

"Joe's a guy who doesn't give himself much chance, lady. He doesn't eat right or sleep right or do anything right that he can do wrong. He oughtn't even be playing a lousy piano in a joint like this."

"Perhaps he needs someone with him."

"He's getting along all right. I went to see him this morning, and he was all right. He needs to eat and sleep a little, that's all."

"Just the same, I think I had better go and see him. Don't you think it would be a good idea if I went?"

"No. I think it would be a good idea if you let him alone."

"Why?"

"Because he's already got all the trouble he needs."

"Do you think I want to bring him trouble?"

"What you want is something I couldn't begin to guess, lady, but what you'll do is something else entirely. You remember what I said when you walked in here out of a black fog night before last? I said you looked like a Martini and smelled like a Martini, and I was mostly just joking, but there was something else you looked and smelled like, and I'll tell you what it was, and this time I won't be joking at all. You looked and smelled like trouble, lady. Bad trouble. Joe's got all he needs without you bringing him any more, and you ought to leave him alone,"

"Why are you talking to me this way? I thought we were becoming good friends, and now you are saying these cruel things to me."

"We can't be friends, lady. Not you and me. You're one thing, and I'm another, and that's the way it is. I mix you Martinis, and you pay me for them and drink them, and we talk a little and maybe kid each other a little, but that's all there is, there isn't any more. Maybe you think it's different with Joe, and maybe it really looks a little different on the surface, but underneath it's the same with you and him as it is with you and me. You make a little of what passes for love, and you think what a big difference that is, but there's no difference, not really, and all he's really done is mix you another Martini."

"I don't believe I want to sit here and listen to you say such things," she said.

"I don't blame you, lady, and I'm sorry I had to say them."

"Do you want me to leave?"

"You can stay as long as you like, and you can leave when you want."

"I don't suppose, under the circumstances, that you'd care to mix me another Martini."

"It's my business to mix Martinis for anyone who wants them. You're no exception."

"Very well. I'll have another."

When it was in her glass, she drank it slowly, finishing it in silence. Then she pushed the glass away with the tips of her fingers and stood up.

"It's apparent that you dislike me," she said, "and I'd better go."

"I don't dislike you, lady. Just the contrary."

"In spite of what you said?"

"In spite of it."

"Perhaps you didn't really mean it"

"I meant it. Every word."

"In that case, I must go even if you don't dislike me and want me to."

"If you're going to see Joe, I might as well tell you where he lives. It won't make any difference as far as he's concerned, and it'll save you some time."

"You're very kind, I'm sure, but it isn't necessary for you to tell me. I've been there before."

"I thought you probably had," he said.

She went out and got into the Jaguar and drove toward Washington Square, toward the house in which Joe Doyle lived, and she had no difficulty at all in reaching it, in spite of her condition now and the condition she had been in the first time she had gone there. Her assurance was rather astonishing, everything considered, and she even remembered exactly the floor and exactly the door, and she knocked on the latter without the least thought of being mistaken, and she wasn't. Joe Doyle opened the door and looked at her across the threshold, and whatever surprise he may have felt, he didn't show.

"Why are you up?" she said. "You're supposed to be in bed."

He grinned wryly. "Ever since yesterday morning? I've been up twice since then."

"I didn't mean that. I mean because you're sick. I went to the place you work, and the bartender told me you fainted last night and were home sick."

"Yancy likes to talk. It gets to be a habit with bartenders."

"He likes you and worries about you. I can tell. He dislikes me, but he likes you very much."

"Don't let Yancy fool you. It's just a professional attitude."

"No. It's true. He said you don't eat right or sleep right or do anything right that you can do wrong."

"All right, all right. Never mind Yancy. What are you doing here?"

"That's surely obvious. I've come to see you."

"Visiting the sick?"

"As it turns out, I am, but I'd have come to see you anyhow."

"What do you want?"

"First of all, I want to come in. Don't you know it's very rude to keep someone standing so long outside your door?"

"I don't think you'd better."

"Come in?"

"Yes."

"Why?"

"I just think it would be better if you didn't."

"Will you kindly tell me what's wrong with me? Everywhere I go, everyone wants me to go away again."

"I didn't say I want you to. I said it would be better if you did."

"Oh. I see that I misunderstood. Well, now that you've explained it, I'd still be happy to come in, if you'd only ask me."

"All right. Come in."

He stepped aside, and she walked past him into the room with a warm feeling of familiarity with it and all its contents, and this was pleasant and rather unusual, for often when she walked into most rooms, even rooms she'd been in many times or even lived in, she had a feeling of being a stranger who had never been there before. Turning, she looked at Joe Doyle, and the light was now fully on his face, which had not been so when he was standing in the doorway, and she saw that he did look sick, exhausted, the flesh drawn in his face and making him appear not so much an older man as a young man who looked older than he ought to look.

"You need someone to take care of you," she said.

"Look," he said, "I appreciate your concern and all that, but you're giving too much credence to Yancy's talk."

"Its not that. It's the way you look. It makes me want to cry. Do you know that it's been a very long time since I've wanted to cry?"

"I'm all right. All I need is a little rest."

But he was not all right, and he needed far more than a little rest. What be needed was something that neither she nor anyone else could ever give him. Turning she crossed to a worn sofa and sat down at one end, right against the arm, and looked gravely at a bright framed splash of hot color that might have been a copy of a Gauguin.

"What was it you were playing on the phonograph?" she said. "You remember. Over and over when I was here before."

"I don't know. Why?"

"I want you to play it again."

"I'd play it if I could remember. Maybe you could hum a little of it."

"All right. I'll try."

She hummed a little, softly and off-key, still looking at what was probably a Gauguin copy, and he listened, watching her and smiling and wanting suddenly to laugh.

"That's enough," he said. "See if this is it."

He went to the phonograph and put on a record and started it spinning. After the first few bars of music, she nodded and looked from the Gauguin copy to him.

"That's it," she said, "Now come and lie down and put your head in my lap. Please do."

She had about her the compelling quality of an earnest child. It would have been no more than perversity, he thought, to refuse what she asked. He lay down on his back on the sofa with his head in her lap, and she began to rub his forehead lightly with the tips of her fingers, and. she felt then, for a few minutes, closer than she had felt in a decade to the girl in the vision of the street and the father, closer than she would ever feel again.

"Are you happy that I've come back?" she said.

"I don't know. I think so."

"It's quite remarkable that I have. Usually I never want to be with a man a second time."

"Why with me?"

"I'm not sure. I don't believe it's wise to try to diagnose something like that, as if it were a case of something. I only knew I wanted to be with you a second time, and I know now that I'll want to be with you a third time, and every time I'm with you from now on I'll be thinking about being with you next time."

"You think so?"

"It's true. You'll see."

"You have a husband. Have you forgotten? Husbands complicate matters."

"How do you know I have a husband? I don't recall mentioning him."

"You didn't. Maybe it's just because your not having one would be better luck than I'm likely to have."

"Well, you mustn't let it make you feel bad. I'll simply have to arrange things."

"Is it so simple?"

"Not actually. Sometimes it may be quite difficult, but I'm prepared to do it. I'm quite clever when I need to be. You'll see."

"All right. I'll believe it for the present."

"That's fair. It's only necessary to believe it each time for as long as the time lasts. Now it's this time, and we believe it, and it's all right. Everything's all right."

"How about between times? Between times I probably won't believe it at all."

"You'll have to try. After a while you'll begin to believe it even between times. Tell me. Were you angry when you woke up and found me gone?"

"No."

"Why not? You'd have been justified. It was really rather rude of me to go away without a word."

"I wasn't asleep."

"Oh, now. Of course you were asleep. I looked at you carefully several times. I even counted your ribs."

"I was awake. Even before you got up."

"If you were awake, tell me what I did."

"When I first saw you, you seemed to be pointing toward Mecca."

"What?"

"You know. The way Mohammedans pray. On their knees and bending way over."

"Oh. Is that when you wakened? I must have looked perfectly ludicrous."

"No. Curiously charming. What were you really doing, by the way? I've been wondering."

"I was trying to read the time on your wrist watch."

He began to laugh softly, and she continued to rub his forehead and waited for him to stop.

"Is it so funny?" she said.

"Yes."

"But charming?"

"Yes."

"That's good, then. Do you know what I'd like to know?"

"No."

"I'd like to know all about you as a boy. Where you lived and what you did and all about everything."

"I was a very dull boy. It was dull where I lived."

"I can't believe it."

"Take my word for it. I'd rather talk about you."

"Oh, no. I don't even like to think about me, let alone talk. It's too depressing."

"Tell me about your husband."

"That would be even more depressing."

"Is he rich?"

"Yes. He's very rich."

"Is that why you married him?"

"That's one reason."

"What others?"

"Nothing important. It was a kind of convenience. It solved a few problems for some people."

"Including you?"

"Well, it's very nice to have lots of money. I don't think I'd care to live without lots of money."

"I see your point of view. Not having lots of money is a problem that's worth solving, even by marriage."

She sat quietly, stroking his forehead and looking from his face to the Gauguin copy and back again, listening to the music with a feeling that was like the one she used to have when she listened as a girl in summer evenings to the music of countless cicadas.

"I'm sorry that I won't be able to stay all night," she said.

"That's all right. You needn't apologize."

"It wasn't au apology. It was a regret. I want to stay, but I can't."

"I understand. Even a marriage of convenience requires certain concessions."

"Are you being bitter about it?"

"No. Why should I? It's none of my business."

"Do you suppose if we had met years ago that we'd have fallen in love and been married?"

"No."

"Why not?"

"Because I didn't have any money then and have never had any since."

"That would have been a handicap. I admit it. At least, however, we might have fallen in love. Falling in love doesn't require any money."

"It requires money to make it last."

"I suppose you're right. Yes, I'm certain that you are. I have lots of money, though, so it's no particular problem for us."

"That's a nice way to look at it. Very generous. Is it your money or your husband's?"

"Well, it's his, actually, but I'm permitted to use all of it that I want."

"Even on another man?"

"I'm not asked to submit a statement of expenses. It isn't necessary for him to know how I spend the money."

"I see. He seems to be quite liberal, to say the least. Maybe he doesn't deserve to be deceived."

"No, no. You don't understand at all. It's impossible to think of Oliver as being liberal. It's just that he's always had so much money that he's never learned to consider it important."

"I doubt that I'd ever be able to understand that."

"Yes. That's so. It's possible only to people who have always been rich."

"Anyhow, the money aside, he must be liberal regarding you in other respects. What I mean is, you seem to do a lot of moving around on your own. Aren't you ever required to account for your time?"

The conversation had now become suddenly threatening, and she wished that he had not asked the last question. It compelled her to think of how Oliver had known last night precisely where she had been the night before, and to wonder if he would know tomorrow where she was tonight. This was something she did not wish to think of, and she refused to believe, in spite of what she had thought, or said to Edith, that he was having her followed or possessed supernatural powers to know what it was clearly impossible for him to know normally. It was much more likely that he had learned what he knew by accident. Yes, that was almost certainly it. Someone had seen her and followed her, someone she knew who did not like her and wished her harm. This person, whoever he was, had told on her to Oliver out of pure malice, and the more she thought about it, the more she became convinced that it was probably Milton Crawford, for it was just the sort of mean trick Milton would be capable of playing when his vanity was hurt. Of course. It became clearer and clearer as one thought about it. Milton had seen her leaving the place they had been, and he'd followed her and told on her. It might seem rather incredible that anyone would go to all that degrading trouble just to play a mean trick, but not if you knew Milton, and she was convinced, because she wanted to be, that this was the explanation for everything.

"Well," she said, "he frequently asks me where I've been and what I've been doing, but I'm always able to explain things satisfactorily."

"You mean that you're an accomplished liar."

"I don't think it's fair to put it that way. I'm only doing good to everyone concerned by not telling things that would get everyone disturbed and cause a lot of unnecessary trouble."

He closed his eyes. The tips of her fingers worked a kind of cool, dry magic.

"Oh, Jesus," he said.

"What? Why did you say that?"

"Never mind. I'm just wondering if you're sublimely rational or completely in left field."

"I'm sure I don't know what you mean, and I don't think I care to. What I think is, we're wasting too much time in talking about depressing things. As I said, I can only stay for a while, perhaps until eleven or twelve, and I'd like to talk about something cheerful or nothing at all."

"All right. What shall we talk about?"

"I'd like to talk about what we'll do tomorrow, and I've already decided what it will be."

"Is that so? Tell me."

"I've decided that we will drive out on Long Island in my Jaguar. It's plain that getting out of the city would be very good for you, and it's fun to drive out somewhere in a Jaguar. Have you ever done it?"

"I've never owned a Jaguar."

"You'll love driving out on Long Island in one. Wait and see."

"What if I were to decide that I don't want to drive out on Long Island in a Jaguar?"

"Are you serious?"

"No."

"You'll go?"

"Yes."

"Good. That's settled, then. I've also got an idea about what we might do the weekend. Would you like me to tell you?"

"Yes, I would."

"Well, I have a friend who has a house in Connecticut, and I'm sure it would be all right with her if we went up there and used it. Have you been in Connecticut?"

"Probably not to the same places in Connecticut that you've been."

"Oh, Connecticut isn't very big. You can hardly go there at all without going practically everywhere."

He began to laugh again very softly, scarcely audibly, stopping after a minute or two with a strangled sound in his throat.

"Why are you laughing again?" she said.

"I don't know. I have a feeling that I shouldn't be laughing at all."

"Will you go to Connecticut with me?"

"Can you explain a weekend to your husband?"

"I'll think of something. Probably this friend who owns the house will be willing to say she wants me to go up with her. Will you go?"

"I have an idea that I will."

"That's sensible. Do you see how good I am for you? The bartender where you work said I would be bad for you, but you can see that it isn't so. Already you're laughing and looking forward to doing things."

"I told you about Yancy. He worries too much."

"That's true. He means well, but he worries too much. What time is it?"

He lifted his left arm so that he could see the watch on his wrist.

"Almost nine-thirty. Why?"

"I was wondering how much time was left before eleven or twelve. I'm sure I can safely stay till twelve. It's becoming rather tiring, sitting here this way, however. I think it would he more comfortable for both of us if we moved over to the bed."

There was no denying the validity of this, and so they moved, but after a while they went to sleep while the music on the record kept repeating itself, and it was after one when she wakened and went away.

CHAPTER 11

Thursday on Long Island was wonderful, a fine day, and they drove from Jamaica to the North Shore and all the way along the North Shore to Orient Point, where they had a very interesting time in a secluded place, and the next day, Friday afternoon, they drove northeast into Fairfield County, Connecticut. They went directly to the Early American house of Charity's friend, which had been arranged for, and they were alone there that night and the day after, and in the evening of the day after, which was Saturday, they lay side by side on a pair of chaises longues on a terrace and felt domestic, as if Joe had just a little while ago got off the 6:02 from the city. From where they were on the terrace, they could see across quite a lot of grass to a bluestone drive that ran down to the road through a split-rail fence with a hitching post beside it. The split-rail fence didn't keep anything in or out, and nothing was ever hitched to the hitching post, but they were pretty and effective and were something nice to look at in the cool evening.

"Exurbia," Joe said.

'What?" Charity said.

"I said Exurbia. You know. A place beyond Suburbia where people live."

"Oh. Like in the book, you mean. I didn't read it, because I hardly ever read anything at all, but I remember people talking about it at cocktail parties and places, and some of them were quite angry. The ones who live here, I guess. My friend, Samantha Cox, who owns this house, said that it presented a very distorted picture of things, but she was forced to admit in fairness that it was very clever. Samantha makes quite a point of being absolutely fair about books."

"Well, I gather that your friend Samantha isn't a real Exurbanite. It was probably easier for her to be fair than it was for some of the others."

"That's true. Samantha only comes out for short periods every once in a while. She really prefers to live in her apartment in town."

"Why does she bother with the house at all, then?"

"It's no particular bother. She has lots of money and can afford it easily, and she feels that it's important to her career."

"Career? Does she have a career?"

"Oh, yes. Didn't I tell you? She's very serious about being a TV actress, but she hasn't had much luck at it yet."

"Sorry. I don't get the connection."

"Lots of important TV people live in Fairfield County. Don't you remember that from the book?"

"Yes, I do, now that you mention it. TV and advertising."

"That's the reason she keeps the house. She has parties sometimes and invites certain people to them."

"I see. Wasn't it fortunate that she hadn't planned a party for this weekend?"

"It was. It was very fortunate."

"How does it happen that you don't have a country house of your own?"

"I don't care for one. I wouldn't want to live here or come here as a regular thing, and I have no other reason like Samantha's to make it worthwhile."

"Wouldn't your husband care to live here either?"

"Oliver? Not at all. Oliver wants to live in the same place all the time and do the same things over and over. He's really quite abnormal about it. He has a kind of schedule that he keeps. That's why it's possible for me to go around different places with little or no interference."

"Even on weekends?"

"Yes. Isn't it convenient?"

"At least. Do you really believe that he's ignorant of what you do?"

"Well, most of it. Anyhow, even when be learns something, it doesn't seem to make much difference in the long run."

"That's convenient, too. Do you think he's learned anything about us?"

"I'd rather not talk about it."

"Why not? Because he has?"

"To tell the truth, someone saw us that first night and told him, and I'm of the opinion that it was Milton Crawford. He's the one I was with when I walked away and blacked out and went to where you were. Milton's just the kind of sneak who would tell on someone if it suited him."

"What did he say?"

"Milton?"

"No. Your husband."

"Nothing much. He was sarcastic and nasty, the way he can be, but now it's over and forgotten."

"Oh, God. Just over and forgotten and nothing more to it."

"I've told you and told you that Oliver's odd. If you knew him, you'd understand. You can't expect him to react to anything the way someone else probably would."

"Thanks for telling me anyhow."

"Are you angry because I didn't tell you sooner?"

"No. I'm not angry."

"I didn't want to worry you, and I was afraid, besides, that you might decide it would be better if we didn't see each other any more."

"I have no doubt at all that it would have been better."

"You see? If I'd told you, you would have refused to see me."

"I don't think so."

"In spite of Oliver's knowing about the first night?"

"In spite of it."

"Why?"

"Because I couldn't have. Because I'm weak or strong or don't care. Because I've wanted you constantly almost the whole week I've known you."

"Isn't it marvelous, the way it's lasted? I've wanted you all the time, too, and as far as I'm concerned it's very unusual. I'd not have thought in the beginning that it was possible. Do you think it will go on and on until we die?"

"For me or for you?"

"For both."

"No."

"For either?"

"Not for you."

"For you?"

"Possibly. It won't have as far to go in my case, you see, which makes a difference."

"Don't talk like that. You know very well that it makes me sad. Anyhow, it has lasted this long and is still lasting, and I don't want to talk about it, or my husband, or anything depressing and unpleasant like that."

He turned his head to look at her and saw that she had been looking at him all along. Reaching for his near hand, she smiled the smile that was somehow sad even when she was relatively happy. She was wearing a white blouse and short white shorts, even though it was quite cool now in the evening, and her skin was smoothly golden all over, where it showed and didn't show, for the color had been acquired by lamps in privacy and not by the sun, which she didn't particularly like and generally avoided.

"What do you think it would be amusing to do tonight?" she said.

"Honestly?"

"Of course honestly."

"What we did last night."

"Well, naturally. That's assumed. I meant *besides* that."

"Nothing especially. Do you have an idea?"

"There are always lots of parties around different places on Saturday night. It's true that we haven't been invited to any, since no one knows we're here, but we could undoubtedly find one where we would be welcome if we wanted to go."

"Do you think we'd better?"

"I guess not. I don't much want to go, anyhow. Do you?"

"I don't want to go at all. I'd rather lie here and hold hands and look at the split-rail fence."

"It's very pleasant, isn't it? And that's another surprising and unusual thing. Ordinarily I'm not content to sit quietly for any length of time. Ordinarily I'd much rather be going somewhere and doing something exciting."

"I'll go somewhere with you if you want to go."

"No. I agree that it's much more pleasant here than it would be anywhere else. It's beginning to get quite dark, isn't it? It reminds me of under the trees on the street where I lived as a girl. That was in another town in another state. Light filtered through the leaves into the shadows and there were thousands of cicadas in the trees."

"I thought you were a native New Yorker."

"No. Not at all. Why did you think so?"

"I don't know. I just assumed that you were."

"Well, I'm not. I lived in another town in another state."

"Tell me about living there."

"I don't think I want to. It would depress me. It's better here and now than it's ever been anywhere else at any other time. Don't you think so?"

"Yes. I think so. I was even thinking that it would be pleasant and easy to die here. Just lying here looking at the split-rail fence. It's strange. You're subject to the absolute indifference of the universe, and you take comfort and courage in a split-rail fence."

"It's nice, I admit, but I don't think you need to be so gloomy about it. You seem determined to make me sad, and I wish you wouldn't do it."

"I'm sorry. I wasn't feeling gloomy or trying to make you feel sad. As a matter of fact, I'm feeling very happy."

"Truly?"

"Yes. In my frame of reference, at least."

She lifted his hand and pressed it flat against her breast and held it there. Between the hand and her heart was only the thin fabric of her blouse. After a moment, she slipped the hand inside the blouse, and the heart quickened and became urgent, pounding in his palm.

"Darling," she said, "the bartender was wrong, wasn't he? I've been good for you, haven't I?"

"You've been good for me for almost a week."

"Did you like it out on Long Island? Did you think it was good on Orient Point?"

"I liked it on Long Island. Especially on Orient Point. You told me how it would be, and that's the way it was."

"Was it better on Long Island or is it better now in Connecticut?"

"I don't know. How can you say one time in one place is better than another time in another place when they're both as good as they can be?"

"No, no. Surely one is a little better than the other. Nothing is exactly the same as something else."

"On Long Island I think it's better, and in Connecticut I think it's better. Whichever place we are."

"That's good. You've said exactly the right thing, for it means that right now is best of all so far. Darling, it's really becoming quite dark. Do you think we could be seen if anyone happened to come along unexpectedly?"

"I think we could."

"Well, I don't believe I can continue to lie here like this much longer."

"We could go inside."

"It would be a shame to have to. It's much nicer outside."

"Would you like to take a walk until it becomes darker?"

"Walk to where?"

"Just down to the fence. We could lean against it for a while and be part of the stigmata. A split-rail fence needs someone leaning against it."

"What's stigmata? I don't like the sound of it"

"It's all right. Stigmata are the things you find around a certain place that are characteristic."

"Really? I thought it meant something bad."

"You're thinking of stigmas. That's different. Stigmas are marks of disgrace or something like that."

"All right, then. We'll be stigmata. First, however, I think we should have a Martini. We've sat here for quite a long while without having any at all."

"I'll mix some. The shaker's empty."

"If you get up to mix the Martinis, you'll have to take your hand away from where it is. I'm not certain that I want you to do that."

"Not even for a Martini?"

"Well, I suppose one can't have everything all the time. After all, mixing Martinis isn't anything permanent. It's only a temporary interruption at worst."

"True. I'll mix them."

He got up and walked a few steps to a table that was nothing more than a thick circle of clear glass on wrought iron legs. The shaker and bottles and glasses and a bucket of ice were on the table. He mixed the Martinis in the shaker and poured two into two glasses and carried the glasses over to the chaises longues.

"I'm not as good at this as Yancy," he said, handing her one of the two.

"Yancy's a superior bartender," she said, "and he makes superior Martinis, but his judgment isn't always reliable as to who's good for whom."

"That's right. Yancy's mortal and therefore he is fallible."

He resumed his place on the longue, and she replaced his hand, and they drank the Martinis slowly, and it got a little darker.

"Are these all the Martinis?" she said.

"No. I thought it was as easy to mix four as two, and that's what I did."

"That's the way I usually think about it. It seems a shame to waste the energy and the space in the shaker."

"Shall I pour the other two?"

"Yes, pour them. After drinking them, we'll walk down to the fence and be stigmata, and then it will surely be dark."

"Martinis are stigmata too, when you come to think of it. They're just as much stigmata as hitching posts and split-rail fences and people."

"Everything and everyone are stigmata."

"Correct. As stigmata, let's drink these last two stigmata."

He got up again and poured them, and they drank them, and afterward they walked down the bluestone drive to the split-rail fence. Leaning against the fence, they listened to some kind of bird making a sad sound in the gathering darkness, but neither of them knew what kind of bird it was.

"Tomorrow is Sunday," he said.

"What about Sunday?" she said.

"We have to go back."

"Oh. I suppose we do. I suppose it wouldn't be wise to stay any longer. Anyhow, Samantha agreed to let me use the house only for the weekend. If I didn't keep the agreement, she might become annoyed and say something to somebody."

"Would she do that?"

"Samantha's capable of it. I don't trust her very much, to tell the truth. I only asked her for the house because I couldn't think of anyone else who had one that was suitable. She's sometimes malicious and does sneaky things."

"In that case, we'd certainly better not annoy her."

"Yes, we'd better go back tomorrow. However, there will be other places we can go at other times. You see how it is? Far from not wanting to see you again, I'm already planning how it can be arranged."

"I'll have to go back to work Monday night."

"Playing the piano?"

"That's my work."

"That's true. It is, isn't it? Somehow one doesn't think of playing the piano as being work exactly."

"It's work, all right. Sometimes it gets to be very hard work."

"I suppose it does. The hours and the people and all. Do you like it? Do you wish you were doing something else?"

"I never wish I were doing something else besides playing the piano. I wish all the time that I were playing the piano differently in a different place."

"Why don't you, then?"

"Its not that easy. I'm as well off playing where I am as anywhere else they'd let me play."

"What do you mean?"

"I mean I'm not good enough to do what I'd like to do, even if there were time to do it."

"I think you're extremely good. When I was there that night and heard you suddenly start playing, I thought you were wonderful."

"Thank you, but I'm not."

"Are you sure? Perhaps you are merely lacking confidence."

"No. It's just tricks, what Chester and I do. It's clever sometimes, but it's never really good."

"I refuse to believe it. I don't like to hear you talk about yourself that way."

"I'm sorry. I'll stop."

"Monday night I'll come listen to you play, and it will be very good. Will you play something especially for me if I come listen?"

"I'll play everything especially for you."

"Perhaps it better hadn't be Monday, though, after all. For the sake of appearances, after being gone for the weekend, I think I'd better stay home Monday night. I'll come Tuesday."

"All right. Tuesday."

"Will you let me go to your place with you afterward?"

"If you want to."

"I'll want to. I'm positive already of that. Are you positive that you'll want to let me?"

"Yes. Quite positive."

"That's arranged, then. And now we must stop thinking about tomorrow or Tuesday or any time but now, and you must stop being despondent and critical of yourself. Do you agree?"

"I agree."

It was now as dark as it was going to be. Stars were out, but no moon. The sad-sounding bird was vocal in the darkness.

"Well, please don't just stand there," she said, "What do you want me to do?"

"I want you to hold me."

"Like this?"

"No. Put your hand here. Right here."

"Like this?"

"Yes. Oh, yes, yes. Darling, can't we go now? Right now?"

"By the road? Someone might come."

"I don't care."

"Afterward you would."

"Oh, God, God, God! Don't you want to? Are you going on and on finding reasons not to?"

"I want to. On the terrace. Let's go back to the terrace."

"All right. Right, darling. But hurry! Please hurry!"

So they went back to the terrace, hurrying as if they had only a few minutes instead of all night.

Chapter 12

Bertram Sweeney was ten minutes early for his appointment at three. He sat in the outer office with Miss Carling and cursed himself for having arrived before the appointed time. He had cursed himself a dozen times before for the same reason, and every time he had sworn that he would never arrive as much as five seconds early again, and then, sooner or later, he did. He knew very well that Farnese was doing nothing beyond his closed door, and he had come to interpret the unnecessary waiting as a sign of Farnese's contempt. He wondered what would happen if he were to come late just once, but he never quite had the nerve to try it and find out, and what he decided was that he would come late the very last time, the day he came to kill Farnese, if that day came. He liked to think of killing Farnese. Of all his fantasies, the only ones that gave him more pleasure were those concerning Farnese's wife.

Now, waiting and cursing himself and Farnese, he watched Miss Carling. He didn't like Miss Carling. The only thing that kept him from hating her was the exhaustion of his hatred in the hating of so many others with priority. He was aware that she loathed him, found him physically revolting, and after the passing of the first feeling of pain and degradation that this reaction always aroused in him, it delighted him that she did. In his mind he became a kind of vulgar and artless Cyrano, exploiting his ugliness to elicit her horror. He kissed the back of her neck and pinched her bottom and whispered obscenities in her ear. He rocked with laughter at her terror and disgust. He would not kill Miss Carling the day he killed Farnese, but he might, for the pleasure of it, make her grovel for her life. The memory of her fear would expunge the memory of her disdain. Afterward he would always hear her pleading for Sweeney's mercy instead of telling Sweeney arrogantly that he was early and would have to wait.

It was almost time to go in. The clock on the wall above Miss Carling's severe head showed two minutes before the hour. Well, it was going to be an interesting report, the very best yet, for several pages of the notebook in Sweeney's coat pocket were filled on both sides with Sweeney's cramped writing. It would even be worth the waiting, the humiliation and contempt and effluvial disgust, and in the last two minutes of the waiting, Sweeney closed his eyes and anticipated the turbulence, all the more violent for being controlled, that he was going to arouse in the man he served and hated and dreamed of killing. Abortive laughter began and grew. With appreciative malice, as if he were expressing his gratitude, he began to curse Farnese again. Slowly, one by one from his full repertory of obscenities, he selected and pronounced in the barest whisper the appropriate words.

At three precisely, Miss Carling looked across at Sweeney and nodded once sharply to indicate that he could now go in. Sweeney did not see her nod, for his eyes were closed and he was not at the moment faced in her direction, but he had developed a kind of sensitivity to Miss Carling's movements, feeling what he didn't see, and he stood up at once and walked across to Farnese's private door and let himself in. Farnese was sitting behind his desk in his usual posture, his fingers laced in front of him on the desk's top, his eyes focused on the fingers. He didn't look up or speak or give any sign whatever that he was aware of Sweeney's presence, and Sweeney, crossing to the chair, resumed his inaudible obscenities. He sat down heavily and removed his notebook from his coat pocket and waited.

"Make it concise," Farnese said. "Give me only essentials, please."

Sweeney took a deep breath, releasing on the breath the last vile word, and began his report. He did not read verbatim from his notes, and this disturbed and angered him, for he took pride in the detail and accuracy of his observations and would have preferred presenting them exactly as he had set them down. He was all the more angered because he knew there was no real necessity for brevity. Farnese was a phony son of a son with nothing to do that needed doing, but he always had to act, nevertheless, as if the time he gave to Sweeney was taken from other matters much more important and pressing. What Sweeney wanted to know was, what the hell was more important and pressing than a prowling nympho wife? Nothing was more important and pressing, that was what, and Sweeney knew it, and Farnese knew it, and both of them knew that the other knew it, and who the hell was fooling who? Well, Bertram Sweeney wasn't fooled for a minute, that was sure, and it was really funny the way the stinking phony sat there like a God-damn stone, trying to act as if nothing he was hearing made any difference in the long run, and all the time his guts were in an uproar and he was sick to death inside with the rising violence of his fury. Realizing this, Sweeney felt almost compensated for the butchery of his report. His resentment gave way to his silent internal glee.

"Wednesday afternoon," he said. "I followed subject, Mrs. Farnese, to a restaurant on Fifth Avenue. She was alone. She drove a Jaguar car. I waited until she left the restaurant and then followed her to an apartment building on MacDougal Street. Subsequent investigation disclosed that she went to the apartment of a Mrs. DeWitt, a divorcee. She was there for approximately three hours, after which she again left alone and drove in the Jaguar to the small nightclub in the Village which is known as Duo's and which I had occasion to mention in my last report. Leaving Duo's, still alone, she drove to the residence near Washington Square which I also mentioned in my last report in connection with the piano player known as Joe Doyle. She remained in this residence until approximately one o'clock. She then returned home."

Pausing, he lifted his eyes to the little barometer of Farnese's passions, the fine line of scar tissue along the lower mandible. The tissue was already livid, but Farnese's face was in perfect repose. His laced fingers held one another quietly on top of the desk.

"Thursday?" he said.

"Thursday morning," Sweeney said, "approximately eleven o'clock. Mrs. Farnese left in the Jaguar and drove directly to the residence she had left at one o'clock of the same morning. She went inside and remained there until almost noon, at which time she came out in the company of Joe Doyle. They crossed the East River into Kings County and drove east to Jamaica. Since my area of operation is restricted by your orders to New York City, I turned around there and came back. At regular intervals during the rest of the day, I called the apartment on Park Avenue to see if Mrs. Farnese had returned. The maid said she hadn't. At nine o'clock that night I went to Duo's to see if Joe Doyle was there or was expected. He wasn't there and wasn't expected. The bartender told me that he was on sick leave and wouldn't return until Monday. Tonight, that is."

"I know what day it is," Farnese said.

"Yes. Of course." Sweeney's thick lips formed the shape of a sound that was not part of the report. "From Duo's I drove to the residence of Joe Doyle. The Jaguar was not parked in front or in the vicinity. I parked across the street and down the block where I could watch the house. It was about a quarter to eleven when they returned. At twelve-thirty Mrs. Farnese left alone and went home."

Sweeney paused again, awaiting comments, but Farnese had none to make. He unlaced his fingers, flexed them, replaced them.

"That's enough," he said.

"What?" Sweeney said.

"I said that's enough. The rest of your report would be superfluous."

Sweeney folded his notebook slowly, leaving a fat index finger between the pages as a marker. He felt as if he had been slapped in the face, and his resentment was commensurate.

"I don't understand," he said.

"I'm quite easily understood, I believe. I already know how my wife spent the weekend. Do you find it incredible that I should learn something about my wife without your professional assistance? I'll tell you how I know. I know because my wife has the obvious mind of a perverted child. Her deceptions, even when she elaborates on them, are transparent. Friday she informed me that she was spending the weekend at the Fairfield County house of Samantha Cox. She went there, all right, but not with Miss Cox. She went with this Joe Doyle. Isn't that true?"

"She sure as hell went to Fairfield County. As you say, with Joe Doyle. I don't know what particular place in the county they went to, because I left them at the line."

"I know. Your area of operation is only the City. All right, Sweeney. Your devotion to orders has been sufficiently established. When you're speaking to me, however, please avoid profanity. I don't like profanity. I think I've told you this before."

Sweeney didn't reply. He lowered his eyes and removed his index finger from the notebook in a sign of complete capitulation. His report and his pride were now thoroughly mutilated, and he sought expression for his feelings in the deepest and vilest cavity of his brain. Farnese, after silence, spoke again. His voice was soft and measured, as if he were weighing his thoughts and words with special care.

"Mr. Doyle has become a fixture," he said.

"He hangs on," Sweeney said with concealed relish.

"Yes." Farnese unlaced his fingers and made a tent of them, placing their tips together with a careful exactness that seemed to reflect the quality of his thinking. "It's unfortunate. As you have reason to know, I am, for reasons of my own, exceedingly tolerant of my wife's social activities. There are times, however, when it becomes advisable to interfere, and I'm inclined to believe that now is one of the times."

Sweeney was offended by Farnese's oblique approach to brutality. It made him sick. He had no such reaction to brutality in itself, however. In the pustule world, he had suffered and administered it far too often himself to make of it a particular issue. It was only the indirection, the tone and posture of sadistic piety, that offended him. There was a kind of minor salvation from the worst of hell, he thought, in calling a spade a spade.

"The same as before?" he said.

"Yes. Do you still have your contact with Mr. Chalk."

"Sure. Chalk's always available."

"Arrange it."

Sweeney put his notebook away in his pocket. He sighed and coughed and wiped his thick lips with a soiled handkerchief. He sat staring intently at the handkerchief as if he expected to find it stained with blood.

"The price will be up," he said.

"It was up last time."

"I know. From five hundred to seven-fifty. This time it'll be a thousand. That's Chalk's schedule."

"Very well. A thousand."

"When do you want it?"

"As soon as possible. Tonight?"

"I don't think so. Chalk's a careful organizer. He doesn't like to be pressed. Maybe tomorrow night."

"All right. Take care of it and let me know."

"Sure. You want to be there?"

"Yes."

"I'll talk with Chalk."

He heaved himself to his feet and stood waiting for a few seconds to give Farnese a chance to say anything more that he might want to say. Apparently Farnese wanted to say nothing, for he remained silent, and Sweeney walked out of the office and past Miss Carling in the outer office and down ten floors to the street. It was a long descent that taxed the endurance of his obese body, and he did not ignore the elevator because he enjoyed the exercise. It was rather because the small steel box in its deep shaft was suddenly the fearful instrument of a developing encroachment. Cornered and confined in his own gross self by what he had become and was and could expect to be, he was aware of a claustrophobic fear that he didn't understand and refused to admit.

In his car, a plain black Ford, not new, he drove to lower Broadway and was lucky enough to find a spot to park. He was compelled to walk two blocks, however, to reach his destination, which was a small cigar and tobacco shop. This shop was operated by the man named Chalk, and Chalk himself, in a continuation of Sweeney's luck, was sitting on a high stool behind a high glass counter. He was a thin man with a curiously flat face, plastered hair so glossily black that it was plainly dyed, and skin that looked burned out by some former terrible fever of the flesh, brittle and checked and gray-white, the color that his name denoted.

In Chalk's shop you could actually buy cigars and tobacco and cigarettes and numerous items essential or incidental to smoking, but the sale of this merchandise, although he made a profit from it, was not Chalk's principal source of revenue. Most of his income came from the sale of marijuana, which was distributed in cigar boxes by half a dozen pushers operating from his rear room. Besides this, he was usually prepared to contract various lucrative odd jobs. Like, for instance, the odd jobs he had done for Bertram Sweeney acting as the agent of Oliver Alton Farnese.

"Hello, Chalk," Sweeney said now, placing one elbow on the metal frame of the glass counter and leaning heavily.

Chalk nodded. "Hello, Sweeney," he said. "Watch the glass."

"Sure," Sweeney said.

He shifted his weight a little as a concession to Chalk's concern, but he didn't remove the elbow. Chalk watched him with a worried expression until it became apparent that the glass was safe, at least for the present, and then he relaxed and sucked noisily at the sodden end of a dead cigar.

"What's on your mind, Sweeney?" he said.

"I was wondering if Cupid's around."

"Not now. Couple days since I've seen him."

"I didn't mean that. I mean, is he available?"

"Could be. He usually is. You got a job for Cupid?"

"For someone. Client of mine wants a guy taken care of."

"How much care of?"

"Nothing final. Just a good lesson he'll remember."

"Oh. I see. Just dressed up a little."

"That's right. You interested?"

"Depends. What client, for instance?"

"Same as last time. Same as time before last. Farnese."

"Jesus! That guy must hate a lot of people."

"He hates the ones his wife likes. That's a lot."

"This would be the third job. It'd run to a grand."

"I know."

"You better tell him."

"I already told him."

"Okay. Who's the guy he wants handled?"

"Name's Joe Doyle. You know Duo's? It's a little joint down in the Village near Sheridan Square. Doyle plays the piano there. A young guy. Ugly. Real thin. Looks like he doesn't eat regular."

"A lousy piano thumper? Honest to God? How'd a guy like that ever make Park Avenue?"

Sweeney shifted his weight again, and the frame of the glass counter creaked beneath it. He felt angry, filled with a tepid and sluggish resentment, as if Chalk were referring facetiously to the betrayal of Sweeney himself. Which he was, of course, in the crossing of Sweeney's worlds.

"Who knows?" Sweeney said. "Who predicts a woman? Anyhow, it's neither here nor there. Doyle's the guy. He sleeps up in the Washington Square area, but I figure it would be better if you snatched him at Duo's, when he comes out from work. He quits around one, usually, sometimes earlier, now and then later. He keeps his car parked in the alley behind the place and goes out the back way when he's through. That would be the time and place."

"Not tonight. It's too quick."

"No. I figured that. Tomorrow night."

"I'll see. You want Cupid in particular? I've got other reliable boys willing to work."

"I like Cupid. There's something poetic about him. He looks the part."

"He does. He sure as hell does. No denying that."

"Tomorrow night, then. Cupid working. He'll have an audience."

"I'll fix it," Chalk said.

Sweeney moved, shoving his bulk erect. He took out his soiled handkerchief and wiped his mouth and stared down through the glass into the case.

"Gimme a couple of those Roi Tan blunts," he said.

"Sure, Sweeney," Chalk said. "Twenty cents, please."

Sweeney dug out a couple of dimes and dropped them on the glass. Chalk produced the blunts and rang up the dimes, and Sweeney walked out into the street and back to the plain black Ford. In it, he drove to the shabby hotel in which he kept a room. He went up to the room and let himself in with his key and sat down on the edge of the bed. He removed his hat and rubbed his scarred scalp and began looking at the picture of Charity Farnese that stood beside the bed on the night table.

And at that instant the first world disintegrated and became the second world, and Sweeney stood with arms akimbo on the white sand beach beside the whispering sea, and his body was straight and strong and golden in the hot white light of the sun.

Charity was running down the beach. Lightly, lightly, scarcely disturbing the sand. She cried out once, his name, and he turned with his heart pounding and swelling to see in her face the light of anticipated ecstasy. Then the second world was in an instant, without warning, distended and blurred and bursting apart. It vanished completely in a pink froth and was gone for a minute and then returned. The sun returned, and the sea and the sand, and Sweeney was standing where be had stood. But he was now, in the second world, the first world Sweeney. His body was blue-veined and bloated, a profanation of light.

Charity had stopped running. She stood in the sand as still as stone. On her face, instead of ecstasy, was an expression of utter loathing.

Sweeney closed his eyes and lay back across his bed.

CHAPTER 13

Monday was not one of Charity's better days, but neither, on the other hand, was it one of her really bad days, and on the whole it was just a day in between. She wakened in the middle of the morning and lay thinking for a while of Connecticut, how fine and exciting and yet restful it had been there with Joe Doyle, but this was not good, for it made her begin to want Joe again, and it was much too soon to begin this, for it was far too long a time until Tuesday night. If she began thinking about him and wanting him already, it would make the passing of time much more difficult to bear, and she was quite likely to do something precipitate and unfortunate instead of waiting patiently and sensibly as she had planned. In order to avoid this, she began thinking of what she could do to fill in the rest of this day that she had now started. The first thing that occurred to her was breakfast, and she was surprised, the moment it occurred to her, to discover that she was really quite hungry, which she scarcely ever was at the beginning of any day, no matter what time she began it.

She got up at once and had a shower and dressed and then went out to the dining room, where she ate a substantial breakfast, even including an egg, that would eliminate the necessity for lunch. The breakfast was served by Edith, who said good morning in a respectful voice and didn't say anything more all the while she was serving and Charity was eating. She hovered about, however, usually in a position in which Charity could not see her without turning her head, and this made Charity uncomfortable. She wished that Edith would go away, but she didn't say anything about it until she was ready for a second cup of coffee and a cigarette, and then she said something as politely as she could with the definite intention of not being unpleasant.

"Edith," she said politely, "I wish you would go the hell away."

"I beg your pardon, Madam?" Edith said with a rising inflection which implied that she had either not heard correctly or could not believe what she had heard.

"You heard me quite clearly, Edith," Charity said. "I said very politely that I wish you would go the hell away."

"Certainly, Madam. Is there anything more I can do for you before I go?"

"No, there is nothing more you can do. I am only going to have a second cup of coffee and a cigarette, and I am perfectly capable of doing it without any help from you."

"Shall I pour the coffee?"

"I'll pour it myself, Edith. I'll also light my cigarette myself."

"Very well, Madam,"

Edith walked around the end of the table and across the room to the door. She stopped there and turned and smiled and stood with her hands folded under her breasts in the kind of posture taught to offensive children by teachers of elocution. It was a kind of posture that was meant to be ingratiating but only succeeded in being annoying,

"I hope you had a pleasant weekend, Madam," she said.

"I had a very pleasant weekend," Charity said, "I went with Miss Samantha Cox to her house in Connecticut."

"So I understood, Madam. I was certain that I saw Miss Cox drive past on the Avenue Saturday afternoon, but obviously I was mistaken, since she was in Connecticut."

"Obviously you were, Edith."

"Probably it was only someone who looks like Miss Cox and happens to drive exactly the same kind and color of car."

"It's more probable that you are trying to be malicious and troublesome, Edith, which I understand clearly."

"Pardon me, Madam. I'm sorry if I've offended you. Would you like me to make your bed while you're having your coffee and cigarette?"

"Yes, you may go make my bed, Edith, and please don't help yourself to any of my things while you are there,"

"Very well, Madam."

Edith smiled again and unfolded her hands and went out, and Charity poured a second cup of coffee and lit a cigarette and was furious.

The bitch! she thought. The sneaky, unreliable bitch!

She wasn't thinking of Edith, however. She was thinking of Samantha. It was just like Samantha to have driven right by the place innumerable times and to have made no effort at all to be inconspicuous during the time she was supposed to be in Connecticut, and it was Charity's opinion that she had probably let herself be seen deliberately. You simply couldn't rely on Samantha to do her part faithfully in anything, and it was bad luck that she had been the only one with a suitable house to borrow for the weekend. She was more than unreliable, as a matter of fact. She was absolutely treacherous when it pleased her to be, with no conscience whatever, and it wouldn't be the least surprising to discover that she had actually called Oliver on the telephone on some pretext just to let him know that Charity had lied about going with her to Connecticut. But if this were done and she were charged with it, she would simply be too contrite and exuding apologies for being so careless and forgetful and utterly undependable, which she wouldn't have been deliberately for the world, of course, and she was absolutely a bitch, bitch, bitch!

While thinking of Samantha, she had been drawing deeply and methodically on her cigarette without realizing what she was doing, and suddenly she became aware that her tongue was hot and the cigarette was tipped with a long red coal that was almost half as long as what was left of the cigarette itself. She crushed it in a tray and drank the coffee in her cup. She was beginning now to wish that she hadn't eaten such a hearty breakfast. It had tasted good, and she had enjoyed it, even the egg, but it was beginning to feel like a mass of sodden facial tissue in her stomach, and she couldn't imagine how it had got as far as it had, or how it would ever get the rest of the way it had to go.

Well, it served her right for being such a glutton. Ordinarily she had very little taste for food of any kind, and she ate lightly as a necessity whenever her body demanded it, and she simply couldn't understand people who made a big issue of eating, a kind of religious ceremony, with all kinds of specifications as to how things were to be prepared and served. It was disgusting, when you stopped to think about it, making such a thing over eating flesh and eggs and things like that, a lot more disgusting than some of the natural appetites some people professed to find disgusting, and anyone who did it, as she had just done it, deserved to have an uncomfortable stomach at least.

Getting up abruptly from the table, she went out of the dining room and into a hall and down the hall to a library with two or three thousand books that no one ever read. Once she had gone through a period of resolving to be something different from what she was, and then she had decided to start reading the books in the library with the intention of becoming dedicated to a reclusive life, and she had actually taken a few of them down and read snatches in them here and there, but she had never got around to starting one at the beginning and reading through to the end. It was just as well that she hadn't started, anyhow, because the period had been pretty brief, and she probably wouldn't have had time in the length of it to read a whole book. Now, starting Monday morning to wait for Tuesday night, she put several records on the hi-fi and sat down in a chair to listen.

Not that she really listened. Not, that is, with an understanding of scores and a genuine appreciation of execution. The music simply became a part of her emotional content and gave a kind of splendid quality to things remembered and anticipated that had not really been splendid at all, or would not be. Eventually, this effect became flattened, and she became bored. She wondered what she could possibly do with the rest of the day without going out somewhere to do it. There was nothing she could do with it, she decided. Nothing in the apartment. She had determined as a matter of sagacity to stay home until tomorrow night, but it would surely do no harm to go shopping, which was something she had not done for quite a long time, and so she went to her room with a freshly made bed and dressed appropriately and went.

There was nothing she needed or especially wanted, but then she thought that she would buy a new gown to wear tomorrow night for Joe Doyle, and this became at once a rather exciting venture. She tried to decide what he would probably like in the way of a gown, and she realized that she didn't have the least idea. It was astonishing. They had actually known each other intimately for a long while, almost a week, and she did not know about him such a simple thing as what he might like in the way of a gown. Perhaps this was significant, and it bothered her slightly for a moment because she thought it might indicate a deficiency or basic indifference in their relationship. But this was not true, she assured herself, and what it really indicated was a kind of stripped and unqualified acceptance of each by the other. What she would have to get was something that she especially liked herself, and the chances were, since they were so compatible and acceptable to each other in all ways, that Joe would like it too.

She went to a salon and looked at some original gowns on two sleek models, and by a stroke of uncommon luck the third one on the first model was a gown that she knew immediately was exactly right and that she must certainly have. It was simply designed and seemed to be precariously secured, which added a quality of anticipation to its effect on whoever was watching whoever was almost in it, and it was a gown, most importantly, which clearly required other prerequisites than merely the considerable sum of money it took to buy it. After paying for the gown and arranging to have it sent, she went to two other places and bought lingerie in one and shoes in the other, which she also arranged to have sent, and then it was definitely late enough to have the Martini she had been thinking about, between other thoughts, all afternoon.

In the cocktail lounge that happened to be nearest to where she bought the shoes, she sat at a small round table in cool shadows and drank one Martini quickly and another slowly. While slowly drinking the second one, she began to think deliberately about something she had been deliberately not thinking about, or at least trying not to think about and this was what Oliver might know about the weekend, and what he might say or do about it when she saw him this evening for the first time since returning last night. She didn't see how Oliver could possibly know anything, unless Samantha had given it away, damn her, but Samantha couldn't have given away anything specific, at least, because she only knew that Charity had used the house, not with whom or why, although she could surely guess the latter. If it turned out that he knew about Joe's being there, or about Long Island or the night before Long Island, then that would be additional evidence of an abnormal capacity to learn things, or of some method of systematic spying, and she didn't know which of these would be worse, but either would be too bad. They were both threatening and frightening, and that was why she had deliberately not thought of them, and she would not have thought of them now if she had not been compelled by the time and supported by gin.

Having considered the issue at last, whether Oliver would know anything or not, she felt a strong compulsion to find out as quickly as possible, and for that reason she wanted to be home when he arrived at six, which it would be in less than an hour according to the tiny watch on her wrist. Resisting the desire to have a third Martini, she left the lounge and returned to the apartment and went directly to her room. After she had changed into something more casual and comfortable, there were only ten minutes left of the time before Oliver would return on schedule to dress and do whatever else he regularly did before going out again this particular night of the week for dinner and bridge at his club. Or was it Tuesday night that he went for dinner and bridge? She was uncertain about it, but it didn't matter, anyhow, for she definitely remembered that he went somewhere for something this night.

She had intended waiting here in her room, but in considering his coming and what might happen, she remembered what had happened the other time, the time about a week ago right after he had told her all about her first experience with Joe, and so she decided suddenly to wait instead in the living room, where the same thing might still happen again but was less likely. Going into the living room, she sat on a sofa and looked at pictures in a magazine and spent the remaining minutes, and when Oliver arrived at six she was vastly relieved to see that he was quite normal and apparently not suspicious or angry about anything.

"Hello, my dear," he said. "How are you?"

"I'm fine," she said. "Do I look as if I were not?"

"On the contrary. Your weekend in the country seems to have agreed with you. Perhaps we should have a place of our own. Not in Fairfield County, however. I think I'd prefer Bucks."

"Well, I'd not prefer either one as a regular thing. As a regular thing, I prefer the city. We'd only want to go to the country now and then, and it would hardly be worthwhile having a place for no more than that. It's always possible to get invited to someone's house when you want to go."

"You're right, of course. I didn't really offer my suggestion seriously."

He walked over and sat down on the sofa near her, turning sidewise to face her in an unusually companionable position. He was behaving so graciously, as a matter of fact, that it made her uneasy and inclined to listen sharply for significant nuances in his voice.

"Did you and Samantha get along all right?"

"Perfectly. Usually I can't tolerate her for more than a few hours at a time at most, but this time we didn't have the slightest difficulty."

"That's good. Who else was there?"

"You mean all the time or just everyone who happened to come and go?"

"Oh, I wouldn't expect you to account for all of Samantha's casual visitors. Just the guests."

"There were only three besides me. There were a couple, a Wesley Bussy and his wife, who were from Hollywood. He has something or other to do with motion pictures, production or administration or something like that, not acting or directing or anything. An executive is what he is. His wife's name is Andrea, and she went to Hollywood from someplace like Texas to become an actress, but he saw her there and married her, and she's given it up. Acting, I mean. Neither of them is anyone you'd be likely to hear about."

She said all this naturally, with a perfect accent of truth, and even the names, which were imaginary, were produced without hesitation. To anyone who heard her give such a performance and knew all the while that she was lying, which was frequently the situation, it seemed an incredible accomplishment, but it was not actually as remarkable as it seemed. The truth was, she often amused herself by thinking up names and circumstances that might become useful to her, and when she needed to tell something convincing in an emergency, they were always available. She was really rather proud of her ability to file them away in her mind, and she was very particular about the names, evaluating them carefully to be certain that they were neither too common nor too odd, which would have made them excite suspicion in either event. The only thing that concerned her sometimes was the feeling that she had, in lying to someone it was necessary to deceive, given certain names to certain imaginary people that she had previously given to other imaginary people who were obviously altogether different in all other respects. She tried never to use the same name over in telling lies to any given person, but she couldn't always be sure she hadn't slipped. She was sure now, however, of the Bussys. She had only imagined them recently and had definitely never used them before.

"Were they interesting people?" Oliver said.

"No, they were very dull. They were bores, as a matter of fact. Especially her. A number of years ago she won several of these beauty contests you are always reading about in which someone becomes Miss something-or-other, and she seemed to think this was important. Everyone knows perfectly well that such contests mean hardly anything, but she kept referring to them all the time as if having won them was an exceptional accomplishment"

"I'm sorry you were bored. Was the other guest any better?"

"Yes, he was. He was much better, He's a professor in a university somewhere and is apparently quite poor, but he's writing a book that may make some money for him."

"What's his name?"

"Clyde Connelly. I don't remember what university he teaches in, but I believe it's somewhere in the Middle West, like Ohio or Illinois or some-where, and if I'm not mistaken he is on sabbatical leave next year and is going to Europe. He came to New York to see a publisher about the book and met Samantha at a party they had both gone to with someone else. You know Samantha. She is always picking someone up and cultivating him for a while and then dropping him. This professor is good-looking and not very old, and it's probable that they're having an affair."

"You think so?"

"Yes, I do. I think it's probable."

"Are all your friends always having affairs?"

"Oh, no. Not always. I didn't intend to give that impression at all. If you think they are, you're mistaken."

He laughed and reached over and squeezed her nearer knee in a sudden warm gesture.

"My dear," he said, rising, "I know practically nothing about your friends, and I think about them just as infrequently as I can."

He stood looking down at her, smiling, and her feeling of uneasiness returned and grew, not because of what he had said or the way in which he had said it, but simply because his geniality was rare and excessive and therefore suspect.

"I must go change," he said. "Are you going out this evening?"

"No. I thought I'd stay in and go to bed early. I'm rather tired after the weekend and all."

"Good idea," he said. "I'll not disturb you when I come in."

When he was gone, her uneasiness began to diminish slowly and after a few minutes was gone. There had simply been no evidence at all that he was informed on her affair, and it was impossible to believe that he was capable of such convincing and monstrous deception. Besides, what would have been the point of it? It was obvious that everything was all right, that there was nothing to worry about, and she began to regret, now that she had convinced herself of this, that she had not planned to go see Joe Doyle tonight instead of tomorrow night. She was tempted to go tonight any-how, regardless of plans, but perhaps it would be wiser, since she had com-mitted herself to staying in and going to bed early, to wait another twen-ty-four hours.

The time would pass. Tomorrow she would find something to do, though she didn't know what, and tonight she would have a simple dinner alone and two or three Martinis afterward, and then she would watch television in bed. Television was commonly so utterly dull that it would probably put her to sleep after a while without the help of soporifics.

CHAPTER 14

Tuesday was a day that was somehow spent.

In the afternoon, the gown and other things were delivered, and she tried on the gown in her room to be sure that it was actually as exciting as she had thought it was in the salon, and it seemed to her that it was. Often she would get enthusiastic about something that she saw and bought, and then later, when she saw it again in different circumstances, she couldn't understand how she had been so mistaken as to have wanted it, but this time, to her relief, the gown was still right and exciting and just the thing to wear when she went to see Joe Doyle.

After trying it on and looking at herself for a long time in a mirror, she took it off again and laid it across the bed in readiness for later, and then there wasn't a thing left to do that was tolerable, but it was essential to do something, for doing nothing was most intolerable of all. In this kind of situation, she usually ended up doing things to herself, brushing her hair and trying new effects with her face and fixing her fingernails and toe-nails, things like that, and she started now doing all these things. Fortunately, this was all meticulous work that required careful attention and had the incidental result of making time pass quickly, and she had just finished with the nail of the little toe on her left foot, the last thing to be done, when Oliver came home and knocked on her door, and she was genuinely astonished to realize that it had become so late so soon.

But there was something terribly wrong. She felt it the moment Oliver came into the room. He closed the door behind him and stood leaning against it, watching her, and the wrongness was immediately present and felt and growing to such enormous dimensions that it seemed to fill the room and press in upon her from the walls. Not that he said anything or did anything or appeared to be in the least angry. He appeared, in fact, to be unusually congenial, as he had been yesterday, and he smiled and nodded his head, watching her, as if he approved of what he saw.

It was strange and irrational how the feeling came over her. One moment she was doing things to herself to pass the time until she could do what she really wanted to do, and everything was all right and getting better, and the next moment everything was all wrong and getting worse, and there didn't seem to be any reason for it or anything she could do to stop it. She had experienced the same feeling before, however, the sudden terrible conviction of imminent disaster that had no apparent relationship to circumstances as they were at the time, and a doctor at one of the parties where she got most of her spiritual and psychiatric guidance had told her, after an intimate consultation in a corner over several cocktails, that it was a kind of free-floating anxiety that occasionally attached itself to a specific incident or person. This was nice to know, of course, but it wasn't very effective as therapy and did little or nothing to alleviate matters whenever the free-floating anxiety attached itself afterward to something or someone specific, as it was now attached to Oliver at the door.

What's wrong?" she said.

"Wrong?" He straightened and walked three steps into the room. "Nothing's wrong, my dear. What makes you think there is?"

"I don't know. I just had a feeling when you came in that something was."

"You're mistaken. Everything is fine. Are you planning to go somewhere tonight?"

"I was thinking that I might. I went to bed early last night, you know, and now I'd like to go somewhere and do something."

"Do you have something definite arranged?"

"Oh, no. Nothing special at all. There's always somewhere to go that doesn't require special arrangements."

"That's good. It's good, I mean, that you haven't committed yourself to anything definite, for I've planned a little surprise for you."

"Surprise? What kind of surprise?"

He smiled, tracing with the tip of an index finger the thin scar along his mandible, and she watched him with a conviction of personal peril growing stronger and stronger in her morbid certainty of all things going wrong, It was surely a kind of minor revolution when Oliver disrupted his schedule for anything whatever, and it raised the question of whether the disruption was a sign of a change in their relationship which he intended to be good or was, on the other hand, a development of the danger she had sensed and believed, and in either case it threatened to spoil the night she had planned and was therefore bad.

"Dinner and dancing to begin with," he said. "Afterward I have something rather unusual in mind. I think it will amuse you."

"What is it?"

"If I told you now it would spoil the surprise. I want you to anticipate it, my dear."

"Well, I know you don't really like to do things like this and are only doing it now for my sake. It's very kind of you, I'm sure, but it isn't necessary."

"On the contrary, I'm quite enthusiastic about it. Do you think I'm incapable of enjoying anything out of the routine?"

"You'll have to admit that you always plan things ahead very carefully and hardly ever deviate from them."

"That's true. I like an ordered life, as you say, but I've been thinking that perhaps you should be included more often in the order. I'm afraid I've been neglecting you shamefully, my dear, and you've been exceedingly generous and understanding about it."

This remark seemed to indicate that he was only trying to alter their relationship with good intentions, which was a relief from fear but would certainly become a great nuisance if she permitted it to continue, for it would prevent her from going places and doing things as she pleased, or at least as frequently as she pleased. It was extremely unlikely, however, that Oliver would deviate from his established order for any length of time, and the acute problem now was tonight, how she could possibly go to Joe Doyle while Oliver was imposing himself upon her in this extraordinary way, and her going, which had up to now been no more than desirable, became imperative as it became imperiled.

"Thank you very much," she said, "but I don't think I'd care to become part of an order. I prefer to do things more spontaneously."

"I know. We are quite different in that respect. An adjustment will demand concessions from us both. Is that a new gown on the bed?"

"Yes, it is. I bought it yesterday, and it was delivered this afternoon."

"It's nice. I'm sure you'll look charming in it. Were you planning to wear it tonight?"

"Yes. I was trying it on before you came."

"I'm sorry I didn't come earlier. No matter, though. I'll see it on you later when we go out together."

"Are you certain you want to go? If you prefer, we could go another night when you have more time to prepare for it."

"No, no. It's all arranged. We'll go to the Empire Room for dinner and dancing, and later we'll have our little surprise."

He moved toward her suddenly and took her by the shoulders and kissed her on the mouth with a lightness and tenderness that were rare and would have been deeply moving in the kiss of anyone else. In his, they were somehow frightening, the qualities of mockery. She was ravished by the kiss as she had never been by his occasional brutality, and at the same time, paradoxically, she felt far more rejected than all his customary coldness had ever made her feel. Worst of all, she was compelled to recognize with an exorbitant sense of loss and despair that he was determined to take her with him to the Empire Room and wherever else afterward he had planned, and there was nothing, nothing at all, that she could do to prevent it.

"We'll leave at a quarter to eight," he said.

He released her and went out, and she sat on the edge of the bed in her despair and tried and tried to think of something she could do to save the night, to make it possible still to go to Joe Doyle, but she could think of nothing, and she knew that there was nothing to be done by her or anyone else in the world. It would be necessary, then, to call Joe and tell him that she couldn't be there, and why she couldn't, and how terribly sorry she was, and that she would surely come as soon as she could, which would be tomorrow if she could possibly manage it.

Having decided to call, she tried to remember if there was a telephone in his room, and she couldn't remember any. If there had been one she would certainly have remembered it, and so she concluded that there wasn't, which meant that there was a house phone in the hall that would probably be listed under the name of whoever owned the house, and the trouble was that she didn't know who owned it. Then it occurred to her that he might be at Duo's already, where he worked, and that she could at least leave word for him there if he wasn't actually there himself to be talked to.

She turned in the classified directory to the nightclubs and found Duo's number and dialed it, and while she was doing this she kept hoping very hard that Joe would be there to be talked to, for she wanted to tell him personally how much she wanted to come and how sorry she was that she couldn't. It was imperative that he understand this and believe it, for he was inclined to lack faith in her anyhow, and he might decide that she had simply had enough of him, which wasn't, surprisingly enough, yet true. After she had finished dialing, she waited and waited while the phone rang in long bursts at the other end of the line, and she had about concluded in despair that Duo's was one of those places that absolutely ignored telephone calls whenever it suited them, but then, just as she was preparing to cut the connection, someone answered. It was Yancy.

"Duo's," he said. "Yancy speaking."

"Hello, Yancy," she said. "This is Charity Farnese. You know. The dry Martini."

"I know."

"Where in the world have you been? The phone rang and rang, and I was about to hang up."

"I was here all the time. I was busy."

"Well, I'm glad I waited. It just shows you that it doesn't pay to give up too soon, doesn't it?"

"Not always. Sometimes it pays to give up as soon as possible."

"I'm not sure I know what you mean, and I don't think I want to know. What I do want to know is, is Joe there?"

"Joe Doyle?"

"Of course Joe Doyle. You know perfectly well I mean Joe Doyle. Please don't be so evasive, Yancy."

"Sorry. He isn't here."

"Do you suppose he will be there soon?"

"I don't think so. Not soon."

"Do you know his telephone number?"

"It's a house phone. I don't know the number."

"Perhaps you could tell me the name the number is listed under."

"I can't. I don't know it."

"Are you merely being contrary, Yancy?"

"No. If I knew I'd tell you."

"Thank you. That's very kind of you. Will you please give him a message from me when he comes in?"

"I might."

"What do you mean, you might? Will you or won't your?"

"It depends on the message."

"Please tell him that I won't be able to come tonight. Something has developed that makes it impossible."

"I'll tell him."

"Tell him also that I'm truly sorry and will see him as soon as I can. Will you tell him that?"

"Reluctantly."

"What's the matter with you, Yancy? Do you still think it's wrong for me to see him and that no good will come of it?"

"You know what I think. I told you."

"Well, in the beginning there may have been an excuse for your scepticism, but now there is none whatever, and you are only being stubborn and unpleasant. I can tell you that some good has already come of it, and Joe will tell you the same if you will only ask him."

"Not me. What's good or what's bad is for you and Joe to figure, and you don't owe any accounting to anyone but each other and maybe your husband. I just decided. Good-by, now. I've got customers."

He hung up without giving her a chance to say good-by in return, and she listened for a few moments to the humming of the wire and hung up too. It was still earlier than she needed to start dressing for the evening, but she started anyhow, because there was nothing else to do and doing something was a necessary defensive mechanism, taking a long bath and brushing her hair for a long while deliberately. Finally, after everything else was done, she took the new gown off the bed and hung it in a closet and selected another, which she hardly looked at, and put it on. She was compelled under the circumstances to go out with Oliver if he demanded it, but she was not compelled to wear the gown she had bought particularly to wear for Joe Doyle, and she was not going to do it. She would think of something to say in explanation if Oliver noticed it was not the new gown and said something about it, and that, of course, as it happened, was the first thing Oliver did when he knocked on the door at a quarter to eight and entered.

"I thought you were going to wear the new gown," he said. "Or did you buy it for a special occasion?"

"No," she said. "I decided it isn't suitable for the Empire Room, that's all."

"Really? I thought it looked quite suitable."

"No. It's not suitable at all."

"Whatever you think, of course. The gown you're wearing is nice. You look lovely in it."

"Thank you."

"It's time to leave now. Are you ready?"

"Yes, I'm ready."

Edith let them out of the apartment and closed the door silently after them, and they went down to the Avenue and found Oliver's Imperial, which had been ordered around, waiting for them at the curb. They drove on the Avenue to the Waldorf-Astoria and went immediately to the Empire Room and were shown to the table that Oliver had reserved. She should have known, of course, that he had made a reservation, but she had not considered the details of the situation that carefully, and now that they were exposed and she was compelled to consider them in spite of herself, she was possessed by a most terrible feeling of absolute impotence. Without consulting her or conceding anything whatever to her rights or wishes, he had reserved the table and the night and her, and all the time that she had been planning to make certain things happen, quite different things had actually been happening already and were still happening, and there had been nothing she could have done to change the order of events then, before she even knew about it, and there was nothing she could do to stop it or change it now. Nothing at all. What she had hoped and almost believed yesterday and earlier today, that Oliver's unusual geniality was only a sign that he might become a nuisance and not a menace, she no longer hoped or believed in the least. She was resigned to disaster, and as her resignation increased, her fear diminished. She hardly cared what the form of disaster might be precisely, or when, exactly, it might come.

A waiter placed a menu before her, but she had no interest in it. She pushed it away with the tips of her fingers as if it were something contagious. Oliver watched her, smiling. He traced and retraced lightly the line of his scar.

"Will you order now, my dear?" he said.

"I don't believe I care to order," she said. "I'm only interested in having a very dry Martini immediately."

"Would you like me to order for both of us?"

"If you wish."

It was apparent that dinner was part of the established order in which she was involved and impotent, and it would be quite futile to say that she did not want it or to resist it in any way. While Oliver ordered from the menu, she thought of her Martini, which she wanted desperately, and looked around the room, which she did not like. She never came here voluntarily and would have been depressed, even if everything else were all right, at being brought here under compulsion. It was not that there was anything wrong with the place itself. It was only that she and the place were not compatible. It was always filled with people who were supposed to be important or interesting or both, and they always seemed to be working very hard at being whatever they were supposed to be, and she always had, watching them, a very strong feeling that there was actually no such thing as importance and that anyone who assumed it or pretended to it was a kind of imposter. It was her experience, moreover, that the most interesting people were usually found in places where no one expected to find them, and that these interesting people, when they were found, hadn't the faintest idea that they were interesting. This experience had been supported by her study of bartenders in odd places, as well as by other contacts in other places she had gone to accidentally or on purpose, and it was her impression now that by far the most interesting person in this incompatible room was the attractive Negress who was singing sultry songs in a tigerish manner. Charity was sure that the singer was someone she ought to know, for anyone who sang songs in the Empire Room was bound to be someone that everyone ought to know, but she couldn't think of the singer's name, although she was positive it was a name she would recognize if someone mentioned it.

Her Martini was served and she nursed it with a kind of greediness because she knew that it would be difficult, if not impossible, to get another before dinner. Oliver did not have a cocktail. She had never seen him have a cocktail or a drink of any kind in all the time she had known him and been married to him, which was about the same amount of time in either case.

"Are you enjoying yourself?" he said.

"Yes," she lied. "It's very pleasant."

"You don't seem to be. You look bored."

"I'm sorry. I don't particularly care for this place. It depresses me."

"Really? You just said it was pleasant."

"I was only being agreeable. I would never come here if I had my choice."

"I should have consulted you I suppose, but I wanted it to be a surprise. We've gone out together so seldom that I don't know the places you like to go."

"Well, you probably wouldn't like the places I like, so it would make no difference anyhow."

"Perhaps you could convert me." He reached out and touched her right hand, which was lying palm down on the table, and his eyes glistened for the first time with overt malice. "As I said before, I'm feeling quite guilty for having neglected you. It might be amusing for both of us to become more familiar with each other's habits."

"I don't wish to interfere with your life. It isn't necessary for you to make concessions that you don't really want to make."

"You're too generous. It only makes me more determined to emulate you." He touched her hand again and laughed, and the malice in his eyes was in the laugh also. "However, here is our dinner, and I hope you are pleased with what I ordered. Afterward, we'll dance. It has been a long time since I've danced with you, hasn't it? I'm sure I'll be awkward in the beginning, but you must be patient until I improve. The music is by Nat Brandywynne, I believe. Are you familiar with his orchestra? Do you like it?"

"I don't know. I don't think I've beard it."

"Well, no matter. To tell the truth, we are only killing time as pleasantly as possible until we can go to the special event I've arranged for you. However bored you may be by all this, I promise that you'll not be bored by that. I promise that you'll find it most interesting."

He looked across the table at her, waiting for her to ask again what the special event was to be, but she did not ask because she was afraid to know, because she knew by feeling already that it was going to be, whatever developed specifically, the bad end of this bad night in which waiting and waiting and waiting was to be one of the worst of all bad things. Dinner was served, and the remains of dinner were taken away. Afterward they danced, and their dancing was a kind of cold and acceptable social sodomy. She refused after the first time to dance again, and so they sat and sat and did not even talk, and eventually it became eleven-thirty and time to leave.

In the Imperial, she shrank against the door and closed her eyes as a frightened child closes his eyes in the night, trading one darkness for another, the living and breathing outer darkness of a thousand threats for the sealed and solacing inner darkness secured by the thin membranes of the lids. She was conscious of moving, of riding for a long time on different streets, but she had no sense of direction, and when the car stopped and she opened her eyes at last, she had no idea of where she was, except that it was an incredibly dark and narrow and filthy street that turned out not to be a street at all, but an alley.

"Where have you brought me?" she said. "What are you going to do to me?"

"Do to you?" He took her face between thumb and fingers and turned it up and around and looked down into it smiling. "What a fantastic idea. I only brought you here to see something amusing. I told you that."

Releasing her, he got out of the car and came around to her side and opened the door, and she got out beside him. A bulky shadow separated itself from the deeper shadow of a recession in a crumbling brick wall. The shadow moved toward them and became an obese man, and she had the most peculiar feeling that it was a man she had seen somewhere before, but this was probably only a contingent of terror and not so.

"You didn't say you were bringing anyone," the obese man said.

"Was I obligated to inform you?" Oliver's voice was a soft expression of utter animosity, and Charity was aware that between these two men, in whatever strange relationship they had established, there was deep and abiding hatred. "Are you suggesting that I have no right to bring my wife as a guest if I please?"

"It's not smart," the man said. "It may be dangerous."

"I think not. And if you're worried about its compromising your usefulness in the future, you needn't worry any more. I had already decided that your usefulness has been exhausted." Oliver turned his head slightly toward Charity. "My dear, this is Mr. Sweeney. You'll hardly believe it, I know, but you and he are old friends after a fashion. Isn't that so, Sweeney?"

The man called Sweeney didn't answer. Turning, he moved back to the dark recession and disappeared. Guided by Oliver's hand on her arm, Charity followed and saw that there was in the recession a metal door which was now standing open, and she went through the doorway onto the concrete floor of a long dark building, a single enormous room, that was or had been almost certainly a garage. High, small windows at the far end were like blind eyes reflecting the feeble light from a lamp on the street outside. A single dim bulb burned in a conical tin shade at the end of a cord descending from shadows at the ceiling and cast upon the stained concrete a dirty yellow perimeter of defense against the darkness.

Sweeney brushed by, opened a door to a small enclosure that was mostly glass above a low wall of rough boards fixed vertically. The enclosure projected from one side of the room and was or had been the improvised office of what was or had been the garage.

"In here, please," Sweeney said. "It will probably be a while yet, so you had better sit down and take it easy."

"Yes, my dear," Oliver said. "Here is a chair with a cushion beside the desk. I'm sure you will be quite comfortable in it."

She sat down and folded her hands in her lap. It was hot in the small and dark enclosure, but she felt icy cold. Quietly she waited for the bad end of the bad night. Regret she felt, and fear and despair, and the greatest of these was despair.

CHAPTER 15

The drum and the piano were tired. In the shag end of the night, in the rise and drift of sound from a litter of people at a litter of tables, the die-hards, the last dogs, the ones who never wanted to go home, their voices lagged and faltered and fell silent. The drum, in the end, had the final word. The piano, too tired to care, declined to answer. The litter heard no silence that was not its own.

In a tiny room off the short hall to the alley, Chester Lewis put a hat over his wiry hair, lit a cigarette, looked with his expression of chronic surprise at the miracle of thin blue smoke that issued from his lungs.

"It wasn't good tonight," he said. "I wasn't with it."

"You were all right," Joe said. "You were fine."

"No. It wouldn't come. Not the good stuff. What came was gibberish."

"You're tired, that's all. We're both tired."

"That's right, Joe. We're both tired. We're a pair of tired guys, Joe."

"Everyone gets tired."

"Everyone doesn't stay tired."

"All right, Chester. You better get some sleep and forget it."

"Sure, Joe. You better, too."

"I'll get along in a little."

"You going to play again?"

"I don't know. Maybe not. Maybe I'll skip it."

"How about a sandwich and a glass of milk somewhere?"

"I don't think so, Chester. Thanks anyhow."

Chester drew on his cigarette, examined with astonishment the miracle, of smoke.

"We've been good partners, Joe. You think so?"

"I think so, Chester."

"I needed you. You came along just right."

"We needed each other, Chester. It was right for both of us."

"Yeah. I guess so. We've never said much to each other, though. There are lots of things we could have said that we never did."

"Just with the drum and the piano."

"That's right. The drum and the piano. You hear what the drum was say-ing tonight, Joe? Tonight and last night?"

"I heard it,"

"The piano didn't answer, Joe. It didn't say a word back. Just changed the subject."

"There wasn't anything to say."

"Yeah. I guess not. Nothing to say." Chester dropped his cigarette on the bare floor and stepped on it, reducing his little miracle to a dead butt. "Maybe we're more than partners, Joe. Maybe we're friends."

"We're friends, Chester,"

"Funny how it begins and goes on, isn't it? What makes and keeps two guys friends, Joe?"

"I don't know. It's hard to say."

"Probably it helps if each of them pretty much minds his own business."

"Probably."

"Sure. That's what I've been thinking. Well, be careful. Be real careful. I think I'll be going along now, Joe. Goodnight."

"Goodnight, Chester."

Chester went out and back to the alley, and Joe went out after him and up to the bar where Yancy was.

"How's everything, Yancy?" he said.

"No complaints," Yancy said.

"I'll have rye and water."

"You sure? No Martini?"

"You heard me. Rye and water."

"I had a notion you'd switched to Martinis. Funny how I got such a notion."

"Very funny, Yancy. I'll laugh later."

"You needn't bother. Truth is, I don't think it was funny myself." Yancy poured rye and added water and set it out. "I got a message. I'm supposed to tell you something."

"All right. Tell me."

"She can't come. Something happened. I'd have told you sooner, but you were late getting in and I didn't have the chance."

"What was it happened?"

"I don't know. Something to prevent her coming. She said she was sorry, and she sounded like she really was. She said to tell you she'd come as soon as she could. Tomorrow, maybe."

"She telephoned?"

"That's right. Between six and seven. Nearer six, I think. She sounded all right, just like she was sorry."

"Thanks, Yancy."

He drank some of the good strong rye and water and sat looking into what was left. Behind him was the sound of the last dogs in the litter of the night. Between now and daylight were five long hours. In five hours a man could count perhaps twenty-two thousand heart beats.

All right, he thought, all right. There was a night and a part of a night

in the room, and there was most of a day and a night on Long island, and
there was a night and a day and a night and a day in Connecticut, and now
there's the finish, the end, nothing more. Whatever there was and however long it lasted, it was more and longer than you thought it would be
or had any reason to expect it to be, and so you had now better have your
rye and water and go home and to bed, and if you can forget it in the little time that's left for forgetting, that's something else you had better do,
and if you can't forget it, you can at least remember it and her with kindness and pleasure and pity, for she will probably need kindness and pity
and the remembrance of pleasure far more in the end than you will ever
need them.

In the depths of the golden rye and water, she raised her face and looked
up at him sadly from under her hair on the heavy side, and he lifted the
glass and emptied it of the rye and water and her.

"You still here?" Yancy said.

"I may be here for quite a while. What's the matter, Yancy? You need the
space?"

"I didn't mean that. I meant you looked gone. Like part of you had
walked off and left the rest of you."

"I was thinking."

"Well, that's a bad habit to get into. A guy gets along pretty well until he
starts thinking too much about things, and then he's in for trouble.
Trouble with himself, I mean, which can sometimes be the worst kind of
trouble there is. I read a poem about that once. According to this poem a
guy can survive pretty well on a diet of liquor, love and fights and stuff like
that, but the minute he starts thinking he's a sick bastard."

"Is that the way the poem went?"

"Well, not exactly. That's just the general idea."

"I didn't know you read poetry, Yancy."

"Of course you didn't. You didn't even know I could read. You thought I
was just an ignorant, illiterate slob."

"Not me, Yancy. I've always had the greatest respect for you. I value your
friendship and solicit your counsel."

"Oh, sure, sure. Funny boy. What if I told you to go to hell?"

"You won't."

"That's right. I won't. Where I'll tell you to go is home, but you won't be
in any more hurry to go there than the other place. You got no brains to
speak of, that's the thing about you."

"Sometimes, Yancy, one place is much like another."

"Yeah. I know that myself. You want another rye?"

"Yes."

"I thought you would. I was only doing my duty to my lousy conscience.
You going to play requests tonight?"

"I don't think so. I don't feel like it."

"I know you don't feel like it. You didn't feel like it earlier with Chester, far as that goes. You were working."

"It's uncanny how you know things, Yancy. You must have some kind of special power or something. It makes a guy feel uneasy."

"Well, I know when something's fun and when it's work, and playing the piano used to be fun for Joe Doyle, at least part of the time, but now it's all work and when anything gets that way, all work, it's no good any longer and ought to be stopped. Why don't you quit, Joe?"

"Maybe I ought to quit eating and paying rent, too."

"There are other ways to eat and pay rent. There are other places to go than a lousy club every night, and there are other things to do than play piano for a lot of God-damn tramps and lushes with nothing better to do than get maudlin over some cheap little tune that stirs up some cheap little memory."

"I admire you when you're eloquent, Yancy. You're real impressive."

"Okay. I ought to know better than to try. Maybe you'll think about it, though. Maybe you'll think about all the other things there are to do."

"I know there are other things to do, if you know how. I don't know how. All I know is how to play the piano, and I don't know that a tenth as well as I wanted to and tried to."

"Forget I said anything. I tell you I ought to know better, and then I try again before I can even get my mouth shut, and what I learn from the effort is that I ought to know better. It's your business. If you want the last thing you see to be a bloodshot eye and the last breath you breathe to be a lungful of second-hand cigarette smoke, it's your business."

"Thanks, Yancy. What you say brings us to an interesting question, and it happens to be a question, believe it or not, that I've done quite a bit of thinking about at one time or another. The question is, Yancy, what do you do with what's left of a life when only a little's left. When I was a kid in high school I took a course in public speaking. We got up and talked about things. One of the things we talked about was this particular question of what we would do if we only had so long to live. Only a little while. I remember some of the things that were said, including what I said, and it was all foolishness. Everyone was running around in his little talk doing the little thing he liked the very best, and that just isn't the way it is, when the time comes. No, Yancy, they're doing pretty much what they were doing yesterday and the day before and the day before. They're doing what they've always done and know how to do. They're playing the piano, Yancy, the same as me."

"Here," Yancy said. "You need another rye." He mixed it with water and pushed it across the bar. "You call me eloquent? I'm practically a mute, sonny."

"It's the rye, Yancy. It's two ryes on an empty stomach. And maybe something else a little. I won't say I haven't thought about it, though. About what I'd like to do best the last thing. There are several things I've thought about, and the trouble with all of them is that they're things that have already been done and can't be done again. You know what one of the things is I've been thinking about and wanting to do? I'll tell you. Listen to me and two ryes, Yancy. Two and a half ryes. I've been thinking about how I used to walk on hot summer afternoons out from town to the creek for a swim. That was when I was a little kid and lived in a little town, long before I got big and started living in this biggest of all big towns. I'd walk out about two miles on a country road, and the dust was white and hot under my feet, and it raised clouds around me as I walked. It got in my throat and made me very thirsty, and being thirsty was a great pleasure, because it made so much cooler and better the water that I drank from a well on the farm that the creek ran through. I drank the water from a tin dipper that hung from a nail driven into a tree a few feet away, and then I walked down across fields to the creek and swam naked, and afterward I came back and had another drink from the well and walked home. You can see that this is something a man might want to do again, Yancy, but you can also see that it's something he can't possibly do. Not again. He can't do it again because it requires a certain time as well as certain circumstances, and time is something that can't be done over."

"Cut it out," Yancy said. "Goddamn it, I was just suggesting it would be better for you if you went somewhere and did something that would give you a little peace and quiet and you could keep decent hours doing. I didn't ask for any hearts and flowers, Goddamn it."

"Excuse me, Yancy. I'll have another rye."

"The hell you will!"

"Are you refusing me service, Yancy?"

"Call it what you like. You've had three ryes already."

"I know how many ryes I've had. I can count up to three ryes as well as anybody."

"Three are plenty."

"Am I creating a disturbance, Yancy? Have I given you any reason to discriminate against me? It seems to me that you are being very highhanded, if you don't mind my saying so."

"I don't mind at all. You can say anything you like, and you can drink as many ryes as you like, and I'm damned if I'll try to talk sense to you ever again."

"Thank you, Yancy. You're a very understanding bartender."

"Superior, sonny. Superior's what I am. I've been told by an expert."

Yancy supplied the fourth rye and water with a kind of angry abruptness of motion that plainly expressed his disapproval, and Joe looked into the tiny golden sea in a crystal bed and saw again the face of Charity smiling up at him with sad finality. He lifted the glass and tipped it against his mouth, and she slipped over his tongue and down his throat as easily as an aspirin tablet.

"Hey!" Yancy said. "Take it easy."

Lifting the empty glass against the light, Joe looked through it, into and through the empty crystal bed of the vanished golden sea. He felt for a moment purged of his sins and wholly well, shriven by rye and cured of his ills by the swallowed vision. Then, instantly afterward, he felt terribly sick. He was sick to his stomach and afraid that he was going to humiliate himself by vomiting on the bar. Closing his eyes and mouth tightly, he bowed his head and sat very quietly until his stomach stopped churning, or stopped, at least, churning so violently. He became aware after a minute or two that Yancy was repeating something he had said before.

"You sick, Joe?" Yancy said. "You sick?"

"No." Joe lifted his head and set the empty glass, which he had continued to hold, gently on the bar. "I'm all right."

"The hell you are! You're sick. You feel like fainting again?"

"I'm all right now, Yancy. Four quick ryes on an empty stomach are too many. You were right as usual. In a minute I'm going home."

"I'll tell you what. You go lie down in your back room, and I'll drive you home after closing."

"I can drive myself. Thanks anyhow, Yancy."

"You have one of those fainting spells while you're driving, you'll pile up and kill yourself, that's what you'll do."

"Don't worry about it, Yancy. I'll get home all right."

He slipped off the stool suddenly, and his stomach began to churn again immediately with the movement, and he stood gripping the edge of the bar until it and his stomach settled and became still in a precarious resumption of their proper places and conditions. Yancy watched him warily. Anger and anxiety were equal parts of Yancy's expression.

"Okay," he said. "Maybe I'll read about you in the papers."

"Not me." Joe shook his head and managed a grin. "You'd never find a couple lines in all those pages."

"Sure. Big joke. Go ahead and be a hero, sonny. See who gives a damn."

"All I want to do is go home, Yancy. Does it take a hero to go home?"

"Go on home, then. Go on."

"I'm going. Right now."

He turned and started carefully across the room among the tables, some of them empty and some still occupied by the last sad dogs of the night. Yancy stood watching him for a few seconds, and then, prompted by remembrance of something he'd wanted to mention, he walked around the end of the bar and followed. In the short hall to the alley, he caught up.

"I don't need any help, Yancy," Joe said. "I keep telling you."

"Who's helping?" Yancy said. "I just thought of something I wanted to tell you, that's all."

"What's that?"

"A guy was in here asking about you. Last Thursday, it was. A fat slob with a bald head with little scars all over it. Ugly bastard. You know him?"

Joe stopped just inside the alley door, thinking and shaking his head.

"I don't think so. I can't think of anyone I know who looks like that."

"Well, he was in here asking about you. Where you were. When you were expected back in town. Things like that."

"Maybe he wanted to sell me some insurance or something."

"More jokes. More big laughs. You in the market for insurance?"

"Not quite. I'm not considered what they call a good risk."

"Just be careful you don't get to be an even worse one."

"Worrying again, Yancy?"

"Over you? Hell, no. I told you it wasn't worth the trouble. Anyhow, he's probably just a guy who's got fat and dropped his hair since you knew him somewhere sometime, and since you don't seem to give a damn who he is or why he was here, I'm sorry I bothered to tell you. Go on home."

Yancy turned and went back through the hall to the front room and the bar, and Joe, opening the door and pulling it shut behind him, stepped out into the alley and stood for a moment breathing deeply of the night air. Even the effluvium of things that gather in alleys seemed crisp and pure and invigorating after the stale air of the club. Lifting one arm, he placed the hand flat against a brick wall, and a coolness crept from the brick into the hand and seemed slowly to move up the arm into his body. He wondered if it were true that the coolness did so move into him, or if it were only, instead, a matter of suggestion. His stomach was feeling much better. He was reasonably sure now that he was not going to be sick after all.

Letting his arm drop to his side, he began to walk carefully along the wall toward the space in which he had left his car, and he had reached the space and almost the car when two men took shape in the darkness and moved toward him. He thought at first that they were merely going to separate and pass on either side and go on, but they stopped abruptly with him between them, and he was forced to stop also by strong hands gripping his arms. He understood then that the positions were accomplished by design and that the two men were in effect the jaws of a sprung trap in which he was caught for a reason not yet clear.

One of the men was a kind of exemplary average. He could have walked all day on a hundred streets without being particularly noticed or remembered at all, and even now, in the dark alley, he was not impressive, except that he was, in his implicit purpose, a threat. The other man was, on the other hand, a monstrous deviation from the average. He was the result of a terrible joke played by a gland on an organism, and if he had walked one street for one-half of one hour, he would have been noticed and remembered reluctantly by everyone he met. His appearance was brutish. Huge head with jutting stony jaw. Enormous hands and feet that swung and shuffled with a suggestion of anthropoid power. The total effect was one of deformity, distortion and disproportion of bones, and there was a name for it, this glandular joke, but Joe couldn't think of the name or precise cause, only that the soft bones of extremities continued to grow when other bones did not.

"Hello, Lover," the monstrous man said. "We thought you were never coming. We waited and waited and we thought you were never coming."

He pronounced the term of endearment lingeringly, fondling it with his tongue as if he were loathe to release it, laughing softly afterward as if it were a joke at least as good as the one that had been played by a gland on him. Average laughed too, a brief burst of air that was more like a snort than an expression of amusement

"Cupid's a comedian," be said. "Always with the humor, that's Cupid. You'll like him."

Joe stepped back, trying to release his arms from the hands that held them, but he was not strong, could not hope to prevail or even compete, not even with the unusual strength that is created by the strange chemistry of fear.

"What do you want?" he said.

"You, Lover," Average said. "Like Cupid told you, we been waiting and waiting."

"Why? What do you want with me?"

"Well, it seems you been a bad boy. It seems you been keeping company you had no business keeping, and someone figures you ought to be ashamed of yourself. Someone figures you ought to be taught what happens to bad boys who keep the wrong company."

Cupid lifted his enormous free hand and cupped it beneath Joe's chin, tipping the head back and looking down into the tilted face with an expression that was a caricature of affection. His voice was an incongruous croon.

"I like you," he said. "We're going to be good friends. Lover and Cupid are going to get along fine."

Average laughed again, the explosive snort, and Joe felt shriveled and incredibly old and sick with shame, knowing now that what he had thought was dead had yet to be killed. Park Avenue ending in an alley. After the North Shore and Connecticut, violence and degradation in some dark corner. Most shameful of all in the evaluation of himself, a fear of physical pain that he had never accorded the anticipation of death. Despite this, aware of what was certainly coming, be felt a desperate and incon-sistent urgency to get it over with as quickly as possible.

"All right," he said. "If you've been hired to give me a beating, why don't you do it?"

"No, Lover." Average gave Joe's arm a little squeeze. "We can't do it that way. Not here in the alley. We got a nice place all set up for it. You can see how it is. You been doing someone wrong, and this someone wants to be sure you get what he figures is coming to you. Since he's paying for it, he's got a right to be sure. You admit that's fair? Come along quietly now with Cupid and me. We'll take you to this nice place where no one'll bother us, and everything will be fine. You'll see. Everything fine."

They walked together down the alley to a side street and got into a wait-ing sedan, Average behind the wheel, Joe and Cupid in the back seat. Average drove slowly, apparently in no hurry to get to the nice place or anyplace, and after a few minutes he began to whistle cheerfully through his teeth. Cupid leaned back and opened his mouth in the shape of a laugh, but he began to make, instead of the sound of laughter, a very soft crooning sound, oddly musical, that might have been made by a mother to comfort her child. The sedan, under the guidance of Average, turned many corners and traveled on many streets, and after a while Joe no longer had any idea of where they were or might be going, except that the streets were narrow and littered and dark, lighted at long intervals by inadequate lamps at the curb.

Average whistled and Cupid crooned, and the shameful fear of physical pain was a malignancy in Joe's mind. Watching Cupid from the corners of his eyes with a slyness made acute by growing fear and diminishing time, he began to think positively of escape, how he might accomplish it, and then, all at once, in a slight change of circumstances in his favor, he was acting instinctively without slyness or calculation or any regard for chances or consequences. The sedan slowed for a corner, turning left, and in an instant he was clawing at the handle of the door beside him, in another instant was sprawling headlong into the street. Vaguely conscious of fire in his flesh where it was seared by asphalt, he doubled and rolled and came onto his feet running.

Ahead of him was a high board fence stretched between two shabby buildings, and in the fence a wide gate sagged open on a length of chain. Hardly slackening his speed, he slipped through the opening and ran down an aisle between high piles of scrap iron and steel to another board fence at the rear. He ran along the fence to his right, pounding the boards with his fists in search of a gate, but he reached the juncture of fence and building, and there was no gate. Reversing himself, he ran back along the fence the other way, still pounding the boards, now beginning to sob softly, but still there was no gate. He looked up to the top of the fence, but it seemed incredibly high and impossible to scale, and there was, moreover, no time to try, for Average and Cupid were coming into the yard from the street, and it was imperative to hide from them at once.

Sinking to his hands and knees, he crawled along the building behind the piles of scrap, and after half a minute he found a sanctuary, a small hollow in one of the piles, and he crawled into this and vomited and lay very still, sucking in his breath between clenched teeth and releasing it slowly, a little at a time, to avoid making the slightest noise.

Average and Cupid ran down the aisle to the rear fence. Joe listened to the pounding of their feet and measured the distance between him and them by the sound. He knew very well that now was the time to act, that he should now get up and make a break for the front gate and the street and perhaps someone on the street who would save him, but he couldn't move, could find nowhere in himself the strength or will to take what was plainly his best chance, and so he continued to lie quietly in his false sanctuary, sucking his breath between his teeth, the sour taste and smell of his own vomit on his tongue and in his nostrils. He could hear Average and Cupid examining the length of the fence. He could hear their footsteps, hear their fists beat upon the wood for evidence of a gate or a loose plank through which he might have gone.

"Maybe he went over the top," Cupid said.

"No," Average said. "I don't think so. It's a high fence, eight feet at least, and we'd have seen him going over. Probably he's hiding somewhere in this junk."

"It's not nice of him to cause us so much trouble," Cupid said. "Why did he want to run away and hide and cause us so much trouble?"

"Never mind that," Average said. "What we got to do is find him. If we don't, we're in big trouble. Chalk don't like guys to fumble a job. It's bad for business. You take one side of the yard, and I'll take the other. He's got to be in here somewhere."

Obediently, Cupid started through the piles of scrap on the side of the sanctuary. His huge feet shuffled slowly, scraping against the hard ground and disturbing a piece of metal now and then with a sharp clatter. Coming closer and closer to the sanctuary, he began to talk in his soft, incongruous crooning way.

"Come out, Lover. This is Cupid, Lover. Come out to Cupid, Lover."

The crooning voice was more terrifying than a curse as a threat of evil. Joe pressed his face against the ground and covered his ears with his hands, and then he could not hear the terrible soft threat any longer, could not hear the shuffle of feet coming nearer and nearer, and after a few moments in the silence and darkness achieved by hands and closed lids he began to have a strange sense of peace and security, and he was lying so, in the false security of the false sanctuary, when great hands took hold of him gently and lifted him up and held him erect.

"Here's Lover," Cupid crooned. "Poor Lover's dirtied himself. It wasn't nice of you to run away and hide and cause Cupid so much trouble, Lover. Cupid's angry because you ran away."

Average came across the aisle from the other side of the yard. Saying nothing, he took Joe by one arm and started immediately toward the street. Joe did not resist. He had no longer any desire to resist or to suffer again the unbearable ordeal of escape. In submission, he achieved a kind of miraculous detachment from whatever was happening or might happen to Joe Doyle, an emotional immunity to Joe's fear and Joe's pain and Joe's ultimate end, whatever it turned out to be. In the car, he leaned back beside Cupid and closed his eyes and sank briefly into exquisite physical lethargy. Charity was waiting for him in the vast, illimitable night behind his lids. She smiled at him sadly, and he could see, shining like traces of phosphorous in the darkness, the paths of tears across her thin cheeks. He nodded and returned her smile and tried to make her understand without words the miracle of acceptance and submission that had made all right everything that had been, a few minutes ago, all wrong.

The sedan turned a corner and stopped at last, and Cupid, crooning again, took him by the arm with his incongruous, monstrous gentleness and helped him out onto the sidewalk. They were standing now near the entrance to an alley. Average got out on the street side and walked around the front of the sedan and went into the alley without looking back, as if he had forgotten entirely that anyone was with him. Cupid and Joe stood waiting on the sidewalk, Cupid crooning and Joe quietly with his head bowed in a posture of prayer or reflection, and after a minute or two Average returned.

"It's all right," he said.

Together, Joe between the two, they went into the alley and past a parked car and into an enormous room with a concrete floor. Small windows were glazed with faint light at the far end. At the rear, near the alley entrance, a weak bulb in a conical shade cut a circle of light in the darkness. Joe stood in the light under the conical shade, his arms hanging, his head still bowed in the prayerful posture. He thought he heard, somewhere in the room, a whisper of movement, a ghost of sound, but it was not significant, whatever it was, in his present vast indifference. Cupid had taken off his coat in the darkness and stepped into the light without it. He was smiling and saying something, and Joe raised his eyes and listened intently in an effort to hear clearly what was being said, but for some strange reason he could not quite understand. He saw that Cupid was wearing a pink shirt with very thin white stripes, and he thought that the shirt was silk, but he wasn't absolutely certain of this, either. He saw also that Cupid's eyes actually seemed to be red, and this struck him as extremely odd. He wondered if it was just a trick of light and shadow. The eyes of Siamese cats looked red in certain circumstances, he knew, but he had never heard of the eyes of a man looking red in any circumstances whatever. He was so fascinated by Cupid's red eyes that he did not even see Cupid's huge fist when it was driven at his face. He was only aware of splitting flesh and splintering bone. Not even precisely of these. Only of the monstrous, incredible pain of them. Crying out with the pain, he fell spiraling in an immeasurable thunderous night to the concrete floor.

Aware after an age that he was on the floor, he decided that the floor was a good place to be. He thought that he would simply remain forever on the floor. Someone, however, did not want him to stay there. Someone was asking him to get up, pleading with him in a crooning voice, but he knew perfectly well that this was only a trick, an effort to get him to do what he did not want to do, and he could avoid this simply by lying very still and pretending that he didn't hear. This did not work, however, for whoever was talking was now also lifting him to his feet and holding him erect, and he was suddenly ashamed that he was not even capable of standing on his own feet without help. He spread his legs, trying to establish a balance. Deliberately, with a great effort, he raised his head and tried to focus his eyes. It was a foolish and painful thing to do, which would surely accomplish nothing, but he was compelled by an irrational conviction that it was somehow essential to pride and manhood to stand erect and see clearly in that instant.

It was the instant he died. Cupid's second and last blow detonated above the bad heart that was ready to quit, and Joe collapsed again in a final recapitulation of pain and engulfing darkness. The. pain was as brief as the instant of dying, but the darkness endured with death.

CHAPTER 16

Oliver knocked and opened the door and came into the room. Charity was lying on her back on her bed. Her eyes were wide open, staring at the ceiling. She didn't look at Oliver when he entered. She didn't stir in the slightest.

"There's a man here to see you, my dear," Oliver said.

"I don't wish to see anyone," Charity said.

Oliver walked over beside the bed and stood looking down at her. She was fully dressed, wearing even her shoes. Her wide-open eyes were hot and dry and unblinking. They continued to stare at the ceiling.

"I'm afraid you had better see this man whether you want to or not," Oliver said. "He's a policeman."

"Why does a policeman want to see me?" she said. "I've done nothing that should be of any interest whatever to a policeman."

"Of course you haven't, my dear. He's only trying to get some information about a man who was killed. This man's name was Joe Doyle. The policeman seems to have some evidence that you and the dead man knew each other. Naturally, he wants to ask you some questions."

"Am I required to answer his questions?"

"I think you are. After all, he's really being very considerate. He might have forced you to go to police headquarters"

"All right. If I'm required to answer them, I'll come."

"I'd like to make a suggestion first, if you don't mind. Please be very careful of what you say. There's always a danger that an inexperienced person may incriminate himself or others in these things when there is really no need for it at all. It would be most unfortunate if you were so careless."

"I know. You needn't worry."

"I'm not worried, my dear. Not for myself. I'm only thinking of your welfare."

"Of course."

"I'll be with you all the time, supporting you, and I'm sure there's nothing to be concerned about. Shall we go in together?"

"Yes."

She got up and smoothed the skirt of her dress and pushed back the heavy side of her hair. She did not look at Oliver at any time. Walking with a kind of rigidity, as if she had been drinking too much and were exercising the greatest effort to conceal it, which was not true, she walked out of the bedroom and down the hall into the living room, where a man rose at once from a chair to meet her. He was slender, below average height, with sparse, sandy hair brushed straight back from a high fore-head, and his eyes were covered with thick, rimless lenses. He leaned slightly forward from the hips, which gave him the appearance of peering intently at whomever he was merely looking, and he had, she learned after a moment, an odd habit of pinching the lobe of his right ear with the thumb and index finger of his right hand. He did not conform at all to her idea of a policeman. To her, he looked much more like a clerk in a depart-ment store, although he was not dressed quite well enough for it, and he was so palpably uneasy that she felt sorry for him and wanted immedi-ately to say something to reassure him.

"My dear," Oliver said, "this is Mr. Bunting of the police."

"Lieutenant," Bunting said.

"Excuse me. Lieutenant Bunting. He would like to ask you some ques-tions."

"How do you do," Charity said. "I'm sure I can't imagine what I could tell you that would be of any help to you."

"Well, it's just routine, Mrs. Farnese." Bunting sounded apologetic. "You know how these things are."

"No, I don't," Charity said. "What things?"

"Oh, police matters in general. It's necessary to investigate them, you know. I'll not disturb you any longer than necessary. Perhaps it would be better if we sat down."

"Certainly. Please sit down, Lieutenant."

Bunting hesitated with an air of desperation and then sat down slowly in the chair from which he had risen. Afterward, Charity went to anoth-er chair and sat down too. They faced each other across five feet of deep pile. Oliver continued to stand.

"I understand that you knew a man named Joseph Doyle," Bunting said.

"Do you?" Charity said.

"Yes. He played the piano in a nightclub called Duo's. You're familiar with the place, I believe. The bartender there told me that you and Doyle became acquainted there one night about a week ago and later left the club together. He said you saw each other at other times."

"Is he certain of that? That we saw each other at other times afterward?"

"Well, no, he isn't, as a matter of fact. He can't prove it, that is. He assumes it, but he feels sure you did." Bunting shot a glance at Oliver Farnese and looked more apologetic than ever. "I don't want to embarrass you, of course."

"I am not embarrassed, Lieutenant. I only want to know if you are accus-ing me of something just because someone chooses to make assumptions."

"I am not accusing you of anything for any reason." Bunting pinched the lobe of his ear, glanced at Oliver Farnese and back to Charity. "I thought it was understood that I'm only after information. I'm not very good at saying things, however, and maybe I didn't make my position clear. What do you say we start over? Joseph Doyle is dead. Maybe it was murder, but more likely it was manslaughter. He was found yesterday morning in an alley. His jaw was broken and his face and lips lacerated, and several teeth were loosened. He had been struck, from the evidence, by the fist of a strong man. But it wasn't this blow that killed him. He had been struck a second time in the body. Above the heart. Post mortem showed that he had a bum heart, and it was the body blow that he didn't survive."

"He had rheumatic fever as a boy," Charity said.

Bunting smiled at her, pinching the ear lobe, and silence stretched out for seconds. His attitude seemed suddenly more relaxed, suggesting that everything would now surely be pleasant and productive for everyone since he had clarified his position and his problem.

"That's fine, Mrs. Farnese," he said finally. "I knew you would want to cooperate with us when you understood the circumstances."

"I'm willing to cooperate," she said, "but I still don't understand how I can help you."

"You do admit that you knew Joseph Doyle?"

"What do you mean, admit it? I don't like the way that sounds. You make it sound as if it were something shameful or incriminating or something."

"No, no. I'm sorry if I gave that impression. I only want a statement as to whether you knew him or not."

"It has been established that I knew him, and it is perfectly clear that you know all about it. I don't see why you keep going over and over it."

"Sorry. If you will only be patient a little longer, I'll appreciate it. Was this night at the Club about a week ago the first time you met Doyle?"

"Yes. I had been somewhere else and went in there to have a Martini and think about things. He was playing the piano, and someone else was playing a drum. It was quite clever, like a conversation that you kept trying to understand. Afterward, when it was quite late, Joe Doyle played requests on the piano, and I asked him to play a particular song. I thought he was very good, but he said that he wasn't. We had Martinis together at the bar. At least, I had a Martini. He may have had something else."

"I see. Did you leave the Club with him?"

"Yes."

"Did you see him again after that night?"

"I don't know that I should answer that. I can't see that it makes any difference."

"Perhaps you're right." Bunting looked miserable, and the lobe of his ear was red from the mauling of thumb and finger. "I hope you believe that I have no desire to embarrass you, and that I have no interest at all in your personal affairs. Let me come to the point directly. Do you have any idea who might have killed Doyle?"

She was silent, sitting with her hands folded and her bead bowed. She wondered if he would hear, as she did, from some remote and indeterminable source, the soft, incessant sound of cosmic weeping.

"No," she said at last. "How could I?"

"I thought he might have mentioned someone who held a grudge against him. Something like that."

"No. Nothing of the sort. He didn't talk about other people he knew or what had happened to him before we became acquainted. As you see, I learned practically nothing about him."

"Except that he had had rheumatic fever as a boy."

"Yes, of course. He told me that. Also that he wanted to be an exceptional pianist, but didn't have the ability. I thought that he was very sad about it, not having the ability and all, and I felt sorry for him and tried to make him feel that it was still possible, but he didn't believe me."

"I see. It's tough, sometimes, learning to accept our limitations." Bunting looked embarrassed again, as if he were suddenly aware that his remark sounded presumptuous. He had not looked at Oliver Farnese since his one previous glance, but at this moment he somehow gave the impression that he was deliberately, with an effort, refraining from looking. "There is one other point I'd like to mention, Mrs. Farnese, if you don't mind."

"Not at all. You may mention whatever points you choose."

"Thank you. According to my information, you had arranged to see Joseph Doyle at the club where he worked on the night he was killed. Night before last, that was. Between six and seven o'clock, you called the Club and talked to the bartender and asked him to relay the message that you would be unable to come. Is that true?"

She would have lied about this if there had been any chance at all for a lie to be believed, but there wasn't any, not the slightest, and so the only thing she could do was to tell the truth, or at least part of it, and try to make what had happened seem as natural and insignificant as possible.

"Yes," she said, "it's true. I called and said that I couldn't come."

"May I ask what made you change your plans?"

"Why do you continually ask if you may ask? Since you are obviously going to ask whatever you please, its rather ridiculous and a waste of time."

"You needn't answer any of my questions if you don't want to. Not at this time, anyhow."

"Later, however, you would force me to answer them. Is that what you mean?"

"I hope it would not be necessary."

"In other words, if you were inclined to be honest, it is exactly what you mean. Well, it doesn't matter, for I don't mind answering at all, and I only wish you would not try to pretend that things are different from what they are."

"I apologize. Please tell me why you were unable to go to the Club that night."

"There was a very simple reason. I had promised I would go hear the piano and the drum again, because I liked them and wanted to, but at the last minute my husband wanted me to go out somewhere with him instead, and I felt compelled to go."

Now Bunting did look sidewise at Oliver Farnese for verification, and Farnese smiled and nodded. It was apparent from his serenity that he found nothing disturbing in his wife's activities and did not object in the least to her interest in pianos and drums and whoever played them.

"That's right, Lieutenant," he said. "We went to the Empire Room, where I had made a reservation. I suppose you can check that if you feel inclined."

"I'm sure it won't be necessary." Bunting sighed and stood up. "I won't intrude any longer, and I appreciate your kindness. These things are tough. The toughest. You find a body in a street or an alley, and there doesn't seem to be any reason for it, no leads, no connections. We'll be lucky if we ever get anything definite on this one. I mustn't impose my troubles on you, however. I've already been bother enough, I'm afraid. Thank you again for your kindness, Mrs. Farnese. You've been very patient."

"Not at all," she said.

For a moment she was afraid that he was going to offer to shake hands on leaving, and she was exorbitantly relieved when he did not, turning abruptly, instead, and starting for the door with Oliver following. She remained motionless in her chair, her hands folded in her lap, and pretty soon Oliver returned from the door and stood a few feet away looking at her amicably.

"You did quite well, my dear," he said. "I'm proud of you."

"Are you?" she said.

"Yes, I am. You were admirable. I've never heard anyone avoid the truth so cleverly. You had poor Bunting on the defensive from the beginning."

"I wasn't trying to put him on the defensive. I only wanted him to get finished and go away."

"I can understand that, my dear. You've gone through a difficult time. I was certain, however, that I could depend on you to be sensible. You're feeling tired and despondent now, but you'll recover in a little while. I've noticed before how remarkably durable and resilient you are."

"Thank you very much."

"You owe me no gratitude, my dear. You have earned everything I've said."

"And done?"

"Yes. Said and done."

He laughed and took half a step toward her, and she wondered what she would do if he were to touch her. Perhaps she would begin to scream, she thought, or rake him with her nails, or merely be sick on herself and the carpet. He did not touch her, however. He stood for a second with one foot before the other and one hand lifted toward her, but then he lowered the hand slowly and drew the forward foot back.

"I think you had better rest now," he said. "If you don't mind, I'll go to the office for the rest of the afternoon."

"I don't mind. Please go where you wish."

"Will you be all right?"

"Certainly."

"It disturbs me to be off my routine. I want to resume it without any further delay, and I hope that it will not be necessary to disrupt it again soon."

She didn't know if this was a warning or not, but it was of no great importance. She sat without moving or answering, and he turned and went out of the room, and she continued to sit with her hands folded after he was gone, and she was still there, in the exact position she had been in when he left, when he returned and crossed the room and left the apartment.

Now I will think very carefully about everything that has happened, she thought. It is absolutely essential now to think clearly and sanely and not to allow myself to become deceived by emotion or excessively depressed by what has occurred and can't be helped. Let me see how it was exactly. I went accidentally to the place where he worked, which was nothing for which I can be blamed and was no offense of any kind, and I saw him there and heard him play the piano, and I thought that he was beautiful and played beautifully, and I loved him, I did love him, and now he is dead because of it, but that is no reason to accuse myself or to assume responsibility for what I did not want or directly do.

I did not want him to be hurt or to die. All I wanted was to make him happy and to be happy myself, and that's what I did and almost was. He said himself that he was happy, that each time we were together was the best time of all, and this was good. It's true, of course, that it would not have continued indefinitely, or even much longer, which I'll not try to deny, but it was good for the time it lasted and better than no good at all. This is only logical, that something is better than nothing, and it is surely not my fault that it ended badly.

So. I have reasoned calmly and rationally, there is no question about that, and it is clearly preposterous for me to have this terrible and oppressive feeling of guilt, as if I had personally done a great wrong or had deliberately permitted the great wrong that was done. Commitment to grief is one thing, and commitment to guilt is another. That's the distinction I must understand and believe. I saw him die, however. There's no getting away from that. I saw him beaten and killed by a monster, and I said nothing afterward to anyone, and just a little while ago when the policeman was here I still said nothing, and the reason I have said nothing and will say nothing is because I am afraid of Oliver, and I know that he would find a way to destroy me if I gave him cause. I could go away, of course, but he could certainly find me if he wanted to, and even if he couldn't I still wouldn't go away, because there is no place for me in the world but this place and no way to survive but this way. I'm a coward, to tell the truth. I do not care to make a gesture that would change nothing that has happened and would only make things worse.

There. I have faced things fairly as they are, and myself as I am. There is supposed to be a kind of catharsis in this, and one is supposed to feel much better after having done it. In a little while, if I sit here quietly, I shall surely begin to feel better.

She sat quietly and waited to begin feeling better, but she didn't feel better at all, and pretty soon it was impossible to wait any longer for anything or to stay any longer in the apartment than it would take her to change her clothes and get out. Unfolding her hands and rising, she walked stiffly to her room with the strangest and most disturbing sense of being precariously contained, as if the slightest exaggerated motion would cause her to fly apart in all directions. In her room, she changed her clothes and brushed her hair and came out again to the telephone and called down to the garage for the Jaguar. When she got downstairs and outside to the street, the Jaguar was there, and she got in it and drove away, and then for the first time she began to think of where she would go, and she knew, even as she began to think, that she was going to Duo's, where Joe Doyle had worked, and this was for some reason imperative, something she had to do.

It was after four o'clock when she got there, and Yancy was at the bar. He saw her enter and watched her approach, and then, just as she reached the bar, he turned his back and spoke to her reflection in the long mirror behind a row of beer glasses.

"Get the hell out of here," he said.

"What?" she said.

"You heard me," he said. "Get the hell out of here and don't ever come back."

She stared past him into the mirror, meeting his eyes sadly, and he was almost convinced for a moment that he had hurt her inexcusably and should be ashamed of himself.

"Why are you abusing me?" she said. "Don't you believe that I am as sorry as you for what happened?"

"No."

"Do you believe that it happened because of me?"

"Yes."

"Is it because you hate me so much that you want to think so badly of me?"

"I don't hate you. What would be the use? It would be like hating cancer."

"If you don't hate me, why don't you look at me?"

"I don't want to look at you. I don't want to see you or talk to you or have you near me. I'm sick of you, and I'm afraid of you. You're contagious. I told you before what you were, and I told Joe, but it didn't do any good, and now it'll never do any good. He's dead, and there's no way of proving who did it, I guess, but you know and I know why it happened, that it was because of you and what you are and did. I wish it had been you instead of him, but it wasn't, and probably that'll be all right, after all. In the end, you'll probably find a harder and slower way to die."

She shook her head from side to side, as if she would not believe that he was saying such cruel things to her, and the heavy side of her hair moved slowly back and forth over one sad eye.

"All right," she said. "I can see that I had better go away. Good-by."

He didn't answer, and she turned and walked to the door and stopped and looked back, but he continued to look into the mirror silently, and so she went on out and got into the Jaguar, and it was remarkable how she had begun suddenly to feel. She felt vastly relieved and lightened, purged and almost exonerated by Yancy's castigation. Driving away in the Jaguar, she started thinking about somewhere else to go in order to avoid being alone, and she decided that Bernardine DeWitt's apartment on MacDougal Street was the closest place that appealed to her, and so she went there.

She was admitted to the apartment by the maid, and there were, as usual, several people talking and moving around and drinking cocktails, but Bernardine wasn't among them. Perhaps she had merely gone off somewhere for a few minutes, or even for a few hours, which wouldn't be exceptionally odd of Bernardine, who was very casual about guests, but it didn't matter, anyhow, where she had gone or when she would come back. Everyone would simply drink as much as he wanted, and leave when he was ready.

Charity had one Martini quickly, and then took another to carry around the room. She had drunk about half of it and spoken amicably to three or four persons when she came to a young man in a corner. He was sitting alone with an empty glass in his hand, and he had an interesting, angular face and stubborn hair that went in different directions in several places. She stopped and looked down at him, pushing her hair back on the heavy side with the hand that did not hold her glass.

"Hello," she said.

He stood up with a kind of awkward, spasmodic motion, as if he moved by sections, one after the other. He returned her look with fierce intensity.

"Hello," he said. "I was just watching you."

"Were you? Why?"

"Because you're the only woman here worth watching."

"Do you really think so? Even if you don't, it was a charming thing to say. I don't believe anyone has ever said anything so charming to me before."

"Please don't accuse me of being charming. I was only telling the truth. I'd like to paint you."

"Are you a painter?"

"Yes, I have a studio in the Village. You needn't ask who I am, however, because you've never heard of me."

"Possibly I'll hear of you in the future."

"Possibly. It doesn't matter. Will you come to my studio and let me paint you? I couldn't pay you, of course. I'm very poor."

"I wouldn't want you to pay me."

"Will you come, then?"

She heard in his voice the same kind of urgent fierceness that she saw in his eyes. She was aware of the stirring of incipient excitement.

"Perhaps," she said. "Let's sit down and talk about it."

THE END

Interview with Charles Runyon
BY ED GORMAN

Stark House is publishing its first three-fer this summer—three Gold Medal novels long in need of reprinting. I wrote the introduction to Charles Runyon's THE PRETTIEST GIRL I EVER KILLED, a masterful suspense novel that puts Runyon in the top ten of GM writers in such company as Lawrence Block, John D. MacDonald, Charles Williams, Vin Packer, Richard Stark, Malcolm Braly and a handful of others.

At the time I wrote the introduction I was told that Runyon was dead. Not so— he's very much alive.

Q: The obvious mystery to those who were following your career—when did you stop publishing and why?

A: In 1980, Jove published my novel, *The Gypsy King*, which I thought represented my highest effort, a cut above the genre sf and mystery novels I had been publishing. I was never content with working at the level of my last published work, but at the same time I wasn't sure which way to go with my future work. To fill in the time while deciding, I went back to the University of Missouri and picked up a Master's in Creative writing, in case I might need to work before my sales picked up again. However, the hiatus stretched on, and teaching did not blend with writing as well as I had hoped. Writing was still my preferred profession, but the path back to publishing was a rocky one, and nobody laid down a red carpet for me any more than they had at the beginning. Somehow the word got out that I had "passed on" in 1987, and the thought intrigued me, much as it once intrigued Tom Sawyer. What if I tried to reenter the field, not as an older writer reentering the field after a long lay-off, but as a fresh new face with reams of new ideas? However, thanks to you, Ed, that experiment has now been abandoned, or left to others to carry out.

Q: Can you give us a sketch of your life?

A: A rough sketch would show the young writer growing up on a farm in Worth County, Missouri, the most insignificant county in a not-too-significant state. I couldn't wait to grow up and leave the farm like most boys, but ran away from home at age 16 to work on a ranch in West Texas.

So we come full circle; 60 nears later I am back in Texas. The intervening years included army service in Korea, Germany and Indiana, J-school at Missouri University. I just missed a job on the National Geographic and instead went into industrial editing. It was either that or poetry which paid nothing. While working for Mr. Rockefeller's old outfit in Chicago an agent to whom I had been paying readers' fees for five years—Scott Meredith—suddenly started making sales. I lost no time in quitting my job and announcing that I was now a full-time writer. With a new baby and no income, I borrowed a lakeside cabin and sat down to write my first book. After sending it off to my agent, I took off for the West Indies, found an almost deserted island, and lay back to await the gentle shower of royalties. It didn't quite happen that way, but it was only a few months before the book sold to Ace; my reaction was to charter a yacht and take the wife and kid on a tour of the islands. I returned to New York suntanned but broke, still expecting the gilded life of a best-selling writer.

Q: How about a sketch of your publishing career? Was writing something you'd always wanted to do?

A: Since I was about 8 years old, and realized how easily (comparatively) words came to me. Before that I wanted to be a doctor, until somebody told me you had to go to school for endless years. I was already making preparations when in High School I took typing; the only other "boy" in my class was a pianist. (For the rest of the nitpicking career details, I'm sending an updated bio out of Contemporary Authors.) [see below]

Q: Do you recall your first sale?

A: Of course; it was a short story called "First Man in a Satellite" to *Super Science Fiction* in 1957—fifty years ago! This was about the time the Russians sent up Sputnik so I was undeservedly credited with being a harbinger of the Space Age. I got a personal rejection from John W. Campbell, with his signature slanting across the bottom of the page as if tracing the path of a tumbling tumbleweed. He disparaged the whole idea of a midget in a space ship, adding that Lester del Rey had already done it—better. Editors didn't care about writer's sensibilities in those days. I still treasure the letter.

Q: Which gave you more satisfaction as a writer—science fiction or crime novels?

A: It's the sf novels and stories that I remember with the most affection. The crime stories and novels were more neatly wrapped up, while the sf novels and stories open onto worlds of other plot possibilities.

Q: What was the genesis of *The Prettiest Girl I Ever Killed?*

A: I was making notes for the book while spending the summer in my old home town of Sheridan, a place with an almost one-to-one correspondence to the Sherman of the book. The characters were pulled from the scenery of my past, specific incidents belonging to a real person could be welded to a fictional person without the need to improvise more than details of the plot. It was very liberating and exhilarating, to find that I could shape my own reality, as long as I kept it within the realm of the believable. (Actually, the story is not as bizarre as it may seem; my home town is near the little town of Skidmore, famed as the home of the hog-stealer, arch-bully, pedophile and murderer MacElroy, who was finally "executed" by a shotgun blast in full view of thirty townspeople. Not a single one of those citizens stepped forward to identify the shooter. Someday, I may get around to doing that book.)

Q: *Prettiest Girl* is invariably likened to the novels of Jim Thompson but when I reread it recently my take was that there is a fundamental difference between your book and just about anything Thompson wrote. Your killer in control of himself—unlike many of the Thompson protagonists who seem hard-wired to be at the mercy of themselves—and he's even a bit droll and sardonic at times. In other words, he can stand back and look at what he's doing objectively. The cumulative effect of this subtly but powerfully underscores his madness. Given the verities of paperback originals, this was an original approach. Did you think of it that way? Or are you even conscious of your writing decisions? Evan Hunter always said that he tried not to analyze what he was doing. He was afraid it would hamper his spontaneity.

A: I will have to read some of Jim Thompson before I comment on the difference between us. I always write in a close autobiographical style, even though I often change the pronouns to third person. When I finish a book, I always feel like a hollowed out lobster, all meat and flavor taken out, and nothing but dry pulp left inside. That's the reason I usually get in a few weeks of total leisure between novels; the creative energy needs time to rise to a level where I can begin pumping again. I think Evan Hunter is right in not analyzing his methods; the creative imagination is a shy, faery creature, and doesn't like the cold light of appraisal.

Q: Sometimes you sound almost dismissive of your crime fiction. Your science fiction seems to be your true love. Are you unhappy when people say they prefer your crime fiction to your sf?

A: No, I just assume that these are non-sf-readers by nature. As long as I could treat these crimes as merely head games, I could get considerable pleasure out of working out the problems. Having been a police reporter, I had a good grasp of the routine and the jargon, as well as tons of material. But I can date exactly when my preferences changed; in 1967 my younger brother was murdered, and the whole messy scene got involved with the stupidity of Vietnam and the decay of the courts, with the result that the murderer walked out of the courtroom smirking. This was too similar to the stuff I had been doing, and although I had many projects in the works, I never felt good about doing that sort of killer-oriented thing again.

Q: You've written some of the most remarkable opening chapters in suspense fiction. The first five thousand words of *The Dead Cycle*, for instance, put me in mind of The Doors' "Riders on The Storm." Except that where the song is from the innocents' point of view, this is from the Riders point of view. There's a mythic quality—almost of the old west—of the robbery gone wrong, an elderly clerk shot dead by one of the Riders, and them now desperately trying to get to the Mexican border. This is so much more realistic than much of the neo-noir we see today because the turf is real and you know this turf, the small-town Midwest. But it's the underbelly of the Midwestern small town you usually use. Was this intentional given that it's the setting of so many of your Gold Medal novels?

A: Sometimes I wonder if I'm really a fiction writer. The motorcycle story was based on an unusual honeymoon my wife and I took, riding double on a Harley through the back roads of Mexico in 1957. Add another couple, a murder, a stash of cash and some loose gash and you get The Death Cycle. It was fun to write, and to know that every bone-rattling jolt on that old Harley was paying off in hard core realism.

Q: *The Black Moth*, which is set on a college campus, is a notably different private eye novel in that the protagonist is a p.i. masquerading as a professor. But even here, in a more refined setting than you usually use, the writing stays hard as hell. Your books are proof that tough guys don't have to swagger or be violent to prove that they're tough. They're hard asses and no less so when they don academic robes. Was Black Moth based on your early experiences teaching college courses?

A: At the time I wrote *The Black Moth* I had never taught a college English course, but it definitely foreshadowed my later career. The idea was to have a series of vicious murders taking place amid the mannered politeness of an exclusive girl's finishing school. And in Columbia, Missouri, where I did my journalism study, there was Stephens College, the very model of such a school. My undergraduate years of dating Stephens girls paid off in some interesting characters and loads of verisimilitude. One of the fallacies of the lay person is that you can "create" characters out of whole cloth. With me, it's more of a cut-and-paste.

—April 2007

Runyon, Charles W. (1928—)

Personal: Born June 9, 1928, in Sheridan, Mo.; son of Monte Charles (a farmer and schoolteacher) and Nina (a schoolteacher; maiden name, West) Runyon; married Ruth Phillips (a student nurse) January 29, 1955; children: Charles W., Jr., Mark, Matthew; grandchildren: Zach, Nathan, Walker; great-grandchildren: Osias. *Education:* Attended University of

Missouri, 1947-50, 1953-54, Indiana University, 1950, and University of
Munich, 1951-52.

Career: Former newspaper reporter in Columbia, Mo.; Sinclair Pipeline
Co., Independence, Kan., editor, 1954-57; Standard Oil Co., Chicago, Ill.,
editor, 1957-60; freelance writer, 1960—. *Military service*: U.S. Army, 1948-
50, 1951-53. *Awards*: Edgar Allan Poe Award from Mystery Writers of
America, and best book of the year award from Missouri Writers Guild,
both for *Power Kill*.

Additional: *Death Cycle* and *The Prettiest Girl I Ever Killed* have been made
into motion pictures.

The Prettiest Girl I Ever Killed

BY CHARLES RUNYON

Prologue

The name of the game is Death.

Most people play without knowing, like sleepwalkers dancing to slow faint music. A few play with full awareness of the game and its inevitable end. Bernice Struble thought she was playing the adultery game, but I taught her that it was only a variation of The Death Game.

I noticed that she'd started coming into town every day between nine and eleven a.m. Her husband was at the depot getting ready for the ten o'clock freight. After it left, he'd be clearing up cargo and checking bills.

Bernice did no shopping; met no friends. By the tenth day my interest was engaged. I watched her park at the curb and sit smoking a cigaret. One plump arm lay along the window. Her short fingers beat a desultory tattoo on the side of the car. Her lips looked swollen and sensuous as they pursed and pulled on the white cylinder. Her eyes were moist and hot, measuring the men as they passed. After a time she got out of her car, flipped her cigaret into the gutter, and strolled along the two blocks which made up the business district of Sherman. She carried her bosom high and forward, with its salient points clearly etched against her white-and-green print dress. I watched her amble past the Square Deal grocery store, past the Purina feed store, Grant's Recreation Parlor and Pool Hall, Stubb's Tavern, Slavitt's Repair Shop and Auto Salvage. She cut left just before she reached the schoolhouse. As she crossed the highway toward the park, the sun reflected off white gravel and gave her dress a brief transparency. In five years she'd be coarse and dumpy, but now she had no need to stretch and compress her flesh with latex and elastic. The soft rolling shape beneath Bernice's dress was Bernice; she was dealing it straight, letting you know in advance, and if you were disappointed later it was your own fault for not looking.

In the park she sat on the wooden steps of the weather-blackened bandstand, cooled by the shade of gigantic elms. It was a hot day in late June; already the thermometer had topped ninety. She smoked another cigaret, then rose, walked across the grass, got into her car and drove out of town. The Strubles had twenty acres and a house two miles east of town. I waited a half hour and no cars followed. I wondered: Was it a mating ritual, or was she simply a woman with nothing to do? She had no close friends in town; a depot agent with two-year tenure never becomes part of a Missouri farm community. Her husband was a mild young man with a taste for beer and a passion for shuffleboard. I weighed the risk and found it non-existent. I got in my car and drove west, then I cut back and took the old south road across the river, drove east two miles and came back toward town on the blacktop. I turned south on the Braden Gravel and reached their house, an old-fashioned two-story structure with tall narrow windows.

She was sitting in her front yard on a plaid blanket drinking a glass of red Kool-aid. I pulled off onto the track worn beside the mailbox and called: "Where's Bill?"

She rose from the blanket and came forward.

"He's at the depot," she said, opening the wooden gate. She negotiated the plank laid across the grader ditch and came up to the car, resting her forearms along the open window. "He don't come back till around noon. He meets the ten o'clock, then he goes up to Stubb's and has a beer, so he don't come home till around noon."

Her face held no expression. Her two front teeth were prominent; not protruding, but larger than the others. I noticed streaks of flour on her dress where she'd wiped her hands after baking. I felt a pulse of excitement; she'd been in her kitchen cooking something for her man, and here I was about to...

It was hard to keep from breaking into a foolish grin. "Won't be home until noon, eh?"

"No." It's hard to convey the exact tone of her voice. It showed no coyness, no arch, teasing flirtation. She was like a child saying, *I want ...*

"You want to take a ride?"

I think she'd already made up her mind; she glanced up the road toward the main highway, then opened the door and slid into the car. I'd just pulled out onto the gravel when she said: "I didn't bring my cigarets."

"I've got some."

Thirty seconds later she pointed to a dirt road leading toward the river. "You can turn in there."

When we were bouncing along the track beneath the cotton woods, I glanced over at her. Beads of perspiration gleamed in the fine white hairs of her upper lip. Despite her neutral tone, she was excited; this was the only adventure she knew.

Before we reached the river she pointed to a thicket of willows. "There," she said. A breathy tautness had altered her voice.

I killed the engine and set the brake. As she got out of the car I asked: "Who'd you come here with before?"

She shook her head. "That'd be telling."

"Point is, he might show up."

"Huh-uh. He left the country."

Then I knew who it was: Wayne Bergen, a truck driver who delivered gas and diesel fuel to neighboring farms. A tall, easygoing bag of bones with an insolent manner, he'd been fired two weeks ago for getting drunk on the job—just before Bernice started showing up in town....

She led me twenty yards into the thicket and stopped in a small clearing. Floodwaters had heaped a dune of sand behind a fallen cottonwood. Wild grapes and elderberries draped the tall trees and wrist-thick willows screened us from all sides.

"Keep these for me," she said, shoving her panties in my pocket. "If we hear anyone, I'll roll into the weeds and you can say you chased a rabbit in here."

There were a few kisses, but hardly worth mentioning, like the playing of "The Star-Spangled Banner" before a prizefight. There was also sand and airless heat and mosquitoes. The girl had energy but no art; heat but no style. She seemed to have the nervous system of a dinosaur; one small brain controlling the lower portion of her body, and another in her head. Her face remained the same throughout, eyes closed and mouth open, sweat dewing her upper lip, like a restless child dreaming on a hot afternoon. Poor dumb broad, she had nothing working for her but an extra helping of hormones. I felt like most of me was unnecessary. She'd thrown out her line and I was the fish who'd struck the bait; she'd been sitting there in the yard with the house locked up and it hadn't mattered who came by, Stubby or the banker or Earless Joe who racked halls in the pool hall....

When it was over she shook the sand from her dress and said that if we came again she'd remember the blanket. I knew there'd be a next time, because I had something to make up with her; she'd used me, and according to the rules of the game, she qualified as a victim.

We managed to meet about twice a week. Bernice was addicted to rituals; when I didn't show for three days, she'd come to town and do her invitational walk around the square. So I'd get in my car and drive out. She'd be standing at the front gate as though waiting for the mailman to deliver a package. If there was any traffic on the road, I drove on and came back later. If the road was clear, Bernice got in and crouched beneath the dash until we reached the willows. She went ahead while I waited to make sure nobody had followed. I'd convinced her there was reason to be scared and she loved it. With the truck driver she'd been an animal crawling off under the bushes. Now she was risking all for love, like the heroines of the true confessions she read while waiting for me. This amused me because basically she was a neat little German *Hausfrau*. She used to fold her dress up neatly across her belly so it wouldn't wrinkle. Once I tore her panties, pulling them from my pocket; suddenly I was no longer custodian of her lingerie; she just didn't wear them when she expected me. I'd approach the mailbox and think of her standing there with her legs going up and up without interruption, and my mouth would get dry....

But she was too simple, and by September I'd lost interest in the sex game. The less interest I showed, the more she tried, and the more bored I became....

I watched it spiral up and up; I gave her money and that put the whole affair on a new footing. She was puzzled; I told her to buy herself a dress or something. But we no longer met for mutual pleasure. I kept giving her money, and she strained to pay it off in the only coin she had. But when you try, you can't.

Our last meeting in the willows in October was cramped and shivery, and I said we'd better end it. She said:

"I'll find a place we can meet inside. Don't talk about ending it."

Her dinosaur brain must have been stimulated by need, because she set it up beautifully. I only followed instructions. I drove by her mailbox and she gave me the sign from her window. I parked the car by the willows and walked along the river until I reached their property line. Then I approached the house under cover of a hedgerow. This brought me to the rear of the house. Down three steps, through a door, and I was in the basement. The furnace kept it warm; the presence of her washing machine and clothes hung up to dry filled it with a miasma of soap and wet fabrics. After I was in, she locked the door to the basement. The connubial couch was a rubber air mattress laid down behind the furnace. She asked me if it wasn't better than the thicket and I told her it smelled like a laundry. She said she felt more secure here, and to prove it she undressed for the first time. She walked around, her bare feet leaving damp tracks on the dusty concrete. She wanted me to say something, but I could only wonder how long it would take that blazing furnace to consume her flesh. I wondered if she would swell and burst like a hot dog; if the dark blonde hair would sizzle and shrink to a black kinky mass. In my mind's eye I saw the victim's hat on her head: a black skullcap with a tiny red tassel, like a Talmudic scholar's. Mine was a wide-brimmed corsair hat with an ostrich plume. You've got to have style or the Watcher gets bored. Without style you're only a butcher.

But the rules of the game required a motive, and she hadn't yet given me one. I beckoned her to join me on the air mattress. She strained to please me and afterward she gave me a piece of apple pie. She wanted a pat on the head but I gave her money and she looked like she was going to cry....

The excitement of bringing the game into enemy camp held my interest until mid-December, but the strain was wearing down Bernice. She started complaining about her husband:

"You know I don't like him to touch me any more, but that only gets him worked up. Sometimes he comes out from the depot after the midnight train and wakes me up with his damn poking; or it's after the six a.m. train and he comes in while I'm fixing breakfast and runs his hand up my dress.

It's all I can do to keep from hitting him."

Another time: "Why don't we take off together? Don't say you can't. You'd find a way if you had to."

And finally: "I've waited for you to do something, but you didn't. So I went ahead and did it."

I felt the skin draw tight across my cheekbones. "Did what?"

"I saved the money you gave me. I told my husband I was going to visit my sister in Minneapolis. But instead I'm going to Las Vegas and get a divorce. You can meet me there and we'll get married."

"I can't leave here."

"You'll have to when I tell Bill what's been happening."

I heard a high, faint buzzing in my ears. I thought, with a mild, remote sort of interest: Well, well, look at what I've built, a little death machine. I said:

"Your word against mine."

"Is it? Remember the day you couldn't come? You put the note in my mailbox. I've still got it."

"Unsigned."

"But in your handwriting."

Suddenly I was outside the game; I saw all the pieces strung out on the board below me. I'd put the note in her box without being aware of any ulterior motive; now I saw that my subconscious had been leading me into a trap.

"Wait a few days," I said. "I'll think it over."

"Two days," she said. Something in the German countenance limits expression to either arrogance or servility; there's no middle ground. Bernice's face was wearing the arrogance; now it dissolved into servile apology. "I don't want it this way. You forced me into it."

I smiled, because she didn't know how true that was.

For two days I tried to plan. A car accident... gas... something with the furnace... burn down the house.

My intellect couldn't help trying to take charge even though I knew it was wrong to plan. If the time is right, everything will be laid out. You just assemble the pieces, like a model plane with each part numbered.

When I arrived two days later there it was: The packing had worn out in their electric pump; the cover was off the well and the pump removed to the shop. Meanwhile water had to be drawn up with a bucket attached to a rope. The morning was cold and clear; telephone wires hummed and the sun was a pale disc which gave light but no heat. As I went in, I noticed that ice had frozen around the curb of the well. Beside the basement door stood the tools they'd used to remove the pump.

I told Bernice I'd decided to go with her, and we spent a quarter hour discussing plans. She prepared to consummate the deal on the air mattress but I said no. I knew that if there was an autopsy, the fact that she'd just had intercourse would be hard to explain.

"I'd like a drink of water before I go," I said.

"I'll get it from the refrigerator."

"It would taste better from the well."

She frowned. "We might be seen."

"I'll just be getting a drink of water. Anyway, does it matter? Your husband has to know sooner or later."

That reminded her that she had reason to please me, no matter how ridiculous my request. Her felt house-slippers skidded on the ice as she walked to the well. I was behind her, holding a massive pipe wrench I'd taken from inside the door. I waited until she'd pulled the bucket almost to the top, then I called her name.

She turned. In the moment it took her to focus her eyes on my face, she saw the wrench. I watched the awful knowledge come into her eyes; it was a puzzled kind of sadness. Her jaw dropped as I brought the wrench down. My footing was bad and I managed only a glancing blow on her left temple. She dropped the rope and tried to scramble away, skittering on the ice like a hog on a frozen pond. I swung again and caught her behind the ear. She fell across the curbing, dazed but not out. I put my foot against her shoulder and tried to push her into the well. Her hands clawed at the icy bricks and her short crimson nails held like talons. I brought the wrench down with all my strength. The impact jolted it from my hand, but the blow was good. She dropped headfirst like a bomb from a bomb bay. Cool air puffed up into my face as she went down; her legs were bare and she'd prepared for the as usual. That was a pathetic and touching sight, and the last I saw of her. She struck with a hollow *Chung!* and the bottom of the well exploded into a thousand darting splinters of light. I watched the water until it was a bright silver coin, then I returned to the basement. I cleaned up the cigaret butts and threw them into the furnace. In her bedroom I found her purse; I took out the money she'd been saving and put it in my wallet. I found the note I'd given her and threw it in the furnace. I took the water pitcher from the refrigerator and carried it out to the well. I poured water over the flecks of blood and watched it turn to mush as it froze. I set the pitcher on the curb so it would appear that she'd come out to fill it. I wanted her found quickly; I wanted no mysteries, no inquiries. I thought of the wrench and decided it must be lying at the bottom of the well—unless it had somehow gotten tangled in Bernice's dress. If that had happened... tough. You can't anticipate those things.

I felt calm as I followed the hedgerow back to the river. My crepe-soled shoes left no mark on the frozen ground. There was no way they could trace me; nobody was even aware that I knew her.

She made number ten. I searched myself for elation and found none. It was like reaching into a cookie jar and finding nothing. I was empty.

Later it came, of course. Not elation, but a sort of remembrance. I thought of Bernice and her little *Hausfrau* attitudes: the way she gathered up the tissues and cigaret butts which had accumulated during my visit, bending from the waist and snatching them up like a hen snapping up grains of corn... opening the furnace door with face pinched tight and throwing the little package away with a gesture of rejection... then looking to see if she'd missed anything, biting her index finger with those two prominent incisor teeth. I thought of her brain and its memories of me, now dead. (Within three days she'd been taken from the well, and reburied in her home town nearly two hundred miles away. The well was filled up, and her death ruled accidental.) I thought of the hours she'd spent waiting for me, the hope that must have surged up when she saw me, the habit she'd acquired of washing and perfuming herself in intimate places... something she would not have done if it hadn't been for me. Before she died I had changed her life. In a sense, I had created her....

I have only contempt for those who go out on a dark street and select a victim at random. They are ending a life they do not understand; they are crude and barbarous vandals, like savages who smash a radio. Let an engineer destroy a radio, that is significant. Let him destroy a radio which he has built himself, that is better still.

Bernice had lived her life. At twenty-one she was complete. She couldn't grow into something else, no more than a calf can grow into a gazelle; the genetic materials are not available. Bernice could only have become an older, coarser version of what she was; I could do nothing more with the materials at hand, so I destroyed her.

As weeks passed, the memory of Bernice became a sick sweetness, as when you eat too much pork fat. By killing Bernice, I seemed to have killed myself. I had existed in her mind, and when her mind ceased to exist... what became of the man she knew? I walked the street feeling my feet thud against the concrete and I would wonder whose feet they were. Walls began to waver, as in the heat warp from a stove. I worked harder, fitting my days with labor, creating things I could look at and somehow see myself reflected in—

But these things were only wood and metal and plants rising from the soil. I needed a person, a woman—not in a physical way, but as a partner in the game. My thoughts turned, as they often had before, to Velda.

I can walk past the store and see her behind the counter. Usually the store is empty, and she is alone. This quiet woman in this quiet place fascinates me. I stop and took through the plate glass, most of me hidden by posters Scotch-taped to the inside which announce sales on meat, soap powder and canned goods. An open book lies on the counter before her. She sits on a high stool, one bare knee atop the other, running the point of her pencil through the pale rust-colored hair which she has pulled above her ears and bound up in the back. From time to time she shifts her legs, hooking one foot behind the ankle of the other. She is beautiful in a way which does not immediately strike the eye: her features are almost, but not quite, ordinary: a sheen of gold brightens her red-blonde hair, an emerald tone deepens the green of her eyes; her narrow nose ends in a slight upward tilt; her long smooth jaw suggests a masculine stubbornness. Her upper lip forms a tight unmoving line; the lower swells and protrudes slightly. She lights a cigaret without interrupting her reading, thrusting out her jaw and lilting her head so that the lighter does not flare into her eyes. She draws deeply once and allows the smoke to roll from her nose and lips; then she deposits the cigaret in an ashtray and smokes it no more, only waves away the wisps of smoke which trail across the page.

She does not look her thirty-five years: her body seems to have early acquired a toughness, a resilience which resists the sagging effects of age. Her long crossed thighs show faint ridges of muscle through the dress; her calves are smoothly rounded, free of blue swollen veins which are the stigma of the retail trade. She wears a bibbed white apron over a blue cotton dress; her breasts press full and firm against it.

A customer enters; a bell rings above the door. She closes the book and marks it with a sliver of cardboard; she slides off the stool and stands erect, placing her palms flat on the wooden counter. A diamond-crusted circlet glitters on her third finger, left hand; the large center stone shoots out arrows of blue light. The customer is a talkative woman. Velda converses with her: she laughs—a half-amused chuckle which ripples only the surface—she carries her verbal share of the conversation... but always there is something reserved, some little chamber of emotion she does not open. (The local people have forgotten that she is beautiful; they have seen her so often they no longer see her. A woman comes to town only half as lovely as Velda and all heads turn to follow her because she is new. In a year or two she will also become invisible, condemned to the peculiar anonymity a small town conveys.) Probably this is good for Velda, for she has acquired none of the self-conscious poses of women who are accustomed to attention. She has no false modesty because she knows no reason to feel proud.

All this is speculation. I don't really know her—though I know her as well as or better than anyone else in Sherman, because I have studied her and they have not. At midmorning she often disappears behind the green plywood partition which segregates her office and a small bathroom. She locks the door and remains for sometimes an hour. I wonder what she does in there, but the bell over the front door always rings when I enter. Even when I muffle its ringing—as I did once by winding tape around the clapper—the wooden floor creaked and she came out looking flushed and surprised. (Does she know I am studying her now? Probably not, I am a familiar face; my behavior undergoes no major change, and in minor changes I am shielded by the same anonymity which protects everyone else in this town.) Oh, I'm not teased by the mystery of what women *do* when they're alone... little dabs of grooming, searching out gray hairs, pushing hair masses here and there to see how it would look in a different style, checking for new pimples and wrinkles, squeezing blackheads... But what does she *see* when she looks in the mirror? What image is reflected to her and why does it dissatisfy her? Because there is discontent in the way the lips sometimes curve downward. It could be her marriage, but then she would need only to give some sign of availability and the men would come. Strangers make overtures, true, which she studies and rejects. The rejection is not important, but the study is. She desires, she does not obtain....

Another symptom is her reading. New worlds inside the covers of books. Surrogate experience, proving that reality falls short. Like any avid reader she knows words, good words, big ones. But, living in cultural isolation, she often mispronounces them, or drops them in the middle of a sentence, like a rock which destroys the symmetry of her speech. Her information is spotty, another result of undisciplined reading. She discovers history and devours all she can find on the subject, at the same time lacking even a high school graduate's knowledge of astronomy or philosophy. She is a strange blend of knowledge and naïveté. Normally she talks in a studied, level tone, letting no emotion out, merely communicating. Yet when she is angry, the blunt country words break through, pungent and steaming and barbed with the directness of the hills. The emerald eyes sparkle with green fire, the lips stretch tight across even white teeth, and you see that the words belong to her. You see her as she was when I first saw her, sitting in the back of a Studebaker wagon, her bare feet swinging a foot above the dusty road, She was a woodland creature born and raised in the hills of Brush Creek, taking her first look—not really, but it seemed so—at neon lights and movies and fountain Cokes. She was no beauty then; she had vivid freckles dusted across her cheekbones and the bridge of her nose. Her teeth were small and not quite closed up, with dark gaps between them. Her sunbleached hair was a hue most accurately described as mustard. It framed a long thin face which may have been clean when she started to town, but had since acquired a gray coating of road dust. She wore a dress made from a flowered Parina sack; it lay not quite flat across her chest; her immature breasts did not bounce with the movement of the wagon....

Now she is by local standards a rich man's wife. Nylon sheathes the legs which knew only wool in winter and the wind in summer. She has grown used to imported silk and French perfume and gold which does not turn green; her small hands know the satiny smoothness of new money and the wheel of the powerful, expensive car....

But this latter woman is totally divorced from the poor little hill girl. Velda is either one or the other, she is never a blend of the two.

I see her as a victim. This is as natural as a beautician seeing her with her head beneath a dryer, a policeman seeing her behind bars, or a surgeon seeing her with her stomach cut open. I think of how she would look dead, or in the process of being killed. (She would fight, this is certain; I visualize her as a naked, clawing, spitting savage.) But the picture is unsatisfactory, because she is not ready. Even at thirty-five, she is an unformed, immature woman.

An element is missing, a catalyst which will blend the hill girl with the rich man's wife and make her complete. The element is not me, for I am already in her life, and have blunted my power to affect her without risk. The element is not even in Sherman, for she has adapted to all those who live here, examined them and shoved then aside. The element must come from outside. Until she changes, Velda is immune....

CHAPTER ONE
Velda's Game

When you see a stranger in our town, you know he's come *here*, he's not passing through on his way to somewhere else. Sherman is the end, the jump-off. At the east side of town there's a sign reading: *State Maintenance Ends.* From here west the gravel roads dwindle away into a wilderness of limestone ridges they call the Brush Creek Nation. Ten miles west the ridges slope down into Lake Pillybay, but tourists always approach it from the other side on Highway 30.

That's why I stared at the man who came into the store just after I'd opened. A blond beard hid the lower part of his face; his deep tan was a rarity in late March. I watched him wipe mud from calf-high rubber boots and walk toward the counter. He was young, I could tell from the springy sureness of his walk. He was married; I saw the gold wedding band as he lay his palms flat on the counter. A deep bass voice asked for a can of Velvet and I set it in front of him. He opened it, gouged the tobacco with a long forefinger, and raised it to his nose. He squinted at me over the can and said:

"Velda Groenfelder?"

I shook my head. "Velda Bayrd. I married Louis Bayrd."

His sun-whitened eyebrows rose. "Ah, you've risen in the world. A flat-lander by marriage."

I frowned at him, looking for a familiar face beneath the beard. Only a native would speak of flatlanders with that peculiar taunting inflection.

"You used to live in the Nation?" I asked.

He nodded. There was movement behind the foliage as though he might be smiling, but I wasn't sure. I tilted my head so I could see his face in better light. That mat of beard darkened from yellow on his cheeks to a coppery black beneath his chin. A deep tan gave his blue eyes a piercing brilliance. He might have looked mean but I didn't feel it because of the intelligence in his eyes. Hate and intelligence don't go together.

I shrugged and smiled. "I can't place you. Come out from behind the bush."

"Curt," he said. "Curt Friedland."

My knees went soft at the sound of the name. My smile stuck in place and my cheeks felt like old leather. His eyes drove into me like blue steel rivets. He was leaning across the counter, making me hear it, making me like it. I saw something in his eyes I'd missed the first time I'd looked; a hard reckless indifference. I knew the grin was there now, but it was a twisted taunting thing that said I could think and do what I liked because he didn't give a damn.

I took the can of tobacco and set it on the cash register.

"They sell tobacco in the tavern," I told him. "It's fresher. You'll like it better."

He shook his head slowly. "After fifteen years, Velda? I didn't even think you'd know me."

"I knew your family. Your brother."

He leaned back, still smiling in a way that didn't reach his eyes, smiling like I was a little doll doing all kinds of funny tricks.

"My brother Frank," he said. "Your sister Anne. She's been dead twelve years and Frankie's serving life. And what's all that got to do with you and me?"

"You know damn well what it's got to do with us."

"Code of the hills? The pride of the clan?" He shook his head. "I'm a long time away from cornbread and hominy grits, Velda. I'm surprised you aren't."

I felt hot blood burning my cheeks; I didn't like the way he made my words sound. "They held a trial. The verdict was guilty."

"You believe it?"

"—Yes."

"All right. Stick to it. Don't even think about it." He reached past me and picked up the tobacco; I could have stopped him by grabbing his hand, but I couldn't make myself touch him. He dropped a quarter on the counter and walked away. I was surprised to see that he was over six feet tall and heavy in the shoulders. I remembered him as being thin and pale... but then he'd only been sixteen when he left.

My hand touched the quarter and I started to ring it up. A sudden impulse made me throw it toward the front of the store. It clanged against the window and went spinning off, leaving a tiny starburst on the plate glass. Curt paused an instant, then turned around.

"I suppose Frankie killed Bernice Struble too."

"Bernice? Why... that was an accident. The coroner's jury—"

"Keep believing it, Velda. The authorities are never wrong."

He smiled and walked out. I watched him climb into a mud-caked Ford with a Florida license. His smile was gone now. He backed out and drove away without looking back.

I went into the bathroom and bathed my face in cold water. I put my hand to my breast and breathed slowly, wishing I'd inherited a little less of the Groenfelder temper. I should have been dignified and haughty with Curt: *Really, Mr. Friedland, did you expect to be met by a brass band?*

I touched up my lips and brushed hack the red-blonde hair above my ears. Then I walked back into the empty store, through the warm smell of oranges and floor wax and leafy vegetables. I looked at the calendar: March twenty-third. I pulled a pencil from above my ear and circled it. It's a habit of mine; my husband says I try to hold back time by putting little traps around the dates. I saw that I'd also circled February tenth, the day Bernice Struble fell in the well....

Or was pushed? Oh no, I thought, I won't let Curt Friedland's evil seed take root. The coroner's report had said she died by drowning. Hair and pieces of scalp had adhered to the bricks where she'd scraped her head going down. It was assumed she'd slipped on the ice and fallen in; finger-nail scratches on the curbing indicated that she'd tried to catch herself and failed.

I'd been in Franklin that day, watching my daughter Sharon roller-skate. We'd just gotten home when the line ring came about Bernice. You can't mistake a line ring: the insistent *zzzt-zzzt-zzzt* goes on until presumably everybody picks up their phone to learn what the emergency is. Half the time the operator announces that school is closed or the Eastern Star meeting is canceled, but often it's real tragedy. It rang on April 17, 1947, the day the tractor turned over on Marston and crushed his chest. That date will never be anything else for me, just as June twelfth will never be anything but the date we were supposed to get married. It rang when Marvin Jobe drowned, when Tom Groner's little gal Lotte burned to death on a haystack, and the morning Audrey and Jim were found in their car poi-soned by carbon monoxide. It rang on February 4, 1954, the night Jerry Blake burned to death along with his store. It rang on July 18, 1951, while I sat at home sewing a dress for Sharon's fourth birthday. I lifted the receiv-er to hear that my sister Anne had been found dead in her car outside the Club 75 and that Frankie Friedland had been shot trying to escape—

Gladys Schmit came into the store with her overshoes flopping, uncoil-ing a woolen scarf from around her neck. She pulled off her embroidered mittens, remarked how nice it was to see a thaw after three weeks of snow and ice, then with a birdlike jerk of her head she asked:

"Who was that young man with the beard?"

After thirty years of teaching school, Gladys treated the entire commu-nity as though they'd never left her fifth and sixth grade room.

"Curt..." I said, and the last name stuck in my throat. "Curt Friedland."

Her eyes went round behind silver-rimmed spectacles. For a moment her lips pursed in a childish disappointment which reminded me that Gladys was, after all, pushing sixty.

"I didn't know he was coming back."

I fingered the ball-point pens in the rack and said nothing. Gladys peered at me with a look of bright interest: "What's he going to do?"

"You'll have to ask him, Gladys. I don't know."

"You knew him, didn't you?"

"He was four years younger than I. You couldn't say I knew him."

"Oh." She was frowning, obviously trying to get in touch with her memory. Then, giving an abrupt jerk of her head, she picked up a loaf of bread and brought it to the counter. "He was the youngest of the four, I remember now. His brothers were so rowdy and athletic. Nobody thought there was brains in the family until they brought that intelligence test in, and Curt made the highest score in the state. People were amazed, he was always so shy and polite...."

I thought: Gladys, *are we talking about the same one?* I remembered seeing Curt fight a larger boy on the playground; Curt had seemed to back away, trying to flee in panic, and my heart had gone out to the kid because I thought he needed help. He backed against the barbed-wire fence which ran between the playground and a cornfield; the other boy lunged, flailing his arms. Curt sidestepped abruptly and the boy crashed into the fence. Curt turned and began hammering with his small fists; when the other boy tried to defend himself he ripped his arms on the sharp barbs. The other boy had finally run away crying. with blood streaming from the gashes on his arms and dripping off his fingers. He'd had twenty stitches taken and Curt hadn't a bruise. The boy's parents had wanted Curt punished, but there was nothing to he done; Curt hadn't cut the boy, the boy had cut himself. Only those of us watching realized that Curt had deliberately maneuvered the boy into the fence. I'd stopped feeling sorry for Curt at that moment; from then on I'd pitied those who were deceived by his quiet manner.

Gladys was telling how, as alumni secretary, she'd kept Curt's address up-to-date in order to send him invitations to the alumni banquet. In five years she'd traced him around the world: "Germany, France, Italy, Tangier, Morocco, Mexico. Japan. Hong Kong. Hawaii. Haiti. Costa Rica. I sent him questionnaires for the school paper and he filled in occupations like opium peddler, beachcomber, ship's cook, taxi driver, things like that. I was so relieved when he settled down and got a college degree, then got a job with that research firm. When he started his own firm I thought, Well *finally* one of the Friedlands will amount to something. Then six months ago his questionnaire came back from the West Indies. He'd listed his occupation as fisherman. Now he's here." She pulled on her mittens and tucked the bread under her arm. "Well, Curtis wasn't like his brothers. He won't cause trouble."

She went out with her overshoes flopping and I thought, No, he won't unless he wants to, but I think he wants to....

I didn't mention him to my husband that night; I didn't want to get involved with Curt Friedland, even to the extent of talking about him.

The next day I stood at the window of the store and saw Curt Friedland drive by in an old car, throwing off a pinwheel of dirty slush which stuck to the parked cars. My husband followed in his pickup with his dark-furred arm out the window. He saw me and drew a circle in the air with his finger, then pointed in the direction Curt was going. That meant he was going to show some property and wouldn't be home for dinner. Lou had at least ten places listed but I was sure which one it was: the old Friedland place back on Brush Creek, vacant since the elder Friedlands had moved near Jeff City so they could visit Frankie on weekends.

We would become involved with Curt, I could see that. I wanted to tell Lou, don't sell to that man, but it wouldn't make any difference. Lou would go on selling, buying, dealing, making money regardless of what I did. Regardless of what *he* did, even; Lou was like a snowball rolling downhill which picks up a gob here and a gob there and suddenly you find it's enormous and what can you do with it all...?

A hubbub down the street announced the school's morning recess. Sharon came in like a whirlwind of thick black hair and gave me a hard sell about having supper with Sue before the basketball game. She said her current boy friend would drive her home afterward; I put forth a token resistance but in the end I relented and off she went, a darkly exotic fifteen-year-old image of her father. A group of boys in a parked car called out an invitation, and I felt a tingle of pride at the way she handled it—no kittenish play-anger, just a cool no-thank-you. I thought of my own self-conscious adolescence; I could see myself in worn shoes getting off the school bus from Brush Creek and walking that long fifty yards to the schoolhouse door. My stomach would knot when I saw the cluster of boys around the foot-scraper: I couldn't ignore their taunts. I felt I had to insult them in return or else pick up a handful of rocks and let fly as I passed. Well, Sharon had the advantage of what passed locally for wealth. I doubted that she'd have gone through the same ordeal even without it, having inherited her father's... what? Self-centered poise? Selfishness? Not a kind word at all....

A curious feeling of discontent crept through my mind. I started to add up the tickets on the morning deliveries but my attention dwindled away. A car passed with the sound of fat frying in a skillet and I saw that it was Bill Struble coming back from the depot. Life goes on, I thought. Bill still met the trains, but he'd been dazed and withdrawn since his wife's accident. Nobody knew him well and if he had any suspicions about his wife's death he wasn't saying anything. He'd locked up his house and taken a room in own; he'd put his place up for sale and asked for a transfer, so it was clear he had no love for the city of Sherman.

Across the street I saw that the old men had moved from the inside of the pool hall to the slatted bench outside. Harbinger of spring.... Old watery eyes trailing the young girls drifting in threes and fours toward the schoolhouse. Twenty years ago I'd made the same walk; there'd been different faces but the same ragged Mackinaws, same speckled hands on gnarled canes, blue smoke puffing up from corncob pipes. The town didn't change much; it dried up and got smaller, and each Saturday night a few less people came to town. When I was young, Saturday night had brought clusters of men in faded overalls, faces sunburned up to the middle of their foreheads, dead-white from there to the hairline where their hats had held off the sun. Women in wrinkled stockings lined the benches before the stores, talking in tired murmurs while babies fed from white breasts spilled out through flowered print dresses. There were brawls in the alley behind Cott's dance hall (closed during the war and never reopened) and once there was a shooting. (The date was July 4, 1936, a year of drought and despair and desperate gaiety, free government flour with Dad on the WPA and brother in the CCC. I was sitting on the fender of our old Model-A feeling sick because I'd just seen a boy stick a firecracker in a toad's mouth and light it. I saw the man running up the street with the sheriff behind him. Sheriff Wade was young then but heavy; he was falling behind. Then his forty-five roared twice and echoes thundered through the summer night. The locusts stopped chirring and the dogs slopped barking. In the sudden hush the running man spread his arms in a swan dive and fell on his face. He kicked while blood gushed from his month. It was the first time I'd ever seen a man die, and I realized that in death man has no more dignity than a dog kicked by a mule. The dead man had left another man in the alley behind Cott's with his stomach slashed open. The man got his stomach sewed up and was talking and smoking a cigaret an hour later. But the dead man was a dead-broke drifter and nobody grieved.)

That was the depression in Sherman. During the war boys in khaki staggered in the street and fought in the alley; afterward they loafed around wearing ruptured ducks and pieces of old uniforms. When their unemployment payments ran out, they drifted to Kansas City to pack meat or to California to build airplanes. Sometimes when their parents die they come back and try to farm the old place, but they usually sell out and Lou has another listing.

That night I asked Lou over supper: "Sell anything?"

"Umm... not yet."

Lou had a private rule never to discuss a transaction until it was finished, the deed signed and the money deposited. There was no point in trying to discuss Curt with him even if I'd wanted to; he'd have turned cagey and talked around the subject. When it comes to business, Lou seems to forget I'm his wife.

But the next day I knew the deal had gone through and that Cart

Friedland was settling in Sherman. His wife came into the store just before noon. I knew it had to be her; we don't get two unrelated strangers in a single week. She wore no makeup. Her short, thick-curled hair spilled from the front of her white woolen cap like glossy purple grapes. Her tanned face was narrow; her eyes large and hazel, with an element of softness. They made her look surprised and bewildered, and I wanted to help her.

But I didn't. I watched her push her cart around the store picking up the things you need to restock a house: condiments, spices, flour and canned staples. She wore a preoccupied, totally introverted air, as though unaware that she had the attention of everyone in the store. The bread man had dropped two loaves trying to stack bread and watch her at the same time; the candy man had broken off his discussion with me and was peering over the shelves at her. She wore a hip-length mink jacket and tight tore-ador pants which revealed the abrupt beginning curve of her buttocks below the jacket. She wore the fur as though it were something to keep her warm; a combination of the elegant and shoddy (her ski boots, for example, were scuffed and muddy) made her look as though she'd grown up in wealth and no longer noticed it.

Gladys Schmit must have been watching the store; she came in five minutes later and examined the shelves of pickles. Gladys didn't eat pickles, but that's where Curt's wife was. I heard Gladys ask: "Aren't you Curtis Friedland's wife?"

The girl paused as though thinking it over, then said: "Yes. I'm Gabrielle."

Gladys launched her schoolmarm's interrogation about Gabrielle's career, her husband, and her plans. Gabrielle dodged none of the questions, but answered them in a way which told Gladys only what she knew already: that they'd sold their business in Chicago, spent a few months in the Caribbean, then come here. Gladys attempted to trade confidences; she told about having Curt in school, and how intelligent he was...

"...But so shy and unsure of himself. I used to tell him, go ahead, don't doubt yourself, but he never..."

The girl was not interested. Having defined the old woman's relationship to her husband and decided there was nothing she wanted, she answered in polite monosyllables until Gladys ran down and departed. Then she wheeled her cart to the counter and said to me:

"It seemed like she was talking about someone else. He isn't like that."

She'd done nothing to me except marry into the Friedlands, but I'm really not an outgoing type; I'm narrow and suspicious and mean-tempered, like most Brushcreekers. I busied myself in ringing up her purchases. "People change," I said.

She gave a vague lost smile. "They don't, really."

I ripped off the long ribbon of tape and laid it before her. While I was boxing her purchases, the guilt crept in. After all, she was a stranger in our xenophobic little village and it was pointless to be rude to her. I told her who I was and asked if she'd like to visit some afternoon.

She laid a fifty-dollar bill on the counter and gave me an unblinking look: "Does this include Curt?"

So... she wouldn't let me off the book. I slightly admired her honesty. "I saw him earlier. Didn't he tell you?"

"Yes. He said you'd changed. You used to be friends."

My face felt hot. "It was a long time ago."

"Yesterday," she said. "It all happened yesterday."

I frowned at her. "What do you mean?"

"I've got a man," she said, "who had it all in his hands. Success. Then he threw it away. Why? Because he skipped a turn. He says life is a downhill slalom and if you miss a run the rest of the run doesn't count. No matter how good it is. He thinks he could have saved Frankie if he'd been here, but the air force doesn't give emergency furloughs for murder trials."

I was shocked at the change in her. Instead of a lost, bewildered girl, I was suddenly faced by a passionate, self-assured woman; eyes blazing, coat thrown back and hands on hips, small breasts thrust against a white cashmere sweater. She had a raw physical appeal, a certain savage sexuality which I'd missed the first time.

I lowered my eyes and started counting out her change. "You think Frankie's innocent?"

"I don't question my husband's convictions."

"And he thinks so?"

"Curt doesn't question Frankie's word." She smiled and put the change in her purse. "We all have our little dogmas, don't we?"

I knew what she meant, and I wanted to tell her that I'd wondered about Frankie's guilt—even doubted it—but that I was neither detective nor lawyer... and no matter what happened Anne would remain in her grave...

But I said nothing, and she turned and walked away. I started to call that she'd left her groceries when I saw her speak to a man who'd been leaning against the building. He came in and I saw that it was Guilford Sisk, about six-feet-four of good-natured male with bony wrists hanging from the sleeves of a red and black Mackinaw. He wore his woolen cap pushed off his forehead so the earflaps rested on his ears. He grinned at me self-consciously and jerked his head toward the groceries.

"Those belong to Missus Friedland?"

I nodded. "Are you working for her, Gil?"

"That wouldn't be work," he said with a wink. "No, working for Curt, helping him fix up the old house. It's pretty shot."

That puzzled me, because Gil wasn't one of the men who generally hired out his labor. On the contrary, Gil was one of the biggest landowners in the county. His great-grandfather had come out from Ohio with a Union Army land grant for most of the choice bottomland around Sherman. Gil's grandfather had gradually acquired the rest of it, and there was nothing for their descendants to do but enjoy themselves while the land increased in value. Gil was the last remaining member of the family. He hadn't married; he told me once that he was only interested in one woman and that was me. Yet he'd never proposed in a way that I could take seriously. I enjoyed talking to him because he was intelligent and well-educated; now and then he'd bring up something I'd never heard of, then he'd explain it—not with exasperated patience, as though he were instructing a child, as Lou often did—but with enthusiasm, as though he was as interested in it as I was. I sometimes got the feeling that Gil and I were expatriates in a foreign land, forced together because we could talk only among ourselves. Lou was intelligent too, but he didn't get along with Gil. Our home place was surrounded by Gil's land; Lou wanted to branch out and Gil wouldn't sell. That could have been the reason for the coolness between them, or it could have been me. Gil had never made a pass at me which I could definitely identify, and I had never given him any openings. (I don't think a woman ever gets an offer she doesn't invite, unless it's from a boob, a stranger, a nut who's showing off for friends, or a drunk. No reasonably intelligent man is going to approach a woman without encouragement, and I'd never given it to Gil.) It's true that he had a bad reputation... he'd grown up with fast cars and girls who never said no. Even now he had no respect for the institution of marriage. "A married man's got to uphold the sacred bond of matrimony," he told me once. "He doesn't want someone plowing his own field while he's plowing another' s. Me, what have I got to lose?" But if there'd been a spark waiting to flame up we'd both have known it by now. Nothing could sneak up and surprise us; we'd talked too long and too frankly. He didn't need me, anyway; when he wanted that kind of amusement he'd go down to Kaycee or up to Chicago and bring back a girl to stay a few weeks in his huge three-story brick mansion. He didn't live there, he merely camped in one or the other of its thirty-eight rooms. When he got tired of the woman he sent her home, then plunged into an orgy of work. You'd see him out working on his land, digging post holes, pitching hay and cutting wood, no different than any of his farm hands. He was a strange and rootless man, and despite all our profound conversations, I had the feeling I'd only skated on the surface of his character.

I watched him shoulder the box and I asked: "What's your game now, Gil?"

"With her?" He shook his head soberly. "No game. The kid doesn't know how to play." He stuck a cigaret in his mouth and struck a kitchen match on his thumb. He was full of such overdone yokel mannerisms. "Neither one of them knows how to play, Velda. You might keep that in mind when you're around Curt."

My face grew warm, but I didn't rise to his bait. "Well... what are they doing here?"

He shrugged. "We'll see, Velda. Be patient."

I watched him walk out, and then it struck me. Gil had been Frankie Friedland's best friend. He'd also known Anne not in a romantic sense, but as a member of her group.

And he'd been unable to prove where he was the night Anne was killed.

I felt as though a dismal fog were settling slowly over the community. I didn't want to think about it. I started unpacking soup cans and stacking them in a pyramid.

I was still at it when Ethel reported for work. She was a small erect woman with a hyperthyroid bulge in her eyes. Her husband had once owned the store, but his car had stalled on a rural railroad crossing and he hadn't gotten out in time. She'd sold the store to Louis, but then she'd found time heavy on her hands and come to work for me. Usually she relieved me at one and closed up at six, but today she had something to tell me which wouldn't wait. She'd spent the morning with a sister who worked in the traffic bureau in the county seat of Franklin. The sister had a friend in charge of circuit court records, and guess who had come in that morning and bought a transcript of the Friedland trial....

"Curt Friedland," I said.

Ethel blinked at me, her eyes magnified by thick-lensed spectacles. "How'd you know?"

"The town is in suspended animation. Nothing moves, only Curt Friedland."

"Well... " Ethel's tone was deflated. "He also asked for the coroner's report on Bernice Struble, but that wasn't available. You know what they say?"

"Who says?" l asked.

A wave of her hand included the entire community. "They say he's trying to clear his brother."

I looked up at Ethel, suddenly hating the community for its inability to mind its own business.

"Who says, Ethel?"

"Everybody. And you know what else they say?"

"For God's sake, don't dribble it out. *Say it!*"

The pyramid collapsed, and I walked off and left the cans rolling. As I opened the door to my cubbyhole office, she called after me:

"They say Bernice was probably murdered!"

I slammed the door and lit a cigaret. I tried to work on the charge account ledger, but I couldn't get interested in who owed us money. We had enough money already. I pulled on my cloth coat and walked out. I said good-by to Ethel but she didn't answer. Well, she'd survive the blow.

Driving east in the station wagon, I found myself humming a song under my breath: *Oh-oh, trouble's back in town.* I could only remember one line, but it seemed to fit....

I drove north on the gravel, then turned right and passed beneath a stone archway. The open wrought-iron gates—initialed LB for Louis Bayrd—made me feel as though I were entering a cemetery. I drove up the curving lane which Lou had paved and bordered with evergreens. He'd made his aunt's old farm look like a country estate; white fences enclosed sloping pastures; chunky Herefords grazed amid a shrinking patchwork of snow; a sorrel mare and a black gelding trotted with the car along an old-fashioned rail fence. Towering elms and red oaks flanked a white neo-colonial house and a five-acre lawn sloped down to a pint-sized lake stocked with swans and bluegills. Lou had put up a diving board and planted shrubbery, then had grumbled because Sharon and I didn't use it more. So we'd used it fiercely for a month and Lou had happily gone on to something else: converted the old farmhouse into a workshop, jammed it to the roof with power tools and built a power cruiser. Now the boat squatted on its trailer gathering dust, waiting for summer and sunshine on Lake Pillybay. We'd probably use it two or three times. When did Lou enjoy himself? What drove him? I couldn't answer because he never sat still long enough for me to see him.

The kitchen was polished brick and sparkling copper. I washed the breakfast dishes, opened a can of pork and beans and ate, washing it down with milk. I brewed coffee and drank it with a slow cigaret, feeling the silence of the huge empty house seep into my body. I liked the lonely afternoons at home. Evenings there was Lou, mornings the store, but in the afternoons I led my own life.

I washed the dishes and debated whether to take a bath or a shower. I decided against a bath; it made me lazy and sexual, like a cat licking itself in the sun. Today I needed movement. I showered under water blended to give just a tingle of coolness. I dried myself before the heating vent, letting the warm air caress my skin. I pulled on blue jeans and a sweatshirt and walked down to the pasture. I pumped water for the horses and let them nibble sugar lumps out of my palms. I noticed that the gelding had gotten fat during the cold spell. I took the hackamore off the windmill and pulled it over his head. I rode him bareback, raising my face to the wind and feeling his great muscles roll between my thighs. After a half hour I slid off and removed the hackamore. I could feet the warmth and dampness of perspiration against my thighs. I took another shower and went into the studio Lou had built for me. I pulled the drapes and filled the room with purple twilight. I sat down at the piano and played songs I knew by heart. My fingers moved without direction; my thoughts dwindled away....

Lou came home around eleven.

I lay with my light off, pretending sleep, listening to the sounds as he prepared for bed: slap of wallet on the dresser... jingle of keys, change... *clump-clump* of shoes... clatter of hangers as he hung up his clothes. I visualized him: deceptively small and built like a chunk of stovewood, black hair swirling about his thighs and curling up from his chest in great tufts. Lou was humming. He always did when he performed some task which didn't fully occupy his mind. I strained my ears and caught the tune: *Oh-oh, trouble's bank in town.* I was shocked to realize I'd become so closely linked to this man that Curt's arrival would trigger the same train of thought.

Before he got into his bed, he set the controls of the electric eye which bracketed the drive. When a car passed through the gate, the beam would be broken and the drive floodlighted. Lou wasn't nervous about burglars; he just did it for amusement, like the shop and the boat. I'd asked him before not to turn it on when Sharon had a date, but he did it anyway.

I heard him get into the bed across from mine and light a cigaret, then he said:

"Curt Friedland bought his dad's old place."

There. How the hell did he know I was awake? I sat up and lit a cigaret. I saw the ashtray heaped full of butts and realized how he'd known. Lou never missed the little things....

"Why?" I asked. I was surprised at the coldness of my voice.

"He was born there."

"So were his brothers. They haven't come back."

"A man gets lost, he has to return to the starting place to find himself again."

"You think Curt's lost?"

"Who isn't?"

It was one of my husband's non-answers. Ask him if he's cold and if he doesn't want to think about it he says: Who isn't? Ask him if he likes fried chicken, he says: Who doesn't? Then I get hung up trying to think of somebody who doesn't like fried chicken and I forget the original question.

At that point the floodlights came on. Poor Sharon.

I exhaled slowly, trying to keep cool. "I knew a girl who was whipped when her father caught her with a boy. So she went the whole distance every chance she got. She knew she'd be punished anyway."

"What's that got to do with Sharon?"

"Give her a chance for a normal relationship."

"It's normal to sit in a parked car for hours?"

I sighed. "Yes, Lou. It's normal."

He got up and turned off the floodlights, then lay back down. I was surprised at his quick acquiescence until I realized he probably wanted something from me. Maybe he only wanted to talk about the Friedlands; at least he started that way. They seemed to have no money worries, he said; Curt had paid for the place with a ten-thousand-dollar cashier's check on a Chicago bank and deposited the rest. The van had been waiting with their furniture and Lou had helped them move in. "Nothing fancy," said Lou, "just quietly expensive. A few antiques that his wife shepherded along. I think she comes from money. Also two electric typewriters, hi-fi, tape recorder, adding machine, stuff like that. Curt's firm didn't go broke the way some people thought; he was in opinion research, and he suddenly decided be didn't give a damn about other people's opinions. He sold out and went to the islands, goofed around in a native dugout while his wife made shell jewelry. Then he got the idea of coming back to fix up the old place..."

Lou swung his legs off the bed and sat up. "I like the way he does business. No scratching his head, no hemming and hawing. It's either yes or no and it's obviously final either way. He lets his wife run things on the surface. If he doesn't like it she changes it around until he does. She used to manage the field end of the business, door-to-door canvassers, telephone interviewers, mail questionnaires. She's not a brain, but she's sharp as a knife." He smiled vaguely. "Pretty too."

I gave him a narrow look. His face was flushed—probably from drinking—and there was a rare brightness in his eyes, the pinpointed, dazzled look of someone hypnotized. I had a good idea who'd done it.

"You and Curt worked pretty late?"

"Not too. We took off at eleven and went to the Club 75. Goober Sutton and his wife kept staring at Curt and mumbling to each other. I thought Goober was going to call the law when Curt started bugging him."

"I thought your friend was so cool."

"He is. He did it deliberately, to get information."

"Didn't he ever hear of the friendly approach?"

Lou sighed and stretched out on the bed. "The friendly approach elicits platitudes and false cordiality. Your front is undisturbed; you can sit there lying with your teeth showing in a great big smile. On the other hand, if you bug a man, he's liable to get mad. And when he gets mad he tells the truth whether he wants to or not. Not verbally, but by his actions."

"That sounds like a direct quote from Curt."

"I guess it is."

"You think he's pretty smart?"

Lou stood up and walked around the room, his pajamas flapping. "Look, I don't mean he tweaked his nose or anything. Just shook hands and asked if Goober remembered him. Then he looked around and said, 'You've changed things around, haven't you, Goober?' Goober was beginning to stiffen up. 'We've made several changes over the years,' he said. And Curt said, 'That wall, I mean. You didn't have that partition say, twelve years ago, did you?' Goober looked like he had stomach trouble. He said: 'No, we didn't.' And Curt said, 'You've added a lot of lights to your parking lot too. It's bright as day out there. Not much hanky-panky could go on now.' I could see Goober wishing Curt would give him some excuse to go for that lead-filled club he's got under the bar. Finally Curt said: 'Look, I don't want you to think I hold anything against you. I don't. You told the truth as you saw it, what else could you do?' Remember, Goober testified that Frankie got mean and violent when he drank; he upset Frankie's picture of himself as a good-natured, harmless drinker, and it had a lot to do with the verdict. Anyway, Goober looked like a boiled beet. He opened his mouth but Curt said he didn't have to apologize. Goober blurted that he damn well wasn't *about* to apologize; Curt said he certainly didn't blame him, because there was no need to apologize for telling the truth as he saw it. Jesus... I was about to fall out of the booth laughing. That poor goddam Goober was being led along like a pig with a ring in his nose. Finally he got up and said he was closing for the night and we'd have to leave."

"You enjoyed it, did you?"

Lou smiled. "I like the way he screws people up."

"Sounds to me like he's just trying to make trouble, this hero of yours."

Lou pulled aside the covers and slid into his bed. "Not *just* make trouble, Velda."

"You believe he's trying to clear his brother."

"Naturally," said Lou, stifling a yawn.

"Does he have anything new?"

"I don't think so."

"And Bernice? Does he have any evidence of murder?"

"None that I know of."

"Then what—?"

"Listen, you've gone rabbit hunting with your brother?"

"Yes."

"What did he do when the rabbit ran into a brushpile?"

I frowned, trying to remember. "He threw rocks and made a lot of noise, trying to scare him into the open."

Lou nodded. "And if that didn't work he set fire to the brushpile." Lou frowned at the ceiling. "I'm just guessing, you know. I can't read him at all. He smiles when you can't see anything to smile about. Sort of hangs back, watching you. I don't think his wife understands him either. When she talks to somebody, her eyes keep sliding in his direction to see how he's taking it." Lou paused. "An interesting couple. I thought I'd invite them... "

"Lou." A tone of quiet warning.

"His brother did it, Velda. Curt was in Korea."

"I know that." I was speaking around a pain. "Invite anybody you like. Just don't expect me to entertain them."

"You sound like a Brushcreeker."

"Strange. It happens I am."

"So's Curt."

"Then he'll understand exactly how I feel." I rolled over and turned my back. "Good night."

A moment later the canopy of light between our beds disappeared. I tossed in the darkness and cursed the treachery of my own nervous system. All the girlish uncertainty I thought I'd conquered had only been asleep someplace. Curt's return had brought it popping out like some foolish jack-in-the-box grinning its floppy head at me. I knew that Curt had trapped Lou in a net of curiosity, and I was determined not to be caught the same way. I also saw that Lou didn't care whether he was trapped or not, and I was afraid I wouldn't care either—

Oh hell, let's face it. Curt was too smart, and my little boat couldn't stand much rocking. Give me credit for knowing that much.

Chapter Two

I was standing at the store window next morning when Gabrielle strolled through the park with Sandra Matthews. Sandy was a Brush Creek girl whom the boys used to pick up around midnight and take home the long way. Poor Sandy had the illusion that this was what they meant when they talked about popularity. She'd been in the Club 75 with Frankie the night of Anne's murder, and she'd testified at the trial.

I could picture the courtroom at Franklin; I could hear the muffled coughs and hushed whispers. I smelled musty paper and ancient varnish and I saw Sandy on the stand, so serious that she looked mournful. She wore a navy-blue suit and black patent-leather pumps, the same outfit she'd worn to Anne's funeral. She testified that Frankie had drunk perhaps a half dozen beers and sampled a friend's bottle of bourbon. When the prosecutor asked if Frankie was drunk, Frankie's lawyer objected that Sandy wasn't qualified to judge drunkenness. The judge sustained the objection, and the prosecutor went on to ask what happened when Frankie was told that Anne was waiting in the car:

Sandy: *Well, I was bugged. I mean, he was my date, after all. I asked him why he didn't go out and finish with her for good. I didn't mean—*

Prosecutor: *You meant he should stop seeing her?*

That's what I meant.

What did Frankie say?

For me to worry about myself. He'd take care of Anne.

What do you think he meant?

The defense objected that Sandy's opinions were irrelevant, and the judge sustained it. In cross-examination, Sandy admitted that to the best of her knowledge Frankie and Anne were on intimate terms and hadn't quarreled.

Since the trial, Sandy had acquired a husband named George Bennett, four children, and fifty pounds of fat which trembled as she walked. She still talked about the murder and hinted that she hadn't told all she knew, but nobody listened to her any more.

I watched the two of them together: slim Gabrielle and dumpy, dowdy Sandy with a baby on her hip, haunches rolling, like a plow horse mistakenly teamed with a show horse. The pair sat on a bench in the sun; Sandy dumped a large gray breast from her dress, shoved it into the baby's mouth, covered it with her sweater, and talked. I knew she was babbling about the murder because that's all she ever talked about....

A blue Mercury rolled past with the words FRANKLIN COUNTY
SHERIFF painted on its door. It parked in front of the building where Lou
had his hardware store and real estate office. Sheriff Glen Wade went in
wearing his .38 in a button-down holster on his belt. The visit wasn't
unusual; Lou was a leading citizen and president of the Lions Club; it was
an election year and Lou was supporting the sheriff. Still, I had a feeling it
concerned Curt Friedland. I'd seen Lou leave town a half hour before with
a load of doorframes and roofing—destined for Curt's house, I was sure—
so I wasn't surprised when the sheriff came into the store.

"Hello, Velda," he said. "Know where I could find Lou?"

"I sure don't, Sheriff." The lie surprised me; I thought I'd outgrown the
Brushcreeker's inborn antagonism toward the law.

The sheriff made a show of examining the display of stainless-steel razor
blades. It had been over twenty-five years since I'd watched him kill the
man in the street, but I could never forget that he wore death on his hip.
He couldn't have been more than thirty then; even now he retained the
blunt, beefy good looks of an aging athlete who keeps in shape.

Finally he spoke in a blurred baritone: "I hear Lou sold the old Friedland
place."

The sheriff had small gray eyes; you looked in and it left you sort of
empty, as though you'd failed to locate a person inside.

I forced down an impulse to lie. "So he said."

"The boy bought it outright, they say."

"That's what Lou says."

The sheriff pulled at his belt and shifted his weight to the other foot. "I
don't get over to this end of the county much. Don't need to these days.
Brush Creek's kind of farmed out and the troublemakers have left. People
like your husband keep things in line. But a sheriff isn't worth his salt if
he can't smell trouble in the wind, isn't that right?"

"That's right, Sheriff."

The sheriff looked relieved. "What I was wondering, have you heard any
rumors that might concern law enforcement?"

Something seemed to rip the words out of my mouth. "I heard that
Bernice Struble was murdered."

The sheriff looked pained. "Now, Velda, you know that ain't true."

I shrugged and said nothing, watching his face turn hard and heavy. I
could almost see his massive strength bunching beneath his light-blue
gabardine jacket. Finally he gave a short decisive nod.

"Think I'd better check up on that rumor. See you later, Velda."

I watched him get in his car and drive off toward Franklin. That puzzled
me because I'd gotten the idea he was going after Curt. Then I remembered that he never went into the Nation alone, just as city policemen
never patrolled tough neighborhoods alone. He'd gone to get his deputy.

I glanced over in the park. Gaby and Sandy were gone. I couldn't see Curt's car anywhere around the square. I tried to add up the tickets on the morning deliveries, but I couldn't make sense out of the numbers. I knew what was wrong; my past kept jumping up and hitting me in the face. I picked up the phone and called Ethel: "Can you come in and take over? I've got to rush out of town."

The streaked old frame house sat on a barren hill in the bowels of the Nation. A single pine tree stood beside the house, its trunk naked except for a tuft of green at the top. The Friedland boys had always kept 'coon hounds chained to the tree; they'd also had stretching frames for curing muskrat and mink pelts, and a small graveyard of junked cars and wrecked motorcycles. For ten years the sightless windows had overlooked gullied slopes which resembled the ribs of a starving dog.

Now the house had the bustling disorder of a mining camp. A telephone company truck was parked on the road, and men were stringing wire toward the house. Heine Wentz' drilling rig squatted half-way up the slope beside a pyramid of fresh yellow clay. I didn't see Lou's pickup nor Curt's old car; apparently Gaby hadn't yet returned. I recognized Gil Sisk's hulking figure on the roof and waved; he spat out a handful of nails and called down:

"Lou went to Connersville for plumbing fixtures."

I nodded. Connersville was the nearest large city, forty miles away. "Where's Curt?"

Gil's face spread in a teasing grin. "What you want him for?"

My face felt hot. "It's serious, Gil. Where is he?"

Gil silently pointed his hammer across a flat stretch of ground behind the house. I saw Curt's back outlined against the sky; broad and tan and bare to the waist, with a quiver of arrows across it. Far ahead of him stood an archery target.

I made my way over the rocky ground. A light breeze caressed my face, warm until the sun went behind a fleck of cloud, then sharp with the bite of winter.

"You're rushing the season," I said as I walked up behind him. "It isn't that warm."

He turned, and I was surprised to see that he'd shaved off the beard. His face was composed of straight lines coming together in perfect angles, so smooth that I looked hard for a flaw. There was something unnaturally clean and hard about his face; you couldn't say about him: Here's a thoughtful man, or a sad and morose man. He seemed... blank, like someone in a waiting room. I felt an urge to see some emotion in the face, and to know that I'd caused it myself. Anything would have served, even hatred or disgust.

But he looked at me without change of expression and turned back.

With a single smooth movement, he took an arrow from the quiver and fitted it to the bowstring.

"I've still got the West Indian sun in my system. The cold hasn't touched me yet."

I felt like a bug which had been seized, stuck under a microscope, and set aside. I forced down my annoyance, remembering that I'd been to blame for our awkward reunion yesterday. It was up to me to erase that beginning.

"I... like you better without the beard."

"It was part of my beachcomber costume." A vague smile tugged at his lips, as though he were laughing at himself. "Now I'm on another masquerade."

We were still stalking on the surface. I felt impatient to make contact, to get beneath his shield. I watched his muscles knot as he slowly drew back the bowstring. A dew of sweat shone on his forehead, but his features were composed. Suddenly all his muscles went slack. Zzzzp! The arrow disappeared; I saw it reappear a second later in the second ring out from the bull's-eye.

"I never saw anyone shoot like that."

"It's the Zen method," he said, drawing another arrow from the quiver. "You're supposed to let the release of the arrow come as a total surprise. You aren't supposed to think."

ZzzzP! A second arrow quivered in the edge of the bull's-eye.

"Pretty good," I said. "Zen is a kind of Buddhism, isn't it, like yoga?"

He nodded.

"You sit with your feet in your lap?"

He smiled, an exasperating controlled flicker at the corner of his mouth which made me want to say: For God's sake, let it go, laugh a little.

"Sometimes," he said. "But only when I feel like it."

Mysticism. I don't know why it made me wistful. That was one of the trails I'd never taken and I sort of wished I had....

He turned, and I saw that I'd somehow broken through. His frozen, guarded look was gone. "If you'd like to try, I'll get you Gaby's bow. It's got a lighter pull."

"Not now," I said. "I came to tell you to expect a visit from the sheriff."

He nodded. "I was already expecting it."

I felt disappointed. "Why?"

He fitted another arrow into the bow. "The sheriff has an opponent for office, a bright ex-marine just out of college. I met him the other day and made a small campaign contribution. He was interested in the fact that I used to do public opinion surveys; wanted to know what I thought his chances were. I told him I'd check around and try to give him something he could use in his campaign."

"You aren't even trying to get along with Sheriff Wade, are you?"

"Sheriff Wade is a bloated bag of ego. All he cares is that everything looks peaceful. The county's like a garbage dump with fresh dirt smoothed over it; underneath it's a seething mass of maggots."

"Oh... not *that* bad."

He gave me a glance of pity. "You've been in it so long you don't even notice."

He turned and sent an arrow into the center of the bull's eye. I watched him slide the quiver off his shoulder and unstring the bow, and I tried to understand my own vague feeling that he was right about Sheriff Wade—and the county too.

He picked his sweatshirt off the ground and pulled it over his head. "Actually," he said, "there was never any question of getting along with the sheriff. We were opposed by the nature of things. My tie-in with the opposition is a form of insurance. If the sheriff tries to give me the roust I go straight to the other guy, who'll spread it all over the country. If the sheriff's smart he'll handle me easy."

I looked at Curt curiously. "You always figure things to the fourth decimal point?"

He shrugged. "Sometimes, Velda. I can't help using what I know to control my environment. Sheriff Wade happens to be part of my environment. I do what I can."

We were walking toward the house when I said: "You manage to get a lot of free labor; my husband, Gil Sisk..."

"Tom Sawyer and the fence. They want to find out what I'm doing here."

"What are you doing here?"

He looked at me. "Your husband trusts you, doesn't he?"

It was a statement, not a question. I don't know why, but I suddenly felt stodgy and middle-aged. "He has no reason not to."

Curt nodded. "I suppose he'd understand if we went for a ride—-in your car."

"Of course," I said quickly.

Not until we were on the road, and he'd directed me toward Lake Pillybay, did I wonder: Would I have gone it he'd put it differently? I decided I probably would have; I had nothing better to do.

I drove silently, leaving the steep marginal farmlands behind, ascending slowly along the ridge. Snow lay white beneath naked trees on the slopes below. Curt lit a cigaret and put it between my lips. I accepted without surprise until I realized I'd have resented the intimacy from another man. I understood that I shared something with Curt that I'd never shared with Lou: we had less need for talk; a glance or a word held special meanings which we both understood. It all had something to do with growing up on a rocky farm during a depression....

"Why did you come back?" I asked.

He waved his hand. "This is where it all happened, the first sixteen years of my life. Compared to what the last sixteen have been... dull, repetitive. This is where everything happened first." He pointed to a stream far below. "'There, for example...'" He broke off with a laugh.

"There what? Don't laugh in your beard. You don't have it any more."

"My first lesson in sex."

"Oh?" My stomach went curiously tight. "With whom?"

"Sandy Matthews."

I felt a vague disappointment. "You didn't pick a very high-class teacher."

"No..." Then he frowned. "I'm not sure, though. I was fourteen, Sandy was three years older. She asked me, and I was trapped by pride. I couldn't say no, and I couldn't admit that I'd never done it before. She took me to an old barn we used to have; she acted so funny I got suspicious. I looked up and saw eyes peering in. My brothers had set the whole deal up. I was fighting mad. I tore out of there and was going to beat up the whole crew, but they ran away. Then I went back and I was going to beat up Sandy too. I found her crying, ashamed. She'd been trapped by a dare. We went for a walk and wound up in the ravine, swimming nude. It really happened then... natural and innocent. I was in love with her for several months." He grunted and pulled out his pipe. "It was... sad to see her again. I wanted to talk to her, but she had only one thing on her mind; she wanted to relive that incident by the stream. It couldn't happen, but she wasn't capable of knowing that. She had youth then; freshness and a kind of innocence. That's all she had, and she lost it." He gave me an oblique look as he lit his pipe. "Something happens to people here. Their bodies look healthy, but the minds inside are dead, sluggish and slow, like cold porridge. What does it, Velda?"

I set my jaws and kept my eyes on the narrow gravel road. He was working up to something, and I had an idea it concerned me.

"Remember after the fight, when the boy got tangled in the fence, you said that ten years from now I'd be ashamed. What did you mean?"

"I... I don't remember."

"See? You had something then. I remember seeing you get on the school bus in the mornings with your chin held high, looking aloof and cold. But with green fire in your eyes. You'd date older boys and I'd feel like you feel when you see a boob on a magnificent horse. They didn't appreciate what they had." He paused. "You've changed. You've fallen victim to life's leveling process. You go to the store in the mornings and talk with housewives and deliverymen. Your terms become those of Ethel and Gladys and Sandy—"

"Oh, Curt—!"

"In the afternoons you go home and... what? I'll bet you've started a dozen hobbies in the last ten years."

I thought of my sewing machine, my guitar, embroidery, sketchpad, typewriter...

"What are you, a detective?"

"An observer. Things have to fit together. I see certain facets of your character—impatient eye movements and excessive smoking, for example—and I deduce that you're restless and bored."

"Well, deduce something else. You're wrong."

"Okay. The hobbies indicate an active, searching mind. Is that better?"

"I... yes."

"Same thing. Active mind. Unoccupied. Gets bored. See?" He laughed shortly. "It's only a word game. Don't give it a thought. You can stop here."

We'd reached the point where the road passed the summit of Bald Knob, highest point in the county. Ahead it descended into Lake Pillybay. I pulled onto the shoulder and Curt got out.

"Want to walk up to the top?"

I gripped the wheel and shook my head. "Curt, you're still playing games with me. You said not to worry, but you didn't mean it. I'm supposed to worry. I'm supposed to feel desperately bored, I'm supposed to say: What can I do, Curt? And then you'll say, Well, you can help me solve this little murder...."

He smiled faintly. "No, just think about it. You've had it buried twelve years, Velda. Think of Frankie. Could he have done it?"

I watched him walk up the hill and I thought about Frankie. He was the second youngest of the four boys, next to Curt. He was also the craziest. He had a strong jaw and curly auburn hair which grew thick and wild. I used to feel about him the way I'd felt about Curt the morning before: this man doesn't care; he's on an emotional roller-coaster, he makes me edgy and nervous, the way I get around strange animals. My image of him is of running and shouting, and something to do with violence... a powerful force unbottled—quite the opposite of Curt, who left an impression of steely control. Frankie was violent, yes, but I never thought he was cruel. I've seen him tear a beer joint apart with a whoop and a holler, but he never stopped laughing. Marston and I were parked along the highway late one night when Frankie roared by on his cycle. He must have been going a hundred and twenty; he was just a blur. A moment later another blurred shape roared by. It was Curt. He was barely in his teens and he followed his brother everywhere. I was afraid for Curt, because I figured Frankie would kill them both....

Frankie went with my sister Anne all through high school. She was prettier than I: big hazel eyes and black hair glinting with blue highlights. She had a sleek windblown look which made you think of the girls they put on hood ornaments. During the war Frankie became a flier and was lost over Germany. They'd planned to get married after he came back, not knowing they should have done it before. My dad was to blame for what happened next; the baby became obvious and we'd been told to presume Frankie dead. Dad told Anne to get a husband and she picked Johnny Drew, a reckless kid who'd been discharged from the marines after getting malaria in the Pacific. For six months afterward he sauntered around town in his dress uniform.

I drew my impression from that: an egocentric fathead who'd carried his bluff this far and run out of gas. I was right, but I got no joy out of it. The baby was stillborn, and instead of getting a sensible divorce, Anne went to hell. If Frankie had come back... but none of the Friedlands came back. The oldest, a Navy frogman, was killed at Eniwetok. The second oldest survived the war as a paratrooper, married a French girl, and settled down in Algeria. After Frankie's release from prison camp he flew for oil companies in Arabia and South America. Around 1948 he went to Alaska and started a flying service for hunters and prospectors. Curt quit school and joined him; started flying at sixteen. Sherman was dull without the Friedlands, but in a sense they were still with us. Anne had become a lovely whore. Every family seems to have one member who goes to hell; I remember Anne during those five years as a dull ache in the heart. She never acquired the bloated, baggy look of a honky-tonk queen—which is the usual way for a girl to go to hell in this part of the country—but she was working on it. She made her home in the Club 75, a rambling roadhouse near Lake Pillybay where tourists and Brushcreekers fought and played together. Know that it was an after-hours' place and you've got the scene: booze-red faces and thick smoke; neckties and denim shirts and black leather jackets jostling together; blood and broken bottles in the parking lot; teenagers getting stoned in the parked cars on booze carried out by older cronies; the sound of retching, the muffled thump of thrashing bodies in back seats and the *squee-squee-squee* of car springs; women with dresses up squatting carelessly between parked cars; men's voices thick with guttural rage and a woman's strident screech: *You suvvabitch I'll go home with whoever I damn please—!*

Queen Anne held court in a knotty-pine booth next to the bar, selecting her escorts with the unpredictability of a royal whim, letting them understand there was nothing in her of permanence or love...

Then came Korea, and Curt went over to fly jets. A year later Frankie drifted home to sweat out the war, saying he couldn't run his business without Curt, since only Curt knew how to keep books and make a profit. And Frankie took up his strange affair with Anne. They seemed to fight against being together; each night they'd go in separate directions with separate groups; each morning around three a.m. they'd be sitting together in a booth at the Club 75. Neither of them had the sense to wipe the slate clean and start over....

Frankie, meanwhile, was playing baseball with a local league, whooping it up around the district, and jousting with the law. It was part of a Brushcreeker's heritage to have law trouble. Frankie was jailed for a week in St. Joe for throwing two bouncers out of their own dance hall; he drew another week in Omaha for tearing up a nightclub; he drew thirty-days in Franklin County Jail for resisting arrest. (He'd taken Deputy Hoff's guns from him and thrown them in a grader ditch, then kicked the deputy in after them. Nobody blamed Frankie; the deputy was a vicious little brute who wore two ridiculous forty-fives low on his hips. He used to walk into the Club 75 slapping his club in his palm, daring somebody to step out of line. Frankie hadn't been able to resist taunting him, and the deputy had been waiting when he left the club.) A week after Frankie's release he was sitting in the club with Sandy when Gil Sisk said Anne wanted to see him in the car. At the trial, Frankie explained it when he took the stand in his own defense:

I usually met Anne at the club and took her home. I just figured she didn't want to come in for some reason, so I went out. She'd parked in the dark and I didn't see anyone in the car. I opened the door and saw her lying across the seat. I reached in to touch her and something blew up in the back of my head. I don't remember anything after that.

Defense Attorney: You made a statement to the sheriff after your arrest that you could remember nothing that happened the night before. Is that true?

Sure, but it all came back to me later. The bump on the head blacked out my memory.

You weren't drunk?

No, I felt good.

What do you mean, you felt good?

I wasn't mad at anybody. I was having a ball.

In the cross-examination, the prosecutor asked:

Isn't it true that in the past your idea of having a ball had led to violence, fighting, destruction—

Objection, which was sustained. The prosecutor then asked why he'd run when they came to arrest him.

Frankie: Hell, I didn't run. Those bastards came out to the house, got me out of bed, and asked me to come with them. My head was splitting and I had a bloody lump on it. I decided I'd busted up some joint the night before and there'd be a stink. I got in and the sheriff took off into the hills, driving slow, asking me questions about the night before. Deputy Hoff had his gun out and was trying to look tough. Little by little I realized somebody had been killed. I got jumpy. I knew the deputy would set me up if he got a chance. So when we stopped—we'd been riding a couple of hours, and eventually you gotta stop—

Who wanted to stop?

The sheriff was driving. He just stopped. We all got out and stood there, you know, taking care of our own business, and I looked at the trees ahead and thought, well, what the hell? So I took off. Blam! Right in the back. Two days later I woke up in the hospital handcuffed to the bed.

Frankie had been found guilty. His family had gone broke appealing the sentence, but it had stuck. Now Curt wanted to open it up. I couldn't see that he had any chance at all.

I got out and walked toward the summit of Bald Knob. Years ago, somebody had cut off the oak and hickory timber in the hope of growing crops, but rain and wind had stripped away the soil and left only jumbled rocks and boulders. Curt sat on a large boulder, smoking his pipe.

"Safest place in the world," he said as I came up. "A barren hill."

I looked at the terrain dropping off in all directions. To the east a glint of light marked the Sherman watertower; to the west I saw tiny patches of silver which were the coves of Lake Pillybay. I could make out the gray roof of the Club 75, squatting in a patch of yellow gravel.

I sat down on the boulder facing away from him. A breeze whispered across the summit, stirred the dead weeds, and teased up my skirt. It felt like cool fingers lightly caressing my thighs. My nose filled with the masculine smell of his tobacco; my back touched his arm, and I felt the warmth of his body through the sweatshirt. A knot of tension formed deep in the pit of my stomach; he had brought me here for some reason. Why? I wondered, knowing that if he tried anything, I'd resist him to the last breath; bracing for him but at the same time waiting, curious to see what he'd do....

Finally I said: "Why do you say safest?"

He waved his hand. "Visibility. You can see trouble coming for miles."

I stared at him. "Are you that scared?"

He smiled. "That's not a good word. I've just developed certain habits, never walk into a dark room with your hands full, never stand in a lighted widow, never tell all you know...."

"But you used to be so... reckless."

"Yes. Well, that's something I lost."

He looked down at his feet a moment, then gave a short, humorless laugh. "Anyway, I wasn't really. Look there, remember that dive Frankie used to do?"

He pointed his pipe toward the lake. I saw the sparkle of water below a limestone cliff, and the low ledge from which we used to dive. My gaze drifted up... up to the very top of the cliff, nearly seventy feet above the water. I remembered Frankie racing across the plateau and leaping off with the chilling scream of an eagle. His tanned muscular body had plummeted past the gaping boys on the ledge and struck the water like a rock. A moment later another shape soared off the cliff and streaked down like a pale arrow, passing the ledge so closely my heart stopped, then knifing the water with hardly a ripple. That had been Curt, outdoing his brother but doing it so quietly that few people noticed; they were busy watching Frankie splash toward shore.

"I remember Frankie's dive," I said. "I also remember yours."

"Yes but... did you know that Frankie made it the first time at night, in absolute darkness? Hell, he didn't know he could clear that ledge below, he just jumped down into the darkness and hoped. You know what I did? I measured the ledge, and I figured I had to leap out fifteen feet to clear it. I practiced the jump from lower down until I was damn sure I could make it."

"Yours was better," I said. I looked at him and he was smiling. "It was. Really."

He shook his head. "Not for me. I only did what I knew I could do. Frankie threw his fate into the lap of the gods and jumped. When he made it he knew they were on his side. I didn't understand that for a long time. Gaby did, though. We had a little cliff on our island, oh ... twenty-five feet high. Water roared into a narrow crevice below it. Gaby used to stand there and time her dive so she'd catch a swell at its peak, otherwise she'd land in three feet of water. Well, the night I decided to come back here— I'd been getting the county newspaper and they'd just brought the one which reported Bernice Struble's death—we had a terrible argument. She didn't want me to come back. She went off mad and was gone until dark. I was about to search for her when I saw her silhouetted against the sky at the top of the cliff. My heart jumped into my mouth. She'd never jumped at night and I thought: Lord, even if she catches the wave right she could hit a chunk of driftwood. Off she went. I met her as she came out of the water and said if she felt like that I wouldn't go. She said no, but that if I wanted to deliberately risk my life she'd do the same.

"Then it hit me. Coming back here was my own jump into darkness. I wasn't sure I could succeed. I knew I'd bump heads with the law, not to mention becoming a target for the real killer. Thinking about it... I was scared, but I was exhilarated too. I was shoving in all I had. I was taking the big jump and at the bottom I'd find either life... or death. Everything was simple."

I looked at him and saw the excitement shining in his eyes. I understood the look I'd seen earlier, of not caring. He'd taken his fate out of his hands and now he was free. And in a way I envied him....

Walking down to the car I said: "You came all the way back here just because Bernice Struble fell in a well?"

"Yes." He looked at me and laughed abruptly. "You think that's crazy?"

"Well, I... Yes. Damn right I do. Especially when you say it's murder and you don't have a single measly crumb of evidence—!"

"I have a theory, Velda. To test a theory you have to act as though it's true. Then you start stacking up the facts and if your theory doesn't hold them all you throw it out. When Frankie got sent up, I was sure of one thing; there was a killer loose in Sherman. I expected him to strike again, sooner or later, but there were no more murders. That didn't fit what I'd learned about killers... until it occurred to me that he was clever enough to make them all look like accidents. I started checking, but it wasn't until Bernice's death that I had something to work on. It could have been an accident, I'll admit. But I have to assume it's murder in order to test the theory. You understand?"

"No." I stopped at the car and turned. "The trouble is you start with the assumption that Frankie didn't kill... my sister. I don't have that faith, you know. He wasn't my brother."

Curt pulled out his billfold and gave me a folded square of paper. It was a penciled note faded and smeared from much handling. It began *Dear Angelface:* that was the nickname Curt's brothers had used when they teased him.

Yr. idea sounds crazy, just between us kids. A good honest cop is worth ten smart lawyers; once the law gets an armlock on a man they quit looking. I got convicted and that's it; I'd bet my tobacco ration that every speck of evidence that didn't agree with the verdict has been shoved under the rug. But okay, I'll answer your questions and shoot this out past the censors. She was dead when I got there.

You know how they feel. I couldn't have been wrong. I must have got home by instinct after I got hit on the head. I don't remember. I didn't black out from booze; Gil Sisk can tell you I wasn't drunk, and you know how I always remembered everything, even when I was totally paralyzed from drinking. So what happened to the knife the killer used? The sheriff never found it, and it's rusted away by now. So damn much of this evidence is cold, cold. One thing to look into: Anne was playing some guy for money. I told her once that I'd go back north if I laid my hands on a bundle, and she asked if I'd take her with me. Half shot, I said sure. Maybe I would've too. Anyway, she visited me in the can while I was sweating out my thirty days and asked me when I could leave, because she thought she could raise about five thou. I said, anytime baby. Could be she had it the night she got killed; did the sheriff find any money on her? Strap that fat-assed son-of-a-bitch down and apply a pair of wire stretchers to his you-know-what. I don't think he knows who killed her, but he knows damn well I didn't. Sandy Matthews might give you something. She said once that Anne should be satisfied with the man she had and not bother me.

She wasn't talking about Johnny Drew, since who'd be satisfied with him? If I think of anything else I'll shoot it out to you, but I'm not holding my breath, buddy-o. Some birds here plan on sprouting wings and they want me in the covey. They'll wait six months, so that's how long you've got. After that I'm out of the game, win or lose. *Buena Suerte*, Angelface.

I gave him back the note and started the car. I was biting my lip. "Six months. He didn't give you long."

"No."

"So... that's why you've got Gaby pumping Sandy."

He nodded.

"Well, I don't know about Anne's other man, but I can tell you this. She was found with only seven dollars in her purse."

"It doesn't mean anything. The killer would have taken it, assuming be was the one who'd given it to her."

I turned the car around and drove back toward Curt's place. He didn't have to say he wanted my help. He'd been saying it all morning, in a dozen ways. The next move was mine.

"Let's say Frankie didn't do it. Why do you think the killers still around'?"

"Several reasons. Bernice is one. Her situation was a lot like Anne's."

"Oh? In what way?"

"She had a roving eye, Gil says. A truckdriver friend of his was making it with her for a year. After he left town, Gil went out to see if she wanted a replacement."

"Gil Sisk?" I felt a hot flush of jealousy. "Gil wouldn't want Bernice."

"A feminine viewpoint. Gil said she had a number of interesting... features. No brains, but Gil wasn't wanting conversation. Anyway, she gave him the cold eye, so he decided somebody had beat him there. Could've been Anne's old boyfriend."

"Curt, that's too farfetched."

"Not if you add up the other similarities. Forget Anne was your sister, look at her objectively. She was roughly the age of Bernice. Had the same kind of passive, unexciting husband. She was known to advertise what she had—like Bernice. And at the end she and Bernice both had a secret lover—"

"Oh Lord!" I gasped. "I just remembered, Bernice was in the store a couple of days before she was . . before she died. She'd been saving trading stamps, but this time she waved them away. She said there were better ways of getting gifts, and besides she'd be leaving town soon. That's like Anne telling Frankie she could get a big wad of money. What do you think?"

"It fits," said Curt. We were approaching his place; Gil had gone, probably to lunch. Neither Gaby nor Lou had come back.

"Park behind the house," said Curt. "I want you to talk to Heine a minute."

Heine had shut down his drilling rig and was getting ready to leave for lunch. Heine was a living insult to Hitler's Aryan ideal; short and stooped, with large hairy arms hanging to his knees. He had a dark, wizened face and wiry, tight-curled hair. He also had a local monopoly on well digging, sewer cleaning and plumbing.

"Heine, tell her what you found when you went out to the Strubles' place the day after she drowned."

"What I don't find, you mean?" Heine gave me a black-toothed grin. "My big pipe wrench. Gone. I think somebody steal it. Maybe the sheriff." He winked at me.

"Did you look in the well?" asked Curt.

Heine's eyes widened. "Ah, that well, we fill her up."

"Why?" asked Curt.

"Mister Struble, he said fill up quick, to the top. This is custom, to fill up the wells when people inside fall. Always. Water is no good to drink."

As he drove away, I said to Curt: "You're taking a lot for granted, even if the pipe wrench was in the well. Okay, it could have been a weapon. But you don't know she was murdered, you don't even know she had a lover—"

"No." He sat down on the steps of the wooden porch. "Her husband took a room in town and left her stuff in the house. I'd like to go through it, see if there are any notes, flowers, souvenirs from her lover." He looked up at me. "Struble listed his place with your husband. That means Lou has a key, right?"

I felt my back stiffen. I knew what was coming. "Yes."

"Can you get it for me?"

"Why not ask Lou?"

"A month from now I could. Right now I don't know him well enough."

I looked out, trying to frame my answer. I saw a car approaching, kicking up a long serpent of dust. Gradually I made out the sheriff's emblem on the side.

"Get in the house," said Curt.

"But why—?"

"Go on. I don't want you to cramp the sheriff's style."

I went in and looked out the window; I felt resentful, not because I'd been sent inside, though that was part of it, but because Curt had obviously planned this when he had me park behind the house. I was being used as... what? An impartial witness? An ace in the hole? How did he plan things so far in advance?

The car parked at the foot of the hill, near the crumbled foundation of a barn. Sheriff Wade got out, followed by Deputy Hoff. I felt a thrill of fear for Curt as the two men strode up the hill. Deputy Hoff was the sheriff's nephew, but they looked enough alike to he father and son: hulking thick-necked men, with the deputy slightly taller and broader than his uncle. He'd left off wearing his theatrical forty-fives and now wore a .38 in a holster clipped to his belt, just like the sheriff.

Curt greeted them without rising from the steps. "Howdy, Shurf," he said in an exaggerated drawl. "What brings you out to these parts?"

The sheriff's white teeth showed in a humorless smile. "Drop the humor, Friedland. You ain't Chester and I ain't Matt Dillon. We came out to look around."

"Look away," said Curt, waving at the barren hills. "I see you brought Deputy Hoff, whose fearless gun is all that stands in the way of Franklin County being drenched in the blood of innocents."

Deputy Hoff hunched his shoulders. "Now listen, Friedland—"

"Easy, Bobby," said the sheriff. To Curt he said: "You was just a kid when you left. They say you're smarter than your brothers, but so far you ain't showed any signs of it. You got a rumor started I railroaded your brother to the pen and I don't like that a little bit. You got the county saying the Struble woman got shoved in the well, and her old man's tearing his hair. He ran to me, and I had to go through all the evidence with him again. Now I'd like to know what business you've got in this county."

"That's none of your business, sheriff."

The deputy blurted: "Uncle Glen, let me—"

"No Bobby, he's right. Legally it's none of my business. One thing that is, Friedland, and that's if you got any firearms in that house."

Curt rose slowly. "I didn't know the state had a Sullivan law."

"I don't know what they call it. All I know is I gotta register all the firearms in the county."

"Well, just out of curiosity, how many have you registered so far?"

The sheriff's face froze in surprise, just long enough to convince me there was no such law. His features quickly smoothed over. "That's none of your business, boy. You gonna let us see them guns?"

"I'd like to see something first. Something like a search warrant."

The sheriff's neck reddened. "You aim for me to drive to Franklin for a piece of paper while you stash the guns out in the brush?"

"You can leave Paladin here to watch me." Curt walked slowly down the steps. I couldn't see his face, but his voice look on a strange, velvety menace. "You're not afraid to stay, are you Bobby? I'll set up a target so you can practice with your shootin' iron. You need it, Bobby. Anybody who hits a man in the back when he's aiming at his legs—"

"You better shut your goddam trap, Friedland."

"You did aim for his legs, didn't you Bobby? That's what you said at the trial."

"One more word, Friedland—"

"Go to the car, Bobby," said the sheriff.

"Let him stay." Curt stepped onto the graveled area in front of the steps. "He can leave his gun on. It doesn't scare me. Any son-of-a-bitch who can't shoot better—"

Bobby tore his gun front his belt and snarled. "I don't need a gun for you."

He rushed Curt, starting his wide swing while still a yard away. Curt sidestepped and seized the arm. I saw a blur of movement, then felt the earth tremble as Bobby thumped onto the ground. He lay gray-faced, trying to get his breath. He sounded like a truck trying to start on a cold morning.

Curt backed away as Bobby rose. "The Japanese call it The Gentle Way, Bobby. Judo. The harder you come the harder you land."

Bobby charged with a roar of rage. This time I heard the air whoosh out of his lungs when he landed. Twin streams of dark blood trickled from his nostrils. As he got to his knees, I saw that the sharp gravel had ripped his shirt. Dark patches showed where the blood had begun to soak through. Bobby stood up and shook his head like an angry bull. Blood smeared his face on either side of his nose, giving him a garish crimson moustache. He took a step toward his gun, but the sheriff snatched it up.

"*That's enough!* Bobby, get the hell back to the car."

Bobby stumbled off, wiping his nose on his sleeve. The sheriff drew the gun from its holster. "Curt, I'm gonna have to arrest you."

Curt seemed relaxed, his voice mildly curious. "What's the charge, Sheriff?"

"Disturbing the peace."

"Whose peace? Look around. I'm on my own property."

"You assaulted an officer of the law."

"Hell! He assaulted me."

"I doubt the judge will take your word against mine and Bobby's." He jerked his head down the hill. "Better get moving."

Curt didn't turn his head. "Velda," he said in a conversational tone.

I drew a deep breath and stepped out onto the porch.

The sheriff was taken by surprise, and in that instant I saw... more than I wanted. I saw the eyes of a man who'd killed more than once, and I saw the same look his victims must have seen. A glazed, animal violence. Something inside me shriveled up and went into hiding.

"Your husband know you're here, Velda?"

"No... but I suppose he will."

His face turned cunning. "Not from me, Velda. I know better than to tell a man what his wife does behind his back." He peered at me as though he'd never seen me before. "I thought your sis was a black sheep, the way she rubbed up against trouble. Now I'm thinking maybe it runs in the family."

He slid Bobby's gun back into the holster and looked at Curt. "I arrested you a minute ago. Now I'm releasing you for lack of evidence. You're free to leave the county any time."

"I'll go when I'm ready."

For a moment the sheriff's face held a look of sincere regret. "Yeah, I figured that. You want to be pushed."

I watched the sheriff walk down the hill and drive off. I felt weak and sick at my stomach. I must have staggered because I felt Curt's arm slide around me. I wanted to lean, and lean hard, but I pulled away. "I've got to go."

We walked around the house to the car, and I said: "You deliberately provoked that fight, Curt. They could have come bearing roses, and you'd still have fought. Why? Just tell me why?"

"I had to see them with the wraps off. I wanted to read them in a hurry."

"Did you?"

He nodded. "Bobby's matured some. Twelve years ago he'd have charged me a lot quicker. But still a boob. He's like a dog the sheriff keeps on a leash, valuable because the honky-tonk cowboys are scared of him. The sheriff is smart, but he's been in office too long. He's trapped in details and can't see the forest for the trees. Honest enough—that is, if you offered him a bribe he'd gun-whip you half to death. On the other hand, if he got the word from a respected citizen—just a calm and thoughtful discussion of a particular case—it could turn him off a suspect without leaving him aware that he'd been influenced." He opened the car door for me. "They're typical rural cops, a little on the rough side, a little gun-happy. They're helping the killer, but they don't know it."

I slid behind the wheel. "Otherwise they'd have killed you the first chance you gave them. Did you think of that?"

He gave me a half smile. "Yes. I thought of it."

I met his eyes and I saw that he didn't care. I saw what he meant when he said he'd taken the jump into darkness. He was no longer responsible for his own life. I got a chilly, crawly feeling. I could only think that in not caring about his own, he couldn't possibly care about the lives of others. Especially mine.

I looked out through the windshield. "Curt, I... can't give you Struble's key."

"I... understand."

"No... no you don't. I can't help you, I can't get involved. Maybe I sympathize with you. I think you're doing something great. But I've got a husband, a daughter. I can't get mixed up in it. Please don't get me mixed up in it."

He nodded gravely. "If that's the way you want it."

"I do." I turned the switch and started the car. Curt leaned against the window.

"Just one question, Velda. When Marston got killed on the tractor, why did he go into the ravine twenty feet from the end of the row? Was he drunk? Did he fall asleep? Why didn't he jump clear?"

I stared at him with my mouth open. I could feel the blood drain from my face. "How did you know?"

"I've got reports on every death in the county for the last twenty years. Indexed and cross-indexed. If you'd like to see—"

"No, no! Curt, you promised—"

"Okay. But think about it, will you? Did Marston have any enemies? Could somebody have knocked him out and set the thing up? And Ethel's husband , why didn't he jump out of his stalled car when the train was coming? He could see two hundred yards in both directions. He had no record of heart trouble, he didn't drink. Think of Don Carroll, who accidentally shot himself on his front porch? And Harold Simpson, who supposedly committed suicide in his house. Why would he leave his tractor out in the middle of the field, the way you do when you have a visitor you know won't be long? Think about those things, Velda. Picture a guy who's killed... eight-ten people in the last twenty years. A guy who knows that if you watch and wait long enough, you'll be able to make it look like an accident. Think of him watching you, waiting for his chance...."

I drove off, squirming inside. The day had turned overcast, with an icy wind. It fitted my mood.

The empty house did nothing to ease my mind. I took a warm bath, but it failed to induce my usual somnolent, lazy mood. I darkened the studio and played the piano, and my thoughts drifted to Marston....

Mart was a big, open-faced, good-humored lout who'd been my brother's best friend. He'd teased and pinched and tickled me all through my youth, and the teasing had evolved gradually into caresses, then love. That last spring he'd worked on the farm where we planned to live after we were married. I always packed his lunch and ate with him on the grassy bank beside a stream. That last afternoon, we'd finished lunch and were smoking a lazy cigaret. Mart was saying he had to get back to work, and I was saying of course, and both of us knew we'd make love first because we did every day....

Later, lying on the blanket beneath the branches of a box-elder tree, I held his weight and pressed my fingers into his back; I felt his warm breath against my neck, and noted how the leaves overhead were green and glossy on top, pale and fuzzy beneath. My mind was sunk deep within my body, following the slow surge of sweet sensation—

Something flickered at the edge of my vision. "Mart!" I said.

He raised his head. His pupils were pinpointed.

"Mart, something flashed in that grove of trees on the hill."

Abruptly I was alone, bereft and exposed. I sat up and pulled my dress down over my legs, Mart was standing, hooking his overalls with angry haste. I watched him leap across the stream and scramble up the bank. He loped toward the trees and disappeared behind them. Five minutes later he returned, red-faced and sweating.

"Some kid," he panted. "I just got a glimpse."

He wouldn't meet my eyes, and I knew he'd lied about something. "You didn't see who it was?"

"No," he said too quickly. "You better go now."

I left, feeling a sour emptiness inside me. How could those evil spying eyes spoil the happiness I'd felt? But they had; I felt dirty, sinful and sneaky. I visualized how I'd looked to those eyes: Sprawled and impaled by a hulking, hunching animal with greasy overalls pushed down to his knees. I had a feeling I'd never enjoy sex with Mart again....

And I never had, because he'd been found dead that afternoon. The shock had erased all memory of the prying eyes until Curt had brought up Mart's death. Now I wondered: Could the flash have been binoculars? Not many kids had binoculars. And if a man, wouldn't he fear that he'd been recognized, and couldn't he have knocked Mart out somehow, laid him in the ditch, and turned the tractor over on him?

Sixteen years, I thought. What clues survive after sixteen years? Long ago there might have been a chance; now it was pointless, hopeless speculation....

Sharon came home at five, breathless and excited. She'd met Gabrielle in town and they'd had a coke together and talked. Now Sharon had sworn off dates and resolved to spend her nights studying shorthand and typing. She planned to go to Chicago and become a career woman just like Gaby....

Lou called from Connersville at five-thirty and said there was a new road going in and he thought he'd stay and bid on the dirtwork since he had a couple of idle bulldozers. Sharon and I ate alone, then watched television and went to bed. I took a Seconal tablet, which I rarely do....

zzzzt... zzzzt... zzzzt ... ZZZZT ... ZZZZT!

The ringing dragged me struggling from an ocean of sleep. I shot upright with thoughts of disaster exploding in my mind. The illuminated alarm clock said twelve-fifteen. Lou was asleep, stretched out like a corpse with his nose aimed at the ceiling.

The phone broke off its staccato message. I jumped out of bed and raced for the kitchen with my nightgown streaming out behind me. I lifted the receiver and heard the operator's shrill voice:

"...pronounced them dead on the spot. The three oldest will live but—"

"Who, Sally?" I shouted over a babble of voices. *"Who died?"*

"George Bennett's house burned down an hour ago. Sandy died in the fire along with her baby—"

My stomach lurched. I dropped the receiver into its cradle and pressed my hands to my head. *He doesn't care,* I thought, *He doesn't care who he kills, women or babies....*

My husband's snore echoed softly through the silent house. I walked into Sharon's room. She was asleep, her full lips pouting, the covers kicked down around her feet. Her pajama top was twisted, and a round, woman-ized breast peeped through. Sharon made me feel vulnerable and exposed. I pulled the blanket over her and walked to the window. The darkness hovered outside like a threat. I pictured a pair of loathsome, inhuman eyes looking on, watching—and I knew I couldn't sit on the sidelines.

I pulled the drapes and went back to the phone. To the operator I said: "Give me the residence of Curt Friedland."

CHARTER THREE

Curt's phone hadn't been connected. I hung up the receiver with a feeling of loneliness I couldn't quite understand. What could Curt have given me? Reassurance that it wasn't murder? Confirmation of my own horrible dread that it was?

I wasn't sure, but still I wanted to talk to him. I pushed open the back door and stepped out. The chill air penetrated my thin nightgown and tingled on the flesh beneath. I went back in the bedroom and got my housecoat; Lou still lay corpselike, his snoring unbroken. I slipped on my houseshoes and walked back outside. Lou's red pickup gleamed in half-moonlight just a couple of yards from the back door. I brushed my hand over the cool metal of the hood and smelled the faint odor of gas. I started toward the garage where my car was parked—

"Velda, what's the matter?"

I turned and saw Lou in the door in his pajamas. There was my husband; I should go to his arms and be comforted, instead of chasing off in the middle of the night to see a man I hardly knew.

I walked back and told him: "There was a line ring. Sandy Matthews... Bennett was burned up in their house. Her little baby too."

Lou sucked in his breath. "Poor George. How'd it happen?"

"I don't know."

He was gone from the door. I heard him in the kitchen ringing the operator, then talking. Muffled fragments of conversation came to me: "...totally destroyed? Yes... sure, something will have to be done for them. Get me Harley Grove. Harley? Listen, you know about the Bennetts? Yes. The kids can stay with Mrs. Thompson, I'll make sure it's okay. No, George didn't have any insurance... I held the mortgage... Sure, insured to the extent of the mortgage but it's a total loss to George... get a collection rolling... I'm good for five hundred, well, hell, but it's all we can do...."

I tuned out his voice. This is the way it's done, I thought. Smooth over death with normal activity, samaritan gestures; forget the charred bodies and the monster who lurks in the night....

Lou was behind me again. "Well, I've done what I can." I resented the smugness in his voice. *Lou, death is not a husking bee....*

"Better come to bed, Velda."

"I will... in a minute."

His arms went around my waist, his hands slid between the lapels of my housecoat and pressed against my bare stomach. His breath blew warm on my neck. "I'm pretty sure of getting this road job, Velda. Then I'll be work-ing hard..."

I understood then. My husband's sexual enthusiasm waxed and waned according to no rhythm I could figure; not the moon, not the seasons, not the rise and fall of his business fortunes. Lately he'd gone through a virile phase; now he was serving notice that we approached a period of celiba-cy. To him Sandy's death was a community event; it had nothing to do with us.

"Lou, I couldn't tonight... really."

His hands squeezed, then trailed away. Only a painful after-tingle told me that he'd squeezed hard; that he was angry with me. "Good night, Velda," he said.

I couldn't go to Curt now. Lou would sleep lightly for at least an hour. I went into the bedroom and lay down without speaking to Lou. I remem-ber smoking my fourth cigaret, then it was daylight and Lou's bed was empty....

I drove to town earlier than usual and asked Ethel to take over the store again. I had to bear her rheumatic complaints and her lament for poor Sandy, who was somehow related to Ethel. She agreed finally, but I could see I'd have trouble with her later.

At first I thought Curt's place was deserted; Heine Wentz wasn't there, and Curt's car was gone. Then I saw Gil's black Chrysler convertible parked behind the house. Gaby and Gil stood on top of the hill, at the archery range. Gaby looked gay and windblown in a halter and white short shorts; she *did* have a figure, that girl, and the shorts did nothing but accent the sharp thrust of her buttocks. Gil wore a red shirt and tan slacks; he was obviously not dressed for working today. I felt a tingle of annoy-ance as I approached them; they stood too close together, and I thought that Gaby should be told about Gil's reputation. Somehow learning that Gil had tried to seduce Bernice had altered my opinion of him. I watched Gil's arrow hit the target several rings out from the bull's-eye, and I won-dered if he was using Curt's bow. (I already felt possessive about Curt's things, even his wife.) They were laughing when I went up, but when Gaby saw me, her face turned sober.

"Where's Curt?" I asked her.

Her face became wary. "I think he went to town."

"I just came from there," I said. "He isn't there."

She was looking at me with the question in her eyes: *What do you want with him?* She had a right to it, I guess. Any girl coming back to her hus-band's home town would wonder: What was this woman to my husband in the past? How well did they know each other? Who do I have to watch and who can I ignore?

If we had been alone, I would have explained it all to her; now I only said:

"He asked me to do something for him yesterday. I told him no. I want to tell him I've changed my mind."

"Oh." Her wary expression didn't lift; her eyes slid over to Gil's and then back to mine. "You... could check where the house burned down. He might have gone there."

I should have thought of that first. The Bennetts lived on the river bottom just a half mile from town. George worked at the lumberyard; his land was water-logged gumbo which rarely produced anything but fifteen-foot-high horseweeds. A dozen cars were parked along the lane which led to the house; a crowd of sightseers trampled around the ruins. It had been an old wooden house, with imitation brick siding made of tar paper; it must have burned like a torch. A pall of smoke still hung over the area. I saw two blackened, twisted iron bedsteads, a refrigerator shining blue-gray where the enamel had flaked off, a cookstove and heating stove. Only these items stood erect; all else was a foot-deep layer of smoking rubble inside the foundation walls. I searched the crowd for a familiar face. By the sheriff's car, in the center of the largest group of people, stood George Bennett. He wore no shirt, and his sleeveless undershirt was full of charred holes. Soot blackened his heavy face. I moved closer. Beside him stood a boy of about eight, George's oldest boy, looking wide-eyed at the sheriff while his father talked in a flat grating monotone:

"—You can put it down to that, Sheriff, if you got to have a reason. That goddam kerosene stove. I could kill myself for not fixing it."

"What was wrong with the stove?" asked the sheriff.

"Got a tank on the back, you know. There was a little drip right where the tubing connected to the tank. Time went on, it soaked the floor behind the stove. Last night was a little chilly, so I had the stove lit. I reckon that's where it started."

"Why couldn't your wife get out?"

Heads turned to see who had asked the question, but I didn't have to look. I recognized Curt's voice. He didn't look as though he'd gotten any sleep last night either. His trousers and sweatshirt were wrinkled, and a faint blond stubble glistened in the sunlight. The sheriff saw Curt too, but for some reason chose not to call him by name.

"You folks out there shut up and let me ask the questions." To George he said, "Why couldn't Sandy get out?"

George looked down at his feet. "Well... she come in last night around ten-thirty. She'd been drinkin... quite a bit. I knew she'd left the house without a cent that morning so I tried to find out who bought her liquor. She went to sleep without tellin me. I jumped in the truck and went in to Stubb's to find out who'd got her drunk. The tavern was closed. When I

came back to the house the fire was shootin up higher'n them cottonwoods. My three oldest kids was in the yard. I couldn't get closer'n thirty
feet of the house. I... stood, and... watched the goddam roof fall in on...
Sandy and the kid... Jesus Christ, that goddam stove... "

Sober faces watched George Bennett push through the crowd with his
forearm over his eyes, then a voice said; "I know who got her drunk."

I saw Johnny Drew, Anne's ex-husband. I was surprised, because he'd left
town a week ago saying he was going to work in Las Vegas. He was
dressed in a checkered sport jacket and powder-blue slacks, and he looked
garishly over-dressed in that austere rural gathering. There had been a
time long ago when I'd thought he was handsome, as handsome as Johnny
himself thought he was. But that had been before I noticed the finger
waves he pressed in his waxy blond hair, before I saw the smallness of his
eyes and how close set they were in a coarse peasant face. Since Anne's
death he'd drifted in and out of Sherman; he'd served a ten month sentence on a bad check charge and once he'd tried to hold up the Club 75
with a pistol. Lou had smoothed that one over, perhaps because Johnny
was an ex-brother-in-law. He certainty hadn't done it for me, because I had
only contempt for Johnny. I noticed his red eyes and the lank strand of
blond hair hanging over his eye and I knew he was half-drunk already.
Everybody else was looking at Johnny, including the sheriff, but nobody
asked any questions. They knew Johnny didn't have to be coaxed to tell
everything he knew.

"He's the one," said Johnny, pointing a blunt finger at Curt. "I saw 'em
together last night in Stubb's tavern."

Curt frowned at Johnny, perhaps trying to place him. I heard mutters in
the crowd. *Who's that? Who got her drunk? Curt Friedland. When did he get
back?* Behind it was a low murmur, like far distant thunder, with nothing in
it of friendship or neighborliness. Johnny Drew must have felt the hostility too, because he took a step toward Curt with his fists doubled at his sides.

"I thought the country was rid of the Friedlands. Maybe you need another lesson."

A faint flicker of a smile crossed Curt's face. He neither moved forward
nor backed away. I don't think he expected Johnny to come for him, and I
don't think Johnny intended to—but suddenly the crowd parted and left
a channel leading from Johnny to Curt. There was nothing for Johnny to
do but lower his head and charge. But he stopped suddenly, confronting
the massive gabardine-clad torso of the sheriff. The sheriff knew Johnny
too; he didn't even raise his hands in front of him. Suddenly there was
Deputy Hoff behind Johnny, who cramped Johnny's arm behind his back
and marched him to the car. It didn't look to me like Johnny was struggling; it all seemed to go off half-heartedly, like a stage production in
which the actors aren't enthusiastic about their parts.

The sheriff turned to Curt. "Now. Is it true what he said?"

"Partly."

The sheriff sighed. He spoke for the crowd, not for Curt, in a tone of sweet reasonableness. "Why can't you just say it? Did you get Sandy drunk or didn't you?"

"I bought her a beer in the tavern. I left her at seven-ten. She wasn't drunk then."

"How do you know it was seven-ten when you left her?"

"I looked at a clock."

The sheriff looked at him sadly a moment then turned to the crowd. "All right folks, let's clear out of here. We all got work to do. Doc Chalmers says Sandy and the baby probably suffocated from smoke before the flames got to 'em—"

"What about the man who got her drunk?" It was only a voice; I couldn't see the face.

"I aim to look into that, but I'm afraid that's between him and her husband. It's no crime to buy an adult woman liquor."

He started toward his car, and I was close enough to hear him tell Curt as he passed: "You seem to hang around trouble, boy. Be careful they don't haul you out in a box."

Then he got in his car and drove away, with Johnny Drew glaring at Curt from the safety of the back seat. I started toward Curt, but he was striding rapidly toward his car and people were watching him go and I... I was reluctant to put myself next to him. I was afraid of my reputation in the community, and ashamed of myself because I was concerned about that now. I hurried along a few paces behind him, and he was in his car and gone before I reached him. I told myself, Velda, you'd better stay out of this affair if you're afraid of getting dirty....

I half-expected him to come in the store later, assuming that either Gaby or Gil had told him I wanted to see him. Bat he didn't. I thought of going up to his place, but I'd already done that. By nine o'clock that evening I couldn't wait any longer; I called and Gaby answered the phone. I almost hung up; I didn't like to look like I was pursuing him. But I'd started it already, so I asked:

"Did... Curt come back?"

"He stopped in around four."

Silence then. She was making me work for it. "I wonder... did you tell him—?"

"Yes." Her voice still held the wariness I'd noticed earlier. "I said you'd changed your mind. He said he'd get in touch."

That was it; that was all she could tell me. I wanted something else; my relationship with Gaby was extremely uncomfortable; I was like a business acquaintance and yet I had no business calling Curt. I was about to say something friendly, something which would get our mutual conversations off the exclusive subject of Curt when I heard a man's muffled voice and Gaby's equally muffled answer, as though she'd put her hand over the mouthpiece.

"Who's with you?"

"Gil Sisk," she said.

"Oh... well, goodby." I hung up the phone, feeling resentful. Here I was ready to help Curt and...

Lou came home around ten and wanted to talk about the new job. He seemed in a bright, gay mood and I wondered why, until I figured out in my head that he'd made a couple thousand off the sale to Curt and probably stood to clear ten thousand on the road job.

Next morning the town prepared for the funeral; all the stores would close at noon, and services would be held at one p.m. I heard some resentful talk about Curt from those who knew he'd bought her that beer. They had nothing to go on, but I could feel their latent hostility. If a tornado wiped out the town they'd find a way to blame Curt Friedland because it happened while he was here. That's the kind of reasoning you run into in Sherman....

About ten Curt strolled in with his face closed up tight, his hands shoved deep into the pockets of his Levis. He wore a wide-brimmed felt hat, blue-denim jacket and lace-up boots: he looked as though he'd never left the Nation. I started to speak but he shook his head emphatically and asked for a can of Velvet. He handed me a bill with a note in it. I opened the cash register, spread the note out in the dollar-bill tray and read: MEET ME AT THE BOY SCOUT CABIN ON LAKE PILLYBAY AT ONE P.M. DESTROY THIS.

I started to say that was the time of Sandy's funeral and it would look bad if I didn't go, but he walked out without even taking his change. Gladys Schmit stood at the door and I knew by her expression she wanted him to say hello so she could offer some schoolteacherish advice. Curt went out without seeing her. Gladys's eyes turned cold and I knew he'd lost another friend....

I locked up at twelve-thirty and drove straight out to Lake Pillybay. Curt's caution had made me wary; I knew how it would look if my car were found parked along a country road—new cream-colored Lincoln with sparkling chrome and white sidewalk. Lou had picked it out. I pulled off the road and hid the car behind a clump of hazel brush. I climbed to the top of a ridge and approached the cabin from the rear. It lay at the head of a little cove which was rarely used by the tourists, having a steep shore-line and no gentle slopes on which to build summer cabins. The cabin itself was crudely built of logs, used on summer weekends by our Boy

Scout troop and the rest of the time by assorted tramps and lovers. The relics of the latter were very much in evidence when I got there; bottles and cans and cigaret butts, so I moved to the side of the water and sat on a rock. It had turned warm, and I took off my sweater and sat in the sun. As I waited, I thought: I should have brought a book, or some knitting. The very idea made me laugh aloud. I was excited and trembling inside. I did-n't realize how nervous I was until Curt's voice spoke my name and I jumped at least six inches in the air. I turned and saw him approaching from behind, carrying a flat manila envelope in his hand. By the time he reached me I was calm enough to say:

"I was wishing I'd brought my knitting."

He sat on the ground beside me. "I checked to see if you might have been followed. Took me some time to find your car. Good job."

I felt a faint thrill of gratification. "I could take up bird-watching, carry binoculars and a bird book. That would give me some excuse to prowl the hills alone."

He studied me narrowly, then: "You're kidding, but it's something to keep in mind." He picked up a pebble and tossed it into the water. "Gaby said you'd changed your mind."

I looked down and stirred the dead grass with my foot. "It's not that cut and dried. I want to know more. Particularly about Sandy, whether you think she was one of his victims."

"I'm almost sure. I checked with Stubb Dixon at the tavern. He said she left at eight o'clock, about forty minutes after I left. She wasn't drunk then, so she must have met a man with a bottle."

I nodded. "Sandy had a habit of riding with whoever made an offer. Marriage didn't change that."

"Yes, it could have happened this way: the guy took her home, waited until George left the house, then went in and set the house afire. Or it may not have been the killer who took her home, just a guy who happened to see her. The killer could have been watching the house, waiting for his chance. I looked around, but the crowd had wiped out any sign of tracks. Her body was so badly burned there was no way of knowing how she'd died." He shook his head. "That couldn't be luck. The guy is smart as hell...."

"Why were you with Sandy?" I asked.

"Gaby drew a blank. Sandy kept hinting that she knew something...."

"She's been hinting for twelve years."

"Yes, anyway I met her, and she was still playing coy, wanted me to meet her the following afternoon. We made a date, but she was killed that night."

"I think she was playing you along," I said.

Curt shrugged. "Maybe. But she had certain things in common with Bernice and your sister. Married, playing around on the side. The guy might choose married women because they've got as much reason to hide an affair as the man. Unless they fall in love, that is, then they're likely to say the hell with everything and bring it all into the open. That would give him a motive for murder."

There was excitement in being near a man who burned with a purpose aside from making money and having fun. I wondered if I was really interested in finding the killer or if I just wanted to stay close to Curt and absorb some of his fire; I also knew that I had to give him something in return.

"You seem so certain of murder, Curt. I'd like to know why."

"Got it right here." He tapped the manila envelope. "But let's get out of the open."

I followed him away from the lake shore. Bending down, we entered a crab-apple thicket; the lake was hidden by tall dry grass. We were screened overhead by the brushy twigs of the crab apple. I laid down my sweater and sat on it, drawing my legs up beneath me. Curt sat down beside me and for a moment I wished there were no murders, that we were just lovers who'd come out into the woods with a picnic lunch and a blanket. Curt gave me a curiously penetrating look—as though he'd caught my thought—then bent his head and opened the envelope:

"It's kind of dry and statistical. Are you sure—?"

"Yes. But one thing I'm curious about first. Where were you last night when I called?"

He looked off into the distance. "Searching Gil Sisk's house."

I gasped. "Gil's *house?*"

He nodded. "The night Sandy was murdered... well, let me go further back. There's a hill about a quarter mile away from our house. It's the only one nearby which has a view from a higher level than our house, a natural lookout if somebody wanted to spy on me. So I took some black thread and fastened it to trees and bushes so it ran around the top of a hill at waist level. Sheep and dogs and wild animals could go right under it. A cow or deer couldn't, but they'd leave tracks. Well, the morning after Sandy's murder, the thread was broken. I found footprints, not sharp to identify, but obviously a man's. There were signs that he'd stretched full length and rested his elbows on the ground as though holding binoculars—"

"Why?"

"The marks were side by side. If he'd been holding a rifle, one elbow would have been behind the other, like this." He rolled onto his stomach and demonstrated. I felt a chill, remembering the flash on the hill while Marty and I... If only someone had investigated, before the passage of so many years....

"How did that involve Gil?" I asked.

"Well... I'd noticed that Gil carried binoculars in his car. He said they were for girl-watching on Lake Pillybay, which sounded reasonable—"

"Considering Gil's character," I said dryly.

"Yes, but I wanted to check. So I searched his house; I was looking for some... relic which would show he'd had something to do with these girls. That's a weird old house, you know—thirty-eight rooms, and I barely got started. There's something in every room, going all the way back to his great-grandfather. It was like taking an inventory of the Smithsonian in a single afternoon. I didn't find anything, but I'd like to finish; I'd like to clear him of suspicion—"

"Why?"

"I like him."

"I don't."

He smiled at me. "Since you heard about Bernice?"

"Maybe."

"He also had a few brief sessions with Anne and Sandy. He made no secret of it with me."

My face burned. "The more I learn about him, the more I realize our friendship was a mistake."

"You're jealous."

"I don't think so. Disappointed..."

He laughed. "Velda, you give a man friendship and you expect it to fulfill all his desires."

"It's enough for me."

"It's a different situation. Think what would happen if the reproduction of the race depended on women. How often do they take the initiative?" He shook his head. "Anyway, you don't understand a man's approach. All the time Gil was talking to you about books and philosophy and everything else, he was looking at you and wondering how you'd be in bed, trying to figure out a way to get you there...."

I looked at him and wondered if he was doing the same, but I didn't say it. I said: "You don't believe that. Otherwise you wouldn't have left Gaby there alone with him."

"Gaby's trained. She knows all the approaches. Anyway she had her own game going; she had to keep him occupied until I got back from searching his house. She couldn't submit, because that would have used up her ace in the hole."

I stared at him in amazement. "You're *really* throwing in all you've got, aren't you?"

"What do you mean?"

"I mean... if Gil is the killer, you're risking Gaby's life."

"She has a gun. She knows how to use it."

"She wasn't wearing it yesterday with him, not concealed under her halter and shorts."

He frowned. "I'll tell her to be more careful. But even if Gil was the one who watched the house, he could be a simple garden-variety Peeping Tom. He's taken with Gaby; obviously, since she's a woman. We didn't have curtains up then, and Gaby was sprinting across in front of the windows in the altogether...."

I felt a prickly embarrassment hearing Curt talk of his wife. For a moment I saw them in the intimacy of their home, doing what husbands and wives do, what Lou and I do on occasion. But was it embarrassment, or jealousy, the kind I'd felt about Gil? What did I want, for every man in the county to worship me from afar and be true? A high school attitude, Velda....

I said, apropos of nothing: "Lou was home when Sandy was killed."

He looked at me sharply. "What made you say that?"

"Just... in case you suspect him."

"I suspect everybody—except myself. When did he get home?"

"He was in bed asleep when the call came about Sandy."

"There would have been at least a half hour delay between setting the fire and the line ring. How long had he been home?"

"The engine of his pickup was cold."

His eyebrows shot up. "You *checked* it?"

"I just happened to put my hand on it." My face burned. "Curt, you don't think I'd spy on my husband!"

"No, I didn't think so." He sighed. "Well, somebody killed her right under my nose and didn't leave a clue. We'll have to go back to the others." He pulled the papers out of the envelope. "Here, if you're still interested."

I glanced at the pages dense with figures and printing. "Curt, I'm not a statistician. Just tell me."

He took the pages from my hands. "Okay. Consider four hundred people living in Sherman, another eleven hundred in the surrounding farms. That's fifteen hundred people. Now here... He pulled out a printed sheet. "I've got actuarial tables on accidental death. Scaling it down to Sherman's size, you'd expect something like thirty accidental deaths during the last ten years. We've had forty-two."

"Maybe we're accident prone. It isn't an ordinary community."

"Okay, consider that. Go back ten more years, we're only seven percent above the national average. Go back ten more, we're exactly average. And so on, until we get back to where they didn't keep statistics. We're an average community in everything else. We have fewer deaths from smallpox, influenza, typhoid fever, and so on, just like the nation as a whole. We have more deaths from automobile accidents, slightly more than the nation as a whole. Suicides have gone up nationally; so have they here... but a little more than average. General farm accidents, household accidents, sporting accidents, we're ten to fifteen percent above average."

"What does it mean?"

"Some of them are murders disguised as accidents."

I stared at him. "Curt, I don't have your faith in numbers, I guess. I can't—"

He handed me a sheaf of papers. "Read these and then tell me. They take you back twenty years."

I read:

Lester Lemonn, 53, died of broken neck after car struck loose gravel on shoulder of highway. Presumed he swerved to avoid livestock. (Comment: Steering gear could have been tampered with. No record of autopsy, or of car having been examined.)

I looked up. "Curt, you're not counting this sort of thing, are you? I mean, there are so many accidents."

He nodded. "That's right. So damn many. I'm assuming we have an average number of accidents. That leaves a dozen which were really murders. Go on, read."

I went on:

Sally Niven, 32, found hanged in henhouse. Children at school, husband working. Presumed suicide. Apparently climbed up on box and kicked it away. Motive for suicide: depression, money problems. (Comment: Left no note, no record of having threatened suicide. Situation easily staged, possible rape-murder.)

Theodore Groner, 15, drowned. Swam for boat in middle of cove, apparently suffered stomach cramp. Witnesses in boat; Jerry Blake, Eli Black, Marston Odon, Gil Sisk, Rally Cartright, Louis Bayrd, Johnny Drew, and Harley Grove. (Number of witnesses make accident probable, but stomach cramps unlikely, since water was warm and victim had eaten nothing but peanuts for some time before swimming. Subsequent death of two witnesses Marston and Jerry, suspicious.)

Charles Hall, 19 and *Ruth Payson,* 16, killed when car struck semi-trailer head-on. (Many possibilities here: jimmied steering mechanism, driver drugged with delayed action soporific.)

I looked up. "You mean a sleeping tablet which doesn't take effect until later?"

Curt nodded. "Most of them don't hit you for ten minutes anyway. Put an extra-thick gelatin capsule around it, and it might take a half hour longer. They ate hamburgers at the Club 75 before starting home. The driver could have been drugged then. Hall was known as a fast driver."

"How do you know all this? It happened seventeen years ago."

"Files of the county paper. It's a small enough community so that every death rates a three-column spread."

I returned to my reading:

Marston Field, 22, killed when tractor turned on him. Crushed chest cause of death. (But, he could have been knocked unconscious beforehand, as there were several bruises on him. Ravine was several feet from end of row. No witnesses.)

Anne Groenfelder Drew, 25, found with throat cut outside Club 75. (Murderer still at large.)

I passed those two without comment. We'd been through them already.

Arnold Shaw, 24, and *LaVella England,* 21, asphyxiated in parked automobile. Found in half-dressed condition, presumed that leaky muffler had let fumes seep through floorboard. (Comment: Could have been murdered by attaching hose to tailpipe, running it through bottom of car. No indication that muffler was checked to see that it actually leaked. Couple could have been unconscious when scene was staged, via pills. Double suicide ruled out; couple was engaged and had no problems.)

"But Curt, *two* of them?"

"The killer was probably after only one, but he doesn't seem to care if others go too. Look at Sandy and her baby; the baby just happened to be there."

The next was:

Marvin DeVore, 38, killed in cement mixer. Assumed that he'd gotten shovel caught in it, reached in to get it without shutting down machine. Presumably his clothes caught and he was pulled up inside. Immense weight of rolling cement on blades crushed and mutilated his body, inflicted several deadly wounds. (Comment: Official of cement mixer company states that he's never heard of a man being *drawn* inside from ground level. Falling in from a higher level, or being thrown in, conscious or unconscious, would probably have been fatal. Condition of body precludes accurate determination of cause of death.)

Barney Proctor, 45, killed by train in rural crossing. Engineer stated the car was stopped at crossing; fireman thought driver was slumped over wheel, but wasn't sure. Theory: He'd stalled his car at the crossing, seen the train, and suffered a heart attack. Autopsy revealed nothing; body too badly shattered. (Comment: A farfetched chain of circumstances. Equally reasonable to assume the man was knocked unconscious and his car driven on the tracks. Convenient means of concealing evidence.)

Jerry Blake, 40, died when butane tank exploded in his store. Verdict: accidental death. (Comment: Takes time for butane to accumulate in sufficient quantity to explode. Why didn't Blake smell it? Store burned down, body burned beyond recognition. Cause of death therefore uncertain.)

I looked up. "Curt, I knew Jerry very well. He was Lou's partner. He was the kindest, best-natured guy in town. It's unthinkable that he was murdered—"

"Consider the unthinkable, Velda. Jerry could have learned something, and the killer had to silence him. Don't worry about motive, look at similarities, the mutilation of the bodies. Read on."

I read:

Harold Simpson, 38, died of shotgun blast in mouth. Verdict: suicide. Wife had left him, taken children. Depressed. (Comments: Left no note. Tractor left standing in field, as though he planned to return to work. Blowing a man's head off with a 12-gauge shotgun is effective way of concealing murder by other means.)

Dean Slaughter, 55, suffocated when storm blew barn down, haymow collapsed and buried him in baled hay. Verdict: accident. (Comment: Check it out. Too neat.)

I jerked my head up. "Curt, how in the world could you suspect *that?*"

Curt shrugged. "Hell. The killer could have seen the storm coming and smothered him before the barn ever blew down."

"And then blew it down himself?"

"He could have hammered some rafters loose and weakened the barn enough that a good wind would blow it over. Sure, it's far out. If there's nothing to connect his death with any of the others, I'll mark it off and work on the easier ones."

I glanced down at the next one:

Albert Simmons, gored to death by bull in barnyard. (Probable accident.)

"Probable! Now Curt, really—!"

"It could have been arranged. The man knocked unconscious, the bull goaded. Simmons owned the bull, you think he'd take any risk if he knew the bull was dangerous? If you've ever seen a bullfight, you'd know how easy it is to goad a bull into charging. The killer probably had plenty of time; here in this sparsely populated county, half the people die unseen. How many deaths are listed as heart attacks which were really murder? I didn't even include heart attacks, but I know there are drugs which overstimulate the heart. Say our killer knows his victim has a weak heart; he introduces a drug into his food and pouf! Without an autopsy, who knows? That sheriff is so damn considerate of other people's feelings he won't cut up somebody's next-of-kin without permission. Go on to the next one."

Maynard Schoentgen, 62, body found partly devoured by hogs. Presumed cause of death, heart attack.

"You see?" said Curt. "This man could have died from strangulation, stabbing, or anything. This is like the train wreck, like the fire and the cement mixer, all the evidence has been obliterated."

I felt a strange coldness at the back of my neck as I went back to my reading. The sheer weight of evidence was beginning to convince me:

Adlai Neilsen, 42, died in plane crash five minutes after takeoff from pasture landing strip. County officials, CAB, ruled death accidental through malfunction of aircraft. (What caused malfunction of aircraft? Unknown.)

Ben Burger, 54, and *Elbert Sim, 60,* found dead from exposure. Both known drunks, left tavern with bottle during blizzard, presumably passed out in cold. (Comment: Could have been followed, drugged.)

Vera Ballinger, 43, electrocuted by massage machine. Short found in wiring. (Comment: Be wary of electrical mishaps unless they're witnessed. Death can occur any place, then the business arranged to look like an accident. This includes following:)

Bryon Danley, 40, electrocuted in home welding shop. Working alone, late at night, found next morning.

Bernice Struble, 21, dead in well, death by drowning, while unconscious. Unconsciousness induced by striking head on bricks; hair and pieces of scalp found there. (Comment: Difficult to see how glancing blow could produce unconsciousness. Also more likely she'd lose her footing while pulling up the bucket, rather than after she'd pulled it up. Another shaky chain of circumstances.)

That was all—except for poor Sandy, who hadn't yet been added. I handed the papers back to Curt and felt a cold shiver pass up my spine:

"Curt, that kind of thinking scares me. If there are people like this, then nobody's safe. I'll be suspicious of people who come into the store; afraid to let Sharon stay out late. It's like... a wolf following a caribou herd, waiting to pull down the cripples. Like a snarling beast lurking outside the circle of light."

He was putting his papers away. "He's there, Velda. He looks just like anybody else, just like you and I."

"Look, I know we're backward in Sherman, but at least we're *civilized*."

"Sure. The French thought they were civilized with their gold tasseled cushions and learned debates in the Sorbonne. At the same time Giles de Rais was killing 2,000 people, almost depopulating a province of France. Only 60 years ago in Chicago a certain Doctor H. H. Holmes confessed to killing twenty-seven people in a single year. Actually they figured he killed over a hundred—and he sold their skeletons to medical schools."

"But this man ... you say he's been twenty years..."

"He's smart. So far there've been only doubts. Doubts pass. People forget."

"But what could be his motive?"

"I think we make a mistake in looking for a motive. It could be anything. He wanted to kill, he built his own motive. Maybe he wasn't even aware of what he was doing; he worked himself into a position where he had to kill simply because he wanted to kill."

Suddenly I glanced at my watch. I was used to having the afternoons creep by; I was amazed to see that it was four-thirty. Sharon would be coming home in a quarter hour; now of all times I wanted to be near her and assure myself she was safe. Even the woods seemed prickly and hostile. I picked up my sweater and wrapped it around me. "Curt, I've got to go."

"Yes." He rose and put his manila envelope under his arm. His face wore a watchful, waiting look. I knew what he was waiting for.

"I'll help you if I can Curt. But don't ask me to take any risk. Not that I'm scared; I mean, certainly I'm scared, but I've got more than myself to think about."

He nodded. "There's something you can do. Take some of these cases. Anne was your sister. Jerry Blake was your husband's business partner. Marston was your fiancé. Ethel works for you. Find out all you can without seeming too interested. I don't want him to get suspicious."

"But... what am I supposed to be looking for?"

"I don't know. Some common denominator. Something that ties them together. Somebody they were all intimate with, or somebody they'd all had trouble with. I don't know... It seems ridiculous that he got away unseen every time. If we find out that the same person happened to be nearby when two or three of the accidents occurred, we'll have something to go on."

Just before we parted at the top of the ridge I asked Curt: "You still want the key to Bernice's house?"

"It's better than breaking in."

"All right," I said. "I'll try to have it tomorrow morning."

I drove home and picked up Sharon, telling her I had to come back to the store and work on the books. In the store I talked to Ethel, trying to find a casual way of bringing up her husband, but there was no need. Ethel had gone to Sandy's funeral; her mind had been turned to thoughts of death:

"So few people there, Velda, I couldn't help but think about Barney's funeral. Churchyard full of people standing, I was just sorry it was a closed casket, poor Barney was so cut up. I remember cars parked all the way down to the river bridge from the cemetery. He had so many friends."

"What was he doing the day he died?"

"Fishing. You know he'd rather fish than eat, that man. There was a water hole under the railroad bridge, where he usually went with Gil Sisk, who never had much to do, or Johnny Drew, who could have done a lot but never did. Barney didn't care much who went with him as long as there was fishing involved."

"Were either of them with him that day?"

"No. Johnny got mixed up in a dice game down behind the depot and Gil... funny, I remember that day just like it was yesterday. Gil stopped by the store to say he couldn't make it because he was going to Kansas City, but Barney had already gone. Gil didn't even know Barney had been killed until he got back a week later.

At home I thought about it. Both Gil and Johnny Drew had known that Barney planned to fish under the old railroad bridge. Gil had also gone unexpectedly to Kansas City the night Anne was killed. And Gil had sometimes helped Mart on the farm; they were the same age, and had run together all through high school. Gil had known that I brought Mart's lunch to him. (What about those binoculars, that girl-watching on the lake? Tie that in with the glint of glasses on the hill.)

The thought upset me. Even though I was disappointed in Gil, the thought of him being a murderer... that would imply that I'd been totally blind—

Johnny Drew was another matter. As prospective brothers-in-law of similar age, he and Mart would be expected to be friends. But it hadn't worked out that way. Johnny Drew used it as an excuse to borrow money from Mart. He also knew about the farm and the fact that I brought Mart's lunch. The day Mart was killed, Johnny had been drinking in a tavern. Nobody had kept track of his comings and goings. He'd been connected with Jerry Blake too. He and Lou had hired him to work in their store, but they'd had to let him go. Lou hadn't told me why, but I'd assumed he'd either been stealing from stock or from the cash register. Lou and I never discussed my brother-in-law if it could be avoided; it left a bad taste in my mouth. But Johnny was one person who could have approached Anne's car outside the Club 75 without alarming her. That was the same night Johnny—Oh God! What horrible tricks the subconscious plays. He'd tried to rape me that night, and I'd completely forgotten about it. Now I recalled him banging on the door at ten p.m. Sharon had been asleep and Lou had gone to Omaha with a cattle shipment. "Where's Anne?" he yelled. "Where is that goddam woman?" I could tell through the door that he was drunk. I told him to go away or I'd call the police. He calmed down and asked if I could just let him in, because he wanted to call the club and see if Anne was there. I was young and naïve then and I let him in. The moment I opened the door I knew I'd made a mistake. His eyes were glazed and red-rimmed; it was clear that he was too drunk to see. He made a grab which tore my nightgown off my shoulder; he called me a dirty name which I'd heard him use on Anne. I told him I wasn't Anne, but he was past hearing. He was ripping the nightgown right off my body and I made the mistake of trying to fight him. All I had were fists and finger-nails, and Johnny was so drunk that only a bludgeon would have stopped him. Finally I gave up trying to fight; I tore myself free of the nightgown and left him holding it. I ran into the bedroom and slammed the door. He pounded on the door awhile and cursed me—he was still calling me Anne—then he wandered outdoors. I locked all the doors and windows and called Lou's hotel in Omaha; Lou had gone out to eat and so I told the operator to have him call back. I went to sleep beside the phone and Lou called up at three a.m. He said the clerk had forgotten to give him the message when he came in and what was wrong? I looked out the window and saw that Johnny's car was gone and the danger was over; I felt like a fool-ish, hysterical girl and said I just wanted to talk. So we'd talked—briefly—and next morning Anne had been found dead and I'd forgotten all about Johnny's visit. But I remembered that Johnny liked to sit in taverns and tell anybody who'd listen what a great Jap-killer he'd been in the islands. . .

Excited, I got Curt on the phone. His first words dampened my enthusi-asm:

"Velda, listen, just remember that this is a party line. Okay?"

"Oh." Suddenly I sensed a dozen ears listening. I'd been using the party line for years and it had never bothered me before. "Well, remember what you said about looking for a common denominator? I've found one: Johnny Drew."

"Got it. Thanks." He hung up, and so did I. I felt disappointed; phone calls were so unsatisfactory.

Lou came home at eight, tired. He'd gotten the road job and had been out all day with surveyors. I drew his bath and fed him supper and waited until he was snoring softly. Then I snagged his key ring off the bureau, and carried it into the kitchen. I found one key with a tag taped to it marked *Struble*. From my own key ring I took a similar key, switched the tags, and put it on Lou's key ring. Then I tiptoed into the bedroom and replaced Lou's key ring on the bureau. If somebody else wanted to see the Struble place tomorrow... tough.

I got in bed and felt a hundred little nerves quivering in my body. I thought of taking a Seconal, but no, that would make me groggy tomor-row and I needed all my alertness.

Lou still lay with his nose pointed at the ceiling, the blanket pushed down past his hips. Black hair stood up in tufts between the buttons of his silk pyjamas. There was a wall in my mind blocking me off from what I'd just done; I didn't want to think about it.

I was starting my second cigaret when Lou's voice said: "Velda."

There was no inflection, nothing. I was sure he'd seen me. I thought, How will I explain it, what excuse can I possibly give him?

"Yes?"

"Why don't you come over here?"

I felt relief. So... that was it. He'd gone to sleep, rested a bit and perhaps had a dream... there was no explaining his urges, perhaps there was no explaining those of any male.

"It's... late," I said.

"You weren't asleep anyway, were you?" No need to answer that; he'd known I wasn't. "Don't come if you don't want to."

Thank you, Lou. But then I knew I'd feel guilty; here was a man who worked hard to provide a nice house and luxury and all the money I could spend....

I slid out from beneath the covers and stood on the mat between our beds. I seized the hem of the nightdress and pulled it off over my head. The air felt cool on my body.

I sat down on the edge of the bed. He didn't move. There is a mental-physical shorthand, a combination of movements and attitudes which comprise the unspoken sexual language of long-married people. I knew what he wanted. I put my palm on his stomach, felt the thick matted hair press against my pain.

"Put the light out, please," I said.

The light went out. In the dark, I can sometimes pretend I am on the black gelding, riding through the night with the wind in my face. This time it didn't work. I felt guilty because I was glad when it was over.

Next morning at ten Curt came into the store and asked for a can of Velvet. I rang it up and gave him his change. With it was the key to the Struble place. He raked it smoothly off the counter and slid it into his pocket.

I said: "Are you—?"

He stopped me with a quick shake of the head. He pointed to his ears and then at the walls, the stacks of canned goods. I understood then; he was afraid of hidden microphones. I took out a piece of paper and I wrote: *Are you going out now?*

He shook his head, wrote under it: *For Gaby, to stand watch.*

I will, I wrote.

Again he shook his head and put down one word: *Risk.*

I wrote: *Pick me up back door one-half hour.* Then to choke off further argument, I crumpled the paper and shoved it in my apron pocket. He lifted his shoulders, then nodded and walked out.

He was waiting in the alley a half hour later. I locked the back door—Ethel had her own key to the front—and stepped into his car. I hunched down between the front seat and the dash, regretting that I hadn't thought to wear slacks. I had to hike my skirt up to my hips to stay hidden, but it didn't matter; Curt looked silently ahead as be drove out of town. His old car sent exhaust fumes up my nose; I was perspiring, probably from excitement. I felt like a juvenile sneaking out on her first date. After a long time Curt tapped me on the shoulder and I sat up, gulped fresh air, and took the cigaret he handed me. We were on a rarely-used dirt road which crossed the river via a rattle-trap steel bridge and met the gravel road which passed the Struble place.

While he drove, I asked him about Gil Sisk and Johnny Drew.

"I haven't cleared Gil yet," he said. "And Johnny Drew seems too stupid. If he were in a city he'd be a small-time hood running errands and trying to look like a big-shot torpedo. Here he's nothing. Anyway, he's dropped out of sight. Maybe the sheriff scared him out of the county. I've spent the last two nights scouring his old hangouts, but nobody's seen him."

He slowed as we passed the Struble house. In the back yard I glimpsed the mound of naked earth which covered Bernice's next-to-last resting place. He turned off the highway and onto a dirt track leading toward the river. Our tires crackled on the sticky gumbo. Patches of ice lay beneath the trees—all that remained of snowbanks. He stopped beneath the cottonwoods and switched off the engine. A curve in the lane hid us from the road. "Now," he said, "we follow the river until we come to a hedgerow. Then we follow that up to the Struble house."

I stared at him. "How do you know so much about it?"

"Aerial photos," he said. "I bought copies from the outfit which surveyed the county last year. Next time you come out to the house I want you to take a look at them."

I stepped out of the car and saw immediately that my heels wouldn't make it. I took off my shoes, then peeled off my hose too. Curt stood waiting, and I flushed with guilt because I was slowing him down. Gaby would probably have had the foresight to wear flats and jeans. As we walked on, the icy mud crawled between my bare toes and reminded me of the high school walkouts we used to take on the first warm day of spring.

Silently we made our way up the hedgerow to the house. Curt left me crouched beneath a spirea bush while he opened the front door with his key. I was to whistle like a bobwhite —the only bird I could imitate—if I saw anybody coming. I couldn't seem to get comfortable; spirea bushes spread out impossibly close to the ground, and a slick mound of ice remained beneath them. I squatted with my bare feet sliding on the ice—feet which had once been calloused but now were soft and tender—and I felt the cold ascend like water percolating upward, reaching my ankles, my calves....

It had reached my thighs when Curt reappeared and said, "Let's go." I followed him on legs which were stiff as stilts, down to the hedgerow, where I again slowed him down because I had to beware of thorns. When we reached the river he started on, then he looked back at me. I was red-faced, sweating, and puffing, so he found a clump of willows and said: "Here, let's rest a minute."

We sat down and lit cigarets, and I asked: "Did you find anything?"

"Nothing, which is significant in itself."

"Why?"

"All her things were there, receipts, appointment slips, matchbook covers, hairpins, perfume, photographs and letters and everything else relatives take when they go through the effects of a deceased person."

"So?"

"So her relatives hadn't gone through it. But someone had. Her things were jumbled, disarranged; the lining of her purse was ripped loose. The sheriff didn't search, I'm sure; he didn't even suspect murder."

"It must have been the killer."

He nodded. "Another scrap to add to the evidence that she was killed. I was nearly certain of that already." He looked at me. "Ready to go?"

"I... guess."

Maybe because there was disappointment in my face, I don't know, but he bent down and touched his lips to mine, very lightly. At least I suppose it was a light touch, even though I felt an electric current passing through my body. I must have been in a sensual state from the mud squishing through my toes, or the excitement of our stealth, but I had to remind myself that I shouldn't, mustn't slide my arms around his back and press him against me. I kept telling myself *no no no* until he drew back his head. I looked at him and I regretted that his eyes... that he had trained them so well that they showed nothing of what he felt. When he spoke I didn't have the faintest idea what he was talking about....

"It's a way station, you know. A point in a journey to a destination. If we're not going to make the whole trip, we shouldn't even get on the train."

I realized then he meant the kiss. I was aware of the leaves arching overhead and the river flowing by at our feet, brown and muddy now with the flow-off from melted snow, and I thought, Well, who's getting off? Then I realized he'd said this in order to give me time to think, so that I'd know exactly what lay ahead. So I thought of Sharon and Lou... and Gaby too, and all the people who would be involved, and I said, "Then I guess you'd better not kiss me again."

He stood up and held down his hand for me. In his eyes I saw that I'd dissembled too late. I read the knowledge that I was available, willing, that he had only to provide a time and a place and the proper conditions. I knew that later, in an hour or a day I would be grateful to him, but now I was only disappointed and angry at myself for being so vulnerable....

I rejected his hand and got up by myself. We walked toward the car in silence.

Ten feet from the car he stopped and motioned me back with a violent gesture of his hand. I watched him tiptoe forward, peering at the ground. He took a piece of paper off the windshield where it had been held beneath the wiper like a traffic ticket. Then, stepping in his same tracks, he came back to me and unfolded the paper. It was a penciled note which said: GET OUT OF TOWN OR GET KILD. TAKE YOUR CHOISE.

"Stay here a minute," he said.

I stood holding the note while he searched around the car in ever-widening circles. He walked out to the road and then back. "Gone," he said. He squatted clown and looked beneath the car, then got a long stick and released the catch on the hood. Without touching the car he examined the engine. Then he poked the stick through the open window and pressed the starter. The car grumbled and lurched, then stopped. I let out my breath, slowly, and only then realized that I'd half-expected an explosion.

"Okay," he said. "Get in. But don't step there."

He was pointing to a sharply defined track in the soft mud. I looked at it and then looked at Curt. "He left a footprint?"

"A beautiful footprint. Too beautiful."

I frowned. "Why?"

"It's probably a red herring. Look here." He placed his foot beside the print. The other mark extended an inch beyond his shoe. "I wear tens. This must be a twelve. And the ribbed sole is like they put on engineer's boots. It's all too distinctive, too traceable to be real."

"What are you going to do?"

"Take you back to town, then go home and get my plaster and make a cast of the print. It's something to look for, even though the shoes are probably buried someplace by this time."

We were driving along the gravel when I said: "Well at least the note narrows it down. You know the man's illiterate."

He threw back his head and laughed. "Sure, it narrows it down. It tells me the man is a damn sight from being illiterate. Look at the note. He can't conceal the fact that he's used to printing. So be uses his left hand to write the note. Make an 'E' with your fingernail there." I did. "See? You made the vertical bar and the bottom horizontal bar in one motion, then attached the other two horizontal bars. That's the way this guy did. A semi-illiterate who draws his letters would make the vertical bar and then the three horizontal bars all separately. Now notice how his right-handed habits carry over. Make an 'A' with your nail." I did. "Okay, on the left diagonal line, you started from top to bottom, then retraced the line back to the top and came down again to make the right diagonal. So did this guy. You can see the double line. The slant shows he wrote it left-handed, but as a matter of fact he was right-handed, otherwise he'd have done the right diagonal first. Same with the 'V' and there's the 'E' again. See what he's told us about himself?"

I looked at Curt. "What?"

"Not a damn thing... except—" He paused and frowned. "Except that he understands the game. This note accomplishes no purpose at all except to make the game more interesting for him. Now he's expecting me to carry this note around the county, searching for matching paper, trying to get samples of handwriting. . ." He laughed abruptly, took the note and shoved it in his shirt pocket. "Yes, he understands the game."

I stared at Curt. "Is that all it is to you? Just a game?"

He turned to me, and there was a strange glitter in his eyes. "Life is a game, Velda. It ends in death. So does this. Now we could get bitter and morbid about it, or we can relax and swing—"

"Or we can check out."

"*You* can. You want to?"

"No." I said it quickly, without thinking, but I realized I meant it. "It just seems to me you've got the odds against you now. He knows you, and you don't know him."

"I will someday."

"When? How?"

"When he tries to kill me."

"Suppose he succeeds."

"That's my game," he said. "To see that he doesn't."

CHAPTER FOUR

I expected Curt next morning but he didn't show up. I was disappointed because I wanted to know if he'd learned anything from the footprints. Gaby came in around eleven; before we knew it we were talking on a level of honesty which I'm sure neither of us intended. That was during our conversation at the cash register; there was a cold drizzle outside and Gaby wore a hooded black raincoat which made her took drawn and tired. I remarked that she was no doubt working hard getting moved in—the kind of social babble you carry on while you're ringing up purchases—and Gaby said she was. I asked if Curt was getting the place fixed like he wanted and only then did I realize that I'd forcibly turned the conversation to her husband.

"He... hasn't been home much lately," said Gaby.

I looked at her and saw a flicker of terror in her eyes, a look which told me she was younger than I thought and had never encountered this kind of problem before. She covered up quickly by throwing back her hood and fluffing out her hair with a quick shake of her head. Then she said:

"At least it's better than having him get bored. When he gets bored he kicks everything to pieces just to see it fly apart."

I didn't want to go that deeply; I pulled back. I asked with a smile: "What does he break up, furniture?"

"No. That was his brother Frankie's specialty, breaking up bars and things. Curt's more subtle." She looked down and fiddled with her billfold, snapping and unsnapping the catch. "He got bored with his research firm, and that's no longer operating. He got bored living with a certain couple while he was going to college and when he left they got divorced. Toward the end they weren't speaking to each other, only to Curt. You'd never get him to admit he had anything to do with that, but I think he did. He's that way about human relationships. He sees a social setup the way a mechanic might see a motor, and he sort of..." she made a fluttery motion with her hands, "...jiggles the wires around to see what will happen."

Suddenly I realized she didn't understand Curt, even though she'd been trying for oh, how many years? She'd built up a vast store of knowledge about his reactions to given situations, but he was still a stranger to her; like an unknown animal in a cage. You know that if you stand around cracking your knuckles, it will turn ferocious. Though you don't know why it turns ferocious, therefore you can't say you understand it, at least you can deal with it. He likes long hair, he hates polished toenails, that's the sort of thing she knew about him.

I had her groceries boxed now and her change made, but she wasn't through. She lit a cigaret and gave me a level look.

"He's had affairs before, you know."

The words sent an electric shock through my body. I felt the heat rise to my face, and at that moment I was sure she knew about our visit to the Struble house and our kiss by the river. *Before* was the key word, that's what made her words apply directly to me—and at the same time made me feel like an insignificant figure at the end of a long line of women. The girl was clever, in spite of her youth.

"Has he?" I asked. "What did you do?"

"Waited. They didn't really compete with me. No more than a... supermarket competes with a gas station. He goes to them for something different than he gets from me."

"What?"

"Excitement, the game, the chance to work out his mind on somebody new—"

"And sex, naturally."

She shrugged. "It isn't the important thing. He never chases a woman for sex. If he does, it's not because he desires them."

I was interested, now that we'd left the specific and gone on to the general. Also I was puzzled. "What reason could he have?"

"To... uh, experiment. To see how sex will affect the woman, or his attitude toward her." She shook her head. "I don't know, really. I just know he's been with women he could have had and he hasn't touched them. Others... vice versa—until he learns what he wants."

"And then what does he do?"

"The same as he does with other people he has no more use for." She held up her palm and blew across it. "He banishes them."

"Banishes them?"

"Doesn't see them. They talk, their words don't reach his mind. He treats them politely, remotely and totally impersonal. I guess there's nothing more frustrating. You can't fight it. Women get drunk and swear at him. He acts surprised. I think he really is because he doesn't realize what he's done to them. When he can't use a person any more, they cease to exist."

I knew what she was doing; she was giving me fair warning: *He wants you only to use you, and here's what'll happen when he gets through with you.* Yet I felt no hostility from her. We were like two housewives talking over a mutual problem; Gaby having the more experience with the problem, she'd led the discussion: *Be sure to whip your egg whites and fold them in separately....*

Sharon came in then and bloomed like a flower when she saw Gaby. I received a perfunctory Hi Mother, then the two went next door to the drugstore. I envied Gaby at that moment—not for her intimacy with my daughter, for a mother gets used to being regarded as dowdy and middle-aged—but for her ability to switch personalities. It wasn't faked; one moment Gaby was an adult woman talking to me about adult matters, the next moment she was a teenager skipping off to discuss records and boys and dating. Gaby was a chameleon, changing her attitudes and personality to suit her environment. I saw that Curt need never tire of her; all he had to do was put her in a new environment and he'd have a new woman....

Gil clomped in for Missus Friedland's groceries. I caught a sour smell of beer on his breath and knew he'd come from the tavern. (I'd begun noticing unpleasant things about him which I'd missed before.) Sarcastically I asked if he and Gabrielle weren't on a first-name basis by now.

"Well now Velda, that's only when we're alone. A smart man never lets on he's high winner in a crap game."

That annoyed me too; not to mention his fake country accent. Immediately I connected it with the note which had been left on Curt's windshield. As Gil walked out, I stared at his shoes. They were big, at least number twelve. I wished Curt would come in so that I could talk to him about Gil. I still couldn't imagine him leaving Gaby alone with a man he really suspected.

The belt tinkled, but it was only Ethel. She took off her raincoat, put away her purse, cleaned her spectacles, and each move was accompanied by a soulful sigh. I didn't ask her anything, I just waited. Finally, after another gut-wrenching sigh, she said: "I didn't sleep hardly a wink last night."

I was supposed to ask why, so I did.

"Thinking about poor Barney. He was always so careful at crossings. And his eyesight was so good—"

"Then how do you explain the accident?"

"He must have been, you know, despondent. He liked Mart a lot, and he never got over finding him dead underneath the tractor."

I felt a chill climb my body; I'd forgotten about Barney finding Mart's body. I must have gone pale, because Ethel asked me what was wrong.

"I was wondering," I said. "Did Barney mention to you that he'd found anything there, or seen anything?"

Ethel looked puzzled. "I'd have to think... "

"Well, think then."

"Why do you want me to think about that?"

"You mentioned that Bernice might have been murdered. Did you ever think your husband might have been?"

Ethel's eyes went wide and round behind the glasses. "Velda! What a terrible thing to say! I won't hear another word." And she wouldn't. She got busy cleaning out the meat cooler and didn't raise her head until I left. I didn't particularly want to go home, but Curt knew my schedule and that's where he'd expect to find me.

I found nothing to do in the house. I would have gone riding but I didn't dare in case Curt called or came by. I was going through all the hardships of a clandestine affair and having none of the fun.

Four o'clock came, and a phone call. Curt's voice said: "Jamboree tomorrow at one p.m."

"What—?"

But he hung up even before I finished the first word. I replaced the receiver with annoyance. Jamboree. What kind of crypticism was that? I puzzled for five minutes, then remembered that Boy Scout conventions were called jamborees. Of course, Curt wanted me to meet him in the Boy Scout cabin....

At noon next day Ethel came in tight-lipped and hollow-eyed.

"I'm quitting, Mrs. Bayrd."

"Ethel, what's the matter?"

Sincerity was evident from the tears in her eyes. "There's no need to talk me out of it, I won't stay in this town another minute. I'm going over to Franklin and live with my sister. She's alone in the house and she's been wanting me to come for a long time."

"Well, of course, if that's what you want. But why?"

"There's something bad going on in this town. Don't ask me, because I won't tell you."

But it was not Ethel's nature to be silent. In the process of getting her things together—I did persuade her to work just one more afternoon—she said that around midnight she'd gotten a phone call. No words were spoken; just a man's voice imitating a train whistle, then laughing. Next morning she'd found a toy train on her doorstep. It had come from a child's playpen next door, and had frightened Ethel to death. "...Just think of the man out there, putting that train on my doorstep... lurking around all night watching and waiting. I couldn't stay another night...."

I mentioned that this proved there was something strange about her husband's death. Why didn't she go to the sheriff? She gave me a hard, narrow look and said: "Maybe it does, maybe it doesn't. Barney's dead and that's it. Being alone you learn you can depend on nobody but yourself. My mind tells me to forget it and that's what I'll do. Whatever you're doing, don't bring me into it. If you do—" her voice became plaintive, lost and weepy. "I'm not a young woman, Velda. I just want him to let me live in peace, that's all. . ."

I left before she started crying on my shoulder. I went out to the lake, parked the car in the same hiding place but approached the cabin from above.

A hundred yards away I sat down behind a clump of buckbrush and waited for Curt to appear below. I'd been there ten minutes when a pair of hands seized my shoulders and jerked me backwards. I arched my back and started to kick when I saw Curt's face grinning down at me.

"Just thought I'd give you a little lesson in camouflage. Don't try to hide in vegetation while you're wearing a blue dress."

Speaking of dresses made me aware that mine had balled up around my thighs. I sat up and pulled it down over my legs. Curt brushed off my back and I could smell pipe tobacco on his breath.

"I thought the killer had me," I said.

"Then you should have screamed," he said. "Best weapon a woman's got is her voice. If you're grabbed, let out the loudest, most blood-curdling screech you can. That usually startles a man enough to make him lose his hold, then you can run."

"Where I grew up a scream didn't do any good. We lived a mile from any neighbors. What's that?"

He'd sat down beside me and pulled out a newspaper clipping. "Front page of the latest county paper. This item here interests me."

A good part of the front page was devoted to Sandy's death, but almost half a column concerned a burglary of the sheriff's office, written in the tongue-in-cheek manner which journalists always use when the police are victims of crime.

IS HIS FACE RED?

A burglary of the courthouse last Sunday night left an embarrassed sheriff seeking an acrobatic burglar who entered the sheriff's office through a third-story window. The sheriff believed it was a prank by a group of boys. Items stolen were:

1. Kit of burglar tools taken from traveler from Minneapolis.

2. Bogus check signed U. Ben Hadde, made out to proprietor of Eat-Rite Cafe.

3. Twenty-two caliber bullet taken from sheriff's arm, received during arrest of auto thief thirteen years ago.

4. Photographic file accrued during the sheriff's 28-year term of office.

5. Fragment of safe blown open at Farmer's Credit Company.

6. Six shares of stock in Reliable Oil Company, a nonexistent firm, which were purchased by various county residents.

7. Assorted pornography impounded from prisoners.

8. Wanted poster for John Dillinger which had hung in office since 1933.

9. Assorted knives, blackjacks, knuckle-dusters and instruments of mayhem lifted from combatants during various peace disturbances.

I looked at Curt. "What does it mean?"

"Item four is the important one, you can forget the rest. I wanted those photos. The one of your sister's body would have been there, so would Mart's and Bernice's and... hell, everybody else I'm interested in. I was trying to figure out a way to get them but the killer beat me to it. Taking that other stuff was a blind, to make it look like a prank." He sighed and folded the clipping. "Well, at least I've got him busy covering up his tracks. One of these days I'll catch him at it." He looked at me. "Anything new?"

"My free afternoons are shot to hell for awhile," I said. "Ethel quit this morning."

When I told him why, Curt looked thoughtful. "I think I see his game. It fits what Gil told me."

"What?"

"He got a call last night, man said it wasn't healthy to work for Curt Friedland, then hung up. Gil called the central switchboard but they had no record of the call."

I frowned. "How could that be?"

"With our old-fashioned party line you can hook onto the line somewhere out in the country and call a person without going through the switchboard. You know how you call others on your line without going through central."

"Yes, but... do you believe Gil?"

He looked at me. "Why not?"

"Well... there's his reputation with women, and the fact that he knew where Mart was working, where Barney was fishing, and so on.... Besides, he wears about size twelve shoes."

Curt lit his pipe in a preoccupied manner. "I made those casts, by the way. The indentation could have been made by a 220-pound man—or by a 160-pound man carrying a 60-pound load."

I shook my head in amazement. "You never accept the obvious, do you?"

"Can't afford to. Gil, for example... the guy is such an airy figure here in the community, nobody notices his comings and goings. Gil's vague about where he goes when he's away... which proves not a goddam thing, because he's vague when he's right here." He stood up. "I'll walk you back to your car. How strong are you?"

"Strong enough to walk," I said, getting up.

"That's not what I meant. Those phone calls could mean he's trying to isolate me, turn the community against me. He might work on you next."

I set my jaw firmly. "I'll let you know when I turn against you. When do we meet again?"

"I don't know. Your afternoons are out, the night..."

I felt a bitter frustration. "What do I do, just exist in limbo until you call?"

"The problem is—look, can you give me a key to the store?"

"Well... I guess. What for?"

"I want to search for bugs. Microphones. That's the only way he could have known you were working on Ethel, by listening in. Once I clear that up we can talk there."

I opened my purse and got out my key ring. Then I stopped. "When are you going to search?"

He shrugged. "Midnight. It's a good hour."

"I'll come and stand watch."

"I won't need it. I'll work in the dark."

My face went hot. "Look, I know I was the one who didn't want risk. But I'd rather be doing something than sitting at home."

After a moment he nodded. "Okay. Wear dark clothing. Go in the back door. Don't turn on any lights. I'll knock once and you let me in. You keep the key, it's safer."

We reached my car and I started to seize the door handle. Suddenly he grabbed my arm and jerked me back. "Wait! Now you get another lesson. You see anything strange about your car?"

My neck hairs rose as I looked it over. Shiny chrome, polished glass, gleaming enamel, all covered by a thin patina of road dust. Someone had written across the door: VELDA BAYRD IS A HORE.

I felt rage pinch my nostrils. "Son-of-a-bitching kids—!"

"Not kids," he said. "Look at the lettering."

I looked, and my rage turned to a chill. The writing slanted backward just like that of the note.

"I see. He knew where we were."

Curt nodded. "He's starting on you, Velda. Better not come to the store tonight."

I set my teeth. "I'll be there," I said. I was scared, but I was mad, mad enough to go after the killer with my bare hands and fingernails....

Curt wouldn't let me in the car until he'd gone through his routine of checking for booby traps. Then he searched for car tracks but the gravel road revealed none. As I drove off—he was going to stay and search the woods—I could feel hidden eyes watching me. I knew why Ethel wanted to run; it was a terrible feeling.

The night began badly. I'd made the date assuming that Lou would be asleep by midnight, but midnight came and Lou hadn't even come home. I didn't want to leave Sharon alone, so I waited. Lou came in around twelve-thirty and said he just wanted to go to bed. I mixed him a drink and he fell asleep before he finished it. I pulled on navy-blue slacks and stuffed my nightdress inside them. It made me bunchy around the hips but I wasn't going to a fashion show. Over that I put a black cardigan. I'd backed into the garage beforehand—I was getting skilled at stealth—so I had only to release the brake and coast down the drive to the gate before starting the engine.

I pulled into the alley behind the store with my lights off. The dashboard clock said one-thirty. It was an eerie hour: the town was dark and silent and a chilly wind whistled around the corners of the buildings. I stopped outside the back door. If anyone saw me I planned to say that I'd come back to lock up the office safe. Curt stepped from a doorway, almost invisible in black. He whispered:

"Go in and close the door. No lights."

I went in and closed the door behind me. The only light came from a streetlamp on the corner. I listened to the sound of my breathing and the hum of the meat cooler. The store was warm and full of familiar smells, but in the dark it seemed alien. I jumped as a knock sounded at the back door. I opened it; Curt was silhouetted in the door a moment, then he stepped to one side and disappeared. I closed the door and turned, trying to penetrate the blackness.

"How can you see?" I whispered.

"Another lesson in skulking, Velda," he said. "Use your peripheral vision. The corner of the eye. Look over there at the cash register. You see me clearly?"

"I see a lumpy shadow, yes."

"Okay, now look toward my voice. I disappear, don't I?"

He did. The next thing I knew he was standing so close I could feel the warmth of his body. My muscles went taut and quivery, expecting his touch. But he didn't move. We stood in darkness amid the odor of celery and cold meats. Curt seemed to be listening. Finally I asked:

"Shall I stand at the front and watch the street?"

"No, you watch the back. Gaby's parked where she can see the front."

"Oh." I felt strangely disappointed. "She knows I'm here."

"Yes," said Curt, moving away. "I'll start with the cash register. The electric system would be a good place to hide a microphone."

I stood by the back door for what seemed like a half hour, listening to the occasional tinkle of metal. I could tell when Curt left the cash register and started tinkering with the meat cooler. The silence prickled at my nerves; when Curt came near enough so I could communicate in a whisper, I asked why he'd quit having Gaby watch Gil Sisk.

"Too risky," said Curt. "Anyway, if he's the guilty party, I want to give him a chance to incriminate himself. He has no really ironclad alibi for the time of any of these accidents, and that's what makes me—"

He was interrupted by two short honks of an automobile horn. "That's Gaby's signal," said Curt.

We hurried out the front door and into the street. A half block away stood Curt's car and Gaby beside it, looking down at the ground. The car looked squat and low to the ground, and then I saw that the rear tires were flat.

"He did it while I was watching the store," said Gaby. "The wind was rattling the leaves in the park, and I didn't hear a thing. But he must have been crawling around the car while I sat there—"

"Your car," Curt told me. "We'll go out to Gil's house."

As I was driving, Curt said he'd seen no point in searching the area; the man had already shown that he was skilled at hiding his tracks. If he found Gil at home, though, he could clear him....

Gil's car was gone. Tacked to the front door, almost as though Curt was expected, was a note written in Gil's huge flowing script: CURT: I HAD TO GO TO K.C. BACK IN A FEW DAYS. GIL.

"That does it," said Curt. "I've got to find out where he is." He turned to me. "You know any of his hangouts, his hotel?"

"He never mentioned any."

"Okay. Now if you'll take us back to town..."

In town Curt said he and Gaby would wait in the car until the station opened and he could get his tires filled. I drove home and crawled into bed as it was getting pink in the east. Lou looked as though he hadn't moved since I left him.

Next morning Gaby came in and asked me to have a Coke with her. I was training a new girl to take Ethel's place, a farm girl named Doris whose husband worked in the grain elevator. I showed her how to use the cash register and joined Gaby in the drug store. We sat at one of the marble-topped ice cream tables which had been there since I was a little girl. Gaby said in a low voice:

"Curt called Kansas City. He's hired a private detective to trace Gil."

Gaby looked tired but no longer frightened, as though she'd gone a step beyond fear. I had an elusive letdown feeling and finally identified it. Since Gaby was telling me this, it meant Curt couldn't see me. Her next words verified it:

"Curt says it isn't safe for you to meet for awhile. He also thinks its better if you don't stay home alone. If your husband isn't there, visit neighbors. Don't let your daughter out alone at night."

"Why is he so worried about me?"

"Not only you. Me too." She jerked her head toward the window. I saw old Tully Robinson and his wife Carrie standing beside Curt's car. They were both Brushcreekers, and I'd known them all my life. Tully had been a brawler in his youth and had once served a term for stealing hogs. Now he was nearly sixty and steadied down. Carrie was a stocky woman with iron-gray hair and biceps as big as Gaby's thighs. She'd been the Nation's midwife for years, but the younger women now used the doctor in

Franklin. She was strong as a man; I remembered seeing her drive mules and strip cane for their sorghum mill. We kids used to eat the sweet sorghum while the foam was still on it. At county fairs Carrie ran the cotton candy concession and Tully the penny-pitch.

"My housekeeper and Curt's hired man," said Gaby. "They're staying with us for a time. Curt says he trusts them implicitly."

"So do I," I said. "But where's Curt?"

Gaby shrugged. "He'll be out of touch until Gil is located. Curt says he's number one suspect." Gaby smiled a bitter smile which did nothing for her beauty. "I liked Gil, but I find myself hoping he's the one. Just to end this damned nightmare."

I looked at Gaby and wondered if I were stronger than she was. I wasn't eager for it to end—perhaps because when it ended, Curt would leave....

CHAPTER FIVE

For a week I had to stay in the store all day while I trained Doris to take over in the afternoons. I didn't see Curt at all, but Gaby came in a couple of times looking pale and Camille-like—particularly alongside ruddy, jovial Carrie Robinson. She'd shake her head when I asked if there was anything new. There was something new, but not in the quest for Gil Sisk. One night a rock smashed the window of Stubb's tavern; attached to it was a printed note saying: THIS IS FOR SANDY BENNETT. Nobody could figure it out except that somebody blamed Stubb because she'd drunk beer there the night she burned. Stubb closed up for a week and went to Excelsior Springs, which contributed to the town's somber aspect. Two mornings later, Bill Struble found a dead dog with its throat cut hanging from the railroad-crossing signal. It was a brindle watchdog—of mongrel breed but mostly boxer—belonging to Fern Blake, the widow of Jerry Blake, who'd been killed when the butane tank blew up in the hardware store. Fern demanded protection, and Sheriff Wade named a special deputy to patrol the area at night. He was Wayne Calvin, a mechanic at Slavitt's auto salvage, Seventh Day Adventist, and about the only unmarried man in Sherman who didn't drink. Tension still mounted; Tillie Sims, 75, who lived alone, saw an eerie face in her window one midnight. Her sister Winifred, 72, who hadn't spoken to Tillie in twenty years, saw a face in her window the following night. The two women moved in together the following day, so it couldn't be said that events were all bad.

The county paper came out that Friday with a three-column headline: PRANKSTER PROWLS SHERMAN.

The story was treated with the Sunday-school type of indignation typical of small-town newspapers. It included a warning from Sheriff Wade that the prankster was guilty of malicious mischief and subject to prosecution.

Just below that story, another tiny headline caught my eye:

CURT FRIEDLAND ARRESTED
RELEASED FOR LACK OF EVIDENCE

Curtis Friedland, former resident of Sherman, was arrested by Sheriff Glen Wade on suspicion of possessing illegal firearms. He was released for lack of evidence.

I pondered the item a minute before I realized it referred to the phony arrest at Curt's place while I watched. Lord! that was how long... over two weeks ago. Two county papers had come out since then.

"Guilt by association," said Curt's voice.

I looked up and saw him standing there. He wore his old denims, but they were deeply wrinkled and stained with red mud, as though he'd been tramping the Brush Creek hills all night. Just seeing him lifted my spirits, but I was depressed by the gray weariness of his face.

"You mean the paper?" I asked.

Curt nodded. "No county sheriff is going to be elected year after year without knowing how to use his local newspaper. He released the story of my arrest knowing the editor usually tries to group all Sherman news together. Most people will just assume that both items were part of the same story. I'm already getting dirty looks."

I folded the paper and shoved it aside. "I've been starving for news, Curt. Haven't you found out *anything?*"

He shook his bead. "The detective's looking. I'm looking. Nothing new."

At the same time he was making writing motions with his hand. I slid a pencil and pad over to him and watched him write: *Tomorrow, five p.m. Your mailbox.*

He went out and climbed in his car. I hoped he'd go home and get some sleep.

That night at seven I got a call from Harley Grove, secretary of the town council. He asked me to tell Lou they were having a special meeting of the council. Lou was supposed to come. I asked what it was about; I'd gone to school with Harley and was shocked when he said bluntly: "Council business, Veda. Just tell Lou to be sure and come."

Lou came in at eight and I relayed the message. Then I watched TV without seeing it until Lou came home at ten. He was chuckling as he pulled off his tie. While I mixed him a drink, he said: "They think Curt Friedland's bringing this trouble. They want him pressured out of town."

I felt like I'd been suddenly thrust among foreigners. That's why Harley hadn't told me what the meeting was about. Where had I slipped up? How had word gotten out that Curt and I were... *what did they think we were doing anyway?*

"How could they pressure him?" I asked.

"Someone would talk to him, buy him out. They... had me in mind." He laughed and tipped back his glass. The ice clicked against his teeth. He lowered his glass and belched. "It's the old story of bell-the-cat. Everyone wants the other guy to do it. I told them they'd better forget the idea before it lashes back. Friedland's no hairy-necked Brushcreeker."

I felt grateful to Lou, and guilty because I was working behind his back. But I explained to myself that Lou and I were going through the period of estrangement we usually have when he starts a new project. He was traveling, buying new equipment, supervising the work. I only saw him late in the evenings, and even then he'd usually be working out in the shop, where he'd installed a desk and an adding machine for a makeshift study.

I was watching the mailbox at four-forty p.m. the next day. My heart jumped when I saw Curt's old car stop—but the car drove off immediately. I trudged out and found a brown manila envelope crammed into the box. It contained a book, *The Prophet,* by Kahlil Gibran, and an aerial photo of the Brush Creek wilderness. The book had certain words circled, and the photo was speckled with numbers written in grease pencil. I took it to the house and tried to fathom the connection between the book and the photo. I couldn't. I decided the key was missing. Damn Curt and his penchant for intrigue....

The phone rang at three a.m. I got up, my thoughts suspended. A three a.m. call meant trouble.

"Hello," I said.

"Velda," said a husky, muffled voice. "Listen carefully and you'll know who I am. You got a sandbur in your butt, remember? You didn't notice until you started to pull on your panties, then you had to have him pull it out. You looked funny standing in the gully holding your dress up with your panties down—they were red, I remember the color—while he—"

I slammed down the receiver. My heart was beating so fast I thought it would choke me. Perspiration trickled down my body and between my breasts. My hands were sweaty; I wiped them on my nightgown and felt an urge to scrub my entire body with soap. The words had stained me with filth....

It had been the watcher. No other living person could have known about that embarrassing incident with the sandbur. I walked into the bedroom and looked down at Lou's sleeping figure. I wanted to wake him up, but I'd have to tell him the whole story of Mart and I, about Curt's project—and what could Lou do?

I drank a glass of straight Scotch and felt better. I regretted having slammed down the phone; if I'd listened longer, he might have let slip some clue to his identity. Even now... I lifted the receiver and heard only the crackle and hum of the wires. I called Central and asked: "Did you just put through a call to me?"

"Uh... yes." The operator yawned audibly into the phone. She slept on a couch beside the switchboard. "It came from Connersville I think. Yes. Connersville."

"Thank you. Get me Curt Friedland's residence."

While she was ringing I remembered Curt's warning of secrecy. But it was too late because Gaby was answering, her voice breathless and urgent.

"Is Curt there?"

Gaby sighed. "No. I thought this would be him."

I felt a brief pity for Gaby; in a sense, she was nearer the danger than I was. "I just got a nasty call from... our friend. From Connersville."

"I'll tell Curt when he comes in."

That was all. Next morning in the store I tried by subtle questioning to learn if any Shermanites had been in Connersville the night before. As nearly as I could learn, none had. Gaby came in and we went for another Coke. She said Curt had left for Connersville as soon as he got home. He planned to look for someone from Sherman, especially Gil Sisk. Then she asked: "Did you figure out the code?"

"Not completely. I know the territory in the photo—"

"He thought you would. The page numbers in the book correspond to the numbers on the photo. When he wants to meet you, he'll give you a quote from the book—over the phone or in a note. The page on which the quote appears will be the number of your meeting place. Find the circled word in the phrase, count from the left-hand margin, and you'll have the time of the meeting."

My head was spinning. "Ingenious."

She gave a wry laugh. "He plays it like a chess game. You should see my instructions on what to do in this or that emergency while he's gone. He covers everything but an invasion from Mars." She paused. "The quote for today is: 'Speak to us of love.' "

I frowned. "Don't you know where the place is?"

She shook her head. "No. Nor the time. You see how it works? A person could overhear and still know nothing. Like me." She gave a crooked smile. "He says there's no need to spread the burden of secrecy."

I drove home after work and looked it up. Page eleven. The word "speak" was circled, fourth from the margin. Four o'clock at site eleven. I dressed excitedly in green slacks and sweater; it would be our first meeting in nearly a week.

The site was a cove so choked with cattails that no boat could enter. I sat down on the bank and smoked a cigaret; I was completely hidden from the lake. Cattails arched overhead, a hill sloped up to a deserted farmhouse, and sheep grazed on the hillside. After ten minutes Curt came strolling down the hill; his eyes were puffy and I decided he'd been taking a nap in the farmhouse while he waited for me. He didn't look any more tired than before; maybe he'd reached a level of fatigue where it no longer showed. He sat down beside me and asked me about the call. I told him in general terms, without revealing exactly what Mart and I had been doing there. I tried to describe the voice, but could only say that it was a man's voice, muffled and indistinct. Curt said he'd seen nobody in Connersville, but that a couple of switchboard operators had promised to keep track of calls to Sherman. They might or they might not; at any rate he planned to spend the night there just in case.

Then he fell silent. I still wasn't used to his total lack of small talk. I got nervous. I looked at the hill, the grazing sheep, the blank windows of the farmhouse like staring eye sockets, and I felt a strange emptiness. I had been eager to meet him... now what? I wanted something more, but I knew no way to break through to him... .

Still, it was our daily afternoon meetings which kept me from leaving town. Because the calls continued during the following week. There was no voice; just a ringing late at night, then a hoarse breathing which gave me chills. I'd listen and visualize Curt out patrolling the neighborhood lines. (His listening post at Connersville produced nothing; only the first call had come from there.) Lou would sometimes be in bed asleep and sometimes out in his study working. If he'd asked me about the calls I'd have told him, but he didn't ask. (He wasn't aware of me really. The road job had bogged down; they'd run into rock outcropping and were blasting it out. With each blast Lou's profit margin dwindled.)

Each morning Curt would call with a quotation or else Gaby would bring it into the store. I'd find the spot on the map and Curt and I would meet. Our seventh meeting wasn't much different from any of the others. It took place in a little hickory grove where I'd climbed trees as a girl.

"Another call last night?" asked Curt.

I nodded. "Like the others. He breathed at me. What's new from the detective?"

"On the night of Bernice's death he went to Kansas City, but there's no record of his having stayed in a hotel."

"Maybe he stayed with a woman."

"As a bachelor, why would he hide it?"

I nodded. "True. Gil would be more likely to brag about it."

On the tenth day I said: "Maybe Gil's a victim. He could be lying dead someplace."

Curt nodded. "Sure. The body could be hidden but not the car. The detective has the make and number. Five-thousand dollar convertibles don't sit abandoned for ten days without being noticed." He looked at me sharply. "You have another suspect?"

"I suspect everybody," I said. "I watch the people come in the store and they all act guilty. Sylvester Bloch mumbles to himself all the time. Fred Goff has a twitch in his face. When he looks at me it's like grasshoppers jumping under his skin."

"We've got more than our share of kooks," said Curt. He was whittling a point on a hickory stick. "Maybe it's inbreeding. In my class at school there were fourteen kids, all descended from three couples." He squinted up at the blue sky between the new leaves. "While I went to school with them they were individuals. People. Since I've been away they've become types, like a Washington Irving story of the New England backwoods. Eli Black was Eli Black, boring and stupid at times, but someone to have a certain kind of fun with. Now he fits perfectly the category of a rural loudmouthed braggart and coward. Marie Herzog was once a moderately attractive, friendly girl, a good dancer, and a girl who'd go all the way in a parked car just to be a good sport. Now she's a frowsy, blowsy, gabbling busybody. Janet was a sharp kid, careful about whom she dated, always on top of the lesson, neat and clean and ready to call attention to the fact that you weren't, but in a good-natured, for-your-own-good manner. She never put out until you'd agreed to go steady. And even then not until you'd hauled her fifty miles to a movie. Now she's a greedy wolfish woman, collecting tinsel in that overbuilt house of hers, pushing her husband until the poor bastard's got a crick in his neck from looking over his shoulder to see if she's behind him. She's a Las Vegas type, the kind you see at horse races and in charge of fashion magazines. Rolly Cartwright was a pudgy little guy whose hands were always sweaty, who was always putting the seam of his pants out of the crack of his ass, who giggled in the locker room and seemed to spend a lot of time in the john. Now I can see plain as hell he's a fag. Gloria's a dyke; she stands over there in the post office and she doesn't watch the men go by, she watches the girls. I don't know where or how she gets her kicks now. In high school she was always the girlfriend of the good-looking chick, the one you always had to bring a date for and the guy you brought always said never again. Just when you were going strong with your date in the movies... she'd nudge your date and whisper in her ear. In a restaurant she'd never go to the john unless your date accompanied her, and then in the john she'd try her damndest to screw up your scene, telling your date you'd gotten fresh or something. Well, she's queer. Look at the guy she married, he's just about as effeminate as you can get without being an overt fag. Somebody should do her a big favor, go over and say, Look baby, your scene is women. Stop fighting it and start making it and you'll be a lot happier."

"Why don't you tell her?" I asked.

He shook his head. "No, actually she wouldn't be happier. Guilt would weight her down. She couldn't be a straight dyke; she'd have to tie it up with a little ribbon of social acceptance.... Maybe she and some young chicks could go off to Africa as missionaries...."

"Curt, while you're analyzing—"

He said it before I finished. "What type are you?"

"Yes."

"You've ceased to be a type and become an individual. Everybody does that eventually."

"But you had me typed?"

"Sure."

"Okay. What?"

"Frustrated romantic, good brain but too easily screwed up by emotions—"

"You can stop now."

He grinned. "Don't want to hear?"

"You... go too deeply, Curt. You miss a lot that happens on the surface."

"Eating, sleeping, talking, what else happens on the surface?"

"Well... emotional relationships. Love..."

"Symbolic," he said. "Sublimated narcissism." He got up suddenly, giving me a pat on the hip. "We'd better go."

This was as near as we'd gotten to a personal relationship; we could talk about sex but we couldn't do anything about it. We were as intimate as old lovers, but we'd never been lovers. I suppose that's why it hurt so much when the community turned against me. I was going to work; the morning was clear and sparkling as a diamond, birds twittered, and the air was full of green, growing smells. Suddenly I stopped. Chalked on the sidewalk in front of the bank were the words:

VELDA BAYRD LOVES CURT FRIEDLAND.

My face burned as I scrubbed it out with my foot. Just then I looked through the window of the bank and saw Bob Sieberling, the vice president, polishing his glasses and watching me. There was no friendliness in his look; I knew he'd seen the words and waited for me to come along and rub them out.

That afternoon I told Curt about it. "I felt I didn't know any of those people... Bob Sieberling... the person who wrote the words... I had a feeling they've hated me for years and all their smiles and kind words were faked."

"Did you notice the handwriting?"

"I..." I blushed. "No, I was so embarrassed, I just wanted it erased—"

"Embarrassed of course because it implied you were the aggressor, the brazen hussy pining for unrequited love. If it had said Curt loves Velda you'd have been flattered—"

I swung at him but he ducked. "Be serious. You think it was the killer?"

"Didn't have to be. Once it starts, others will pick it up. As you say, they've been storing it up. Poor little hill girl marries man for money—"

"I *didn't.*"

"I'm speaking with the voice of Sherman. Blood will tell, they'll say, and point out that your sister Anne was a naughty girl. Some of them have waited twelve years to say I told you so. I'd say it's only the beginning, Velda."

He was right, because the next day Fern Blake came in and said she'd decided to do her trading in Franklin. She'd never been a very levelheaded woman, and I was cool and polite to her. I simply handed her the bill which had been accruing for ten years. We'd never presented it because her husband had been Lou's partner. I think Fern had some chronic illness; she was a pale, bony-faced woman who wore gloves in the hottest summer. She always dabbed pink rouge high on each cheekbone and smelled as though she'd dumped a whole bag of cheap talcum powder over her body. Her hands shook as she ripped apart the ticket. Her voice trembled as she said:

"Velda, for ten years now I've kept my husband's secret. But I've known, and your nicey-nice ways haven't fooled me. If you bother me with this—"

I could only stare at her. "What... *what* are you talking about?"

"I know. Don't think I don't. Just remember that."

She walked out then, and I remembered.... Lou had wanted to borrow money to go into the turkey business; he'd needed Jerry's signature on his note because there'd be a mortgage on the store. Jerry had come out one night while Lou was attending some meeting in Franklin. (I could never keep track of Lou's organizations.) Sharon was a baby then and in bed, and Jerry pulled a pint bottle out of his inside jacket pocket and said he'd wait for Lou. Jerry was a big, thick-necked redfaced man. He was sweating, and I should have known something was wrong. But the Blakes were family friends; Jerry and Lou owned a boat together and we all four spent weekends on the lake, went bowling together and all that. Jerry and I were on a kidding, platonic basis... I thought. Jerry took a couple of drinks then brought up the note. He didn't think he could sign it. I was surprised, because I'd thought it was all settled. Then I shrugged; it was between him and Lou. Jerry drank twice more from the bottle and said it all depended on me. He had a little cabin on the lake which his wife knew nothing about. If I'd tell him when I could get away he'd give me a key. I didn't intend to torture Jerry; I just couldn't understand. Jerry squirmed and finally blurted out that we could meet there and nobody would ever know. I kept my temper; I stood up and said I was going into the bedroom. If he left immediately I'd keep quiet. If he didn't I'd call either Lou or the sheriff. I left the room and Jerry left the house. How his wife had found out, and how she'd managed to find any implication of misbehavior on my part I didn't know. Jerry had been all bluff anyway; he'd signed the note and I'd seen no sign of friction between him and Lou. Of course, I'd avoided Jerry after that and two years later he died.

I was getting sick of the citizens of Sherman. They were more narrow and bigoted than I'd thought. When I told Curt about it that afternoon he asked: "Did Lou know about it?"

"I never told him."

"Could Blake have told him, or Blake's wife?"

"Why would they, Curt?"

He was silent a moment; we were sitting on a ridge where a tilted rock stratum stuck up like the exposed spine of an ancient dinosaur. I'd picked the year's first bouquet and the flowers were slowly drooping in my hand. Finally Curt gave me a sidelong look: "Not many weeks ago you upheld Jerry Blake as a moral saint. What do you think now?"

"The same thing, I guess. Who knows what I might have done unconsciously to give poor Jerry the idea I was available. He might have thought I was flirting when I was just trying to be friendly."

A faint smile flickered around his mouth. "In other words, it isn't immoral for a man to desire you. Whereas if he desires another woman, as in Gil Sisk's case—"

"Oh Curt! Do you examine your own motives as closely as you do mine?"

He nodded slowly. "Yes. As a matter of fact, I do."

I wanted to ask him then what his motives were toward me. I hadn't been much use to his investigation lately, yet I had a feeling there was something he wanted me to do, something he couldn't ask because he wasn't quite sure of me. . .

Gladys came into the store the next morning and started talking about the days when she was my teacher and had great hopes for me, and how I must realize she was interested only in my own welfare, and finally: "You must know, Velda, you're being talked about."

I felt icy cold. "Am I? Concerning what?"

"You surely know, Velda. Apparently I was mistaken about Curt Friedland. He's just like his brothers."

"You happen to be mistaken about me at this very moment, Gladys."

"Indeed. Why is it that I see you driving west out of town every afternoon?"

Gladys wore a weird smile which revealed the orange-colored gums of her false teeth. Her prominent hooked nose and narrow chin stood out in sharp relief, almost like a parody. "Maybe it's because you're a spying old witch, Gladys."

I regretted the pointless insult at once, but it was too late; Gladys strode out with her head high and I knew that whoever didn't already know my shameful story would hear it before sundown.

I looked out the window; a bleak spring drizzle fell on the street. There'd be no meeting with Curt today. The branches of the elm trees drooped under the weight of moisture and I knew exactly how they felt. I went back into the office with the idea of crying, but even that seemed pointless. I called up Doris and told her I was sick, then I went home and drank beer alone all afternoon.

Next day I noticed a coldness in the people who came in the store. None of the usual gossipy conferences around the cash register; now they talked out on the sidewalk, looking inside occasionally at where I was standing.

There was more than one reason for it. A few had stopped trading in the store and left outstanding bills of nearly two hundred dollars.

My father called me up that night. "Stay away from him, Velda. That family's brought us nothing but grief."

"Suppose Frankie didn't do it?"

"I don't give a damn if he did it or not. She ruined her life chasing that man. He's guilty, one way or another. Let him rot in jail, and keep away from his brother."

He hung up. My father had never been much interested in legal subtleties, but all the same, I was beginning to see what a chunk Curt had bitten off.

The next day my brother stomped in. Gordon and I had always been on good terms; the fact that Anne had been between us in age had saved us from any sibling rivalry. He'd competed with Anne instead of me. But today his face was hard.

"Dad called me last night. I told him I'd go tell Curt Friedland to leave you alone."

I blazed up. "You big helpful oaf. Does it occur to you that I'm thirty-five—?"

"Then go tell him yourself."

"What if I don't want to be left alone?"

"Then you oughta be whipped. Too damn bad your husband is a flatlander or he'd do it himself."

He stomped out the door and got into his car. I stood there a minute, then I realized this was an encounter I couldn't let take place. Curt and my brother fighting... how could anything good come of it?

I locked up the store—business had fallen off anyway—and drove to Curt's as fast as I could. When I got there Curt was sitting on the steps and Gordon was standing. Their poses didn't look belligerent; they weren't even talking about me. They were talking about Anne and Frankie. Gordon was saying:

"...doesn't matter who did what. If he hadn't come back she wouldn't have chased him."

"Gordon," I said. "You can't hold Curt responsible for what his brother did."

Gordon turned to me, but Curt spoke.

"That's the way it works, Velda You know that. I am responsible for what Frankie did. But he didn't do anything." He turned to Gordon. "See if you can answer yes to just one of these questions. Did you ever see Frankie hit a woman? No. Was there any reason why he'd kill Anne? Were they fighting? Was she threatening to leave him? No. In fact, it looked like they were going off together. Somebody didn't like that idea. Somebody else—
"

"Curt, Frankie's lawyer said all this. It didn't save him then, how can it save him now?"

"With proof—"

"Proof! You'll just stir up a stink, I agree with Dad. Let it lay."

"Sure, Gordon. Pretend Frankie's dead. You ever see a prison? Nothing grows around it, no trees, no grass. It's like a poison seeps through the walls and kills all life. Put a man away and forget him. The authorities will take care of him because they're paid to. People outside can assume he's dead; he won't pop up and remind you he's alive. He isn't really. He's got nothing to do in there but watch himself die."

Gordon turned and started away. Curt called after him. "You think he's guilty?"

Gordon shrugged without turning around. "It's out of our hands."

He got in his car and drove away without looking at me. Obviously he'd forgotten what he came for. I looked at Curt. "He planned to warn you away from me. How'd you get him off that?"

"A soft answer turneth away wrath." Curt smiled. "I saw he was mad, but I remembered seeing him in a fight once. You were there. The other guy got him down somehow; you jumped on the guy's back and started pulling his hair and biting and scratching. You were a little savage, all skinny elbows and legs. I didn't want to fight you this morning." He stood up and slid his arm across my shoulders. "Come in. Gaby's got coffee made."

It must have been his fraternal gesture—perhaps his nonchalance—but I suddenly choked up with bitterness. "Curt, listen, if I'm a fool for taking this thing seriously, will you kindly tell me? If it's all a game just... tell me so I can laugh and have a ball too..."

He pulled away and gave me a studied look. "You're really bugged, aren't you?"

"I shouldn't be, I suppose. I'm in trouble with my folks, I've made enemies I didn't want and friends I don't need—"

"You can step out."

"Can I?"

"Sure. Tell them I deceived you. They'll take you back and gladly, because you've done something that makes you interesting. You'll be invited places and women will take you aside to tell you about their affairs so that you'll tell about yours. You'll find life full and complete and with a richness you never dreamed—"

"Oh, shut up." I wasn't mad anymore.

"Seriously."

"Sure. You make the whole community sound like a gabbling chicken coop."

He shrugged. "I see what I see. You want out or not?"

"When I want out I'll get out. I don't need your release."

He smiled, and somehow it all faded away. It always did; you never really came to grips with Curt unless he wanted it that way; it was as though he had spent all his life avoiding traps.

That night, for the first time in weeks, Lou arranged one of his quiet family evenings. He washed the dishes, helped Sharon with her homework, and watched TV. After Sharon had gone to bed, Lou turned off the TV and regarded me with an expression of sadness and pity.

"You know they're talking about you, Velda?"

It was his commiseration which infuriated me; that and the fact that I'd been told so many times.

"How nice," I said. "How utterly suburban."

"You know what they're saying?"

"The worst, I suppose. I'm carrying on shamelessly while you, the faithful husband, slaves away in blind devotion. I'm pregnant with Curt's child, expected to slip off to St. Joe for an abortion at any moment...."

He smiled faintly, and I could see the picture amused him.

"You know," he said, approaching the subject from left field the way he often does, "your family has a strange self-destructive urge. Once a structure shows a few chinks, you yell whoopee, damn the torpedoes, school's out, let's burn the building. Just because one little piece is tarnished, you tear down the whole goddam edifice."

He was talking about our marriage. I didn't want to go into that.

"What are they saying, that I have a weakness for the Friedland family?"

"For violence... destructive men. Maybe you see it in the men, or maybe you bring it out in them, I don't really know."

"Like I bring violence out in you. What a violent man you are, Lou."

A faint smile tugged at the corners of his mouth. "You think so?"

At that moment I didn't know. I said: "You think there's anything in what they're saying about Curt and me?"

"No."

Somehow that only made me angrier. "I see. You are the calm voice of understanding. You only brought it up to remind me of our place in the community, and how we shouldn't do anything to jeopardize our position. I'm expected only to be careful, and if we should decide to sleep together, we should tell you, and you'll make sure that we're discreet about this thing and nobody knows—"

"You can stop now, Velda. Your nose is getting red."

I jumped up and went into the bedroom. While I lay there I could hear him in the kitchen, getting a bottle from the cupboard. I drifted into a half-sleep; I didn't hear him come into the bedroom. Suddenly I felt the blanket jerked off and my nightdress yanked up to my waist. I could hear the rush of breath through his nostrils as his strong hands rolled me and sprawled me on my back. There was no point in pretending to be asleep;

I helped him in order to end it more quickly....

"Every other night, Velda," he said when he rose. "Maybe that will keep you home. That's what all the boys tell me."

Gaby's call awoke me next morning. The eaves still dripped from an early-morning shower. Lou had already left for work and Sharon had gone to the corner to catch the schoolbus. Gaby said:

"Can you come over? It's urgent."

"Has anything happened to Curt?"

"No. One of his traps has sprung. He wants us there. You'll have to come and get me."

She was waiting in front of the house with two suitcases. "He found Gil."

"Found him?" A picture of Gil lying dead in a ditch leaped into my mind, but Gaby's next words corrected it. "He hasn't taken him yet, but he knows where he is. He found out Gil has a cabin on Lake Pillybay. The detective's been watching it. Late last night Gil came back to it. He's still there."

I helped her load the suitcases into my car and asked what they were.

"Recording apparatus," she said. "Just finding the killer won't help Frankie. There has to be a confession, and an impartial witness."

"Who—?"

"You."

As I drove I learned that most of her information had been received in a phone call which instructed her to implement plan 3a. That meant a suspect was cornered and the recording equipment was needed. She showed a sheaf of typewritten pages on which he'd listed plans for various emergencies. One said: *Arrest by sheriff.* It called for Lou to bail him out, and I wondered if Lou really would. Another was labeled: *My death. Clear out without delay. Hand evidence to FBI and forget it.* That one horrified me; I knew Curt thought that way, but seeing it coldly written on paper made it seem almost as though it had already happened.

Gaby directed me to the opposite side of Lake Pillybay, a rolling wooded area which Shermanites seldom visited. Curt was waiting at a crossroads; he looked pale and grim and he wasted no breath saying hello.

"Cabin's down there. Detective Boggus is watching it. You two wait here until I get this stuff strung out."

He took the two suitcases and disappeared into the dripping woods. After a half hour he came back.

"Okay. We'll go in close."

We got out of the car and closed the doors silently. We started down the dirt road; I was too tense to ask questions. Suddenly Curt stopped and motioned us close:

"The cabin's right around this bend. You two go in there—" he pointed to a break in the sumac which lined the road "—and hide where you can see the action. I'll knock on the door and see if I can startle Gil into making a move."

Gaby motioned me to go first; I guess she assumed I was an experienced woods-runner. We crawled through the underbrush; each time I brushed against a sapling it dumped a shower of droplets on me. We were both soaked by the time we came in view of the cabin. It was a sprawling lodge with a green roof and brown siding. The forest surrounded it from three sides, making it a perfect hidden love nest. I wondered how many Sherman women knew the inside of it; I wondered who Gil had with him now. There was no sound; the only sign of occupancy was Gil's convertible standing just outside the door.

I saw Curt walking toward the door, his shoes squishing in the mud. He knocked loudly and waited, his eyes roving the woods. They passed ever us without pause, so I decided we were well hidden.

After a moment Gil opened the door. His eyes widened at the sight of Curt; he stepped out quickly and jerked the door shut behind him. His hairy shanks protruded from beneath a maroon silk bathrobe. He stood blinking in the light, looking rather more embarrassed than scared. His face looked stiff and painted, like a theatrical mask. I couldn't hear the conversation, but Curt obviously wanted to go inside and Gil didn't want him to. Finally Curt squared his shoulders as though he were about to shove Gil aside and open the door. Gil shrugged; he opened the door and called out a name. It sounded like "Bunny" but it must have been "Benny" because a young man appeared in the door. He looked slim and girlish, with long hair and a narrow, large-eyed face which also had a painted look. He frowned at Curt and pouted his full red lips. Curt turned abruptly and started walking away. Puzzled, I heard Gil call out in a plaintive tone which didn't sound like Gil's voice.

"Say, old fellow, you don't plan to noise this around Sherman, do you?"

"No," said Curt gruffly, "I won't."

Gil slid his arm around the boy's shoulders and the two went inside. Their attitudes were those of a husband and wife who'd just gotten rid of an unwelcome visitor and abruptly I understood. My face prickled with embarrassment, whether for Gil or Curt or just for the human condition, I wasn't sure. I looked into Gaby's wide eyes and saw that she understood it too.

At the car, Curt discharged Detective Boggus with a check; he was a short, chubby man with a dozen black hairs combed carefully over a bald pate, not at all my idea of a private detective. Curt loaded the recording equipment in his car—telling Gaby to erase it, since it was useless, and to drive on home. "I'll ride back with Velda," he said.

For a time we drove in silence, then he said: "You understood the scene back there?"

"Yes."

"How do you feel about Gil?"

I had to think, because I'd identified so closely with Curt that I'd felt only disappointment at the failure of his trap. "About Gil? I think... all that muscle, manhood... what a terrible waste."

He laughed abruptly. "That's funny as hell. I've heard men say exactly the same thing about an attractive Lesbian." He sobered abruptly. "But that explains Gil's absences... and why he worked so hard to get a reputation as a ladies' man. I'll have to take him off the list for good. That kid was wearing lipstick; Gil had it smeared all over his face. You wouldn't fake that." He grimaced. "Stop here. I need a drink."

It was a little gas station and honky-tonk; the kind you see around the country with names like Burntwood Inn and Cozy Dell. This one was called Pine Cove Tavern and was crowded (there was no work in the fields because of the rain) with men in overalls and a couple of women in print dresses. We drew stares as we walked to a booth in the back. I felt wicked and daring, and though it was unlikely that any Shermanites would see me, I found that I didn't really care if they did. I told Curt to order me a boilermaker: a glass of beer with a shot of bourbon inside it. He ordered the same for himself and drank silently for a few minutes. Finally he said: "You've been patient, Velda, working in the dark. Now I'll tell you something, but I've got to have your word you'll keep the secret."

"Okay. You've got it."

"Specifically, I want you not to tell Lou."

I stared at him. I was mad at Lou at the moment, but I didn't like the position I was being put in. "I don't know if I should promise that, Curt."

He shrugged and drank his drink. He wasn't going to tell. Finally I asked: "Does it concern Lou?"

"Yes."

"And me?"

"Yes."

"Then you've got to tell me."

"Promise first."

"Curt, I'll throw this beer in your face."

"Go ahead."

"Look, does it... I mean, if I don't tell Lou, will it get him into trouble?"

"No."

"He won't suffer?"

"The incident is done and past. If it were known in Sherman, people might smile, but nobody would blame him. It will only add to your fund of knowledge concerning your husband, but nothing which will work to your advantage."

"God, I've got to know. I promise not to tell Lou."

"Okay. Remember that night you met me in the store, and I searched for hidden microphones?"

"Yes."

"Lou followed you."

I gasped. "No!"

"I watched after you went in, remember? He drove his pickup past the head of the alley and parked somewhere. Later he came back and stood in the shadows. He didn't see me watching him."

"You didn't say anything then."

"I was waiting to see what he'd do."

"He didn't let the air out of your tires?"

"No. He was there all the time. When Gaby honked, he disappeared."

I felt angry and prickly. "Damn him. Of all the sneaky..." I looked at Curt, who was smiling. "Why did you tell me this now?"

"I need some information from you."

I looked down at my drink. I felt depressed. "About Lou?"

"Yes."

I shook my head. "If you suspect Lou you... you're crazy. He was in bed when the phone calls came. He was home the night that Sandy was killed. He was in Omaha when my sister Anne was killed. He was in the alley the night the air was let out of your tires—"

He was nodding. "I know all that, Velda. But he's a common denominator. He was Jerry Blake's partner, and Jerry Blake made a pass at you. To a jealous man that's a motive for murder right there...."

"He isn't jealous. And he didn't *know*."

"We aren't sure. Even if he didn't he profited by Jerry's death. He took over the store; he had partner's insurance on Jerry and he collected that. And when Ethel's husband died he bought another store cheap. I don't know his relationship to Anne, but there was Mart. He married you when Mart was killed—"

"Curt, I won't listen to another word."

"All right, let me put it another way. When Gil Sisk faded out as a suspect, it left me with nothing"

"Johnny Drew."

"Okay, Johnny Drew. Anne was about to leave him, that's a possible motive for killing her. But how can you tie him with the others?"

"He worked for Jerry Blake and Jerry fired him. Okay? And Mart... I don't know. Once Johnny said he'd been in love with me all his life. That could have been drunk talk, or it could have been true. There's something else. Johnny gambled a lot, and sometimes he was terribly lucky. Once he took Anne to Bermuda on his winnings. She came back alone, wired home for money because he'd lost again. He used to disappear after he'd make a killing. People figured he was living up his winnings, but who knows? To me he's a prime suspect."

"Okay. But he's disappeared."

"Find him."

"I will, but I need some more help. Your husband's a smart man, probably smarter than you think. I could use his help. If I clear him I can trust him."

"Is that why you've been playing games with me? Waiting until I was ready to spy on my husband?"

"Spy?" He looked thoughtful. "Okay, call it spying if you like."

I had a giddy sensation which didn't come from the liquor I'd drunk. I'd just looked into myself and it was like looking down a deep well; I found to my surprise that Curt had timed me perfectly, because I was ready.

"What do you want to know about Lou" I asked.

"Everything," he said. "Everything you know."

CHAPTER SIX

When I told Curt about Lou, I told myself I was simply laying to rest Curt's suspicions about him. But I suppose it was partly to examine my own feelings about Lou. It's hard to explain my motives; it was like two radio programs going at once, each drowning out the other.

Lou came from a small town near Connersville. He used to visit his aunt here during the summers. He played with the Brush Creek boys: Eli Black, Rolly Cartwright, Mart and Gil and Johnny Drew and Frankie and Teddy Groner who'd drowned, but he'd been gone every winter and he never really belonged. He seemed to endure an initiation every spring when he'd come to visit his aunt. She was a fanatical Methodist, and each summer she'd launch Lou's visit by trying to indoctrinate him into the church. I remember seeing Lou in the churchyard in necktie and shiny patent leather shoes wearing a frozen smile while the boys ran up to spit on the shoes. After a few weeks, Lou's aunt would drop the church routine, but Lou never completely made it with the boys. During the war he was 4-F because of a heart murmur and that cut him off even further. He came to Sherman to run his aunt's farm, then he ran Jerry Blake's store when Jerry joined the Navy. Lou started making money, and people resented that. One fight I remember . . not really a fight—with Johnny Drew.

"What happened?" asked Curt.

"It was at Gable's tavern where the Brushcreekers went—the quiet drinkers used the other one. I was fourteen then, and I'd gone in to see Dad—on Saturday night he'd drink beer and I could figure him for a dime provided I got there before my brother and sister had cleaned him out. I used to hang around awhile; it was an exciting place, always a few servicemen, loud talk and sometimes a fight. On this night Lou was sitting at the bar drinking a beer. I didn't notice him until Johnny Drew came in. He was just out of boot camp, wearing his marine dress uniform with marksmanship medals all over it. He saw Lou in civvies and decided to have some fun. He said, 'What's wrong, Lou? You have an eardrum punctured?' Lou murmured something which nobody else heard, and Johnny said: 'I don't see how that could keep you from fighting.' 'Well, the Army thought so,' said Lou. And Johnny said: 'It couldn't keep you from stepping over into the park and having a friendly little match?' Lou said he'd rather drink his beer. Johnny turned to the crowd and said: 'Whaddaya think, this civilian would rather drink his beer.' Then he laughed and knocked the beer in Lou's lap. Everyone got quiet waiting to see what Lou would do.

He reached in his pocket and pulled out a knife. The blade wasn't more than two inches long, but the quiet way he did it, kind of sad and regretful, caught everybody's attention. He jabbed it into the bar in front of him and ordered another beer. He didn't even look at Johnny, but Johnny got the message. He walked out and never bothered Lou again. That's the way Lou worked; I've never seen him lose his temper. It's like something he keeps in a bottle and lets loose only when it will do some good."

"Yes," said Curt. "He's a rich man now."

"Well, he made it honestly. He started with the farm his aunt left him, then bought into the hardware store when Jerry came back from the Navy. He had a talent for being in the right place at the right time. Take the turkeys... when the big feed companies started offering inducements to get people to raise turkeys, Lou borrowed money to get into it: ten thousand poults the first year, fifty thousand the next, a hundred thousand the year after that. Suddenly the whole county was raising turkeys, and Lou stepped out. That year the bottom dropped out of the turkey market and those who were still in lost their shirts. Not Lou. And construction.... when the government started subsidizing farm ponds, Lou bought a bulldozer and started digging. Everybody wanted work done; things had fallen apart during the war and everybody was rolling up their sleeves to put it back in shape. Lou bought more equipment; he built roads and reservoirs and a string of small airfields to get ready for the big air age. The air age never panned out. You can see some of the fields be built, weeds coming up around the concrete, a ramshackle hangar, a couple of peeling piper cubs. Some people went broke, but not Lou. He'd taken his profit and gone on to something else. Somehow he knew when to get in and when to get out. The fact that he happened to make money when certain people died means nothing. He made money at everything."

As we were driving home, Curt asked: "How about Mart's death."

I thought about it. "Lou took me out a few times while Mart was in the service, but he didn't seem serious. Never really tried anything beyond a single goodnight kiss when he took me home. I was going to marry Mart, and he seemed to accept it. In fact, he sold Mart the farm we planned to live on after we were married. When Mart died Lou took me to the scene of the accident and showed me that he'd bulldozed off the bank so that no more accidents could happen."

"And just happened to cover up the evidence," said Curt. "I wonder who told Struble he should have the well filled in."

My face felt hot. "You're twisting everything up, Curt. Lou just gets a kick out of helping people behind the scenes. Like the sheriff. . ."

"He helped the sheriff?"

"Loaned him money or something. I don't know."

"And I suppose the sheriff shows his gratitude."

"Well... not directly. When somebody in Sherman has trouble they often ask Lou to smooth things over with the sheriff. Like Johnny Drew when he passed some bad checks—"

"What did Lou get out of that?"

"Nothing, for Pete's sake. Maybe a feeling of importance, I don't know. Curt, don't get me started looking at motives. I have to look at what a man *does*. Lou showed up pretty good after Anne's death. My folks never had any other home, but here they were surrounded by painful memories. Lou had a farm fifty miles away and he made Dad a proposition; he could live on the place for life and give him a tenth of the crop. It was twice as good a farm as the one they had here."

"Are they happy there?" asked Curt.

"Are you looking for trouble?"

"No, but people uprooted at that age—"

"Maybe they'll adapt. They don't like it there, but who knows whether they'd like it here or not?"

"Why'd he pick a farm so far away?"

I realized that everything I said in defense of Lou could be turned against him. Curt could have said that Lou wanted my folks out of the way so that Anne's murder would be forgotten. I didn't believe him.

But that evening I looked at Lou sitting under the reading lamp and realized that I had no idea of what went on in his head. He *could* kill; any man could kill if he thought he had to. Our country's wars have taught us that if nothing else. I thought of Lou creeping up while I slept; I damned Curt for planting this little seed of horror....

Next day Curt wanted me to take him to see Lou's mother. I wondered how I'd explain the visit, but I needn't have worried. Lonely old women don't question the rare arrival of visitors. Lou's mother was a starchy white-haired woman living in a prim white house on an elm-shaded street.

She told Curt what a well-behaved boy Lou had been; always went to church, always did his homework. I'd heard it all before, so I concentrated on stifling yawns until she displayed some relics of Lou's eight-year-old interest in taxidermy: twenty little white mice, almost perfectly preserved.

Curt looked at me and smiled; I wondered what his suspicious mind was making of this. Personally, it made me realize what a strange, lonely childhood Lou had had.

That night I talked to Lou about Bernice Struble. I told myself I was personally curious, but I'd reached the point of not being sure whose motives I was acting on, my own... or Curt's. Lou didn't seem interested in the subject but said yes, he'd told Struble the well would have to be filled.

"You wouldn't expect people to drink out of it. Would you, Velda?"

I had to admit that I wouldn't.

The next night I was surprised to see Curt's old car coming up the drive. Curt and Gaby stepped out dressed for visiting, Curt in slacks and knit shirt, Gaby in a wraparound skirt and blouse. I met them at the gate and my face must have revealed worry because Curt said: "Just a social call. Relax."

I didn't relax, because I knew Curt had come to study Lou. I must admit that Lou seemed pleased to see them; he kept the glasses filled and led the conversation.. I found that I wasn't the only one on edge. Gaby was watching Curt and acting on his signals. She'd reach for a third drink and abruptly refuse it; she'd start telling a story and suddenly change the subject. I began picking up his signals; a slight pinching of the lips and a movement of the eyes. Lou missed them, I'm sure. I saw them because Curt didn't try to hide them from me.

Maybe it was curiosity, but I didn't want to leave Curt and Lou alone. When Lou took him out to see the shop, I went along. It was weird to hear Curt lead the conversation into the subject of wire taps and hidden receivers: "With transistors and printed circuits," said Curt, "you could hide a receiver in a cigaret lighter. If somebody wanted to spy on you, you'd never be out of earshot."

When Lou showed Curt his guns, Curt asked questions and showed polite interest, but it was clear to me that he was studying Lou and not the guns. I'd always felt that Lou bought guns just for the joy of possession, but Curt led the conversation to killing. "I don't like guns particularly. As tools for killing they're so damned... noisy. If I were going to kill a man I'd never use a gun."

"What would you use?" asked Lou.

Curt smiled. "That would depend on the situation. I'd kill a man only if he were trying to kill me, and then I'd use... whatever I had."

"You might happen to have a gun," said Lou.

"If I did, it would be because I expected to need it. And if I expected to need it, I might create a situation where I did. The subconscious plays funny tricks."

Lou nodded, but I was puzzled by Curt. It seemed to me that if Lou *were* the killer, he would *know* that Curt suspected him. Then I remembered: Curt wanted the killer to make a try at him.

Later they talked about the killing instinct; I don't know who led the conversation into it, Curt or Lou, but suddenly Lou was saying he'd never been in the service so he didn't know if he could kill or not. He'd always been awed by the way the Army made killers out of ordinary farm boys-

—

Curt shook his head. "They- don't *create* killers, Lou, they educate the one that every man has inside him."

Lou raised his brows. "Seems like a risky business. They can't be sure they've got him de-educated. One minute the killer's a patriotic citizen; suddenly there's an armistice and the killer becomes an antisocial beast."

Gaby laughed. "You should get Curt to show you the psychiatric study they did on him. They didn't think they could get him to stop."

"Stop what?" I asked.

"Stop kill—uh, fighting."

An awkward silence fell in the room. Gaby drew back in her chair and I think she regretted her words because the psychiatric study was obviously a touchy subject with Curt. But it was out and he had to deal with it.

"They gave me a clean bill," he said. "I got an honorable discharge, finally. But like you said Lou, I resented those bastards in Washington who think they can turn a man into a killer by pushing a button that says go. Then turn him into a decent taxpayer by pushing one that says stop. I wanted to show them that I controlled my own switch. So I let the fighting machine run on a little while until they got panicky, then I got tired of the game. I shut myself off." He rose from his chair and walked to the table, poured his glass full of straight bourbon. He looked at me over the rim and for a second there was something in his eyes I didn't like. Then he went on: "For a while it would get turned on again without warning. Other guys could turn it on, but only I could shut it off." You'd never know Curt was excited, except that between each sentence he'd drink. I found myself sitting on the edge of my chair. "Now I control both ends," he said, taking a drink. "I turn it on." Drink. "I shut it off." Drink. "It's a comforting feeling to control your own killer. Everybody should do it." Drink. "But to do it you have to let him run loose until you know him well enough to get a halter on him. Takes a war to do it, Lou. That's where you're at a disadvantage."

He smiled, set his empty glass down on the table, and walked back to his chair. I felt an immense relief, because I felt he'd re-experienced the entire war while he was talking to us. I resolved never again to ask him about the Army or the war because of the way his eyes went flat and dead....

I glanced over at Lou and saw a studious look in his eyes. I realized that just for a minute they'd switched roles; Lou was the observer, and Curt was the subject. . .

After they'd gone Lou sat with an untouched drink in his hand looking at the empty TV screen. I showered and dressed for bed; as I passed Lou's chair he asked without looking up:

"What do you think of him?"

I paused. "He's like you, Lou, in certain ways."

Lou jerked his head up. "How so?"

I sat down on the hassock and tried to define my vague feelings. "I don't mean physically. You're opposites there; he's tall and blond, you're short and dark. But you have the same way of talking, those long rushing declarations when nobody can get a word in edgewise. And you both have an uncanny way of shifting the burden of proof to the other person. You get the other person talking, explaining, apologizing, then suddenly the guy gets a puzzled look in his eyes and wonders why he's apologizing...."

When I paused, Lou said: "Go on."

"Well, neither of you seem to have close men friends. You think weird thoughts, all that talk of death and killing. You don't tell jokes. You don't *enjoy* things... at least not the way I see enjoyment. I don't understand what goes on inside either of you, only the parts you let show above the surface. But Curt seems... tighter, somehow. He cares more about things... doesn't dissemble quite as well...."

Lou smiled vaguely. "He's nine years younger. Give him time."

The meaning of that burst on me suddenly: I thought, my God, Curt is nine years younger than Lou. I'd actually considered them the same age, and I thought: If they're even now, where will Curt be when he's Lou's age? At that moment I regretted that I wouldn't be there to see it, because I felt that he'd leave me far behind.

Lou's curiosity was engaged, and the next night he took me to see Curt and Gaby. There was a farmhouse near Curt's—Lou had the place listed for sale—where the attic was full of bats. Lou liked to sit and shoot them as they darted out at sunset. It was like a skeet shoot, only trickier. Curt was reluctant to do it, and I thought he was squeamish. But Lou insisted, and Curt took the gun. Bang, he took one shot and got one bat. Then he handed Lou the gun and said: "That's all. I won't push my luck." Lou took five more shots and only winged one. When all the bats had flown, Curt said he thought he'd go up and board up the hole, but Lou said: "Leave it open. They'll come back."

Curt smiled and said. "I see. Then we'll have more to shoot tomorrow."

I'd never thought of it like that but Lou's deal with the bats seemed suddenly sadistic and perverted. Before it had seemed like harmless fun.

Afterward Lou said: "He doesn't like killing, you notice that? He just likes talking about it."

I looked at Lou. "*Should* a person like it?"

"No, certainly not." Lou chuckled to himself; he seemed oddly self-satisfied.

I felt uncomfortable watching the two together, each studying the other. Occasionally I'd pick up fragments of weird conversation. Curt saying: "Life is telling yourself a break will come, tomorrow will be better. Suicide is deciding it won't come, or if it does it won't be worth a damn." And Lou asking: "Suppose you decided, how would you do it?" Curt said: "I'd choose to wait for death from some outside agency. Then each day would be profit, reckoned from the day I decided." Lou laughed. "It's altogether too sane.

When you really decide on suicide, you're nuts. Right now you're sane, so you plan simple painless methods. But if you ever really do it, you'll be kooky, so naturally your methods will be kooky too." "Yes," Curt agreed finally. "And you'll probably take a few people with you."

A week passed; Lou spent less time at his work and no longer puttered in his shop at night. I was torn between worry and willingness to see Curt under any circumstances. Lou would get in the car in the evenings and say, Well, shall we go to a show or what? And I'd say, Whatever you want, Lou. And my stomach would knot up because tonight I wouldn't see Curt, then Lou would say, Shall we stop and see Curt and Gaby? And my tongue would stick to the roof of my mouth because I knew before the evening was over Curt and Lou would be sizing each other up, like a pair of tom-cats. Everything was a kind of contest, like the water skiing. Lou had been skiing for years and was far better than average. He asked Curt if he'd ever skied, and Curt said: "I've tried a couple of times." From then on Lou could-n't rest until he got him on a pair of boards. I stood on the bank and watched his first wobbly, wallowing attempts. An hour later I watched his smooth gliding ease; a day later I saw him slalom and carry Sharon on his back. Lou strained to stay ahead of him, but I could see it was useless. Then, just when Lou and Curt were exactly equal in skill, Curt said: "I'm beginning to lose interest in the sport."

I thought about that. I realized that if he'd gone on to surpass Lou, I might have pitied Lou and resented Curt. But when he didn't go ahead, he got all the credit and none of the blame. He was as superior physically as if he had, yet he didn't have to bear the burden of having put Lou down.

I still hadn't figured it out completely, though. One afternoon we were shooting the basketball at the net Lou had tacked onto the garage for Sharon. Curt dropped ten in a row which just whispered through the net. He seemed to forget the rest of us were there; we were just co-spectators in his drive to attain perfection. Then he seemed to remember that we were keeping score; he started clowning and missing shots. Lou beat him, but everybody knew Curt could have won. I had a feeling Curt was trying to infuriate Lou, in a way which left Lou no excuse to be angry. Curt was so blithe and easy about it, the way he shot the arrows. Lou got pretty good with the bow, but never as good as Curt—and Curt was always ready with a lame, unhelpful excuse:

"Your arms are too short; you need a lighter bow." I felt like screaming at Lou, For God's sake get off the physical kick; you're just playing into his hands. But Lou didn't seem to notice; trying the tablecloth trick was his own idea. Curt watched Lou do it twice, breaking a plate and two glasses. Then he walked to the table and jerked off the cloth with one hand. He didn't even ripple the cream in the pitcher. He treated it as an accident and wouldn't try it again; but I knew that somehow Curt had practiced, then had worked Lou into trying it first. When we were alone I asked: "Are you always on top?"

He smiled. "'There are better men. I met them back in the days when I was trying everybody out."

"That must have shocked you."

"It was a sobering lesson. It taught me never to deceive myself."

I couldn't figure out Curt's game with Lou. I wondered if *he* knew; I felt that we were all four in a driverless car hurtling downhill toward certain disaster.

Gaby felt it too; she got a bright nervous glitter in her eyes. Her cheeks grew hollow and she cursed the town: "Goddam dusty stinking little pigpen." I suspected she was hitting the bottle secretly, but she kept it all from Curt. She made me promise not to tell, then told me she'd gotten nasty phone calls at the same time I'd been getting them.

"Why didn't you tell Curt?" I asked.

"I was supposed to," she said. "I was supposed to rave and scream and get scared so Curt would pull out. That's why I didn't."

I had to admire her courage; slim, elfin creature. She'd never really had her nose rubbed against life before. She couldn't have been more than twenty-five. I felt sorry for her, but at the same time envious, watching her and Curt together. I saw him kiss her in the car, and I tried to remember how long it had been since Lou and I had done that. When we'd leave their house, they'd stand on the front porch together and Curt would slide his arm across her shoulders. There was something basic about that; a gesture of solidarity in front of the home which hints that everything's good inside.... When they left our house, I always walked Curt to the car, and Lou walked with Gaby. I'd make these comparisons and I'd feel a prickle of discontent.

One day Sharon came to me with a problem. It was Sunday; Lou and Gaby were out riding, Curt and I were sitting on the blanket in front of our house. Sharon had been told by a boy she liked that he preferred short hair. Sharon wanted to know, Should I cut it, or would that make me seem too eager?

I said: "Well, I'm not a boy. Why don't you ask Curt?"

Curt looked at me curiously, then at Sharon: "I'm afraid I didn't have a normal boyhood. Why don't you ask your dad?"

She left to do that, and Curt kept looking at me. Finally he said quietly: "He's her dad, and nothing I do will change that. I don't tamper with things I can't change."

"I know." I felt everything coming down on top of me, covering me with confusion. I jumped up. "I know he's her dad, and I know he loves her. And she loves him. I just wish there were more understanding between them and less emotion. I wish you were—" I turned away suddenly, my face burning. "My God, this thing is getting out of control."

He shook his head. "No, it isn't."

"But... it has. You've gotten so involved in your little game with Lou you've forgotten—"

"It's all one game, Velda."

I stared at him. "But I thought by now you'd clear him—"

"On the contrary. I've noticed that the phone calls have stopped since I've been staying close to Lou."

My mind started spinning. I couldn't put two thoughts together. "Then... how can you leave Gaby alone with him so much?"

"I'm usually within calling distance."

"Not now. They've been gone an hour on the horses."

He nodded. "I know. Put your ear to the ground."

I lay my ear against the ground and heard the faint thudding of hoofs. I looked at Curt. "What would you do if they stopped?"

"Go find them," he shrugged. "But it isn't necessary now. Sharon went for me."

It made me furious that he'd used my daughter. "Damn you. You treat everybody like bugs under a glass."

He reached up and took my hand. I looked into his eyes and saw that the pupils were large and black, with only tiny rims of blue around them. "Hold yourself together, Velda. Something's going to break soon."

I hoped so. I was tired of lying in bed every night and adding up the score: This counted for Lou, that counted against him. Was he, or wasn't he? I'd added it a hundred times and never got enough on either side to settle the account. I doubted that any wife had ever been faced by such a problem.

The following night all my suspicions of Lou were wiped out. It was ten o'clock. Lou was out in the shop; Gaby and Curt had just left, and I was sitting with one eye on the TV and the other eye on the clock. Sharon had ridden the gelding to visit a girlfriend who lived two miles up the road; I'd been against letting her go, but Lou and Sharon had both opposed me, so I'd given in.

The phone rang, a hesitant ring which told me it was being cranked manually and not by the switchboard, which has a push button. That meant a call from somebody on our line. Since those weird calls had always come on our line, I lifted the phone fearfully.

"Mrs. Bayrd," said a woman's voice. "This is Crystal Miller. Can you come up? Your daughter's here."

My heart stopped. The Millers lived just a half mile up the road. "Is Sharon hurt?"

"She's... not hurt, but—" She started to say more but stopped. "You'd better come right away. That's all I can say."

I ran out the door and called to Lou. The door opened, and he was silhouetted by the light behind him. "Lou! Sharon's up at Miller's! Something's happened!"

We wheeled into the Millers' lane and stopped; Bert Miller came out of the square white house and sauntered down to meet us. He was a retired railroader who wore greasy overalls and smoked a corncob pipe which was unbearably rancid even if you liked pipes—which his wife didn't. "She's inside," he drawled as though this were a social visit. "I don't think you folks need to worry. Some kids threw a scare into her, I figure. I found her hammerin' at my door, her shirt half torn off. She was bawlin'..."

Lou strode past him toward the house, then Bert said: "I called the sheriff; he's on his way."

Lou paused in midstride, then nodded abruptly and went on. I walked behind him, into a neat living room which smelled of waxed linoleum and sassafras tea. The sassafras wafted up from a glass in Sharon's hand. She sat in an armchair, pale and puffy-eyed, wrapped in a large plaid bathrobe. Crystal Miller stood behind her with bony arms folded across her chest, her pale gray eyes fixed on me.

"You shouldn't let your daughter out at night, Mrs. Bayrd, with all those strange things happening."

I ignored her and went to Sharon. "What happened, baby?"

Sharon took a deep breath and blurted: "I was riding Lightning down the road and a bright light flashed and Lightning jumped and I fell, and—"

She stopped abruptly. "Go on, Sharon," I said.

"Don't rush her, Velda," said Lou. "Just tell the story, Sharon. No hurry now."

Sharon looked down at the tea. Tears started running down her cheeks. "Mother . . . I can't drink this."

I took the tea and handed it to Crystal Miller. Her lips pursed with disapproval, but she took it.

Bert Miller said: "A shot of whisky would—"

"Shut up, Bert," snapped his wife.

"Go on, Sharon," I said.

"Well... I lay in the road with the breath knocked out of me. Then something... ran over from the side of the road, growling like an animal."

"A dog?"

"Oh *no*. It was a man, I know that, but the sound was like an animal. It started tearing at my clothes... my shirt. I started kicking and screaming, and it was tearing at my Levis... but all of a sudden it ran away."

"Ran away?"

"I guess my screaming scared it off."

"But... he didn't do anything?"

"Yes he *did*, Mother. He tore off my shirt and ripped my jeans—"

"But he just ripped them? He didn't... I mean afterwards—"

"Oh, Mother!" Sharon started sobbing.

"Velda," said Lou. "You're not getting through." He came forward and helped Sharon out of her chair. "Let's go in the other room and talk."

The door closed behind them and I heard Lou's soothing voice. After a minute Bert Miller cleared his throat and said if I could use a drink, he'd just walk out to the barn. But Crystal told him to shut up, she wouldn't have the stuff in the house; Bert shrugged and we sat in awkward silence for five more minutes. A car purred to a stop outside, then the sheriff came in, bulking huge in creased gabardines. He pulled off his hat and said: "Hello folks, Velda. Where's the girl?"

Lou and Sharon came out, Lou with his arm around Sharon's waist. He said: "Sorry you got called out on a wild goose chase, Sheriff. The girl just fell off her horse."

I stared at Lou. The sheriff said: "Hell! I heard she got raped."

Lou turned to Sharon. "Baby, tell the sheriff what happened."

"I..." Her voice was husky from crying. "I fell off the horse and tried to catch him and tore my clothes in the fence."

I gasped. "Sharon! Why did you tell that story?"

She looked down, refusing to meet my eyes. "Because... I'd stayed longer than you said, I didn't want to he punished."

"But I never... you knew you wouldn't be—"

The sheriff cleared his throat. "I'll be getting back, unless..." he looked at Lou "...you think I ought to look into it?"

Lou shook his head. "No, I'm sure it happened like she said."

I watched the sheriff leave, too dazed by events to say anything. Lou drove the pickup out of the lane, with Sharon sitting between us. On the road he stopped and said: "Drive on home. I'll check the area for tracks."

I stared at him. "You mean... her story was true?"

"Yes."

My mind buzzed in total confusion. "You mean you covered it up to keep it out of the paper? You think your standing in the damn community is more important than our daughter, for *God's sake?*"

Lou sighed. "Velda, I know exactly what I'm doing. You remember the Covin girl? It damn near ruined her life when they took that boy to court for raping her."

"But the sheriff could have helped quietly—"

"Don't argue, Velda. Take Sharon home and put her to bed."

He slammed the door and walked down the road. I drove Sharon home and drew a hot bath for her. As I bathed her, I saw that the struggle had been far more violent than she'd led me to believe. There were bruises on her breasts and neck. My throat ached when I saw the finger marks on the lower curve of her stomach. He'd reached down, grabbing for the soft tender womanhood. I felt prickly and nervous handling her body; the child seemed suddenly to have become a woman, full-breasted and fledged and desired by men—so desired that they used force to take what they wanted. I thought to myself: *It may be a game for Curt, but it's no longer a game for me.*

As I tucked Sharon in bed, I asked: "You know what he was trying to do?"

"Mother, of course. I'm fifteen."

I wondered how she knew—then I recalled that I had known when I was fifteen, but couldn't say how I knew.

"He didn't do it though? You're sure?"

"I'm sure. It was the Levis. He couldn't tear them, and I kept my legs crossed."

I heard the door slam. I said goodnight to Sharon and left her. Lou said he'd found signs of a scuffle on the gravel and a button off her shirt. But there'd been no tracks on the gravel and none on the shoulder. He said goodnight to Sharon, then fixed a drink and sat down.

"Velda," be said heavily, "it's time we had a talk about this investigation of Curt's."

"He told you about it?"

Lou shook his bead. "I've watched it in operation, Velda. You can't dissemble as well as you imagine. Go ahead, call him up. I think he'll be ready to talk."

Curt asked a hundred questions about Sharon—exact time, location... so on... but I couldn't say much on the phone. Lou's eyes were on me constantly. At last Curt said he'd be over as soon as be could. When I hung up Lou said:

"He doesn't trust anybody, does he?"

"He's coming," I said.

I dreaded the next few hours: all the days Curt and Lou had been together I'd felt they were building up to some kind of ultimate encounter. I was afraid it might come tonight and I had a feeling they were too evenly matched to do anything but destroy each other. I watched Lou setting out glasses and putting ice cubes in a bowl as though it would be a social gathering; he seemed strangely exhilarated in view of what had happened to Sharon. I discovered that my underclothes were damp with perspiration; I took a shower and put on clean clothes. When I came out of the bedroom, Curt and Gaby were there. Lou was reading from Curt's list of accidents, sipping his drink from time to time.

Curt sprawled in an armchair with his heels on the floor in front of him, holding his glass with both hands and peering at the light through the liquor. Gaby was smoking, rolling the white cylinder between her long fingers. She gave me an expression of sympathy and asked if Sharon was asleep. I said yes, then I sat down on the hassock between Curt and Lou.

After a minute Lou tapped one of the papers. "Teddy Groner," he said. "You'll have to take him off your list of murder victims."

"I'd be interested to hear your reasons," said Curt.

"I was there, as you've noted. The day we went out in the boat Teddy said he wasn't feeling good and he sat on the bank. We didn't notice he'd start-ed to swim out until he was half-way there. Ten feet from the boat he stopped swimming. He looked at me and I saw terror in his eyes. Then he slipped under the water. The others thought he'd just dived under the boat to come up on the other side, but I wasn't sure. A second later, when he didn't come up, I realized he'd had a cramp. I dived in. The water was murky and I could see only a dark shape drifting down. I tried to reach it, but my lungs gave out. I came up for air and yelled at the others and they started diving too. None of us saw him. It wasn't until they were dragging the cove for his body that I noticed the blood dripping off my fingers. I realized I'd been bleeding like hell all this time; I'd torn my arm on a nail getting on and off the boat while we were diving for him."

He held out his arm and showed Curt the scar on his forearm. I'd seen it before, a jagged crescent of shiny scar tissue. Curt leaned forward and examined the scar minutely, so long that Lou withdrew his arm, looking uncomfortable.

"Okay," said Curt. "Scratch Teddy. I don't need him anyway."

Lou read on, and after awhile said: "Here's another one—Jerry Blake."

Curt raised his brows. "You're sure it was an accident?"

Lou shook his head. "I'm almost sure it was suicide."

I was shocked. "*Jerry?* Why would he kill himself?"

"He was sick," said Lou. "Bad heart. He had... five, ten years if he took it easy. On the other hand he might go any minute. Only his wife and I knew. Jerry brooded a lot; he might have lived a moderate life if everything had been normal, but somehow the idea that he couldn't drink and could-n't hell around... well, Jerry just had to do it, that's all. Bought a cabin on the lake and took girls there. Got a helluva scare once when he had an attack there and the girl ran off and left him. Jerry told me about it; said he was afraid of kicking off while he was in the sack with some strange woman... embarrass his wife, raise hell with her future. Not long after that he went down to the store to do some late work; I was there, but I left early. You remember that night, Velda? I came home and said Jerry was acting strange. I was about to go back when I got the call that the store was on fire."

I nodded; remembering the night. I remembered early the next morning, when Lou had come in begrimed with smoke and said that Jerry was dead, and I should forget what he'd said about Jerry's strangeness.

"We were heavily insured," Lou went on, "and the insurance company tried like hell to prove it hadn't been an accident. They finally gave up. I found out later that the books were short by five thousand dollars... that's how Jerry had financed his high living. But if you mention it outside these walls I'll deny it. I don't think you'd be able to prove anything where the insurance company couldn't."

Curt looked tired. He stood up. "Don't bother to read any more."

Lou shrugged and handed the papers back to Curt. "Don't you have anything else?"

"Nothing," said Curt. "Let's go, Gaby."

Curt left with a strange, frozen expression on his face. I would have liked to talk to him, but there was no way I could see him alone; I felt tired and totally incapable of sleep. Somehow my irritation turned against Lou.

"You... smug citizen. Why didn't you give him the benefit of the doubt?"

Lou spread his hands. "What was I supposed to do? Say I was convinced when I wasn't?"

"You had your mind made up before."

"That isn't true." He squinted at me. "Did he hook you into helping him with that flimsy evidence?"

"He showed it to me—"

"But he has *nothing*, Velda. Couldn't you see that?"

I felt confused and angry. I started pacing the room, my fists clenched. "Why don't you just say I'm stupid. Tell me I haven't got the brains to deal with him?"

"Okay, you're stupid. You don't have the brains to deal with him."

"Ohhhhh." I threw up my hands and went into the bedroom. I lay down on the edge of the bed and lit a cigaret. After a minute Lou came in, calm and judicious, shaking his glass so the ice rattled.

"Velda, I understand this thing. Curt can't accept the guilt of his brother, so he's built up this fantastic theory in an attempt to deny it. He's smart in other ways, smart as hell, so naturally you assume he's right about this. But tell me, has he turned up one shred of concrete evidence? One single uncontradictory particle of proof?"

"Yes," I said, sitting up. "There was the note on his windshield—" I stopped abruptly. I didn't want Lou to know about our burglary of the Struble place. But Lou was nodding.

"He showed it to me. Curt said the handwriting was faked. Why couldn't *he* have faked it?"

"Oh Lou! And those phone calls in the middle of the night—"

"Couldn't he have made them?"

"But why?"

"Simple. Curt hates the county for what it did to his brother. He's trying to stir us up, get us to fighting each other." Lou chuckled, looking into his glass "Did I ever tell you about his experiment with the rats?"

I recalled that a couple of weeks ago Curt had wanted to trap some wild rats for an experiment. Lou had gotten the materials to build the cage and had helped him trap them in an old granary. But I didn't know what the experiment was about. "No," I said.

"He painted the tails of one group red and left the other group just as it was. Then he watched them exterminate each other—just like people."

I remembered Gaby's words: *"When he gets bored he kicks everything to pieces just to watch it fly apart."* I got out of bed and paced the room a couple of times. "Lou, your theory that he's doing this for revenge... it's just as fantastic as his—"

"You agree that his idea is fantastic?"

"It's fantastic that a killer has run loose for so many years."

"Too fantastic to be true."

"What about Sharon? Curt didn't attack her!"

"No," said Lou soberly. "That's something else again. I'll learn who did, and I'll take care of him myself. There's no need for official action."

I stopped and drummed my fingers on the bureau. My mind was fogged by the suddenness of events; I couldn't sort out my thoughts. Maybe a day or so on the lake, doing nothing but thinking...

Lou came up and put his hand on the nape of my neck. It was clammy cold from his glass. "Velda, you've let yourself get too deeply involved. Take Sharon and visit your mother for a few days. She can recover from her scare, and you from your... infatuation. ."

I walked away and went into the living room, away from the voice of sweet reason. After awhile I lay down on the couch and closed my eyes; I'd decide tomorrow, I told myself, after I talked to Curt...

Next morning he came into the store with Gaby. It was rare for the two of them to appear together. Gaby's eyes were red and swollen and I thought she'd been crying.

"Hay fever," she said in a congested tone. "I cad hardly breed."

I looked at Curt. "I may visit my mother for a few days, get Sharon away."

He nodded absently. "It might be a good idea."

I felt as though I'd been told: *Thank you, your services are no longer required.* But I couldn't be sure until I talked to him alone. That evening I left Lou working in his shop and drove out to their place. We sat on the front porch—all three of us, and I told him about Lou's reaction. Curt was noncommittal and vague; I felt like a third wheel. It was a hot night; mosquitoes whined in my ears and the leaves hung still as a painted backdrop. It was the kind of evening when the earth makes you feel like a stranger who doesn't belong. I felt a vague sadness, as on the last day of vacation, or at the end of a love affair. Around nine Gaby went inside to grill some cheese sandwiches. I had just turned to Curt when I felt it; a faint shimmering, a tightening of the air. A shock wave ruffled my hair, then a thunderous blast blew the doors open and shattered the windows. By the time I recovered my senses Curt was gone. Then I heard him inside the house shouting Gaby's name.

I ran into the kitchen. Curt was on the floor beside Gaby; her blouse hung in bloody shreds, and blood oozed from her face and neck. My nose filled with the stench of gas and the salty reek of blood. Curt looked up; I read the fear and guilt in his eyes and I thought, Gaby is dead, and Curt will never forgive himself. Then I saw his lips moving and I realized I'd been deafened by the explosion. I bent closer and shouted: "Is she alive?"

"Yes!" he shouted. "But losing blood. First aid kit in the bathroom. Then get your car up to the door."

I did as I was told. He tore up her skirt to make tourniquets for her arms and held his thumbs to the pressure points of her neck. As he carried her to the car, I saw the trail of blood she left on the wooden porch and I thought, She'll never make it.

I took the short cut to Connersville past Lake Pillybay. The third time I slid around a curve, Curt said in a calm voice from the back seat: "Don't rush. I've got the bleeding under control."

I slowed down and asked: "What happened?"

"Oven blew up. There was a fruit jar inside; slivers gashed her head and arms. She must have been bending over when it happened; the cuts all point downward."

"Curt, do you think—?"

"I think, yes. But I'll look into it later."

At the hospital they rushed her into the emergency room. A couple of minutes later an intern came out. "She needs whole blood. You know her type?"

"AB," said Curt. "Rh-negative."

The doctor winced. "That's rare. We may have to put out a radio call—"

I jumped up. "That's Lou's type. Rh-positive."

"Call him," said Curt.

I called Lou; he answered on the extension in his shop. He said he'd bring Sharon and come right over. He must have broken all speed records; I had no idea his pickup would go that fast. Within twenty minutes he was lying on a table next to Gaby. They had her bandaged so that not even her eyes showed. I could see an inch of her forehead above the gauze; it was a pale deadly yellow beneath her tan, but the doctor said her greatest danger was shock and loss of blood. He thought she'd live.

When we were back out in the waiting room, Lou said: "I think I know how it happened."

Curt turned from his pacing. "How?"

"I sell the same kind of stoves, you know. The oven has two walls, and the area between them is packed with insulation. If something should happen to the insulation—say mice ate it—gas would collect in the dead air space until it exploded."

It sounded reasonable to me, but Curt shook his bead violently. "Somebody knew she had hay fever. Somebody sneaked in and turned on the oven while we were talking out front. He knew she couldn't smell. He tried to kill her."

His tone was flat and metallic, like stones falling on a slate roof. He turned his back to us and looked out the window. Lou whispered to me:

"You'd better go and visit your mother. He's liable to go over the edge."

I looked at Curt's stony face; I didn't believe he was in danger of going over. On the other hand, he didn't seem to need me. I looked at Sharon sprawled awkwardly asleep in a tubular aluminum chair. My folks lived only fifteen miles away, closer than Sherman. I decided to go.

My parents are the old-fashioned type; they greeted my wee-morning-hours arrival with open curiosity, but postponed their questions until breakfast. By this time they'd decided I'd quarreled with Lou. They disapproved—not of the quarrel, but of my departure. Groenfelder women have traditionally stayed on the home ground and fought it out toe-to-toe with their spouses. I didn't want to bring up Anne's death and I didn't want them to know what had happened to Sharon, so I let their misapprehension stand.

That afternoon I called the hospital, but they wouldn't let me talk to Gaby. The head nurse crooned that she was out of danger but receiving no calls. I asked for Curt, but they could give me no help and they gave me his number in Sherman. I called there and got no answer. I rang Lou and got the same negative result.

Another day was all I could take. I left Sharon there and told Mother I was going home to Sherman. Instead I went to Connersville. The receptionist at the hospital said I could see Gaby during visiting hours, in thirty minutes. I sat down to wait. The only other person in the room was a man whose face was three-fourths hidden by his newspaper. The visible one-fourth was enough for identification; I'd seen those sparse, carefully combed black hairs before.

"Boggus," I said. "Detective Boggus, what are you doing here?"

He put down his paper and moved to a chair beside mine. "Guarding the patient," he said. "Seeing that she gets no unwanted visitors."

"Somebody could sneak by in a hospital uniform."

He pursed his lips and smoothed his hair. "Well... I wanted to sit in the corridor but they wouldn't let me. I couldn't help that, could I?"

"You know where Curt is?"

"I'm not supposed to say." Unnecessarily, he added: "I don't know." After a moment he cleared his throat. "Incidentally, is he straight?"

"How do you mean?"

"I mean in the head. The lady upstairs got hurt when a stove blew up.

Okay, it could be attempted murder like he says, but a stove's a damned awkward weapon. I can't help remembering that the last killer he staked me out on turned out to be a fag and his boyfriend. That's why I ask if Friedland's straight."

I saw the receptionist beckoning. "He's straight," I said, getting up. "Don't sleep on the job."

The receptionist told me Room 220. I went up and found Gaby lying flat on her back, her neck and shoulders bandaged. She gave me a dreamy, drugged smile. "Velda... they say I won't be scarred."

"Good. Where's Curt?"

She frowned as though trying to place the name. "He was here... was that yesterday... ?"

I saw she was too dopey to talk sense. I took her hand and squeezed it. "I'll find him. Don't worry. Detective Boggus is downstairs."

"Boggus." She giggled. "Have no fear, Boggus is here." Suddenly her voice raised in alarm. "Velda, Curt went back to that terrible place. They'll kill him there. They hate him, all of them. . ."

I walked out into the corridor, silently cursing hospital officials for drugging patients just before visiting hours. Then I had a chilling thought: Maybe it hadn't been the hospital. I found the floor nurse in her lighted cave down the corridor. "The patient in two-twenty, did you give her a drug?"

The woman gave me an icy frown. "Who are you?"

"I'm her sister-in-law. It's very important."

She consulted a chart. "Yes, fifteen minutes ago she received codeine. It would make her somewhat... hazy. She was complaining about the stitches, you know. She had nearly fifty."

"Thank you." I decided I was worrying too much. As I left the hospital, Boggus lowered his paper and gave me a nod, which was supposed to be reassuring. It didn't help, because Gaby wasn't my big worry now.

A quarter mile from Curt's house I could see the place was dark. I parked the car at the entrance to a cornfield and hiked the rest of the way. I was surrounded by silence as I stepped onto the front porch; I waited a moment, then the cicadas resumed their hysterical trilling. I took off my shoes, tiptoed forward and put my ear to the front door. It gave silently. I pushed it open and called Curt's name softly. There was no answer. I walked up to the second floor; the bed rooms were empty. A ladder led up to the attic where Curt had fixed up a study. I climbed up and pushed open the trapdoor. Above me Curt's voice hissed from the darkness: "Keep down!"

I slid out onto the floor and lay flat. The darkness in the studio was stygian; Curt had done the walls in black. I lay for a moment letting my eyes acclimate, then I used my peripheral vision as Curt had taught me. Curt sat on the floor beside the window with a rifle across his knees. I thought of a spider sitting in the middle of his web, waiting for someone to come along and twitch it.

"I think I've got him," said Curt. "He's out there watching the house. Smart of you to come in without using your lights. Might have scared him off. How's Gaby?"

"She's fine..." Suddenly it all seemed like a play. There couldn't be a killer out there watching the house; this was Sherman in the year 1964, not the Dark Ages....

"How do you know he's out there?" I asked.

"Phone wires cut," said Curt. "Electricity off. He wants me to run for it. That's why he didn't try for you."

I had a prickly feeling that Curt was crazy. Wasn't that the way paranoiacs were, everything had to fit their fantasy? Maybe the light company had cut off his lights, maybe a phone wire had fallen down. Wouldn't that be just as logical? I felt an urge to humor Curt, to do nothing to shake his fantasy.

"Who is it?" I asked.

"We'll soon know." Curt lit a cigarette, wedged it into the front sight of his rifle, and passed the glowing end along the window. *Pwwinnng!* A bullet crashed through the window and tore into the shingle roof.

The shock was so great that for a moment I thought the slug had struck me in the stomach. Immediately all my doubts disappeared. There's nothing quite as convincing as solid lead. There was a killer out there; there was a murderer loose in Sherman. I realized how soldiers must feel when they're on the front line and the awareness hits them: My God, they're trying to kill *me!*

"What are you going to do?" I asked.

"Capture him. Get a confession."

I was about to ask if he'd quit suspecting Lou but he silenced me: "Shh. He's coming in."

I looked but I saw only darkness. "How do you know?"

"I feel him," said Curt in an intense whisper. "He's scared, uneasy, but he's excited too. He likes the idea of killing me.... He's choked up with desire, the kind you feel for a woman. He's coming on in a crouch... soon he'll hit the trip-wire. It's attached to a couple of flash units, the kind they use for photographing game. I think that's what scared Sharon's horse. I looked around the spot and found pieces of melted plastic. They use it to coat flashbulbs so they won't explode—there!"

A brilliant flash showed a stocky, bunched figure turning away as though about to run. Curt flicked a switch; a spotlight stabbed down. Curt's voice rang out into the night.

"Hold it or I'll shoot!"

The figure froze.

"Turn around!"

I held my breath as the killer turned. It was Johnny Drew.

"We caught a rabbit," said Curt. "The wolf is still loose."

INTERLUDE

The Killer's Game

Control is the key. My father killed himself when I was eight, but not before he taught me control through his own lack of it. Noise drove him into a rage; he must have had a brain tumor but nobody knew. He kicked apart my games and cursed me when I laughed. I devised secret games, and I learned how to laugh deep down inside. I drank poison after he died; they thought I didn't understand; they kept saying, Don't ever do that again, it'll kill you, don't you understand? I understood that they were afraid of death. I wasn't, because it seemed like something that had already happened to me. It made me stronger than them because they were afraid and I wasn't. That's when I hit upon the game. Later I figured out that your own death ends the game. You keep it going as long as you can. That's one of the rules.

The year after that Teddy Groner and I built a campfire near the haystack. I was fascinated by the way the orange tongues of flame could lick something and make it shrivel and die. I yelled, Feed it feed it, and started throwing hay on the fire. Teddy screamed and tore at my arms. I looked up and saw his five-year-old sister Lotte on top of the stack, but I couldn't stop. After awhile the yellow tongues licked her and she fell. I had to move back but Teddy stood frozen. Afterwards his face was blistered and his hair burned to a crinkly mass which flaked and fell off under your fingers. He remembered nothing. I told Teddy's folks I'd been off across the pasture when the fire started, and Teddy couldn't deny it. Teddy was never right after that, but you couldn't tell it for awhile. He hated me; sometimes he'd charge me blubbering and swinging his fists, but he never knew why. When we were twelve we built a house of grass and sticks and sat inside smoking cigaret butts. The little house caught fire; there was no danger but Teddy ran in terror. When the fire was out we went to Teddy's house to tell his mother but she said he was in bed sick. He was out of school for two months. After that he stuttered, played with trucks like he'd done when he was six years old. But I could never be sure that someday he wouldn't remember that fire. When we went swimming that day, we took Teddy with us. He was supposed to stay on the bank but you couldn't depend on Teddy. He started swimming out to the boat, then he dived down. I knew he planned to swim under the boat and come up on the other side. I slipped off the other side and caught him as he rose. He was out of air so he didn't struggle long....

One thing led to another. The little girl's death led to Teddy's, and then I was never sure of the other boys who'd been on the boat. There was Mart, that big red-necked peasant whose only hold on Velda was that he'd laid her first and she wasn't sure the other boys had what he had. I watched them together out on their farm, and I knew that's all she wanted from him—even though she'd told herself it was love and family and children. Those picnics she used to fix... she never ate a damn thing because she couldn't wait until lunch was over and they could get on with the real reason she'd come out there. Afterwards—Mart never saw this part but I did—she'd kneel down over the stream and wash herself, then straighten her clothes and go home looking demure as a bride. I was sure Mart had seen me the day he came running up the hill. That afternoon I went back with a hammer. The tractor made so much noise—he had an old John Deere—that he didn't know I was behind him until I climbed up on the drawbar. I cracked him behind the ear and he stumped down in the seat. I stopped the tractor, pulled him off and dragged him to the gully. Then I plowed four full rounds (you don't think about what can happen while you're vulnerable, you just try to cut the time as short as possible) in order to finish the section of land he'd marked off. Then I drove the tractor to the edge of the gully, cramped those little front wheels, and jumped. The tractor came down on top of him, the steering wheel crushed his chest. I wiped my fingerprints off the wheel, brushed my tracks out of the sand and left. On the way back to town I met Barney Proctor on his way to take Mart fishing. (Barney didn't really like to fish; he just wanted to get away from Ethel.) He found Mart's body and apparently forgot about meeting me. But it was Teddy Groner all over again; someday he'd remember and wonder what I was doing out there. I waited until he was fishing alone under the railroad bridge. I split his skull with an axe while he was baiting his hook (at twelve-forty-five, which gave me fifteen minutes before the one o'clock freight). I'd always wondered how it would sound; like a huge steel door crashing, like a mountain of tin cans falling down. The train took care of the evidence. Actually, that was the only real emotional kick in it; the rest was the sort of intellectual satisfaction you get when everything clicks into place, the knowledge that all seams are straight, no loose ends are left to snag you while you aren't watching....

Anne was different. She looked like Velda—except that Velda gave an impression of control. Her claws were sheathed, her lips covered the sharp white teeth. With Anne you noticed the teeth first, and you knew she was a meat-eater. She might have been different, but Frankie pulled her cork and her true nature burst through the Southern Baptist upbringing. I began to notice how often she was the object of a fight. While two brawny

louts battered each other there sat this tender young morsel on the sidelines with her legs crossed protecting that little muff which was the object
of the brawl and looking vaguely bored by the whole thing. While blood
and gore splashed on the floor, she'd be casing the joint to see who was
next. I was younger then; I didn't understand the game as well. I knew it
well enough to see Anne's game, but I didn't have a clear picture of my
own. Maybe Anne did... or maybe it was instinct that turned her eyes in
my direction. I know that any man will have a weak moment sooner or
later, and I knew if I put it off until I couldn't help myself, she'd be in control. So I took her when I really didn't give a damn one way or the other:
it was at the lake on the Fourth of July. Everybody was there; the coves
were full of boats and skiers—though not as many as these days. I nosed
my boat up to one of those floating beer joints they launch every holiday
and called out to her: "Get in, we'll go for a ride." She shrugged and got in;
five years had passed since Frankie left but she still hadn't found anything
worth caring about. I nosed through a screen of cattails and into a secluded cove; from the main channel it seemed to lead into a slough, but there
was a clearing in the middle of it. I killed the engine, pulled the bottle out
from under the seat, and gave it to her. Schenley's Black Label, a little
warm from the sun, and she took it down a good inch on her first pull. I
slid my arm around her and started to kiss her but she stiffened up: "You
bring me here to kiss me?" "No." I said. "Then why did you bring me here?
Go on. Say it." I said it and she laughed. "Most guys are afraid to say it. I
guess I'll let you." She had on a two-piece swimsuit, I don't remember what
color. She just peeled off the bottoms and slid forward in the seat. Then she
looked at me and waited; the rest was up to me. At one point in the operation another boat came nosing into the cove; I bent under the dash like I
was repairing a loose wire, but Anne raised the bottle in a toast. The other
boat circled and left (it was a tourist couple also looking for privacy) and
they never suspected that Anne was sitting there with her bare bottom on
the seat. Anne looked at me with a lopsided grin (she'd had three more
slugs of warm whisky) and said, "Finish what you started—if you can."
She had style, Anne did. She dangled her hand in the water the whole
time. Afterward she rolled out of the boat and hung in the water, then
reached in and got the bottom of her suit and pulled it on... all very casual and debonair, as though she were an experienced, high-class whore and
not just a twenty-three-year-old rural honky-tonk queen. . .

   She never came to me; I had to go to her. She knew what I was after (at
the time I played the sex game to the fullest, believing it was the only game
I had going) and she liked to make me crawl. I set up a meeting in Kansas
City; she was to meet me in the room, but she picked up a belligerent
drunk in the hotel bar and brought him with her. I was supposed to fight
him and drench the place with blood, but I just took out my knife and said

to him: "You're in over your head, buddy. Shove off." He crabwalked backwards out of the room. Anne was drunk and thick-lipped; I knew she hated me then because she clawed me and dared me to use the knife on her. She started yelling and throwing things and I knew she wanted the hotel people to come and she wanted it to be in the papers and spread all over the home town. She wanted the whole world to come crashing down on her head and mine too....

I gave her money and she shut up. After that it was a game to see how much money she could get from me. The money was only a way of keeping score, like holes in a cribbage board. Every time I saw her she'd present me with a bill. She told me she didn't give a damn for me or money; she'd give Frankie every cent she got, but he wouldn't take it. He took nothing from her and she offered everything. I began to hate the name Friedland. On that last night she sent me a note to meet her in Connersville with five thousand dollars. She didn't say or else, but I knew. When I met her, she said Frankie had to leave town before he got in bad law trouble. She wanted enough money for both of them to start up elsewhere. I gave her a check—it didn't matter because I knew the game had run out. I followed her when she left, knowing she'd meet Frankie. (There was no plan in my mind; I was just watching for an opportunity.) She stopped outside the club and sat in her car. I pulled around the other side of the club and parked four cars away with my lights off. Soon a boy came out headed for the outside john. I heard Anne tell him she wanted to see Frankie. When he went inside, Anne lit a cigaret; I jumped out of my car and ran up while she was still blinded by the flare of the match. I put my left hand over her mouth and nose and jammed her head back against the seat. The cigaret burned my palm but I didn't know it until later. I already had my jackknife open in my hand. I whispered, "Goodbye, Anne," and then jabbed the blade in below her left jawbone. I yanked it toward the right as hard as I could; her head jerked and flopped; there was a gush of blood and a whistle of air and a gurgling sound. I got the check from her purse and went to my car for the heavy jack-handle. Frankie came out and spoke her name, then leaned into the car. I clubbed him in the back of the head and watched him fall on top of her. I hit him again and drove away. I stopped at a river and washed off the blood and got rid of the knife. Then I stopped at a roadside restaurant and ate a thick steak and potatoes. It was only then that I noticed the burn on my hand. It wasn't shaking at all.

But after Bernice, something warned me: That's one too many young, pretty, loose married women. One of these days somebody will come along and add two and two. It turned out to be Friedland; that fact gave me a weird feeling of powers outside my comprehension. I felt as though the fates were pulling my strings and all I could do was babble and make the proper hand motions....

Sandy was a thing I had to do. She and Anne had traveled in the same crowd, and it was possible Anne had said something about me. I kept putting it off because Sandy didn't interest me, but when Friedland came back... well, in a sense he killed her. I picked her up as she started to walk home from the tavern with her baby. I gave her a drink and drove her around, watching her suck on the bottle. It was clear from the way she trusted me that she suspected nothing. But after I left her at the house— then George tore into town—I knew Friedland could make something of the fact that I'd driven her home. I went into the silent house, tied Sandy's hands and feet, and woke her up. I wanted to talk to her first, but she was disappointingly drunk. I just held my hand over her nose and mouth; she twisted and turned in the bed for only a couple of minutes. Air is such a precious thing, we die so quickly without it. The baby started whimpering then; I was afraid it would wake the others and there'd be three more to deal with. Some people aren't cold enough to be true humanitarians. I am; I smothered the baby too. Then I dropped the match on the floor behind the stove, watched it flare, then left. Some players would hang around and sweat it out: Are they really dead? Did I leave a clue? I threw it in the lap of the gods and left, and once again they took care of me.

But still, the act was pointless from the beginning. Curt Friedland pushed me into it, and I don't like to be pushed.... No, it's not a question of liking, but of uncertainty. I'd never before been up against a man who understood the game, and I wasn't sure of the rules. The one good thing about the new development was Velda. She occupied the ideal listening post in the community and Friedland needed her. I'm not sure how he worked her into his game; perhaps she worked herself. If she'd loved Mart she would not have been vulnerable to Curt but she didn't, otherwise she'd have gone the same way Anne did. The Groenfelder girls love only once, and when they lose their man, they die in essence. Velda didn't die; she was still looking. Men saw the searching look in her eyes and thought they were the object—Johnny Drew, Jerry Blake—but they weren't. Curt seemed to fill the bill. Maybe Velda was attracted by the coldness which enabled him to manipulate people, and by his reckless disregard of life which brought him nearer and nearer the big question mark. Given another environment, another historical setting, Friedland would have been a superb professional killer. (He'd administer death gently, like a blessing, as it should he done.) Maybe Velda was drawn by the smell of death. Whatever it was, she changed, matured, and now she glows with life purpose. Friedland was the catalyst Velda waited for, and I...

CHAPTER SEVEN

Velda's Game

I'd never seen a man questioned before, but I know if I'd had anything to hide, I'd have told Curt before the night was over. He was a cold unfeeling machine; to him Johnny Drew was a locked box which had to be pried open. He tied Johnny to a chair in his black-walled studio and questioned him until I thought I would scream at the repeated questions, each one asked in a hundred different ways. Each time Johnny failed to answer, Curt slapped his doughy checks. I could see the object wasn't to hurt him physically, but to wear him down by repetition, the way the Chinese do with drops of water.

"Where've you been hiding?" Slap. "Did you kill Anne?" Slap. "Who're you working for? You've got four hundred dollars in your wallet. Who gave it to you? You're carrying a Husqvarna .270 rifle. Where'd you buy it? How'd you get these scratches on your hands? Who told you to kill me? How'd you make those phone calls? What's a phone jack? What's a bug? A transistor? Are you right-handed? You don't have insulated clippers. Who cut my electric wires for you?"

Johnny started out trying to sneer, but after an hour his face was a gory mask. His lips were cut on the inside and blood was drooling from his mouth.

"Maybe he isn't working for anybody," I said finally. "Maybe it's his own idea."

"Johnny doesn't have ideas. He's a boob. Aren't you a boob, Johnny?" Curt slapped Johnny's head back against the chair. "You don't know electronics, you don't know how a stove works, you don't know a goddam thing. The other guy set it up; you were just the voice on the line, the muscle, while the other guy walked around the community and showed his smiling face at the right time. Wasn't that it, Johnny?"

"Water..." said Johnny. "Give me a drink."

"That's encouraging. First words you've said. Velda, go down and get a glass of water."

I followed my flashlight beam down through the dark house to the kitchen. The furniture still lay on its side and dark stains remained where Gaby's blood had leaked. I got the water and hurried back upstairs. Curt took the glass, turned his back a moment, then held the glass to Johnny's lips. Johnny took a swallow, then coughed and spat.

"Salt water. You bastard!"

"You get fresh water when you talk. Ready?"

Johnny wasn't ready. Curt stood him up against the wall and got out his bow and arrows. They were barbed hunting arrows, not the round target points we'd been using. He fired three arrows around Johnny, one of them so close that it pinned his shirt to the wall. Greasy sweat rolled down Johnny's face, but he remained silent.

Curt handed the bow to me. "Take a couple of shots, Velda."

"I can't shoot, Curt. You know that."

"That's Johnny's worry."

My knees shook as I got up and fitted an arrow into the bow. Johnny faced me with his mouth open, his eyes wide. "Velda, you wouldn't—"

I don't know whether I would have or not. Curt may have wanted me to bluff, but I was pulling back on the bowstring and my fingers were sweaty... I lost my grip; the string twanged and an arrow quivered in the wall a foot from Johnny's ear.

"Good shot, Velda. Take another."

"Curt, I didn't aim—"

"Aim this time. For his belly. Even if he's punctured, he'll live long enough to talk—"

"No!" Johnny's face was gray behind the blood. "I made those phone calls. I hid out in Connersville."

"How'd you get your instructions?"

"A bartender gave me an envelope with money and instructions."

"Who gave them to him?"

"A kid delivered it. That's all I know. . ."

"Not enough, Johnny."

Curt walked to the wall and slammed Johnny down in a chair. I couldn't tell what he was doing; his body blocked my view. I saw Johnny's head forced back and I heard him gag. After a moment Curt stepped back and set a pill bottle on his desk.

"Those pills are to speed up your heartbeat, Johnny. It'll pound faster and faster until it bursts. It'll fill your insides with blood until you can't breathe. You'll choke to death on your own blood."

Veins stood out on Johnny's head. His face twitched. I picked up the pill bottle and saw that it contained Dexedrine tablets. They'd speed up Johnny's heartbeat, but they weren't fatal.

"Feel the heart pounding, Johnny? It takes fifteen minutes. Feel the blood racing? You can still talk...."

Johnny licked his brown-crusted lips. "If... if I talk, what?"

"I'll give you pills to counteract these. They'll carry you into dreamland."

"Okay... I... got instructions to kill you. He said you'd be here, the lights off and so on. I got four hundred in advance and would get another thousand when the job was done."

"How'd you get the instructions?"

"By... telephone."

"You didn't get the money by telephone."

"They... it was given to the bartender in an envelope."

Curt jumped to his feet. "What was the name of the bar?" He gave Johnny only a second to answer, then asked: "What did the bartender look like? Blond or brunet or bald? What time did you pick up the money? You can't answer, can you? I'm tired of screwing with you. *Tired,* you hear? You slimy goddam snake!"

His open hand caught Johnny's jaw and dumped him from his chair. I thought Curt had lost his temper, but then I saw it was only a pose. Curt helped Johnny back into his chair and spoke in gentle, friendly tones. "You've never heard of the Italian rat torture, have you, Johnny? They put a pair of hungry rats in a cage which fits around a man's neck. First the rats eat away the ears, then the nose, then the eyelids. Then they go for those bright shiny eyes. You can't look away, Johnny. You can't close your eyes. You have to stare at those sharp yellow teeth biting into your eyes the way you'd bite into a peach. I just happen to have a pair of hungry rats...." He went to the corner and folded back a piece of heavy canvas. Beneath it was a metal bird cage containing two lean gray rats. They cluttered excitedly as Curt carried them toward Johnny. My stomach turned over. Curt held the cage against Johnny's cheek; the smell of blood excited them; they squealed and leaped against the side of the cage, their yellow teeth slashing. Johnny groaned and slumped in his chair.

Curt shook him; he lolled, a dead weight. Curt put the rats back beneath the tarpaulin, then threw the glass of salt water in his face. Johnny didn't move. Curt sat down and lit a cigaret.

"What are you going to do?" I asked.

"Wait until he wakes up." He glanced at his watch, then peered at me. I felt as though I'd been dragged over plowed ground against the furrow; I must have looked that way because Curt said: "It's three a.m. There are beds downstairs. You can lie down and rest. I'll wake you if I need you."

I climbed down the ladder and went into the bedroom. I lay down on Curt's bed, amid the smell of his tobacco and after-shave lotion. I didn't intend to sleep, but I did. Dawn glowed warm in the windows when I awoke. The house was draped in silence. I climbed up to Curt's studio, pushed open the trapdoor, and shoved my head through. The gruesome scene struck me all at once, like a hammerblow between the eyes. I gave a little shriek and let the trapdoor fall. I clung to the ladder breathing hard. Could I have imagined the sight? Fatigue, loss of sleep, could that have made me see Johnny Drew lying on the floor with the feathered shaft of an arrow protruding from his chest? Numbly I pushed open the trapdoor; it was real, Johnny Drew was cold meat, as lifeless as a roll of canvas. Although I'd never seen a corpse outside a coffin, I knew there was no point in checking Johnny's pulse.

I lowered the trapdoor and ran downstairs; there was no sign of Curt on the first floor. I ran out the front door and tried to stop, but my momentum was too great. I ran into the arms of Sheriff Wade, who said, "Velda, what the hell—?" I stared into Lou's wide, dumbfounded eyes and I felt my head swimming, the earth tilting. The light faded, and I thought, How corny and feminine, to faint at a time like this....

I awoke in my own bed, and there was young Doctor Nash, with a thin moustache and a greasy bedside manner he must have learned from TV. He was dismantling a hypodermic needle and putting it into a tray. He smiled at me—a process which divided his moustache into separate hairs—and said: "Just lie back, Mrs. Bayrd. I've given you a sedative which should let you rest all day."

"Doctor, you didn't..."

My head whirled suddenly. When it cleared the doctor was outside the room talking in hospital tones to my husband. I wanted to get out of bed but I was caught in a pool of lassitude as heavy as sweet molasses. My lids drooped shut and I was looking into a well spiraling down and down. A light glowed at the bottom like a tiny coin; somebody's face smiled up at me. *Just drift down,* said a voice in my head, *drift down.* I drifted down: I wore a filmy garment which drifted around me like cobwebs. It was Curt waiting down there for me; his hands stripped the lace from my body and he laughed: "Can't you ever say what you want, Velda? Won't you ever be honest with yourself?" I was naked, and his hands passed over my body leaving trails of fire. Horrified, I watched Curt unzip his trousers; he came toward me and I saw that he held a huge hypodermic needle in his hand. I put my hands down to protect myself, saying: "No, I don't want to sleep; I want to know what's happening..." Suddenly there was Gaby dressed in a nurse's uniform. She seized my hands and pulled them away, saying: "Don't be childish. Isn't this what you wanted?" Curt laughed and jabbed, and I felt it go all the way in, up through my stomach and into my lungs until I couldn't breathe....

I opened my eyes; my covers were damp with sweat. A low sun cast a red glow on the opposite wall. *Day is done.* Outside I heard the mewling of dogs. I got out of bed, staggered to the window, and looked out. A panel truck had parked in the drive. Through the wire mesh I saw the mournful lace of a bloodhound. I slipped on my housecoat and walked into the front room to look out the other window. In the front yard stood Sheriff Wade, his deputy and Lou. The sheriff was dressed as usual, but Deputy Hoff was armed for a siege. Two pearlhandled forty-fives hung low on his hips, tied down with leather thongs. Slung on his back was a rifle. I half-expected to see grenades hanging from his belt. Hoff was walking around in small circles, hitching up his belt and spitting on the ground. The sheriff was talking to Lou. Silently I raised the window and listened:

"...like to have you with us Lou, since you're a good hand with guns. He's somewhere over there in Brush Creek. The hounds will find him. But the more men we have, the less chance of anybody getting hurt."

"How about Friedland? You plan to take him alive?"

"He'll get his chance. If he doesn't take it " The sheriff shrugged. "It'll be a better chance than he gave Johnny Drew. Torturing a man in my county..." For a moment the sheriff seemed choked by indigestion, then he said: "How about it? You want me to deputize you?"

Lou shook his head. "First place, I don't know Brush Creek. I wouldn't be much help. In the second place, I don't like hunting a man with dogs, no matter what he might have done."

The sheriff nodded curtly. "Okay, Lou. Whatever you say. Let's go, Bobby."

They jumped in the panel truck and roared off. Watching Lou walk back to the house, I felt proud of him for not joining the hunt. I ran into my room and crawled back in bed just as Lou pushed the door open. "Velda?" I fluttered my eyelids and he came in. "Velda, they're hunting Curt. They wanted to question you but I said that you were asleep." He sat down on the edge of the bed. "I want you to tell me why you were at Curt's house this morning."

"How did you know I was there?"

"Your mother called and asked if you'd arrived home safely. That's when I started looking for you."

I swore at myself for forgetting. Mother always called to see if I'd gotten home all right; she'd been doing it ever since Anne's death.

"But... why'd you bring the sheriff?"

"He just happened to be with me. He had a search warrant for the house; he suspected Curt of burglarizing his office. Now I've answered your questions. You answer mine."

I told Lou that Gaby had given me a message for Curt. I went on to tell him what had happened at Curt's house after I got there. I told him because I wanted a favor from him; I wanted him to join the posse and keep them from killing Curt. Lou hesitated; the deputy might be gun-happy, but he couldn't shoot. If he got close enough to hit Curt, he'd be close enough to take Curt alive. "If he wanted to," I said, then I told him about the fight the two had when Curt first arrived. Lou agreed to go, provided I took the sleeping capsule the doctor had left for me.

"I'm still half-asleep, Lou. But leave it there, and I'll take it."

"No, Velda," he said in a tone you'd use on a feeble-minded patient. "I don't want you tearing through the hills." He held the capsule out between his fingers. "Open your mouth."

I opened my mouth and let him put the capsule on my tongue. I felt like a little baby robin. I giggled and realized I was still giddy from the shot that morning. But I had enough sense to work the capsule in between my cheek and my gums, so that when I swallowed the water Lou handed me, the capsule stayed in my mouth. He left the room, and I spat out the capsule. I went to the window and watched Lou raise the hood of my car and jerk something loose, then climb in his pickup and drive off.

I ran out and raised the hood. I stared at the mass of wiring for several minutes without finding anything loose. I got out the repair manual, opened it to a photo of the engine, and compared the two. There was something visually awry in the area around my distributor. I tugged gently on all the wires until I found the loose one; it was the connection to the coil. I connected it and tried the car; it started. I drove toward Lake Pillybay. I wasn't sure where Curt would go, our last few meetings had been in the open, but he'd once pointed to a narrow cleft in a rock and said there was a cave inside. Frankie had found it once and showed it to Curt; as far as he knew nobody else was aware of it. I pulled the car off the road a quarter mile from the cave and piled branches over it. The distant yap of dogs sent shivers up my spine. I started walking, congratulating myself on my cleverness at outwitting Lou with the capsule and the car. Gradually I became aware of a coldness on my body. Only then did I realize I'd come out naked except for my thin nightgown. It was strange to trudge through the woods without underclothing; occasionally the wind whipped up my gown and gave me a chilling, intimate caress.

But I found the place. A sheer cliff rose up beside a narrow ravine full of dead leaves and humus. No trees grew right in the ravine, which left a ten-foot-wide open space between the woods and the cliff. I stopped at the edge of the clearing and called softly: "Curt."

There was no answer. I called again.

A strong hand gripped my arm. Curt's voice whispered: "Velda, here you are again, wearing white at night."

"I couldn't think of everything. I came to warn you—"

"Shhh. Go inside and wait. I'll see if you were followed."

I squeezed through the cleft and groped my way inside. I smelled dust, decay, bat manure and gas. As my eyes got used to the dark, I saw that the smell of gas came from a tiny butane stove. By the pale blue flame I saw the two suitcases which held Curt's recording apparatus. A coil of wiring lay on the cavern floor, plus a tool kit, a lumped sleeping bag and a case of groceries. I heard Curt come behind me and I asked:

"How'd you move this stuff in so quick?"

"I put it here weeks ago... all but the recording stuff. It was a second line of defense."

I said: "You predict everything, don't you?"

He laughed without humor. "Not quite. Gaby's accident for one thing. Johnny Drew's death for another—"

"You didn't kill him?"

He sighed. "Velda, I've told you. I didn't come here to kill anybody."

"Well, I thought, maybe by accident—"

"By accident Johnny happened to pass in front of the window. Somebody outside was waiting for that moment. It was a good shot. I found Gaby's bow in the brush a hundred yards away. I lost the killer's trail when he waded a stream. I tried to pick it up again, but it was still too dark. When I got back, your husband was there, with the sheriff. What did they do to you?"

I told him about the hunt and the gun-happy Hoff. Curt lit a candle and I saw that his hair was wild, his eyes puffy, his cheeks stubbled. He didn't look as though he'd slept since the night Gaby was injured.

"You know who it is?" I asked.

"Johnny Drew died without talking," he said.

"What do you plan to do now?"

"Stay here until the hunters decide I've left the county."

"I'll stay with you."

"No you won't."

"You plan to tie me up and carry me home?"

He looked at me for a moment, then he handed me a rifle. "Put on something dark and keep watch at the entrance. I'll catch a nap."

I threw a blanket over my shoulders and wedged myself in the mouth of the cavern. I could hear the chilling yelp of the hounds. Once I heard a distant gunshot; I decided something had spooked Deputy Hoff. I pictured Curt trying to give himself up to those men, and I knew he'd die the moment they saw him.

The time dragged slowly. The coldness of the rock seeped through the blanket and numbed my back and buttocks. Breezes found their way up my legs like cold searching fingers. The hour reached midnight, one o'clock. I no longer heard the hounds; I decided the search had been recessed for the night, all the hunters gone home to bed. I felt totally alone, like the last woman on earth. The moon slid in and out of the clouds, creating weird shadows which humped through the forest. The wind whispered and moaned through the leaves. There was nothing human out there; nothing to give me comfort. I went back inside and lay down beside Curt. He slept silently, without snoring. He smelled of clothing worn too long, but I didn't mind. I tickled him with my hair and he snorted, wiping his nose on the back of his hand. He shifted to a new position and put his arm around me. "Gaby " he mumbled. I put my hand under his shirt and rubbed the warm muscular back. He slid his hand down, found the hem of the nightdress and tugged upward. I lifted myself up to help, then relaxed against him. He ran his hands down the curve of my back and touched my buttocks. I suppose that's what made him aware because there was a considerable difference in size. He stiffened slightly but didn't withdraw his arms. "Velda?" He wasn't questioning my identify, but something else. "Are you awake?"

"Yes," I said. "Wide-awake."

I could count on my fingers the times I've enjoyed it... I mean when the flood of emotion picks me up and swirls me to a place of no-thought, no-time, no-existence. With Mart a couple of times, with Lou perhaps once, and there in the cave with Curt. I tried to tell him without sounding grateful or obsequious, but he merely chuckled. "I remember the best food I ever had, it was cold and windy and I'd been driving cattle for half a day. I stopped and had a cold ham sandwich with ketchup and I've never tasted anything as delicious since."

"If you're saying I was sex-starved..."

"I was thinking of the excitement—"

"You rationalize everything until it's meaningless." I stood up and pulled down my nightdress. I thought of the shower I usually took after sex, but I didn't feel dirty. Those sanitary operations belonged to another woman, a certain Mrs. Bayrd. I wanted nothing more to do with her.

"Speaking of food," I said.

"I'll get it."

"Your job is to guard the cave. Go, great hunter."

He went. I warmed a can of Vienna sausage and fried eggs on the little stove. Curt came back and squatted beside the fire and ate from a paper plate. After a minute he said: "It's about daylight. You think you can get out and contact Gaby?"

My heart sank. I didn't want to leave the cave; there were too many problems outside. "You just want to get rid of me."

He shook his head. "Somebody's got to tell her to put plan 'C' into effect. She'll know what to do."

Jealousy is a childish emotion, but there it was. "Why don't you tell me?"

"It's complicated. First of all it means I've got the local law on my back. I've established a certain contact with the state police; he doesn't know you but he knows Gaby. I'm not sure he'd act on your word. Tell Gaby plan 'C', that's all you have to do."

I said I'd try. Curt took a wrinkled plaid shirt and cotton trousers from his sleeping bag and said I could wear them. I pulled off my nightdress, feeling neither shy nor bold to be standing nude before him; just very natural. I let him slide the shirt onto my arms. The cold morning air drew my nipples tight; Curt's touch sent the pulse surging through my veins. I turned in his arms and drew his head down in a kiss; I felt an urge to let my legs go limp and pull him down to the floor with me. I was a glutton, I knew; when Gaby came back there would he no more chances, and I wanted to store up memories for the future. But I sensed Curt's urgency, and withdrew my embrace. While he was rolling up my trouser legs he said:

"Don't go home, you understand? Don't talk to anybody. Just call Gaby and then hide out."

I left, feeling a deep serenity beneath the overlay of urgency. I felt like a college girl sneaking home after a night in her boyfriend's dormitory. I reached the car and drove out, planning to sneak into Sherman and call from the store. Just outside Sherman I rounded a curve and nearly crashed into a pair of livestock loading chutes which had been placed across the road. I slammed on the brakes and skidded to a halt; I looked out the window and saw Joe Riley, former pool-hall bum of Sherman, approaching the car with a deer rifle. A deputy sheriff's badge gleamed on his dirty denim shirt.

"Misses Bayrd. They lookin for you all over creation. Don't move. I'm a legal deputy, 'powered to shoot."

I could only sit cursing my lack of caution while he ran around the car and got in on the other side. "Now jest ease around on the shoulder and out the other side. I reckon I better take you home."

As I drove, Joe never took his eyes off me. Now and then his gaze wandered down to my bosom, and I suspected that Curt's oversized shirt had gaped open to reveal a breast or two. It occurred to me that I might seduce Joe and escape. I noticed his yellowed teeth and realized I couldn't do it without throwing up. Still I tried stopping the car and pretending an urgent call of nature, but Joe smirked and said: "I reckon you can hold it for another mile, Missus Bayrd." So like a sacrificial lamb I drove up our drive and there was Lou and Sheriff Wade waiting in front of the house. There was no sign of Deputy Hoff. The sheriff lumbered over to the car looking angry enough to chew off the barrel of his .38. He yanked open the door and seized me by the arm. "I'm through playin games with you, little lady. Where'd you leave that murderin' sonuvabitch?"

"Sheriff, please—" His hand was a vise biting through my biceps. Lou walked up.

"Hold it, Sheriff. Maybe she doesn't know about Bobby."

"Come on."

The sheriff pulled me out of the car and I had to run to keep from falling. He threw open the back of the panel truck. Deputy Hoff lay inside. He'd swagger no more; an arrow had gone all the way through his neck, just below the ears. In his khaki gabardines, he resembled a deer being carried home to he butchered. I gasped.

"But Curt couldn't have—" I caught myself. "I don't know anything about this, Sheriff. I'm... sorry. About your nephew."

"Nothing gonna bring him back to life." The sheriff was a man stunned by grief, half out of his mind. His voice was gruff. "Thing I gotta do is get the guy who did it. Now you tell where he is and maybe I won't put you under arrest—"

"I don't know *anything.*"

"All right, Velda." He reached for the handcuffs on his belt, but Lou said: "Give me a minute, Sheriff." Lou took my arm and marched me in the house, into the bedroom. He closed the door and seized my shoulders. "Now listen. Don't you understand that Curt's a wanted man? You can't protect him. He killed an officer—"

"He didn't."

"Were you with him last night? Is that how you're sure?"

I kept my mouth closed.

"Velda, you're wearing the proof. Those clothes..."

"Yes, I was with him."

Lou nodded. "All right. Tell me where he is."

"But Lou... they'll kill him on sight. You know that."

"Just tell me. He can give himself up to me. Look." He reached in his shirt pocket and held a badge out in his palm. "I'm a special deputy. I'll bring him in and see that he gets a fair trial."

My eyes caught that crescent scar on his forearm. I remembered Curt staring at it that night; I recalled how emphatically he'd warned me against coming home. I realized the scar couldn't have been made by a nail...

"Velda," Lou was saying. "I don't want to turn you over to the sheriff. I'm trying to help you. For God's sake, think of Sharon, think of your family. You don't want to go to jail as Curt's accomplice. He's ruined himself, but you don't have to follow his example. Just tell me where he is..."

A picture came into my mind; Teddy Groner in the high school group photo, smiling. He had even white teeth, with canines noticeably prominent, extending a quarter of an inch down past his incisors. Looking at Lou's scar I could almost see Teddy's teeth sinking into Lou's arm in a desperate underwater struggle. I thought of other things... Lou practicing with the bow until he could shoot almost as good as Curt... Lou calling me at three a.m. on the night of Anne's murder, telling me the clerk had forgotten to relay my call. I remembered all the electronic equipment in Lou's shop, and the way he always seemed to know what went on in the store even when he wasn't there. I remembered Johnny Drew confessing that he'd made the calls, and realized that Lou's presence in bed did not absolve him of guilt. I thought of Sharon being attacked by her own father and my mind recoiled in horror. I forced myself to say...

"He's in the old Boy Scout cabin, Lou. But I want to go with you."

Lou shook his head. "You're weak, Velda. Your mind isn't working too well. You stay here and rest." He got busy at the little tray beside my bed. "Those pills aren't strong enough. The doctor left something else . . ."

I watched him fill the hypodermic needle and I thought of air bubbles injected into the vein, which kill you so quickly and leave no evidence...

I ran. He was so engrossed in his task that I made it out of the house. The sheriff pulled his gun but hesitated: I guess he'd never shot a woman before. Joe stared at me without raising his gun; I think he forgot he had one. I jumped in the car and drove down the lane, my tires squealing. West of town I skidded around the roadblock and drove on toward the lake. I didn't want to lead them too close to the cave. I drove the car into a corn-field and tried to wipe out the tracks. Then I walked a mile into the woods, crawled into a hazel-brush thicket, and waited. When darkness came, I went on to the cave. I called Curt's name and went in. Curt was behind me.

"Did you reach Gaby?" he asked.

I started to explain, but a brilliant light flashed behind me. Lou's voice said: "Put your hands up, both of you."

I whirled, but saw only a disc of blinding white light. Lou laughed. "I've been with you all day, Velda. You underestimated me, just like you've been doing all your life." His voice hardened. "Turn around and put your hands against the wall. I carry a sawed-off shotgun. I could get you both with one shot."

I turned slowly, and Curt whispered without moving his lips. "Talk. Get him talking."

I made two tries before my voice worked. "You...I can't believe you'd attack Sharon, Lou. You must have had Johnny do that?"

Lou laughed. It wasn't a pleasant sound. If I'd heard it in a crowded restaurant I'd have turned to stare in horror at the man who'd made it. I realized what Lou had kept bottled up all these years; he'd stepped out of the human race a long time ago....

"You didn't think it out, Velda. That little scare wasn't nearly as bad as having her learn I was a mass murderer. Think of her carrying that burden. Your lover was making you look too closely at me, and I couldn't handle you both at once. I had to find some way of turning off your suspicion."

"I don't understand how you used Johnny Drew."

"I caught him stealing from the hardware store. I had him then, but he couldn't kill; he botched the attempt to kill you, Curt, even though he hated you enough."

"Why did you kill the deputy?" I asked.

"To get the sheriff mad enough to shoot Curt on sight. I was intrigued by the idea of having the law do the job for me, but—" He stopped abruptly. "I see your idea; keep me talking until the sheriff arrives, is that it? Sorry to disappoint you, the sheriff went in the other direction, he's five miles away by now. But I don't mind talking. Excuse me while I sit down." There was a pause, then: "All right, move just a little closer together, your shoulders touching, that's fine. You make a handsome couple, you know. I originally had the thought of catching you two in bed together and killing you both. I could have gotten away with it; pillar of the community loses head in fit of jealous rage. But you somehow kept clear of the sex scene—that is, until recently. I sense a new attitude in you, Velda. You've had yourself a nice little tumble and you're happy, aren't you? Happy enough to die?"

My heart stopped, because I knew he meant it. Curt asked:

"How would you explain it?"

"Oh... that you used my wife as a shield. Or perhaps you killed her and then I killed you. Either way I'll be a hero. I never plan in advance...."

Lou kept talking, and Curt drew him out. I listened in horrified fascination while he told about watching Mart and me, about killing Anne and Barney and another girl whom we'd thought had merely run away from home. He'd buried her in the dam of a pond he was building. And Jerry Blake had been simple: Lou's hardware store and the drugstore shared the same storehouse. Jerry was heavily addicted to morphine toward the end; he took to stealing it from the storeroom, shooting himself when he went to the store at night. Lou waited until he'd given himself a shot, then opened a butane tank, hooked up a timed electric spark gadget, and was home before the explosion occurred. Why? His voice was diffident. Lou had concealed Johnny's theft, but Jerry had discovered the shortage and blamed Lou. Gaby's stove... it had happened the way he'd explained, except that Lou was the one who'd taken out the packing.

"Remember how Gaby complained that her oven wouldn't hold heat?" he asked. "The gas built up in there for two weeks before it blew up. It could've happened any time. It had nothing to do with her hay fever."

"Did you plan to kill her?" asked Curt.

"Oh no," said Lou. "Not at that time, anyway. I wanted you to take her out of the game; it was too much trouble to watch both of you and Velda too. Then a couple of days ago, when both Velda and Gaby were gone, and I thought we could have our private little game—"

"But you threw in Johnny Drew."

"A pawn," said Lou. "I was testing your defenses. I didn't know you had Velda."

They were like two friends rehashing a card game. I had to pinch myself mentally to realize that death lay at the bottom of it.

"We could still have the game," said Curt. "Let Velda go."

Lou gave a short laugh. "Impossible. She knows too much, Gaby too...."

"Gaby knows nothing."

"Suspects. That's enough...."

"You have to keep killing, don't you? Once you start it's the answer to every dilemma. How many of those others were murder?"

"Oh, you were right on several. Teddy Groner, as you suspected, bit me underwater. I made up that story of the nail on the spot, then I was stuck with it. I figured it would trip me up someday. The woman who supposedly hanged herself... I made the mistake of thinking she was willing when she wasn't. The man who was eaten by hogs, the one who killed himself with the shotgun, they were theories I wanted to work out... though I told myself I wanted to buy their land cheap—"

"You know how it ends, Lou?" said Curt in a mild tone of curiosity. "You'll meet somebody else with the game and it'll be your turn. That's the only way it can end, with your death. You're committing suicide the hard way."

"Of course," said Lou. "I figured that out myself. But you'll never—"

Suddenly everything dissolved in a thunderous explosion. A terrific weight slammed against my back and threw me against the face of the cliff. Darkness closed in. I was sure Lou had fired and I thought, Heaven is a rocky place. Then I realized I was lying on the cave floor. I felt sticky warmth trickle down my face and knew it was blood running from a bump on my forehead. Hands caught my armpits and hoisted me to my feet; I turned and looked into Curt's face. I was silly from shock; I laughed at the white limestone dust which coated his face, hair and eyebrows. His moist lips looked brilliant red. He looked like a character in a Japanese play. I heard my own laughter echo inside my head, and I realized I was deaf. Suddenly weak, I fell against him and clung for support.

Not until then did I remember Lou. I looked at where he'd been and saw only a slab of limestone.

"Lou—?" I had to shout in his ear. "What happened?"

Curt got the flashlight and shone it on the cave floor. The first thing I saw was the shotgun. Then Lou's hand, clutching the stock. I followed the hand to an arm, and the arm to the vast slab of limestone as big as a grand piano. I saw Lou's head, and I turned away quickly and hid my face. But the image remained; his face was swollen, his eyes bulged like those of a rat caught in a trap. I felt no grief, he had ceased to be my husband and became a monster. For an instant I sensed a whole race of such creatures living among humans, saying the right things and performing the correct actions and all the while playing their little death games. How many women, I wondered, will go to bed tonight with a monster?

Curt took my hand and led me toward the rear of the cave. "There's a rear exit," he was saying. "I sabotaged the entrance in case they trapped me, put a charge of dynamite behind a loose slab. It happened that Lou was sitting right under it."

"How'd you set it off?"

Curt showed me the hidden wire running into his shoes. There was a

battery pack strapped inside his trousers. He took a reel of tape from his
recording apparatus and explained that he'd started the machine as we
entered the cave. He'd known I was being followed, but figured the killer
would talk only if he thought he had the upper hand.

"Did you know it was Lou?"

"I... was almost sure when I saw the stuffed mice."

"So *long*? And you didn't tell me?"

"You had all the information I had, Velda. But you wouldn't believe it.
Come on, let's find a new hiding place. That explosion will draw attention."

We crawled out of a hole just large enough to squeeze through. As I
emerged into the night, a flashlight blinded me. I started to retreat, but
Gaby's voice said:

"Velda, Curt. It's me."

She was standing beside a state trooper, looking almost as pale its her
bandages. I didn't watch as she and Curt embraced. The trooper was a
heavy-necked clean-featured six-footer, the kind of depersonalized All-
American boy you find in state police uniforms. He came over to me and
bandaged my forehead. "I'm Trooper Carson, and you're..."

"Velda Bayrd," I said in a tone which was neither sad nor exultant. "My
husband is dead inside. He's a murderer. Curt has his confession."

A helicopter waited at the top of the ridge. As we flew out, Gaby
explained that she'd tried to phone Curt and had gotten strange responses from the operator; immediately she'd put plan "C" into effect. She'd
known about the cave and had been able to lead the troopers in. They set
us down on the airfield outside Connersville. I started toward the taxi
stand and Curt called after me:

"Where are you going?"

I turned and saw him and Gaby standing together. There was no place
for me between them. I felt bitterness rise inside me. "Do you care?" I gave
him no time to answer. "No, you don't. You were playing the same game
Lou was. It wasn't as deadly as his; it might be more human if it were. With
you there's no emotion. No involvement. You treat us as though you were
some being from the stars. You're cold and cruel and heartless—"

Suddenly I ran out of steam. "No, I'm sorry. You did it to get Frankie out
of jail."

Gaby came forward and took my hand. "Come with us. We'll get Frankie
out and then go to the islands."

I could see that she understood my problem. I wondered how many
times she'd watched women fall in love with her husband. I felt my stubbornness come in and give me strength: "You might persuade me," I said.
"But I've got a daughter. What can I say when she learns her father was a
monster? What will I tell her?"

"To... be strong," said Gaby.

"But I feel that I did it to her. I married him. I..."

I looked past Gaby and saw Curt, his achingly handsome face frozen, and that vague superior amusement in his eyes. Comprehension flooded in like a sunrise. Many people had fallen victim to my husband, but *he* was Curt's victim. My husband had toyed with them, but Curt had toyed with Lou, like a cat with a mouse. I realized that Curt would go on, having discovered the game behind the game, to seek other men like Lou. And next time there'd be no brother to free, just the sheer thrill of... hunting the hunter.

I turned and walked away. Nobody called me back. I didn't really expect it. *Be strong, Gaby,* I said to myself.

THE END

DAN J. MARLOWE BIBLIOGRAPHY

Doorway to Death (1959)*

Killer With a Key (1959)*

Doom Service (1960)*

The Fatal Frails (1960)*

Shake a Crooked Town (1960)*

Backfire (1961)

The Name of the Game is Death (1962)
[pub in UK as Operation Overkill, 1973]**

Strongarm (1963)

Never Live Twice (1964)

Death Deep Down (1965)

Four for the Money (1966)

The Vengeance Man (1966)

The Raven is a Blood Red Bird [w/William Odell] (1967)

Route of the Red Gold (1967)

One Endless Hour (1969)
[pub in UK as Operation Endless Hour, 1975]**

Operation Fireball (1969)**

Flashpoint (1970) [pub in UK as Operation Flashpoint, 1972]**

Operation Breakthrough (1971)**

Operation Drumfire (1972)**

Operation Checkmate (1972)**

Operation Stranglehold (1973)**

Operation Whiplash (1973)**

Operation Hammerlock (1974)**

Operation Deathmaker (1975)**

Operation Counterpunch (1976)**

Johnny Killain series
** *Earl Drake series*

As by Gar Wilson
Guerilla Games (1982)

FLETCHER FLORA BIBLIOGRAPHY

Strange Sisters (1954)
Desperate Asylum (1955) [also pub as Whisper of Love, 1959]
The Brass Bed (1956)
The Hot-Shot (1956)
Leave Her to Hell (1958)
Let Me Kill You, Sweetheart (1958)
Park Avenue Tramp (1958)
Whispers of the Flesh (1958)
Lysistrata (1959)
Take Me Home (1959)
Wake Up With a Stranger (1959)
Killing Cousins (1960)
Most Likely to Love (1960)
The Seducer (1961)
The Irrepressible Peccadillo (1963)
Skulldoggery (1967)
Hildegarde Withers Makes the Scene [w/Stuart Palmer] (1969)

As Ellery Queen
Who Killed the Golden Goose [aka The Golden Goose] (1964)
Blow Hot, Blow Cold (1964)
Devil's Cook (1966)

CHARLES RUNYON BIBLIOGRAPHY

The Anatomy of Violence (1960)
Color Him Dead (1963) [also pub as The Incarnate, 1977]
The Death Cycle (1963)
The Prettiest Girl I Ever Killed (1965)
The Black Moth (1967)
No Place to Hide (1970)
Power Kill (1972)
Something Wicked (1973)
To Kill a Dead Man (1976)
A Killer is a Lonely Man (unpublished)

As Charles Runyon Jr.
Gypsy King (1979)

As Charles W. Runyon
The Bloody Jungle (1966)
I, Weapon (1971)
Pigworld (1971)
Ames Holbrook, Deity (1972)
Soulmate (1974)
Kiss the Girls and Make Them Die (1977)

As Ellery Queen
The Last Score (1964)
The Killer Touch (1965)
Kiss and Kill (1969)

As Mark West
Office Affair (1961)
His Boss's Wife (1962)
Object of Lust (1962)

Stark Houλe Preλλ

0-9667848-7-1 **Lady Killer / Miasma** Elisabeth Sanxay Holding **$19.95**

0-9667848-8-x **The Box / Journey Into Terror** Peter Rabe **$19.95**

0-9667848-9-8 **The Death Wish / Net of Cobwebs** Elisabeth Sanxay Holding **$19.95**

0-9749438-3-5 **Something in the Shadows / Intimate Victims** Vin Packer **$19.95**

0-9749438-2-7 **Pure Sweet Hell / Catch a Fallen Starlet** Douglas Sanderson **$19.95**

0-9749438-4-3 **Murder Me for Nickels / Benny Muscles In** Peter Rabe **$19.95**

0-9749438-5-1 **Strange Crime in Bermuda / Too Many Bottles**
Elisabeth Sanxay Holding **$19.95**

0-9749438-6-x **Damnation of Adam Blessing / Alone at Night** Vin Packer **$19.95**

0-9749438-8-6 **Framed in Guilt / My Flesh is Sweet** Day Keene **$19.95**

0-9749438-9-4 **The Ham Reporter / Disappearance of Penny** Robert J. Randisi **$19.95**

1-933586-00-1 **Blood on the Desert / A House in Naples** Peter Rabe **$19.95**

1-933586-01-X **Brain Guy / Plunder** Benjamin Appel **$19.95**

1-933586-02-8 **Violence is My Business / Turn Left for Murder** Stephen Marlowe **$19.95**

1-933586-03-6 **Shake Him Till He Rattles / It's Cold Out There** Malcolm Braly **$19.95**

1-933586-05-2 **Whisper His Sin / The Evil Friendship** Vin Packer **$19.95**

1-933586-06-0 **The Deadly Dames / A Dum-Dum for the President**
Douglas Sanderson **$19.95**

1-933586-07-9 **Invasion of the Body Snatchers: A Tribute**
ed by McCarthy & Gorman **$17.95**

1-933586-08-7 **A Night for Screaming / Any Woman He Wanted** Harry Whittington **$19.95**

1-933586-09-5 **An Air That Kills / Do Evil in Return** Margaret Millar **$19.95**

1-933586-10-9 **Wild to Possess / A Taste for Sin** Gil Brewer **$19.95**

1-933586-11-7 **My Lovely Executioner / Agreement to Kill** Peter Rabe **$19.95**

1-933586-12-5 **Look Behind You Lady / The Venetian Blonde** A. S. Fleischman **$19.95**

1-933586-17-6 **Underground / Collected Stories** Russell James (10/07) **$14.95**

1-933586-19-2 **Snowbound / Games** Bill Pronzini (11/07) **$14.95**

1-933586-20-6 **A Devil for O'Shaugnessy / The Three-Way Split** Gil Brewer (1/08) **$14.95**

If you are interested in purchasing any of the above books, please send the cover price plus $3.00 U.S. for the 1st book and $1.00 U.S. for each additional book to:

STARK HOUSE PRESS
2200 O Street, Eureka, CA 95501
(707) 444-8768
www.λtarkhouλepreλλ.com

Order 3 or more books and take a 10% discount. We accept PayPal payments.